THE LORD OF
THE RINGS

J. R. R. Tolkien

SPARKNOTES is a registered trademark of SparkNotes LLC

This edition published by Spark Publishing

Spark Publishing
A Division of SparkNotes LLC
120 Fifth Avenue, 8th Floor
New York, NY 10011

Please submit all comments and questions or report errors to www.sparknotes.com/errors

Printed and bound in the United States

ISBN 1-58663-790-8

Contents

CONTEXT

JOHN RONALD REUEL TOLKIEN—called Ronald by his family and friends—was born on January 3, 1892, in Bloemfontein, South Africa. His father, Arthur, had moved his family to Africa from England in hopes of being promoted in his job as a manager at the Bank of Africa. Upon Arthur's death in 1896, however, his wife, Mabel, brought the four-year-old Ronald back to the English Midlands, the region where she herself grew up. Mabel eventually settled in a suburb of Birmingham, where she raised her family with her sister's help.

The Tolkiens' life in the Birmingham suburbs was poor. In 1900, Mabel converted to Catholicism, and in 1904 she was diagnosed with diabetes, which at that time was untreatable. Mabel died shortly thereafter; a Catholic priest who was friendly with the family cared for the orphaned boy. Ronald was placed in a variety of foster homes, ending up in the boarding house of a Mrs. Faulkner.

One of the lodgers at Mrs. Faulkner's house was a nineteen-year-old girl named Edith Bratt, with whom the sixteen-year-old Ronald struck up a friendship and then a romance. The priest forbade Ronald from seeing Edith until the age of twenty-one. In 1911, Ronald was admitted to Exeter College, Oxford, where he specialized in the classics and developed a special passion for philology, the study and comparison of languages.

In addition to the typical course offerings in Greek and Latin, Tolkien studied other, more unusual ancient and modern languages, such as Gothic and Finnish. Also greatly interested in Old English, Anglo-Saxon, and Welsh poetry, Tolkien began to invent and develop entire languages of his own—languages that would form the groundwork for the world of Middle-earth in his novels.

While still at Oxford, Tolkien continued seeing Edith, who converted to Catholicism for him. In 1915, he graduated with a coveted "first," the highest honors. The next year, it became clear that Tolkien would have to embark for France to fight in World War I. He and Edith married before he left for the front. While fighting, Tolkien contracted "trench fever," a form of typhus, and he returned home to England to recover.

While recovering in 1917, Tolkien developed *The Book of Lost Tales,* the stories that would later form his mythology of Middle-earth, *The Silmarillion*. Tolkien lost all but one of his good friends in the war. In his famous 1938 essay "On Fairy-Stories," Tolkien notes the effect of the war on his personal outlook regarding fantasy literature: "A real taste for fairy-stories was wakened by philology on the threshold of manhood, and quickened to full life by war."

After his recovery, Tolkien continued to pursue his love for philology, joining the staff of the Oxford English Dictionary. He took up his first English teaching post in 1920, later winning the prestigious Chair of Anglo-Saxon at Oxford in 1925. By 1929, he had had four children with Edith. Tolkien taught at Oxford for thirty-four years, living a rather reclusive life with his work and developing the mythology of *The Silmarillion* throughout the 1920s.

In 1928, while grading exams, Tolkien absentmindedly wrote on a blank sheet of paper, "In a hole in the ground there lived a hobbit." With this sentence, Tolkien began to imagine what "hobbits" might be like and what they might do. From these imaginings grew *The Hobbit*, a children's story and Tolkien's first published work of fiction. In 1936, a version of *The Hobbit* reached a representative of the publishing firm Allen and Unwin, which published the novel a year later. The novel met with great success, and there was demand for a sequel.

During this period, Tolkien developed a friendship with another well-known Oxford professor and writer, C.S. Lewis. Tolkien convinced Lewis to devote his life to Christianity, although Tolkien, a devout Catholic, was disappointed that Lewis became a Protestant. The two critiqued each other's work as part of an informal group of writers and scholars known as "the Inklings."

Heartened by the profits of *The Hobbit,* Tolkien's publisher encouraged him to start work on what later became *The Lord of the Rings*. Tolkien spent twelve years writing the novel. His initial goal was only to write a very long tale, but as the novel took shape, he related his story of Hobbits to the vast history and mythology of Middle-earth that he had developed in the Silmarillion stories. *The Lord of the Rings,* completed in 1949, was conceived of as a single novel, but published in three volumes—*The Fellowship of the Ring* (1954), *The Two Towers* (1954), and *The Return of the King* (1955)—for logistical reasons.

The Lord of the Rings was such a success that by 1968, Tolkien's fame was so great that he had to get an unlisted phone number and move to the English seacoast town of Bournemouth with his wife. Though the novel made Tolkien a household name in England and

America, he was never a public figure; he continued work on *The Silmarillion* and other tales, leading a quiet life. He remained comfortable with his middle-class surroundings, taking up residence down the road from C.S. Lewis and joined later by the British poet W.H. Auden. Tolkien continued writing until his death on September 2, 1973. His son, Christopher, edited and published *The Silmarillion,* Tolkien's collected mythology of Middle-earth, in 1977.

Over the years, *The Lord of the Rings* has met with widely varied critical reception. Tolkien intended his novel to act as a mythology for England, a group of fantastic tales about the prehistory of a world in which the values embodied those of the common British individual. Tolkien did not wish to retell existing myths or legends, but rather to create new myths altogether, beginning with wholly invented languages and shaping his stories around those languages and their cultures. This complex philological basis for Tolkien's work, while inaccessible to most readers, remains distinct from the simple and universal themes of the story of *The Lord of the Rings.* To some, the simple tale is uninteresting, too long, and artificially archaic. For others, it touches on the very principles of love, friendship, and sacrifice that are an integral part of human life. Scholars and critics continue to dispute whether *The Lord of the Rings* belongs alongside other serious works of modern British literature or whether it remains only a "period piece"—a work of fiction with only passing significance for its contemporary audience.

Regardless of this mixed critical reception, Tolkien's work did much to change English-language publishing in the twentieth century. His publisher, Allen and Unwin, was astonished at the popular success of *The Lord of the Rings,* which it thought would prove too arcane for mainstream audiences, even though *The Hobbit* had already been a hit in 1937. *The Lord of the Rings* proved that there was a huge market for fantasy, not just among young readers, but among adults as well. The earlier dominance of the "serious" novel of ideas—exemplified by Graham Greene, among others—and of the lighthearted novel of social comedy was called into question in the wake of Tolkien's popular tales of an imaginary world. *The Lord of the Rings* was serious writing full of deep social and moral ideas, but it could not be called an intellectual work as previous "serious" novels had been. Tolkien's influence spread even further during the rise of the hippie movement and social radicalism of the 1960s, though he was often dismayed by the way that young counterculture spokesmen idolized his work.

Nevertheless, it is true that Tolkien's tales of Middle-earth present more than just an escapist fantasy about a magic, faraway world. Rather, they give us a view of the world as it was changing in the middle of the twentieth century, forcing us to consider the values that dominated the emerging era. Characters in the novel frequently comment on how the times are "dark," as Éomer puts it in *The Two Towers*—echoing what many commentators said about World War II. The novel is a battle between the forces of good and evil, and the good side is represented by an alliance of various races with diverse customs and interests. The collaboration of Elves, Dwarves, Men, and Hobbits in pursuit of the common goal of saving the world—a sort of primordial version of the United Nations—presents an early vision of the global thinking that characterized postwar society. Cultural differences are present—we hear much about how different Dwarves are from Elves, for example—but they are put aside when collaboration is required. The pursuit of goodness and fellowship across races is part of what makes *The Lord of the Rings* so enduring in difficult historical times.

THE
FELLOWSHIP
OF THE RING

PLOT OVERVIEW

THE FELLOWSHIP OF THE RING is the first of three volumes in *The Lord of the Rings,* an epic set in the fictional world of Middle-earth. The Lord of the Rings is an entity named Sauron, the Dark Lord, who long ago lost the One Ring that contains much of his power. His overriding desire is to reclaim the Ring and use it to enslave all of Middle-earth.

The story of *The Lord of the Rings* begins with several events that take place in *The Hobbit.* While wandering lost in a deep cave, Bilbo Baggins, a Hobbit—one of a small, kindly race about half the size of Men—stumbles upon a ring and takes it back with him to the Shire, the part of Middle-earth that is the Hobbits' home. All Bilbo knows of his ring is that wearing it causes him to become invisible. He is unaware that it is the One Ring, and is therefore oblivious to its significance and to the fact that Sauron has been searching for it.

The Fellowship of the Ring opens with a party for Bilbo's 111th birthday. Bilbo gives his ring to his heir, his cousin Frodo Baggins. When the time comes to part with the ring, however, Bilbo becomes strangely reluctant to do so. He gives up the ring only at the determined urging of his friend, Gandalf the Grey, a great Wizard. Gandalf suspects that the ring is indeed the One Ring of legend. After confirming his suspicions, he tells Frodo that the Ring must be taken away from the Shire, as Sauron's power is growing once again.

Frodo sets out from the Shire with three of his Hobbit friends—Sam, Merry, and Pippin. Along the way, they are pursued by the nine Ringwraiths, servants of Sauron who take the form of terrifying Black Riders. The hobbits spend a night in the company of wandering Elves, who promise to send word ahead to friends who will protect the hobbits. Barely out of the Shire, the hobbits get lost in the Old Forest, where they have to be rescued from a malevolent willow tree, which swallows up Merry and Pippin, and then from an evil tomb ghost. The hobbits' rescuer is Tom Bombadil, a strange, jovial entity with great powers who is the oldest creature in Middle-earth.

The hobbits make it to the town of Bree, where they meet Aragorn, a Ranger who roams the wilderness and who is the heir of the Kings of the ancient Men of Westernesse. Those who do not know Aragorn's true name call him Strider. Frodo tries to keep a low profile at the inn in Bree, but he ends up causing a scene when while taking part in a rollicking rendition of a song he falls, accidentally slips the Ring onto his finger, and vanishes.

That night, Aragorn advises the hobbits not to sleep in their rooms at the inn. In doing so, he saves their lives—for the first of many times. A letter Gandalf left at the inn months before advises the group to head for Rivendell, a realm of the Elves. Aragorn sets out with the hobbits the next day, and with his help they avoid the Black Riders for some time. However, at the top of the hill Weathertop, the Company is forced to defend itself against the attacking Riders. Frodo is wounded during the skirmish.

Frodo's wound, made by a weapon of a servant of Sauron, plagues the hobbit as the Company makes its way eastward. Aragorn is greatly concerned about the power the wound might exert over Frodo. Near Rivendell they meet the Elf-lord Glorfindel, who has been out looking for them. At the last ford before Rivendell, Frodo, riding Glorfindel's horse, outruns the ambushing Black Riders, who are swept away in a flood created by Elrond, the master of Rivendell.

Elrond heals Frodo and then holds a meeting to discuss what to do about the Ring. During this Council, Frodo learns the full history of the Ring. Frodo accepts the burden of taking the Ring to the only place it can be destroyed—the place where it was forged. It promises to be a long, nearly impossible journey, as the Ring was forged in the Cracks of Doom, part of the fiery mountain Orodruin in the very heart of Sauron's realm of Mordor.

At the end of the meeting, the Council creates a group to help Frodo in his quest. In addition to Frodo, the Fellowship of the Ring includes Sam, Merry, Pippin, Aragorn, Gandalf, an Elf named Legolas, a Dwarf named Gimli, and a Man from the south named Boromir.

The Fellowship heads south and attempts to pass over the Misty Mountains via the pass of Caradhras. Their way is blocked by snow and rock slides, and they are forced to divert their path through the Mines of Moria—the ancient, underground realm of the Dwarves. During the journey through Moria, Gandalf falls into the chasm of Khazad-dûm while protecting the Company from a Balrog, a terrible demon.

The rest of the party continues on to Lórien, the forest of the Galadrim Elves, where the Lady Galadriel tests their hearts and gives them gifts to help them on the quest. Frodo, spellbound by Galadriel's power and wisdom, offers her the Ring. She refuses, however,

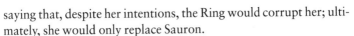

saying that, despite her intentions, the Ring would corrupt her; ultimately, she would only replace Sauron.

Leaving Lórien, the Fellowship travels by boat down the Great River, Anduin. At night, they spot Gollum—a deformed creature that had once owned the Ring but then lost it to Bilbo Baggins in *The Hobbit*—following them. When they reach the Falls of Rauros, the Fellowship must decide whether to head toward Mordor on the east or toward the safety of the city of Minas Tirith to the west.

Boromir, overcome by the Ring's power and desiring the Ring for himself, confronts Frodo. Frodo fends off Boromir and decides that he must go on to Mordor rather than to the safety of Minas Tirith. However, Frodo cannot bear the thought of imperiling his friends on the dangerous journey or allowing the Ring to corrupt them, so he attempts to leave secretly and continue the quest alone. Frodo does not, however, manage to elude Sam, so the two of them set out together for Mordor.

PLOT OVERVIEW

Character List

The Fellowship

Frodo Baggins The main protagonist of *The Lord of the Rings,* a Hobbit of exceptional character. Frodo is also a friend of the Elves, knowledgeable in their language and a lover of their songs. Like Bilbo—or any other good Hobbit—Frodo loves good food and simple comforts, but he is also thoughtful and curious and has a wisdom and strength of character that set him apart.

Samwise (Sam) Gamgee The former gardener at Bag End and Frodo's indomitable servant throughout his quest. Although Sam is not extraordinarily wise or intelligent, his common sense and powers of observation serve him well. Perhaps most important, he is stubborn, brave, and deeply loyal to Frodo.

Gandalf the Grey One of the five great Wizards in Middle-earth, second in his order only to Saruman. Known to most Hobbits only as a creator of fine fireworks, Gandalf is actually powerful beyond their imagination. He is also wise, humorous, kind, and generous, though sometimes short-tempered.

Legolas An Elf from Mirkwood. Legolas is light on his feet and masterful with a bow. After overcoming initial differences that stem from the historical antipathy between their races, he and the Dwarf Gimli become fast friends.

Gimli A Dwarf, the son of Glóin (one of Bilbo's company in *The Hobbit*). Gimli bristles when he feels insulted, but he is noble, stalwart, and brave.

Aragorn   The heir of Isildur, one of the few Men from the great race of Númenor left in Middle-earth. Aragorn is also known as Strider. Before the coming of the Ring, he lived as a Ranger in the North, protecting the Shire and other lands from servants of the Enemy. Aragorn is a formidable warrior and tracker.

Boromir   One of the Men of Gondor, from the city of Minas Tirith in the south. Boromir is a valiant fighter and is always trustworthy in battle, but his pride and recklessness make him vulnerable to the Ring's power.

Peregrin (Pippin) Took A young and somewhat rash Hobbit. Pippin is good-natured and a bit of a smart aleck.

Meriadoc (Merry) Brandybuck A young Hobbit from Buckland. Merry has a temperament similar to Pippin's, though he is more mature and, unlike most Hobbits, not afraid of boats and water.

ENEMIES AND MALEVOLENT BEINGS

Sauron   The antagonist and title character of *The Lord of the Rings*. The Dark Lord Sauron, a servant of Morgoth, the Great Enemy, took his master's place after the First Age. The enormously powerful Sauron is never seen at any point in the novel; he is represented only by images of his Great Eye or the Dark Tower where he resides. He fervently desires the One Ring, which he created long ago and which holds a great part of his power. Sauron is wise, but he only thinks in terms of desire—especially desire for power. He therefore does not understand those who would want to destroy the Ring rather than use it—which is perhaps his only weakness.

CHARACTER LIST

The Ringwraiths Nine minions of Sauron who ceaselessly search for the One Ring. The Ringwraiths—also known as the Black Riders, the Nine, or the Nazgûl (the Elvish term)—take the form of cloaked riders on terrifying black horses. They pursue Frodo incessantly, and are especially drawn to him at any moments when he puts the Ring on his finger.

Saruman the White The head of Gandalf's order of Wizards. Saruman advises the other Wizards not to challenge the growing power of Sauron. Gandalf, who suspects that Saruman intends to join Sauron's forces outright, confirms his suspicions when he travels to Saruman's tower, Orthanc. Saruman does not himself appear as a character until *The Two Towers,* but his presence and influence are clearly felt in *The Fellowship of the Ring.*

Gollum (Sméagol) A hunched, miserable creature who was once Sméagol, a young boy of a Hobbit-like race. Sméagol killed his friend Déagol after Déagol found the One Ring on the bottom of the Anduin River. The Ring corrupted Sméagol and changed him into his current form, the creature called Gollum. Gollum maintained possession of the Ring until he lost in it in his caves in the Misty Mountains, where Bilbo recovered it.

The Balrog A mysterious, gigantic, terrifying elemental demon from deep inside the earth. The Balrog, the "nameless fear" awakened by the Dwarves in the Mines of Moria, emerges from the depths when the Fellowship passes through the Mines, and it ultimately confronts Gandalf in an epic battle. The Balrog, which brandishes an enormous flaming sword and whip, is wreathed in flame and yet exudes shadow and darkness.

Orcs Squat, swarthy, wretched creatures that are seemingly limitless in number and that serve the purposes of Sauron. Hordes of Orcs, which are unable to withstand daylight and therefore emerge almost exclusively at night, pursue the Fellowship through the Mines of

Moria and beyond; it is presumed that the Orcs are also responsible for the death of Balin and the other Dwarves who returned to Moria in an attempt to reclaim the ancient Dwarf realm there.

Bill Ferny   A swarthy, suspicious fellow in Bree who appears to have been paid off by the Black Riders to watch Frodo's movements. Bill Ferny sells the hobbits a half-starved pony at a high price to replace the ponies the Black Riders set loose the night before.

ELVES

Elrond Halfelven The Master of Rivendell. Elrond is descended from a Man and an Elf—thus, "Halfelven." He had the choice to be mortal or immortal and chose the latter. As a consequence, Elrond must leave Middle-earth when the time comes, most likely at the end of the War of the Ring. He is renowned for his wisdom and learning.

Galadriel   The Lady of Lothlórien and perhaps the wisest of the Elves. Galadriel bears one of the Elven Rings of Power and uses it to read Sauron's mind. Like Elrond, she sometimes appears as less a character than an embodiment of physical, mental, and spiritual perfection.

Celeborn   The husband of Galadriel. Celeborn and Galadriel, who both appear to be timeless, ageless beings, rule as Lord and Lady of Lórien, the Elvish forest.

Arwen Evenstar Elrond's beautiful daughter, who plays only a minor role in *The Fellowship of the Ring,* but becomes more prominent later in *The Lord of the Rings.*

Gildor Inglorion An Elf whose approach saves the hobbits from an encounter with one of the Black Riders. Gildor tells Frodo that the mysterious Black Riders are servants of the Enemy and must be avoided at all costs.

Glorfindel   An Elf-lord and friend of Aragorn. Glorfindel, who lives in Rivendell, attends the Council of Elrond, which is called to determine what should be done with the Ring.

Erestor   Another Elf-lord who attends the Council of Elrond. Erestor suggests that the Ring be given to Tom Bombadil, over whom it has no power; the others at the Council, however, worry that even Bombadil could not single-handedly defeat Sauron.

Haldir   The leader of the group of Elves who halt the Fellowship's entry into the forest of Lothlórien. Haldir then leads the Fellowship into the heart of the forest to meet Galadriel.

HOBBITS

Bilbo Baggins   The hero of *The Hobbit* and Frodo's cousin and mentor. Bilbo is clever and loves a good joke or song. The effects of having kept the Ring for so long only occasionally mar his thoughtfulness. Bilbo is an object of curiosity in the Shire for his learning and his wandering ways, and he is trying to write a book detailing his many adventures.

Lobelia Sackville-Baggins   A relative of Bilbo who buys Bag End from Frodo when he leaves the Shire to go on his quest. The disagreeable Lobelia has been trying to get her hands on the house at Bag End for some time.

Fredegar (Fatty) Bolger   A friend of Merry who helps the hobbits move Frodo's things to his new house across the Brandywine River. Fatty stays behind at the house to keep up the pretense that Frodo still lives in the Shire.

Ham Gamgee (the Gaffer)   Sam's father, who lives next door to Bag End. Just before Frodo leaves the Shire, the Gaffer is visited by one of the Ringwraiths, which asks him about the whereabouts of a Mr. Baggins.

Farmer Maggot A farmer who drives Frodo and company to the Brandywine River ferry in his wagon. Farmer Maggot once caught Frodo stealing his mushrooms, so Frodo is afraid of him.

OTHER ALLIES AND BENEVOLENT BEINGS

Barliman Butterbur The innkeeper at the Prancing Pony in Bree. Though a forgetful fellow, Butterbur does finally remember to deliver Gandalf's letter to Frodo when the hobbit passes through Bree.

Tom Bombadil A jovial, mysterious, and powerful being who dances around his small realm, singing songs in doggerel. Tom is extremely old, perhaps immortal, and his origins are unknown. He has great power and is deeply connected to the earth, but he is unconcerned with the world outside his realm.

Goldberry Tom Bombadil's wife. Goldberry has a presence that moves Frodo in a way similar to that of the Elves.

Glóin Gimli's father. Glóin, one of the Dwarves who traveled with Bilbo on the adventures that take place in *The Hobbit,* is present at the Council of Elrond where the Fellowship is established.

Gwaihir, the Windlord The swiftest of the Great Eagles, who rescues Gandalf from the top of Orthanc and takes the wizard to Rohan.

Shadowfax The swiftest of all horses, whom Gandalf tames for his own use.

HISTORICAL FIGURES

Gil-galad An ancient Elven-king who fought in a climactic battle against Sauron ages ago. Gil-galad was killed in the battle, in which Sauron lost the One Ring at Isildur's hand.

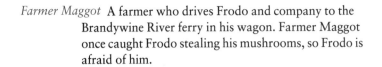

CHARACTER LIST

Elendil   An ancient king of Westernesse who allied his armies with Gil-galad's to take on Sauron. Elendil, an ancestor of Aragorn's line, was killed along with Gil-galad in the battle.

Isildur   The eldest son and heir of Elendil. In the great battle against Sauron in ancient times, Isildur cut the One Ring from Sauron's hand, but then lost the Ring in the Great River, Anduin.

ANALYSIS OF MAJOR CHARACTERS

FRODO BAGGINS

As the Ring-bearer and then principal protagonist of *The Lord of the Rings*, Frodo is endowed with a temperament well suited to resist evil. He is brave, selfless, thoughtful, wise, observant, and even unfailingly polite. Unlike the common run of provincial, self-satisfied Hobbits, Frodo is curious about the outside world and knowledgeable about the traditions of the Elves. As everyone from Bilbo to Gandalf to Aragorn notices, there is something special in Frodo, something that sets him apart from the rest of his race—a fineness, perhaps, or an inner strength. Frodo's goodness, wisdom, and generally impeccable character might make him seem one-dimensional if he were not so frequently wracked with doubt and faced with obstacles he feels unable to surmount. Frodo is not Elrond, nor even Aragorn; he has no otherworldly powers or even physical prowess. Frodo is initially so weak he can barely even get out of the Shire without the help of Farmer Maggot and then Tom Bombadil.

The Hobbit, small and furtive, is a clever inversion of the typical epic hero—an Odysseus or Beowulf—whose strength and bravery equip him in his struggles against monsters and angry gods. In this sense, Frodo can be seen as a very Christian protagonist. Christianity celebrates the power of humility: it teaches that strength of character triumphs over strength of arms, that the path to salvation lies through sacrifice—even self-sacrifice—in the face of a greater power. Frodo's stewardship of the Ring and his heroism, which consists largely of resisting the temptation to use the Ring, exemplify these ideas.

Perhaps what distinguishes Frodo more than any other quality is the sense of remote sadness and reluctance that surrounds him. Unlike Aragorn or even Gandalf, there is no particular glory associated with Frodo. He has a great task, but it is to him simply a burden—one that grows heavier as the quest progresses. While in the Shire, Frodo dreamed of adventure; on his quest, he simply longs for home. In this sense, Frodo is again a different hero than the traditional sort. His great adventure does not feel like an adventure to him; it is simply a task, and an impossible one at that. Frodo does not long for the thrill of exploration or battle or timeless deeds of heroism. As such, his willingness to go ahead with the quest speaks much about the sort of strength of character Tolkien values.

SAM GAMGEE

The loyal Sam consistently serves as a foil to all of the grandeur and earthshaking events that take place in *The Lord of the Rings*. Some readers may find Sam's folksy wisdom and extreme devotion to Frodo somewhat cloying, but these traits do allow Tolkien to keep a little bit of the flavor of the Shire with the Fellowship as it moves toward the dark land of Mordor. Sam is much more the typical Hobbit than Frodo, though Sam, too, displays a great curiosity about the world beyond the Shire, especially Elves. Sam is shy and somewhat awkward socially, but he is ferocious in a fight and clever and quick on his feet. His speech consistently has a modest, awestruck tone. Tolkien, for instance, speaks through Sam when he wishes to capture the particular grace of the Elves simply and directly. Sam also serves as a foil for Frodo's melancholy and fatalism. When Frodo becomes increasingly preoccupied with the great burden of the Ring, he comes to rely more and more on Sam for help. Indeed, throughout even the lowest and most hopeless points of the journey, Sam remains relentlessly pragmatic and optimistic. If it is Frodo's duty to "carry" the Ring, it is often Sam's duty to carry Frodo.

GANDALF THE GREY

Gandalf is a Wizard of surpassing power and wisdom, but when we first meet him he merely appears to be a wizened old man driving a wagon full of fireworks. This mix of the awe-inspiring and the touchingly human defines Gandalf. He is as comfortable at a Hobbit birthday party as at the Council of Elrond, and he counts both the celestial Galadriel and the lowly Barliman Butterbur among his friends. This quality makes Gandalf a more sympathetic character than the sometimes aloof Elves. It also gives him insights that even the wise Elrond misses, as when Gandalf supports Pippin and Merry's wish to be included in the Fellowship on the grounds that their loyalty to Frodo makes up for their lack of experience and strength.

Paradoxically, we see Gandalf grow in power throughout *The Fellowship of the Ring* even as he comes up against obstacles that show him at the limits of his power. He is tested again and again, whether by Saruman or at the Door to Moria or, finally, on the Bridge of Khazad-dûm. In some of these moments Gandalf responds with a blazing magical spell or a feat of wizardry, but in others he triumphs in more modest, human ways. After many unsuccessful attempts to open the Door to Moria, Gandalf finally realizes that the password is a deceptively simple riddle. When he cannot remember which way to go in the tunnels of Moria, he calms himself down with a smoke. As we see later, in *The Two Towers*, Gandalf returns, having survived his battle with the fearsome Balrog and been made even more powerful by his trial. Nevertheless, even at the height of his powers, Gandalf retains his common touch.

ARAGORN

Aragorn, much like Gandalf, hides an impressive amount of power, greatness, and knowledge under a humble exterior. We first meet Aragorn as Strider, the laconic, worn Ranger at the Prancing Pony inn in Bree. As the action moves forward, we see Aragorn slowly transform into the king he is destined to become. Aragorn also displays Gandalf's bravery, kindness, and wisdom—indeed, neither of them appear to have any major faults to speak of. At certain moments, however, Aragorn does display a sort of vulnerability. When questioned about why he does not immediately offer proof of his identity to the hobbits in Bree, one of his answers is simply that he wishes the hobbits would count him as a friend without knowledge of his lineage—indeed, he is tired of being constantly wary. Such an admission is a poignant revelation of a somewhat unexpected trait in such an indomitable woodsman and warrior as Aragorn.

THEMES, MOTIFS & SYMBOLS

THEMES

THEMES

Themes are the fundamental and often universal ideas explored in a literary work.

THE CORRUPTING INFLUENCE OF POWER

Sauron bound up much of his power in the One Ring when he forged it ages ago, and whoever wields the Ring has access to some of that power. The full extent and nature of the Ring's power never becomes entirely clear to us, but we get the sense that the Ring symbolizes a power almost without limits, and which is utterly corrupting. It is immensely difficult for many of the characters to resist the temptation to take the Ring for themselves and use it for their own ends. Regardless of the wearer's initial intentions, good or evil, the Ring's power always turns the wearer to evil. Indeed, even keeping the Ring is dangerous. *The Fellowship of the Ring* is strewn with examples of those who are corrupted by the Ring. The power of the Ring transformed the Black Riders, once human kings, into fearsome, undead Ringwraiths. Gollum, once a young boy named Sméagol, killed his friend Déagol for the Ring and then gradually became a wretched, crouching, froglike creature who thinks only of his desire to retrieve the Ring for himself. During the travels of the Fellowship, Boromir grows increasingly corrupted by the proximity of the Ring, wanting to use its power to destroy Sauron rather than destroy the Ring itself, as Elrond and Gandalf have advised; ultimately, the Ring leads Boromir to desire it for himself. For many, the great power offered by the Ring overrides all rational thought. The power of the Ring is by no means the only temptation in Middle-earth—the Dwarves of Moria, for example, coveted *mithril* too much, and they dug so deep that they awakened the Balrog beneath them—but the Ring is the greatest temptation and therefore the greatest threat.

The Inevitability of Decline

The Middle-earth of *The Lord of the Rings* is a world on the cusp of a transformation. After the events the novel describes, the age of the Elves will pass and the age of Men will dawn. A large portion of the story eulogizes this passing age of the Elves. The Elves and their realms have a beauty and grace unmatched by anything else in Middle-earth. Though the Elves themselves are immortal, as Galadriel tells us, the destruction of Sauron's One Ring will weaken the Three Elven Rings, forcing the Elves to leave Middle-earth and fade away. Throughout the novel, Tolkien gives us the sense that the adventures of the Ring represent the last burst of a sort of magic that will not be found in the world that comes afterward. This later world will be a world without Sauron, but also a world without Lothlórien. Even in chapters about the Hobbits and the lowly Shire, we sense that we are witnessing something good and pure that is, for whatever reason, no longer present in this world. The Hobbits, the narrator tells us, have become somewhat estranged from Men in the times since *The Lord of the Rings* took place, and now avoid us "with dismay."

The Power of Myth

The sense of transience and lost grandeur that pervades *The Lord of the Rings* goes, in part, with the territory in which Tolkien is wading. He writes the novel in a mythic mode, and one of the conventions of myth is that it describes a past that is more glorious than the present. This sense of loss certainly is present in the Greek myths, for example, or in Homer's epic poems that draw on these myths—both of which describe a world in which men and gods mix freely, a world that is no more. Tolkien's own work is something between mythology and fiction, locating itself in a middle ground between a past that is remembered only in song and the everyday present of the reader. This sense of ancientness is constantly present, brought to life in chants, poems, and graven inscriptions. As Tolkien shows again and again—whether with the Elves or with the Númenóreans or the Dwarves—the stories that the characters tell define them. In some cases, as with Aragorn for example, this mythology explains not only where a character comes from, but also where he or she is going. The characters carry their past and their lore around with them, and they are virtually unable to speak without referring to this lore. The twist Tolkien adds is that these "myths," while retaining all of the usual metaphorical resonance and symbolic simplicity, also happen to be true—at least in his world. This sense of reality within the novel, in turn, lends power to even the most everyday occurrences in Middle-earth.

Motifs

Motifs are recurring structures, contrasts, or literary devices that can help to develop and inform the text's major themes.

Songs and Singing

It is no exaggeration to say that *The Lord of the Rings* is literally filled with song. Nearly every character seems to burst into at least one song throughout the course of the novel. Moreover, each song is presented to us in its entirety, with every verse and refrain included. The ubiquity of song in the novel serves a number of purposes. First, the songs link the action of the novel to a distant past, a time long before the written word was dominant over the spoken word. The profusion of songs gives us the sense that the story we are reading is closely tied to something ancient, such as myth or folklore, a body of knowledge or tradition that has been memorized and passed along orally. Furthermore, as the events of which the characters sing are real—at least within the world of Middle-earth—we can easily imagine that, ages later, there will be ancient songs celebrating the deeds of Frodo and the Fellowship. The novel's emphasis on the spoken word also highlights the existence and the sounds of the hundreds, if not thousands, of words—names, place names, terms for emotions, fantastical animals, plants, and other creatures—that Tolkien created in writing the novel. A trained philologist, Tolkien obviously took much care in his invention of the linguistic elements of his universe. One remarkable aspect of *The Lord of the Rings* is that Tolkien's names, without resorting to familiar words, clearly convey the nature of what they describe: is there any question that the mellifluous-sounding Galadriel is benevolent, while an Orc or a Balrog is evil?

The Road

Early in the journey, Frodo recalls how Bilbo always used to warn, "It's a dangerous business, Frodo, going out of your door. You step into the Road, and if you don't keep your feet, there is no knowing where you might be swept off to." This idea of the road as a river, sweeping travelers before it, suggests the means by which Tolkien himself keeps the action of his novel moving—by keeping his characters moving. *The Lord of the Rings* shares this motif of the road and the quest with many of the great epics that precede it, from the *Odyssey* to *Beowulf*; furthermore, the vast majority of all quests depend on a road or journey of some kind or another. The road takes the hobbits out from the familiar confines of the Shire and into the unknown, where, like all epic heroes, they are tested. It exposes them to previously unthinkable dangers, such as the Black Riders and the fury of Caradhras, but also to the unimaginable beauty of places such as Rivendell and Lothlórien. More than a physical means of travel and a narrative means of advancing the plot, the road also emphasizes the fact that nothing stands still in Tolkien's universe; everything is in constant motion. Significantly, the first Elves the hobbits meet are on the road—Elves heading west to the shore before leaving Middle-earth. Time, like the road, sweeps all before it into the distance. Legolas's lament upon leaving Lothlórien sums up the link between the two perfectly: "For such is the way of it: to find and to lose, as it seems to those whose boat is on the running stream."

PROPHECY

Very little happens in Middle-earth that someone, somewhere, has not already prophesied. These prophecies, like the songs that often contain them, link the past to the present, and beyond to the near or even distant future. Like the road, these prophecies move the plot forward, setting up targets for which the plot then aims. These targets are crucial to the remarkable sense of suspense and anticipation Tolkien is able to maintain throughout the whole of *The Lord of the Rings,* which totals more than 1,000 pages in length. In this heavy use of prophecy Tolkien takes a cue from the ancient mythological tradition. Just as Greek heroes such as Theseus and Hercules lived out the predictions of prophecies made long before their births, so do Aragorn and Frodo. The repeated presence of prophecies also shows the great importance of fate in Tolkien's Middle-earth. Things in this universe happen for a reason, though perhaps one that is not immediately clear. Gandalf invokes the hand of fate in his explanation of why Bilbo was the one to stumble across the Ring in the first place. Furthermore, fate is partly why Gandalf spares the wretched Gollum; the wizard has a suspicion that Gollum still has some part to play in the saga of the Ring. The presence of

MOTIFS

such a logic and will beyond the knowledge of any of even the most powerful of the characters is as close as Tolkien comes to implying an overarching consciousness or higher power that controls all of Middle-earth.

SYMBOLS

Symbols are objects, characters, figures, or colors used to represent abstract ideas or concepts.

THE RINGS OF POWER
The Rings of Power represent pure, limitless power and its attendant responsibilities and dangers. The One Ring of Sauron confers almost unimaginable power to its wearer; however, in return, it exerts an immense pressure on its wearer, and inevitably corrupts him or her. The Three Elven Rings, on the other hand, are imbued with a different sort of power, one closely tied to learning and building. Galadriel's ring, for instance, gives the Lady of Lórien the power of sight into the unknown, which she uses to good ends. Galadriel's ability to use her ring responsibly is rooted in the unwavering self-control she demonstrates when she refuses the take the One Ring from Frodo.

THE SWORD OF ELENDIL
The legendary Sword that was Broken once belonged to Elendil, an ancient ancestor of Aragorn's line who died in battle at the Siege of Barad-dûr, the assault on Sauron's stronghold. The sword was broken under Elendil when he died, and its shattered remains have been passed down for generations as an heirloom of his once-great kingdom, now fallen into decay. Aragorn, Elendil's distant heir, carries the fragments of the sword with him. When Aragorn has the sword reforged in Rivendell, renaming it Andúril, it becomes a symbol of Aragorn's greatness and a sign that Aragorn is officially setting out to claim his birthright in the House of Isildur. In a sense, the sword mirrors Aragorn himself. When we first meet Aragorn, he appears to be merely a haggard, weatherworn Ranger, but later he is revealed to be the heir of an ancient and glorious lineage—just as the sword, initially merely a collection of shattered metal fragments, is transformed into a weapon of great beauty and power.

The Mirror of Galadriel

Galadriel's mirror, into which she invites Frodo and Sam to gaze, serves as a symbol of the ambiguity of the gift of knowledge and the ultimate incomprehensibility of fate. Looking into the mirror, one sees events and places that have been, or that are, or that may be—though one is never sure which. It is impossible, therefore, to try to escape what is shown in the mirror, or to alter one's actions to fit the scenes that are shown. The events shown in the mirror will happen, or perhaps have happened already; as such, the reasons or explanations for these fated happenings are largely irrelevant and inconsequential. The only matter of importance regarding the knowledge the mirror reveals is what one ultimately does with that knowledge—whether one uses it responsibly, or toward evil ends. Even Galadriel herself, though a being of great power, has no control over the events depicted in the mirror. At times, the force of fate is indeed great, and no being in Middle-earth has the power to stop it.

SYMBOLS

Summary & Analysis

Prologue

Summary

Dense with detail, the Prologue is an extended introduction to the history and customs of the race known as the Hobbits. According to Tolkien's fiction, their story has been passed down to us in the form of a travel narrative called the Red Book of Westmarch, written by a Hobbit named Bilbo Baggins who journeyed to the East and returned to tell about his trip. Hobbits are small, portly, good-natured, skillful at crafts and gardening, and have impressive appetites. Most Hobbits live in the Shire, an area of Middle-earth to which they migrated from the East more than 1,000 years before the events of *The Lord of the Rings* take place. They were shy even in ancient times, when the events of *The Lord of the Rings* occur, but were originally a bit more active than they are today. Hobbits do not wear shoes, as their feet are tough and leathery and covered on top with curly hair. They are provincial in outlook, for the most part uninterested in the wide world. Their sole contribution to culture has been the introduction of pipe tobacco. They have remained almost entirely on the margins of historical events that have occurred since their migration. However, they can demonstrate surprising toughness and courage when called upon.

The first Hobbit to make a name for himself in the wider world was Bilbo Baggins, author of the travel writings on which *The Lord of the Rings* is supposedly based. As described in *The Hobbit,* Bilbo, at the suggestion of the great Wizard, Gandalf the Grey, went off with the dwarf Thorin Oakenshield in search of a lost treasure. Along the way, escaping from Orcs—a vicious race of squat, swarthy creatures—Bilbo was lost for a time in the mines under the Misty Mountains. Groping in the dark, he stumbled upon a ring on the ground. The owner of the ring, a miserable creature called Gollum, lived in the mines. When the two met, Gollum challenged Bilbo to a riddle contest. If Gollum won, he would get to kill Bilbo and eat him; if Bilbo won, Gollum would have to show Bilbo the way out of the mines. In the end Bilbo won, though his final riddle—"What have I got in my pocket?"—was not, in fact, much of a riddle.

However, Gollum, when he discovered that Bilbo had the ring, flew into a rage. In fleeing Gollum, Bilbo accidentally discovered that the ring made its wearer invisible, and he used this power to escape. Curiously, ever after, in recounting the story of how he came by the ring, Bilbo lied, saying that Gollum had offered it to him as a present. Only when pointedly questioned by the skeptical Gandalf did Bilbo reveal the truth.

ANALYSIS

Tolkien initiates us into the world of Middle-earth in a sophisticated way. The events and background of *The Lord of the Rings* are not simply narrated to us by a detached storyteller who conceived them in his imagination. Instead, the narrator presents his tale as a historical record based upon a variety of different sources: chronicle histories written from the perspectives of both Elves and Men, folklore and oral tradition, and the narrator's meticulous knowledge of the language and customs of the peoples he describes. The narrator assembles all of these disparate materials to create a history that is broader in scope than the history of any one race or people.

We may be surprised to learn that *The Hobbit,* Tolkien's earlier novel, is actually one of the narrator's archival sources, supposedly a part of a larger book we were unaware of called the Red Book of Westmarch. Although *The Hobbit* itself is narrated in the manner of a children's book, we are now invited to believe that the earlier novel was discovered, not created. In presenting the Hobbits' tale in this way, Tolkien follows in the footsteps of many great works of Western literature, such as *Don Quixote,* whose author, Cervantes, pretended to have discovered the manuscript of the novel and published it. There is thus a long tradition of works that claim not to be authored by their authors. One result of this device is that the characters' world and the readers' world are brought closer together. If Bilbo's narrative found its way into our everyday lives, then perhaps we could find our way into Bilbo's world. Although a huge historical gap separates us from him, still we feel that the only difference between the Hobbits' reality and our own is the intervention of a few millennia. The earth he walked on is the same earth we walk on, and the closeness heightens our identification with Bilbo, Frodo, and all the other characters we are about to meet.

The characteristics of the Hobbits are first outlined in the Prologue, and we get a surprising portrait of the creatures that we expect to be the heroes of this narrative. They are hardly noble or majestic in appearance or lifestyle. They are short and dumpy, and most of them live in holes underground. They like food and leisure more than we would expect from the leaders of a mission to rid the world of evil. Our first introduction to Bilbo, recalling events first narrated in *The Hobbit,* underscores this impression, since he is somewhat disappointingly presented. He is not busily arranging his affairs or impressing his peers with his strength of character; rather, he is lost in some mine shafts. Yes, he is on a quest—for treasure—but he is misdirected and unable to find his way. Yet there is a long literary tradition behind this sort of introduction as well. Dante opens *The Divine Comedy* with a scene of himself lost in the woods and unable to orient himself, and his perplexity at the beginning only emphasizes the wisdom he gains later when he does find his way in life. There is an innocence in Bilbo that his clueless demeanor reflects, and that may indicate a capacity for moral heroism. Honesty and candor may matter more than strength or swiftness.

The confrontation with Gollum, though it seemed to be only one of many colorful episodes in *The Hobbit,* now turns out to be central to *The Lord of the Rings.* On a plot level, Bilbo's meeting with Gollum explains the way in which the all-powerful Ring of Sauron came into the possession of the undistinguished Hobbit race in the first place. But on a symbolic level, it also represents the standoff between Hobbit simplicity and alien deception, as the insidious Gollum tries to trick Bilbo with his riddle wager. Bilbo is unaccustomed to verbal complexity, and he has certainly never played a game on which his life depended. He believes in simple deeds, and merely wants to get out of the caves. With all Gollum's cleverness, it seems that Bilbo is fated to lose. But we get a glimpse of the hidden virtues of Hobbit straightforwardness when Bilbo's riddle—"What have I got in my pocket?"—stumps Gollum precisely because it is so simple. It is not a riddle at all, and it infuriates Gollum with its obviousness. Indeed, in the end, Bilbo proves victorious. We see already that the Hobbits' lack of sophistication or worldly wisdom may actually be an asset to them.

BOOK I, CHAPTER I

SUMMARY — A LONG-EXPECTED PARTY

Because of the stories and wealth he brought back from his adventures, Bilbo Baggins is the most famous hobbit in Hobbiton. He is also considered a bit strange, however. The fact that he receives visits at his house, Bag End, from Elves, Dwarves, and the wizard Gandalf make him the object of some slight suspicion. In addition, ever since Bilbo came back to the Shire with the ring—which he has kept secret from nearly everyone—he has not seemed to age at all. In fact, he reaches his 111th birthday virtually unchanged.

When Bilbo announces that he is throwing a grand party for his "eleventy-first" birthday, everyone in the Shire takes interest. After extensive and elaborate preparation, the day of Bilbo's birthday finally arrives. All of Hobbiton has a fine time eating, drinking, and watching the spectacular fireworks provided by Gandalf.

As dinner winds down, Bilbo rises and asks to speak to the assembled guests. The speech is short. Just as Bilbo is starting to lose his audience's attention, he announces that he is leaving, and he suddenly disappears in a flash of light. The party guests are not amused, and they return, muttering, to their eating and drinking.

Bilbo, having used his ring to become invisible, walks back to Bag End, takes off the ring and begins packing for a journey. Gandalf arrives at the house shortly thereafter. Bilbo tells the wizard how excited he is to travel again, to see the world outside the Shire. He says that he has felt worn out recently, "like butter that has been scraped over too much bread." Gandalf reminds Bilbo of the promise he made to leave the magic ring for his favorite cousin, young Frodo Baggins. Frodo is an orphan whom Bilbo has taken under his wing and named as the heir to his home and possessions.

Bilbo, however, is suddenly reluctant to part with the ring, and he even lashes out at Gandalf for pressuring him to keep his promise. Finally, Bilbo gives in, saying that in a way it will be relief to be rid of the ring. Even then, Gandalf has to remind Bilbo one last time to leave the ring behind as Bilbo is on his way out the door. When Bilbo finally takes the ring out of his pocket, he hesitates one last time in handing it over. He drops the ring, and when Gandalf quickly picks it up, Bilbo starts angrily. Bilbo quickly relaxes into a smile, however, and sets off jauntily with his three Dwarf companions.

Frodo arrives back at the house soon after Bilbo leaves. Gandalf tells Frodo that Bilbo has left the ring for him. He warns Frodo not to use the ring and to keep it secret and safe. All the next day, Frodo busily distributes the gifts Bilbo left for various Hobbits, and he deals with all sorts of inquisitive and bothersome visitors. After the gifts have been distributed, Gandalf arrives, seeming troubled, to tell Frodo he is leaving immediately. Gandalf asks Frodo what he knows about the ring, and he warns Frodo again not to use the ring and to keep it a secret.

ANALYSIS

One of the great accomplishments—and much of the appeal—of *The Lord of the Rings* is the exhaustive level of detail of the world Tolkien creates. Middle-earth is full of different races and creatures, each with its own customs, language, history, and mythology. The Prologue, with its anthropological tone, has already prepared us for this unfamiliar world. The Prologue's level of detail—about the Shire's political structure and layout, as well as the habits of Hobbits—not only imbues everything with an aura of real history, but gives the weight of detail to a tale many readers might at first find too fanciful.

The Shire serves as a perfect jumping-off place for the tale. Like many of us modern readers, Hobbits are suspicious of talk of magic and monsters. The Shire, more than any other place in *The Lord of the Rings,* feels familiar, and would have been even more familiar for an English audience fifty years ago. With its cozy homes, small gardens and inns, and portly and good-natured farmers, the Shire is an idealized version of the English countryside in which Tolkien grew up. With its sleepy, complacent air and commonsense values, it appears to be on the sidelines of the sweeping battle about to be fought for the Ring. Perhaps most importantly, the Shire eases us into the fantastical landscape of Middle-earth. We, like Frodo and his Hobbit companions, set out into an unknown and mystical wider world from the comfortable confines of the Shire.

The Shire is not merely a quaint countryside steeped with charm. Though it is a comforting place, there is something severely limited—even stifling—in its provincial mindset. Bilbo and Frodo both appear to note this aspect of the Shire. Later, Frodo admits to Gandalf that he has often grown exasperated with the Shire and its inhabitants. Nonetheless, knowing of its existence during his travels is a comfort to Frodo: "I shall know that somewhere there is a firm foothold, even if my feet cannot stand there again." For all its limits, the Shire and the Hobbits who live in it represent the virtues of simplicity, stability, and determined practicality in the face of the head-spinning events to come.

For readers of *The Hobbit,* the picture of Bilbo presented in Chapter 1 may come as something of a shock. In *The Hobbit,* the elder Baggins is a jolly, somewhat bumbling hero, with great charisma and perhaps greater luck—in short, a character about whom we enjoy reading and with whom we long to identify. In *The Fellowship of the Ring,* however, we see that the many intervening years have changed Bilbo drastically, and not, it appears, for the better. The once-familiar Bilbo, through whose perspective we see virtually every enjoyable minute of *The Hobbit,* suddenly seems very foreign. Within the larger community of Hobbiton he appears to be an outmoded, odd old individual, and an object of great suspicion among the community. Though Tolkien tells us that the typical Hobbit's viewpoint is admittedly provincial, the community does appear to have valid concerns about Bilbo. Why does he receive such strange visitors? Why is it that, even at 111 years of age, he has not physically aged at all? Nonetheless, our hopes remain high for Bilbo's grand birthday celebration—but even that leads to a bit of a letdown when we see how the once-charismatic hobbit quickly loses the audience's attention even during his short speech.

Tolkien intends the new Bilbo to have exactly this sort of disorienting effect, and the author hints that a large part of this shift in Bilbo's character may be due to his possession of the mysterious ring for so many years. Whenever the subject of the ring comes up, Bilbo's behavior becomes strange, unpredictable, and erratic; his words turn defensive and evasive. We learn that Bilbo has kept the ring secret all these years, and we then see that he lies about it and attempts to keep it even after promising to hand it over to Gandalf. We hear Bilbo make the mysterious and perhaps surprising admission that it will, in a way, be a relief finally to be rid of the ring. Together, these elements of the first chapter raise a sense of foreboding about the ring, making us curious as to what exactly the ring is and what role it is to play in the story. Furthermore, as we know that the ring is being passed on to Frodo, we wonder whether it will have the same bizarre effects on this younger Baggins. These suspicions, compounded and made more ominous by Gandalf's tale in the upcoming chapter, hang over the entirety of the story of *The Lord of the Rings.* This masterful and subtle use of foreshadowing on Tolkien's part creates a sense of dread and anticipation, as we wonder and worry whether Frodo will himself fall victim to the ring's spell. This sense of foreboding expectancy drives the narrative forward, making a very lengthy novel breeze by as we await the answers to questions and issues raised here, in the opening pages.

SUMMARY & ANALYSIS

BOOK I, CHAPTER 2

From the beginning of the chapter to the end of Gandalf's story

SUMMARY — THE SHADOW OF THE PAST

> *"I wish it need not have happened in my time."*
> *(See* QUOTATIONS, *p. 82)*

Frodo sees little of Gandalf for seventeen years, until Frodo is nearly fifty years old. Odd rumors from the outside world begin to circulate through the Shire—news about an Enemy whose power is again growing in the land of Mordor, as well as tales about Orcs and Trolls and other terrible creatures. Though most Hobbits pay no attention to such gossip, young Sam Gamgee, who tends the garden at Bag End, is very interested.

Gandalf suddenly returns with ominous news. Apparently, the ring that Bilbo left to Frodo is more powerful than Gandalf thought. Gandalf had guessed immediately that it was one of the Rings of Power, made by the Elven-smiths ages ago, but he had not grown alarmed until he saw the strange effects the ring had on Bilbo.

To test the ring, the wizard takes it from Frodo and throws it in the fire. When Gandalf retrieves the ring from the flames, it is cool to the touch. Fiery letters in the language of Mordor appear on the ring, reading, "One Ring to rule them all, One Ring to find them, / One Ring to bring them all and in the darkness bind them."

Gandalf explains that the ring is the One Ring of Sauron, the Dark Lord. The Ring holds much of Sauron's power, as it controls the other Great Rings. Long before, three Rings were made for the Elves, seven for the Dwarves, and nine for Men. If Sauron should get hold of the One Ring again, nothing could stop him from enslaving all of Middle-earth. The Ring was taken from Sauron long ago, in a great battle between Sauron's forces and the allied armies of the Elves and the Men of Westernesse. Gil-galad, the Elven-king, and Elendil, King of Westernesse, were both killed in the battle; however, Elendil's son, Isildur, cut the Ring from Sauron's hand and took it for his own. The Ring was soon lost in the Great River, Anduin, when an army of Orcs attacked and killed Isildur.

Many years later, but still ages before Frodo's time, the Ring resurfaced. Déagol, a young boy of a Hobbit-like race, chanced upon the Ring on the bottom of the river. His friend Sméagol was with him at the time, and Sméagol demanded the Ring as a birthday present. When Déagol refused to hand over the Ring, Sméagol killed him. Sméagol discovered that the Ring made him invisible, and he used it for spying and thievery. Shunned by his family, Sméagol left home and eventually crept into the dark caves under the Misty Mountains, where he slowly became a hunched and miserable creature. That creature was Gollum, who later lost the Ring to Bilbo Baggins. The Ring, according to Gandalf, was trying to get back to its master, Sauron, of its own accord; it betrayed Gollum just as it betrayed Isildur ages earlier. However, the Ring did not count on Bilbo showing up.

Gandalf learned the story of Gollum when he left the Shire after Bilbo's birthday party. The wizard hunted down Gollum and squeezed much of the information out of him. Then Gandalf made a mistake—he let Gollum go. Gollum made his way back to Mordor, drawn by the power of Sauron. The Dark Lord's minions captured and questioned Gollum, enabling Sauron to connect the Ring to the Shire, to Hobbits, and even specifically to the name Baggins. Now aware that the Ring still exists, Sauron plans to do everything he can to retrieve it.

ANALYSIS

The chapter "The Shadow of the Past" is very dense, providing a detailed account of past events that works in tandem with the Prologue to provide historical roots for the action of *The Lord of the Rings*. Whereas the Prologue focuses primarily on the Shire, "The Shadow of the Past" works on the wider scale of all of Middle-earth. Like the myths and legends and epic poems Tolkien studied as a scholar, *The Lord of the Rings* is full of prophecies and ancient legacies. In Tolkien's work, the past is an unavoidable force in the present; events that occur in ancient history end up determining the future in unforeseen ways. We learn that the saga of the Ring is an ageless one: the Rings of Power were forged seemingly before time, and were distributed to the various races of Middle-earth—Elves, Dwarves, and Men. Sauron, the Dark Lord, was corrupted by his desire to wield the Ring's power—a corruption that has since threatened all those who have come in contact with the Ring, from Isildur to Gollum to Bilbo and, by implication, Frodo himself. More than anything else, the Ring represents power. It gives its wearer not only the magical power of invisibility, but also control over all the other Great Rings. This control is what draws people to the Ring and what makes it so hard for its successive owners to give it up. The Ring's bearers become entranced by and then addicted to the Ring and the power it offers. Ultimately, however, the Ring's power corrupts—and as it is absolute power, it eventually corrupts absolutely. As Gandalf points out, it is significant that Bilbo is able to give up the Ring of his own accord. Bilbo's ability to do so bodes well for his prospects for surviving the aftereffects of owning the Ring.

To Frodo and Gandalf and the other characters we meet, the saga of the Ring is an ancient one. However, we must keep in mind that even the events Tolkien describes in *The Lord of the Rings*—those involving Frodo, which seemingly occur in the present—are themselves ancient and remote, far removed from us as present-day readers. Tolkien hints from time to time that the modern day is separated from Middle-earth not by distance but by time—indeed, Middle-earth and our world are one and the same place, changed drastically and mysteriously by the intervening flow of time. Hobbits, for instance, though rarer now than in the past, still walk among us, but avoid us "with dismay." Throughout *The Lord of the Rings,* we repeatedly get the sense that the world described in the novel is a finer, more magical one that has been replaced by our soulless, mechanized era. In this regard, Tolkien's novel fits into a tradition that includes Homer's *Iliad* and *Odyssey*—epic elegies for a nobler age that take their power from the contrast with the era in which they are told.

Book I, Chapter 2 (continued)

From Frodo's reaction to Gandalf's story to the end of the chapter

Summary — The Shadow of the Past

> *"Many that live deserve death. And some that die*
> *deserve life. . . . even the very wise cannot see all ends."*
> *(See* quotations, *p. 83)*

Hearing Gandalf's story, Frodo is frightened and angry, and he wishes aloud that Bilbo had killed Gollum when he had the chance. Gandalf reprimands Frodo, however, saying that it is precisely because Bilbo did *not* kill Gollum—therefore beginning the hobbit's ownership of the Ring with an act of mercy—that Bilbo was able to withstand the Ring's power as long as he did. When Frodo counters that Gollum surely deserved to die, Gandalf agrees. However, the wizard adds that many who die deserve life, and until Frodo can give them that life, he should be less eager to condemn the living to death. Moreover, Gandalf feels that somehow Gollum still has a part to play in the fate of the Ring.

Frodo asks why the Ring cannot simply be destroyed. Gandalf invites Frodo to try. To his surprise, Frodo finds that he is unable to bring himself to destroy it; instead of throwing the Ring away, he unknowingly puts it back in his pocket. Gandalf warns Frodo that he is already falling under the Ring's power. Frodo asks Gandalf to take the Ring, but the wizard refuses vehemently. With the Ring, Gandalf says, he would become too powerful, and he would inevitably be corrupted like Sauron himself. Even if Gandalf took the Ring simply for safekeeping, the temptation to use it would be too great. Even if he used the Ring out of a desire to do good, it would corrupt him.

Frodo realizes that it is no longer safe for him to stay in the Shire, and that something must be done with the Ring. Gandalf tells Frodo that the Ring can only be destroyed at the Cracks of Doom in Orodruin, the fiery mountain deep inside Mordor itself. Frodo volunteers to keep the Ring and guard it, at least until someone else can be found to destroy it. Frodo quickly realizes, however, that he must take the Ring somewhere else, in order to avoid endangering the Shire. He is terrified of what he has to face, but also somewhat excited to be going on an adventure. Frodo is well aware, though, that the Ring may begin to exert its influence on him just as it did on Bilbo.

Gandalf, impressed by Frodo's courage, recommends that Frodo take reliable companions along with him. At that moment, the wizard happens to catch Sam Gamgee, who has been eavesdropping through a window. Sam is embarrassed, but clearly well meaning, and he has evidently been entranced by the talk of magic and Elves. Gandalf laughingly decides that Sam should go with Frodo on his journey.

ANALYSIS

Frodo's response to Gandalf's story about Gollum, and his regret that Bilbo had not killed Gollum when he had the chance, introduces us to some of the moral complexities of Tolkien's work. Gandalf is the moral arbiter throughout *The Lord of the Rings,* and his views of good and evil are quite stern and inflexible. He firmly

SUMMARY & ANALYSIS

acknowledges, for example, that some living creatures actually deserve to die. This view is harsher than the Christian doctrine of forgiveness for even the greatest criminal, as no earthly being can assume the divine role of judging right and wrong or conferring life or death on his fellow creatures. But, on the other hand, Gandalf reprimands Frodo for wishing that Gollum had been killed, approving of Bilbo's mercy that allowed the monster to escape unharmed. Gandalf feels that some good may come of Gollum someday, that the creature has a role to play in the scheme of fate that Gandalf can dimly glimpse. This notion that even a horrible monster could one day produce something good is closer to the Greek idea of fate than the Christian value of forgiveness.

Gandalf's attitude toward the Ring also, surprisingly, raises moral questions. We might expect the great figure of good in the novel to be able to rise above the wicked power emanating from the Ring, transcending its ability to seduce its bearer into selfishness and greed. If anyone is superior to the Ring's evil, it seems, it should be the morally unimpeachable Gandalf. But, in fact, when Frodo offers the Ring to Gandalf, the wizard pulls back sharply, refusing even to touch it. His explanation is candid and revealing. He says that his power makes him too susceptible, and that his great moral goodness could turn to equally great evil under the Ring's influence. The Ring's power is greater, he admits, than his own moral strength. Gandalf is not set above the Hobbits or other characters in the work; he does not float over the plot like an otherworldly angel. Instead, he is a creature of flesh and blood like all the rest. He is perhaps stronger and wiser and more skilled than most of the others, but he is not perfect, and has the same weaknesses as the others, the same potential for failure.

The introduction of Sam provides a note of levity to balance the grim seriousness of the Gollum story and the task assigned to Frodo. Sam belongs to a long line of humorous characters from literature known as buffoons or clowns, characters who are always out of place or getting in the way, but whose simplicity of origin and speech belie a hidden wisdom often expressed comically. Sam's embarrassment at being caught eavesdropping induces Gandalf to smile—something he rarely does—and endears Sam to us as an ordinary fellow, an unimpressive but well-meaning counterpart to the Hobbit hero. Sam highlights the simple virtues and uncomplicated good intentions that make the Hobbits so easy to love. Moreover, he is drawn into the story of Elves and magic just as we are. He listens

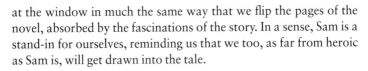

at the window in much the same way that we flip the pages of the novel, absorbed by the fascinations of the story. In a sense, Sam is a stand-in for ourselves, reminding us that we too, as far from heroic as Sam is, will get drawn into the tale.

BOOK I, CHAPTERS 3–4

SUMMARY — CHAPTER 3: THREE IS COMPANY

> *"[Bilbo] used to say there was only one Road; that it*
> *was like a great river: its springs were at every doorstep,*
> *and every path was its tributary."*
> *(See* QUOTATIONS, *p. 83)*

Two months later, Gandalf leaves the Shire to look into some troubling news he has heard. Frodo prepares to leave, though not quickly. On the wizard's advice, Frodo plans to head toward Rivendell, the home of the wise Elrond Halfelven. To that end, he sells Bag End to Lobelia Sackville-Baggins, a disagreeable relative of Bilbo who has always wanted to get her hands on the house. With the help of Sam and his other friends Peregrin Took (called Pippin) and Meriadoc Brandybuck (called Merry), Frodo packs up and moves out that autumn. Just before he leaves, he throws a small party, as he does every year, for his and Bilbo's shared birthday on September 22nd.

Merry, along with another friend, Fredegar (Fatty) Bolger, go on ahead to Frodo's new house, across the Brandywine River in Buckland, with a cartful of luggage. Frodo, Sam, and Pippin plan to follow on foot, taking a few days and camping in the woods at night. Just as they are on their way, Frodo hears a strange voice talking to Sam's father, Ham Gamgee (known as the Gaffer), who lives next door. The voice asks for Mr. Baggins, but the Gaffer responds that Mr. Baggins has already left. Frodo feels that people are getting too inquisitive, and he leaves as quietly as possible.

The second day out, the hobbits hear the sound of hooves on the road behind them. Frodo feels a strange desire to hide, so he leads Sam and Pippin off into the trees. The rider is a tall figure on a large, black horse. He is shrouded in a black cloak and his face cannot be seen. He stops near the spot where the hobbits are hiding and seems to sniff the air for a scent. Frodo feels a sudden desire to put the Ring on his finger. Then, the rider suddenly rides off again. Sam informs

Frodo that it appeared to be the same Black Rider who was questioning the Gaffer the other night.

The hobbits proceed more cautiously, constantly listening for the sound of hooves. As night falls, they hear a horse approaching. Hiding in the trees, they see that it is again a Black Rider. The Black Rider stops and starts to approach Frodo, when suddenly it hears the singing voices of Elves, mounts its horse, and rides off.

The elves approach, and their song ends. One of them, Gildor, greets Frodo. When Pippin asks about the Black Riders, the elves suddenly look worried, and they take the hobbits under their protection for the night. Later that night, the party stops in what seems to be an enchanted glade, and they have a feast. Frodo, who is known by Elves and who knows some of their language, questions Gildor about the Black Riders. All the elf will say is that the Riders are servants of the Enemy and therefore must be avoided at all costs. The party settles down to sleep for the night.

SUMMARY — CHAPTER 4: A SHORT CUT TO MUSHROOMS

When the hobbits awake the next morning, the elves are gone, but they have sent word of the hobbits' journey to friendly ears along the way to Rivendell. Frodo decides to take a shortcut across the fields between Woody End and the Brandywine River ferry, because he is now in haste and does not wish to stay on the road where they can easily be seen. Indeed, not long after leaving the road, the party sees a Black Rider traveling on it. The underbrush is dense, however, and the hobbits make slow progress. Later, they hear two terrible cries, which they assume to be the Black Riders communicating to each other.

Scrambling through bog and briar, the hobbits eventually come upon the fields of Farmer Maggot, of whom Frodo has been afraid ever since Maggot caught the young Frodo stealing his mushrooms. Farmer Maggot welcomes the hobbits and gives them dinner. He then tells them of a strange, dark man who came by earlier asking for a Mr. Baggins. The hobbits, now quite scared, are grateful when Maggot offers to carry them to the Brandywine River ferry in a covered wagon. On the way, they hear hooves approaching, but it turns out to be only Merry, ready to take them across the river and over to Buckland.

ANALYSIS — CHAPTERS 3–4

Like many epics, *The Lord of the Rings* is the story of a quest, and by these chapters the quest has begun. Having firmly grounded his hobbits in the Shire, Tolkien takes them on the road. The contrast between home and the road forms one of the central tensions of the novel. If the Shire means stasis, predictability, self-satisfied boredom, and the comforts of home, the road means movement, unpredictability, and vulnerability. Throughout the novel, the hobbits think back to the Shire in the midst of the alternately strange, perilous, or awe-inspiring sights they encounter. The road also means excitement, and—as we already see in the encounter with the group of elves—wonder. Early in his journey, Frodo recalls how Bilbo always used to say that there is only one road, "that it was like a great river: its springs were at every doorstep, and every path was its tributary." The same road that leads through Hobbiton leads on eventually through Mirkwood, to the Lonely Mountain, and beyond. Despite the fact that the Shire has an atmosphere of safety and remove, it is connected by the road to all the terrors and magic of the outside world. As the hobbits take to the road and make their way out of the Shire, they are almost immediately exposed to unfamiliar elements. Whereas the worst thing Frodo faced in Hobbiton was the greedy Sackville-Bagginses, once on the road, he and his companions are exposed to the much more potent evil of the Black Riders.

Indeed, in these chapters—and in *The Lord of the Rings* as a whole—it is not difficult to figure out who is good and who is evil. The Black Riders, with their shrouded figures, hissing voices, and dread-inspiring demeanor, have evil written all over them. By the same token, the Elves, with their light and clear voices, laughter, "shimmer," and wisdom, immediately appear fundamentally good. As we see later in the novel, the Elves, especially the High Elves, have great power, and they serve as a counterbalance to the evil power of Sauron. If Sauron and his Ring represent corruption, the Elves represent purity. Everything about them, from their voices to the food they eat, is repeatedly characterized as natural and pure. On the whole, good and evil are rarely difficult to discern in the novel.

There is, however, one great complicating factor in the distinction between good and evil—the Ring. As we already know, the Ring has the power to corrupt even the best-intentioned. The Black Riders have some connection to the Ring, as we can infer from Frodo's overwhelming desire to put the Ring on his finger when the Riders are nearby. In this impulse, we see Frodo already falling under the power of the Ring. In Chapter 2, even Gandalf refuses to take stewardship of the Ring, not believing himself able to resist the

Ring's seductive power. In a fictional universe of moral absolutes, the Ring is the one subversive element—the one thing that bridges the gap between good and evil.

Many critics have interpreted Tolkien's exploration of good and evil as a conflict between the natural world and industrialization. Sauron's power is tied up in his Ring, an item that is not naturally occurring, but forged in fire. Elves, on the other hand, a clear force of good, are intimately linked to the forest. The bower where the elves and hobbits stop for the night is an enchanted place and—perhaps more important—an organic one. The great hall in the middle is made of living trees, as are the beds in which the hobbits sleep. Though Tolkien resisted overly allegorical readings of *The Lord of the Rings,* it is hard not to notice his repeated characterizations of the natural as good and the industrial or artificial as evil. Sauron, with his despoiling armies and dark forges, is not unlike the forces of industrialization that overtook the English countryside of Tolkien's childhood—a place for which Tolkien felt immense fondness, as we see in his loving depiction of the Shire. The Elves, who take their power from that natural world, represent the sort of purity and mysticism Tolkien saw in it.

Such a reading of the novel is further reinforced by the fact that Gildor and his company, like many of his fellow Elves, are leaving Middle-earth, going away over the sea to the West. Elves are immortal (unless killed unnaturally), but as their age is passing, they are going into a sort of self-imposed exile. With the Elves goes the fine, glimmering magic they possess. Considering the evident esteem in which Tolkien holds the Elves, it is no surprise that—as Tolkien himself hints from time to time—whatever ultimately replaces the Elves will represent decline more than progress.

BOOK I, CHAPTERS 5–6

SUMMARY — CHAPTER 5: A CONSPIRACY UNMASKED

Merry leads the other three hobbits to Crickhollow, where Frodo has bought a small house under the pretense of moving there permanently, in order to disguise his departure from the Shire. Crickhollow is in Buckland, which, though populated by Hobbits, is very different from Hobbiton or Bag End. Buckland is surrounded by the Brandywine River and the Old Forest, both of which are somewhat perilous. Hobbits from Hobbiton fear water, as none of them can swim, and the Old Forest is strange and frightening, its trees seeming almost predatory. To protect against these dangers, the Buck-landers built a hedge and keep their doors locked at night, which is unheard of in Hobbiton.

The weary travelers are given a bath and supper. Frodo decides that he must finally tell Merry and Pippin that he is, in fact, leaving the Shire for good—a fact that Frodo thought was a complete secret thus far. Frodo is highly surprised when Merry reveals that they have known for some time—not only about Frodo's plans to leave, but also about the Ring and the great peril. With Sam as eavesdrop-per, the other hobbits have pieced together a good bit of Frodo's sit-uation. Frodo does not want to subject his friends to such dangerous circumstances, but Merry and Pippin both insist on coming along. They are his friends and they understand the danger at least as well as he does—which is to say, not very well at all.

Despite his surprise, Frodo is happy to hear that his friends wish to join him. Because of the Black Riders, Frodo decides that the next day they must set out away from the road, cutting through the Old Forest that borders on Buckland. Though the Forest is ominous, at the moment it seems safer than an encoun-ter with the Riders. The other hobbits agree to Frodo's plan. Their friend Fatty Bolger will stay behind to keep up the pretense that Frodo is living at Crickhollow.

That night, Frodo dreams he is looking out a window over a dark forest, in which he hears the sounds of animals sniffing around, looking for him. Then he is on a barren field. He hears the sound of the Great Sea, which he has never heard in real life, and he smells the smell of salt. He sees a tall white tower before him and he struggles toward it to climb it. Then there is a light in the sky and the sound of thunder.

SUMMARY — CHAPTER 6: THE OLD FOREST

The next morning, the group sets off early, through a heavy mist. Merry leads them to the main path into the forest. They plan to head northeast and follow the road at a distance. They enter the Old For-est, but immediately lose the path. The Forest is hot and stuffy, and it seems as if the trees are listening to the hobbits and even moving to block their progress. The hobbits find the path eventually, but it begins to turn in the wrong direction, toward the heart of the Forest. Leaving the path, they find that every time they head north, the trees seem to block their way, only permitting them to go southeast, deeper into the forest.

The hobbits reach the River Withywindle in the middle of the Old Forest. Passing under an enormous, old willow tree, they suddenly feel so hot and sleepy that they sit down. All except Sam fall asleep with their backs against the tree. Sam fights off drowsiness and goes to find the hobbits' ponies, which have wandered off. Sam hears two noises—a splash and a click like a lock fastening. When he returns to the others, he sees that Frodo has fallen into the river at the foot of the tree and is seemingly pinned down by one of its roots. Sam hauls Frodo out, and Frodo says he is certain that the old tree pushed him into the river. Turning around, Frodo and Sam see that Merry and Pippin are caught inside the cracks of the trunk of the tree, which has closed around them. The hobbits smack the tree and then try lighting a fire near it. However, the tree begins to squeeze Merry, who yells that the tree is telling him it will crush him if the hobbits do not put the fire out. Frodo, panicking, runs down the river yelling for help. He is surprised to hear an answer—the sound of nonsensical, jolly singing.

A plump man in a blue coat and yellow boots comes dancing down the path. He calls himself Tom Bombadil, and, seeing the hobbits' situation, appears to be familiar with the tricks of "Old Man Willow." Going up to the tree, Tom sings into the crack and orders the tree to release Merry and Pippin. Old Man Willow promptly obeys. In answer to the hobbits' thanks, Tom tells them to join him and his bride, Goldberry, for dinner. The hobbits, somewhat bewildered, follow Tom along the river as he sings. They come out of the Old Forest into a pleasant clearing, and then go up to a hill where Bombadil's house stands. A woman's voice sings out to them.

ANALYSIS — CHAPTERS 5–6

In these chapters, Tolkien gives us the opportunity to get to know Frodo's companions a little better. They prove to be typical Hobbits in some regards: their love of a bath, their love of food (especially mushrooms), and their stubbornness. But Frodo's companions also seem a bit more adventurous than most Hobbits, less convinced that the Shire is the center of the universe. Merry, especially, seems clever beyond his years, having taken it upon himself to organize the conspiracy to make sure that Frodo does not leave the Shire without them. Though perhaps a bit underhanded, the other hobbits' determination to pry into Frodo's affairs and do what they can to help him is admirable, hinting at the loyalty they display throughout the journey toward Mordor.

Buckland is still within the Shire, but it is not as safe as the comfortable confines of Hobbiton and Bag End. In Buckland, the hobbits are at the edge of the sheltered Shire and therefore closer to the dangers of the wider world. We again see the recurring motif of the road appear in this episode in Buckland: the presence of the road passing through the area is a constant reminder of the nearness of danger and the vulnerability of the Shire. Indeed, the natural world around Buckland is not like the domesticated countryside that surrounds Bag End, but is a more sinister place, with the Old Forest on one side and the Brandywine River—in which, we learn, Frodo's parents drowned—on the other. Buckland, unlike Hobbiton, has need of a protective hedge around it, with guards and gates. This distinction between domesticated nature in the Shire and untamed nature in the outside world is one that resurfaces again and again throughout the novel, notably in the upcoming chapters at the home of Tom Bombadil. Tolkien clearly appreciates the beauty of the natural world, but implies that he favors a more domesticated form of nature to untamed nature, which has the potential to be dangerous and unpredictable.

As the hobbits make their way into the Old Forest, we see that Middle-earth is in many ways an enchanted place. Sauron and the Elves are not the only forces at work, and there are clearly powers in Middle-earth that are not directly concerned with the battle for the Ring. These forces are usually represented by some aspect of the natural world. In Tolkien's world, nature is not usually concerned with the affairs of Men—or Hobbits—and yet nature is almost always distinctly "good" or "evil," only rarely neutral. Even trees seemingly have a will and an influence. Later in *The Lord of the Rings,* we see that trees, perhaps more than any other living thing, represent nature itself for Tolkien. The trees of Middle-earth act upon, control, and even prey upon the people and animals that move among them. As such, nature in *The Lord of the Rings* is not merely a backdrop for the actions of Men and Hobbits, but a powerful, active force in its own right.

Frodo's dream has a powerful symbolic importance. It is a prophetic dream, as it foresees the Great Sea upon which a group of Frodo's friends later sails off westward, as well as presents the white tower that is important in *The Two Towers,* the second volume of the novel. The climbing that Frodo does in the dream prefigures his fatiguing climb to the top of Cirith Ungol, led by the treacherous Gollum. Furthermore, the light in the sky and the thunder foreshadow the spectacle in the heavens over Minas Tirith that signals the end of Sauron's reign of evil in *The Return of the King*. This foreshadowing has the effect of creating an overarching unity in the three volumes of the novel, as events at the beginning refer to and prefigure events at the end. Such foreshadowing also enhances the atmosphere of magic and wizardry that dominates the world of Middle-earth. But perhaps equally important, the mention of Frodo's dream places us squarely inside Frodo's consciousness, showing us the importance of his psychology and mindset throughout the story. His mission will not just be a series of steps he must take, but a personal growth and a psychological expansion as well. The inward focus of Frodo's dreams prepares us to think about his inner state more seriously later in the novel.

BOOK I, CHAPTER 7

SUMMARY — THE HOUSE OF TOM BOMBADIL

Tom Bombadil's house is warm and comforting. The presence of Goldberry, Tom's wife, moves Frodo in a way similar to that of the Elves, but in a homier, less rarefied fashion. Frodo asks Goldberry who Tom is, and she replies somewhat mysteriously that Tom is "Master of wood, water and hill." Tom leads the hobbits to their rooms, where they wash up before a hearty dinner. That night, Frodo dreams of a great tower of stone and a man standing atop it. The man raises his staff, and a giant eagle swoops down and carries him away. Then the dream is filled with the sounds of hooves. Pippin and Merry also have troubling dreams, but they hear the voice of Tom Bombadil in their sleep and are comforted.

The next day is rainy. With relief, the hobbits accept Tom's invitation to stay another day before starting out again. All day they sit at Tom's feet as he tells them stories about the Old Forest, how it resented the animals and people that roamed through it and hacked down and burned trees. Then Tom tells them of the cities that rose and fell on the hills near his house, which have left only crumbled ramparts on the hilltops and grave mounds haunted by spirits called Barrow-wights. Then Tom's story meanders back in time to the very beginnings of Middle-earth. When the story ends, Frodo asks Tom who he is. Tom answers simply that he is "Eldest"—he is older than everything else in Middle-earth, and he even remembers the time before Sauron.

The group eats a dinner even better than the last. Afterward, Goldberry sings for them, and Tom asks Frodo about his journey. Tom has already heard much from Gildor and from Farmer Maggot, whom he greatly respects. Tom asks to see the Ring. To everyone's surprise, when he puts it on his little finger, he does not disappear. Tom spins the Ring in the air and makes it disappear, but then smilingly hands it back to Frodo.

Frodo feels suspicious and a bit annoyed at Tom. To make sure Tom has given him back the real Ring, Frodo puts it on his finger—the first time he has done so. Frodo does indeed disappear, but when he creeps toward the door, Tom seems able to see him nonetheless. Tom calls out to Frodo to take off the Ring and come back. Tom tells the hobbits that it will be sunny the next day. He warns them to steer clear of the barrows (burial mounds) and teaches them a rhyme to sing if they run into trouble.

ANALYSIS

If Tom Bombadil does not quite seem to fit with the rest of the novel thus far, it may be because Tolkien created the character as early as 1933, years before he began *The Lord of the Rings*. Tolkien clearly liked the idea of Tom, and he even tossed around the prospect of making Tom the hero of the sequel to *The Hobbit*. (Eventually Tolkien would write *The Adventures of Tom Bombadil*, a collection of poems, in 1961.) Ultimately, Tolkien ended up transplanting Tom into *The Lord of the Rings*. However, as the novel progresses and grows darker, Tom, in retrospect, may seem to belong more in the children's story of *The Hobbit* than in the more threatening world of *The Lord of the Rings*. Nonetheless, Tolkien did not regret his decision to keep Tom in the final edit of *The Lord of the Rings*; the author later said, "I kept [Tom] in, and as he was, because he represents certain things otherwise left out."

These "certain things" Tom represents are a matter of great debate among Tolkien scholars, as Tom is indeed a mysterious figure. Perhaps the only thing we know definitively about him is that he is joyously immune to the power of the Ring, and therefore a unique, neutral third party in the wider landscape of the War of the Ring that is to come. Tom is something like a male personification of Mother Nature, the master of the land and its creatures, albeit only within his own territory. He clearly has great powers, and the Ring does not affect him, perhaps because he was around before Sauron ever came to Middle-earth. However, Tom refuses to go with the hobbits to fight Sauron, and we get the feeling that Tom's power has perhaps diminished somewhat in the later ages of Middle-earth. Tom's presence, like that of the Elves, contributes to the overall tone of elegy in *The Lord of the Rings,* a sadness for the lost past. Like the Elves, Tom has a power that is closely linked to nature, but with Tom the link is even more explicit. Frodo's feeling when he first steps into Tom's house—that the place has a demeanor that is "less keen and lofty," but "deeper"—suggests this distinction between Tom and the Elves.

The importance and characteristics of Tom Bombadil also give clues about Tolkien's conception of nature. When the hobbits arrive at Tom's house, Goldberry tells them that now they need not worry about "untame things." This wording, combined with the perfectly manicured landscape around Tom's house, suggests that Tolkien does not necessarily view nature as the same thing as wildness or pristine wilderness. Nature, without the controlling hand of man, is unruly and perhaps even unsafe. The most idyllic places in Tolkien's world—whether the comfortable confines of the Shire, the magical bower of the High Elves, or Tom's domain—are places where nature has been tamed. This idea of a domesticated, softened nature is often cited in literature, music, and the visual arts as the ideal of the pastoral. For Tolkien, the pastoral has a powerful appeal.

Tom speaks briefly to the hobbits about the kings of Westernesse, some of whom held kingdoms and fought battles where the Barrow-downs now lie. Westernesse is the land west of Middle-earth, given by the Valar (the angelic gods of Middle-earth) as a reward to the men who fought against Morgoth, the Great Enemy (and Sauron's master), in the First Age. The land of Westernesse is also known as Númenor. Because some of its inhabitants grew restless and proud, they sailed back to Middle-earth and a few fell under the rule of Sauron. Still, they were considered the greatest race of Men in the world. Isildur, who took the Ring from Sauron, was a Númenorean, and it was Númenóreans who lived in the North near the Barrow-downs and fought Sauron's servants from the ancient northern realm of Angmar. Now, however, there are but a few Men of pure Westernesse blood left. As we see later, those who remain have a crucial role to play in the story of *The Lord of the Rings.*

Book I, Chapter 8

Summary — Fog on the Barrow-downs

The next morning, Tom sends off the hobbits, who head north into the hills of the Barrow-downs. At noon, they stop atop a strange, flat-topped hill with a single stone standing in its center. Off to the north, the Downs seem to be ending, which is an encouraging sight, but the hills to the east appear foreboding. The hobbits stretch their legs and eat a full lunch of the food Tom has given them. Unfortunately, their full stomachs, the warm sun, and their fatigue, perhaps combined with some power of the hill itself, cause them to fall asleep.

When they awake, the sun is setting and a thick fog has settled over the Downs. They quickly head back down the hill in what they think is a northerly direction. Frodo believes he sees the exit to the Downs, and he rushes ahead, calling out to the other hobbits. When Frodo reaches what he thought was the gate, he turns to find that he is alone. He hears distant cries and runs forward. He reaches the top of a hill and sees a barrow in front of him. A deep voice speaks to Frodo and says it has been waiting for him. Suddenly, a dark figure appears and grabs him with an icy grip. Frodo falls unconscious.

When Frodo wakes up, he is inside a barrow, under the hills. He realizes that a Barrow-wight has captured him. He is afraid, but he steels himself with desperate courage. Next to him lie the other three hobbits, pale and unconscious, adorned with gold and jewelry and with a giant sword lying across their necks. In the eerie cold, Frodo hears a voice chanting. He sees a long arm walking on its fingers toward the sword. For a moment, Frodo panics and feels tempted to put the Ring on his finger and run away. Unwilling to abandon his friends, however, he grabs a nearby dagger and, with all his remaining strength, cuts off the reaching hand. There is a shriek, and the sword shatters, but the Barrow-wight then makes a growling sound.

Falling over Merry, Frodo suddenly remembers the song Tom Bombadil taught them. He begins to sing and soon hears a reply: old Tom comes crashing into the mound, collapsing the Barrow-wight's chamber. Tom helps the hobbits out onto the grass, where they recover from the Barrow-wight's spell. Tom takes the Barrow-wight's treasure out into the sunlight and leaves it on top of the hill for passersby to sift through. Tom takes a beautiful brooch from the treasure and, looking at it, sadly thinks of the woman who once wore it. Returning their ponies and their packs, Tom takes daggers from the Barrow-wight's treasure mound and gives one to each hobbit.

Tom leads the hobbits out of the Downs and safely to the East Road. He will not pass out of his country, but he directs the hobbits to the nearby town of Bree, where there is a fine inn where they can spend the night. Before they get to Bree, Frodo tells his companions that in front of strangers they should refer to him not as Mr. Baggins, but as Mr. Underhill—a precaution Gandalf earlier reminded Frodo to take.

ANALYSIS

The encounter with the Barrow-wight allows us to learn more about Tolkien's vision of evil. Of course, Sauron emerges as the major figure of wickedness in *The Lord of the Rings,* the being whose nefarious intentions shape the plot of the novel. But Sauron does not have a monopoly on immorality or selfishness, and the presence of the Barrow-wight—or mound demon, as we might call him in more modern English—reminds us that nastiness in Tolkien comes in many shapes and sizes. There is nothing to indicate that the Barrow-wight has any connections with Sauron, or that it is doing anything to further Sauron's aims. The demon is, in a sense, a free agent of evil. Yet even so, there are uncanny resemblances between the Barrow-wight and the Dark Lord. Like Sauron, the wight is in search of jewelry, and is willing to kill to get it. Moreover, the independently moving arm of the wight—which walks spookily on its fingers—may remind us of the severed finger of Sauron, detached when Isildur took the Ring from him. Neither the wight nor Sauron has a personality in *The Lord of the Rings*; they are incarnations of wickedness rather than fully formed characters. They reach and grab with no soul or personality, as if they have hands but no hearts or minds.

The struggle with the Barrow-wight illustrates in miniature some of the major elements of the hobbits' future adventures. First, the idea of fellowship is emphasized when Frodo is left isolated after the wight has captured his cohorts. Frodo has been seen alone in the novel before this point, but he has never seemed quite as lonely as he does when he calls out for his friends and hears nothing but the wind in return. We see that Frodo is not just in the company of the other members of the Fellowship, but is building a real connection with them. Another example of fellowship is Frodo's sudden rescue by

Tom, who has appeared only recently in the narrative. We might have expected Tolkien to use the encounter with the Barrow-wight as an opportunity to showcase Frodo's developing heroic skills—but he does not, for Frodo falls prey to the wight just as his colleagues did. Heroism does not necessarily mean standing out from the others as the strongest; it can go hand in hand with reliance upon others. We see that Tolkien is putting forth a new model of the hero, one who does not insist on doing everything himself, but who can accept aid from others.

The power of the Ring appears as a temptation here, one that must be resisted. We are again shown that Sauron's power is not an external threat, but an internal one as well: it afflicts the mind and heart of its wearer, working its insidious effects from the inside out. During Frodo's confrontation with the Barrow-wight, his first instinct is to put on the Ring, become invisible, and save himself by running away. Of course this would be an effective solution, but it would also be a thoroughly selfish one, as it would ensure the deaths of his friends left behind in the mound. The struggle Frodo undergoes in this episode is therefore not just between himself and a wicked demon, but between two parts of himself—one part that looks to save his own skin at any cost, and another part that cares about those dear to him. We see again that Tolkien's tale is not just about external happenings, but about inward development.

BOOK I, CHAPTERS 9–10

SUMMARY — CHAPTER 9: AT THE SIGN OF THE PRANCING PONY

Bree is a meeting place for the two very different worlds of the Shire and the rest of Middle-earth. Both Hobbits and Big People (humans) live there in relative peace, and there is always a steady stream of travelers of all kinds. Frodo, therefore, feels uneasy when the gatekeeper guarding the entrance to Bree takes a curious interest in the hobbits. The hobbits enter the Prancing Pony, the local inn, and announce themselves to the innkeeper, Barliman Butterbur. The hobbits seem to remind Butterbur of something, but he cannot quite place it.

The innkeeper sets the hobbits up in their room. After dinner, Frodo, Sam, and Pippin go into the main drinking hall while Merry rests in the room. The hobbits quickly become the center of attention in the hall, as the Bree folk rarely get news or travelers from

Hobbiton anymore. Frodo worries about some suspicious-looking characters watching the hobbits from dark corners of the room.

Butterbur points out to Frodo a particularly weather-beaten individual called Strider. The innkeeper says that Strider is a Ranger, a wanderer among the northern lands. Strider makes some pointed comments, and Frodo begins to wonder how much the man knows. Frodo suddenly notices that Pippin, who has had too much beer, is telling the crowd about Bilbo's birthday party—and getting very close to telling the part about the Ring.

To distract the audience from Pippin, Frodo gets up on a table and sings a rollicking song. His ruse works, but as he sings a second time, he falls off the table and accidentally slips the Ring on his finger. The crowd is shocked to see Frodo vanish, and everyone suddenly becomes quiet and suspicious. Frodo slips into the corner and reappears, where Strider, addressing Frodo by his real name and implying that he knows about the Ring, asks to see Frodo later. The people in the hall are not convinced when Frodo steps out of the corner and claims to have simply rolled over there as he fell. They all return to their rooms, and rumors fly.

SUMMARY — CHAPTER 10: STRIDER

> *All that is gold does not glitter,*
> *Not all those who wander are lost...*
> (See QUOTATIONS, p. 84)

Strider follows the hobbits back to their room. He begins to talk, hinting that he knows much about their journey. The hobbits, especially Sam, are inclined to distrust Strider because of his vagabond appearance. However, Strider does indeed seem to know much about the Black Riders, who have recently been seen in Bree. In fact, he saw Black Riders speaking to the gatekeeper a few days ago. Strider also warns that others in Bree, including Bill Ferny—a "swarthy sneering fellow" who was in the drinking hall earlier—are not to be trusted.

Just then, Butterbur knocks and enters. He long-windedly explains to Frodo that he has a letter to Frodo from Gandalf. The letter was supposed to be delivered three months ago, but Butterbur forgot it, and only remembered it when Frodo showed up.

Reading the letter, the hobbits are frightened to learn that Gandalf had sensed imminent danger and wanted them to leave Hobbiton by the end of July, two months before they actually left. The wizard writes that he would catch up if he could, but that they should make for Rivendell as quickly as possible. Finally, Gandalf writes that Strider—whose real name is Aragorn—is a friend who can help them. The wizard quotes a few lines of an ancient poem that is somehow related to Aragorn. Sam is still somewhat dubious, but Strider soon convinces Sam by saying that he already could easily have killed them and taken the Ring had he wanted to. The hobbits agree to take Strider on as their guide.

Merry finally returns, bursting with the news that he has seen a Black Rider while out on a walk. Strider immediately decides that the hobbits must not spend the night in their room. They arrange pillows under their blankets to make it look like they are sleeping in their beds—an attempt to deceive anyone who tries to kill them in the night. The hobbits roll out their blankets in the parlor and go to sleep as Strider keeps watch.

ANALYSIS — CHAPTERS 9–10
Strider dominates these two chapters, though his modest entrance belies his great importance to the novel. At first, his dark, shrouded appearance and knowledge of Frodo's business inspire suspicion rather than confidence. However, we soon see that Strider's down-trodden appearance is due to long years of hard travel, and we learn that his knowledge comes from Gandalf, his own keen ears, and his many years of fighting the Enemy. Moreover, the grandness of the poem that Gandalf ties to Strider's name—Aragorn—hints at the Ranger's greater destiny. In Strider, as in the hobbits, a humble outward appearance hides inner greatness. As we continue to see throughout *The Lord of the Rings*, Tolkien prefers his heroes that way. Even Gandalf, Strider hints, is much greater than the mere clever old wizard the hobbits take him to be.

At this point, then, there are at least two surprisingly powerful figures aiding the hobbits. This fact is not only comforting, but it also suggests that Tolkien's conception of a hero or great man includes the old-fashioned chivalric concern for those who are less powerful. Certainly, the fate of the Ring concerns all of Middle-earth, but Gandalf and Strider have been protecting the Shire since long before the identity of Bilbo's ring was known for certain. For all their involvement in great deeds, neither Strider nor Gandalf loses sight of the fact that he fights the evil power of Sauron in part to protect seemingly inconsequential people such as the race of Hobbits, with their somewhat bumbling, ignorant ways.

In Bree, we continue to see the corrupting power of Sauron and his servants. Both the gatekeeper and Bill Ferny have, it seems, been enlisted by the Black Riders to keep an eye out for Frodo. The gatekeeper appears to obey because the Black Riders have threatened him, whereas Bill Ferny appears to have been bribed. Those who fight against Sauron must have the strength and will to resist both greed and fear, which together make for a powerful combination of incentives.

The general atmosphere of suspicion in these chapters introduces a recurrent motif in *The Lord of the Rings* as a whole. Trust is hard to come by in Tolkien's world. It was not always this way in Middle-earth, however. Characters mention later in the novel that strangers used to be welcomed and trusted before the rise of Sauron's threat and the dark times that his power has brought to Middle-earth. But now we see that even Hobbits from one region distrust those from another. Strider, who later emerges as one of the greatest and most noble heroes in the novel, is distrusted as a vagrant and a scoundrel at first. The notion of trust is made even more complicated by the lies that are necessary to fulfill the mission, including Frodo's deception about possessing the Ring. When Frodo vanishes as he puts on the Ring, the others in the tavern become understandably suspicious of this guest who has powers greater than he has acknowledged.

Book I, Chapter 11

Summary — A Knife in the Dark

Back at Frodo's house in Crickhollow, Fatty Bolger sees dark shapes approach the front gate. He flees out the back door just before three Black Riders break into the house and find it empty. He sounds the alarm, and the Riders flee.

Meanwhile, at the inn, Strider wakes the hobbits up early. Going to their bedroom, they see that their beds were thrown apart and slashed during the night. Furthermore, all their ponies were let loose overnight as well. The hobbits are forced to buy a half-starved pony at a high price, from the suspicious Bill Ferny. They leave with the whole town watching.

A short way down the road, Strider leads the hobbits off into the forest to avoid pursuit. Unfortunately, this path takes them to the Midgewater Marshes, which means three days of bug bites and soggy feet. Still, they are safe until they come out of the Marshes and see the large hill Weathertop ahead in the distance. Strider says that a great watchtower once stood on Weathertop, built by the Men of Westernesse. Now only its ruins remain. After another day, the band arrives at Weathertop. They find signs of a camp, as well as a rock with an Elven rune symbol carved into it. Both signs lead them to suspect that Gandalf passed through the camp recently, in great haste. Strider thinks Gandalf may have been attacked while he was there.

The group rests in a hollow on the side of the hill, and they light a fire. Frodo suddenly thinks he senses five black specks moving on the road far below—the Black Riders. Strider decides they should stay where they are, as trying to move would only make them more vulnerable. To keep up their spirits, Strider tells them old legends and sings them a song of Lúthien Tinúviel, the most beautiful Elven princess, who fell in love with a Man and chose mortality so that she could join him in death.

Suddenly, Sam, who has wandered away, runs back from the edge of the dell and says he feels a strange dread. The group gathers around the fire, facing outward, and watches as several dark shapes come over the lip of the hill. Merry and Pippin throw themselves to the ground in panic, and Sam shrinks to Frodo's side. Frodo suddenly feels a terrible desire to put on the Ring, and he does so.

The black shapes suddenly become clear to Frodo, and he can see through the Black Riders' cloaks. He sees that they have deathly white faces and terrible eyes, and that they are robed in gray and carry swords. The tallest wears a crown, and it springs toward Frodo with a knife and sword. Frodo cries out the Elven names Elbereth and Gilthoniel and stabs at the feet of the Black Riders' king. Frodo feels an icy pain in his shoulder and then suddenly sees Strider leap forward with a burning log in each hand. Frodo takes off the Ring just as he falls unconscious.

ANALYSIS

Despite Frodo's physical weakness and inexperience, he does have the weapon of words at his disposal, which he wields effectively on a number of occasions. After the confrontation at Weathertop, Strider tells Frodo that it was not his sword thrust that hurt the king of the Riders, but rather the Elvish words Frodo cried out as he lunged: "O Elbereth! Gilthoniel!" Elbereth was a queen of the Elves in ancient times, in the First Age of Middle-earth. Her name means "Star-queen" in the Elvish tongue. Though it may seem strange that a mere name would cause the Black Riders to flee, we see again that language is always potent in Tolkien's world. Indeed, Tolkien—who was a passionate student of philology, the study of language—built his entire history of Middle-earth around languages he himself invented. Whenever we see these brief glimpses of foreign words in *The Lord of the Rings,* we must keep in mind that they are not nonsense, but are part of a comprehensive, structured linguistic system. Tolkien's Elvish language—along with the Dwarvish language and the language of Mordor, among others—has a system of characters, grammar, and vocabulary. It is fitting, then, for Tolkien to give great power to language in the world of Middle-earth. This power, however, cuts both ways: though Frodo's Elvish incantation serves as protection, Strider also warns the hobbits against even mentioning the name of Mordor while out in the open and unprotected, as it could bring them great harm.

The Ring displays its powers again here, but also its limitations. When Frodo dons the Ring to escape the notice of the Black Riders, his invisibility comes along with another gift, the ability to see through the Riders' cloaks. He can see their pallid faces and their horrifying eyes, and he observes a crown on the head of the tallest of them. Yet despite the thrilling insight the Ring affords Frodo, Tolkien invites us to wonder about the practical usefulness of this suddenly enhanced vision. Blessed with the power of the Ring, Frodo does not act like a superhero. The others in the Fellowship are more active, whereas Frodo's role is observational and detached rather than participatory or aggressive. Certainly Frodo is less of a threat to the Riders than Aragorn, who wildly brandishes two burning logs as he lunges at them. It may be that the Ring, for all its power and all the knowledge it offers, is not an effective tool in a quest such as Frodo's.

BOOK I, CHAPTER 12

SUMMARY — FLIGHT TO THE FORD

When Frodo comes to, the other hobbits are standing over him. When he put the Ring on, they saw only shadows rushing by and Frodo disappearing and then reappearing, collapsed on the ground. The Black Riders are gone, having been repulsed by Strider's defense and by the Elven names Frodo invoked.

After hearing Frodo's account and examining his wound, Strider becomes concerned—even more so when he finds on the ground the knife that gave Frodo the wound. Strider takes Sam aside and tells him that the wound will soon have an evil power over Frodo, and may well be deadly. Strider goes down the hill and returns carrying leaves of *athelas,* a plant with healing power. He uses the leaves to tend to Frodo's wound, which has begun to spread a cold numbness through the hobbit's side.

Day finally comes. Strider leads the hobbits down from Weathertop and across the road. They suddenly hear two shrill cries from far off. They scramble along in the forest to the south of the road. The next several days are difficult going, and Frodo gets weaker all the time. Strider finds a beryl, a pale green elf-stone, in the path; it appears to have been left for them, and he considers it a good sign. A few days later, they stumble across the three trolls that Gandalf turned to stone on Bilbo's journey many years ago (an episode from *The Hobbit*). This reminder of Bilbo's adventure cheers them.

The party is forced to return to the road to make the last leg of the journey to Rivendell. Soon after they take to the road, they are alarmed to hear the sound of hooves behind them. They hide, but the rider turns out to be not a Black Rider but an Elf-lord, Glorfindel, a friend of Strider who lives in Rivendell and was sent out several days ago to help them. They put Frodo on Glorfindel's white horse and tell him to ride ahead. The hobbit is at first reluctant to abandon his friends, but Glorfindel reminds Frodo that it is he, not the others, whom the Black Riders are after.

Frodo slips in and out of dark dreams as he rides. The party walks on through the night and rests only a few hours before heading out again at dawn. After another hard day's march, they stop again. Glorfindel and Strider, despite their desire to push on, are forced to stop, as the hobbits are exhausted.

The next afternoon, they approach the Ford of the Bruinen River, beyond which is Rivendell. As they exit the forest just a mile before the Ford, Glorfindel suddenly hears the sound of the Black Riders behind them. He cries to Frodo to run for the Ford. Glorfindel's horse, still bearing Frodo, sprints ahead. Suddenly, four Riders, who have been waiting in ambush, leap out from the trees ahead to intercept Frodo before he reaches the Ford. Glorfindel's horse carries Frodo across the river just in time, but there the hobbit waits helplessly on the opposite bank.

The Black Riders begin to cross the river, but their horses seem reluctant. Frodo calls out to them to return to Mordor, the land of Sauron, but the Riders only laugh at him and say they will take him back with them. Then, just as three of the Riders approach the other bank, a rush of whitewater fills the Bruinen and rises up, over-whelming the three in its cascading waves. As Frodo slips into unconsciousness, he sees the other black horses madly carrying their Riders into the rapids, where they are swept away.

ANALYSIS

This chapter brings to a close the first book of *The Lord of the Rings* and the first half of *The Fellowship of the Ring*. Throughout Book I, the hobbits prove themselves rather hapless and in constant need of rescue, whether by Farmer Maggot, Tom Bombadil, Strider, or the raging waters of the Bruinen River. Indeed, it is partly this power-lessness that makes a Hobbit such an appropriate Ring-bearer. As Gandalf earlier explains, if a Wizard such as himself were to take the Ring, it would certainly turn him into another Sauron. Frodo's stew-ardship of the Ring, while it poses grave dangers to Frodo himself, does not bring about the sort of consequences that it would with a powerful being such as Gandalf. Despite their bumbling ways, how-ever, the hobbits also demonstrate a bit of pluck and ability, as we see in Frodo's stands against the Barrow-wight and then the Black Riders, or in Sam's resistance to the wiles of Old Man Willow. The hobbits appear to be adept at learning on their feet.

As Frodo makes his way from Bag End to Rivendell, a group of companions—which is later christened the Fellowship of the Ring—begins to form around him. Whereas at first Frodo thought his mis-sion would be a solitary one, Gandalf decides to send Sam along with him. Then Merry and Pippin join, and finally Strider. More join the party in the upcoming chapters. As we see in the second half of *The Fellowship of the Ring*, however, forces begin to break the Fel-lowship apart as the quest progresses and grows more difficult. This movement from solitude to community and back emphasizes the particular burden of the Ring. Though Frodo needs all the help he can enlist to continue in the quest, in the end the weight of responsi-bility falls squarely on him alone. Tolkien emphasizes the great and solitary weight of the Ring in a number of ways. Glorfindel reminds Frodo of his status and responsibility as Ring-bearer when he tells Frodo that the Black Riders are interested only in capturing him, not the rest of the party. Similarly, the glimpse of the Black Riders that the Ring reveals to Frodo , as well as the dark dreams that his wound gives him, show how he is, in a way, set apart from the rest of the party.

BOOK II, CHAPTER 1

SUMMARY — MANY MEETINGS

Frodo awakens several days later in a bed in Rivendell. He is shocked and delighted to see Gandalf sitting nearby. The wizard tells Frodo that Elrond, the Master of Rivendell, healed Frodo's wound just in time; a splinter of the Black Rider's knife had stayed in the hobbit's shoulder and was working its way toward his heart. If it had reached Frodo's heart, it would have turned him into a wraith, just like the Riders.

Gandalf explains to Frodo that the Black Riders are the Ringwraiths (known in Elvish as the Nazgûl), the Nine Servants of the Lord of the Rings. The Ringwraiths, now undead, were once mortal kings to whom Sauron gave Rings of Power, which he then used to bring the kings under his control. For now, the Ringwraiths have been swept away—though not killed—by the flood of water in the Bruinen River. Elrond, who controls the water running in front of Rivendell, let loose the flood with some help from Gandalf.

Now that Frodo is well, he goes with his friends to dinner at Elrond's table. The hall is suitably magical and impressive. There, he sees the beautiful Arwen Evenstar, Elrond's daughter. Frodo sits beside Glóin, one of the dwarves who traveled with Bilbo years ago (in the adventures chronicled in *The Hobbit*). Glóin tells Frodo much about the history of the Dwarves.

After dinner, the party passes into the great Hall of Fire for music and merrymaking. Frodo, to his surprise, finds that old Bilbo himself is present. The two hobbits talk for a long while. At one point, Bilbo asks to see the Ring, but Frodo is reluctant. Suddenly, Bilbo appears to Frodo as a strange, grasping creature. Bilbo notices Frodo's hesitation and apologizes. Later, Frodo, enchanted by the Elven-songs, falls into a deep sleep. He wakes to the sound of Bilbo singing a song, and the two go to Bilbo's room to talk more. Eventually, at Sam's insistence, Frodo goes to bed in order to be well rested for the Council the next day.

ANALYSIS

Frodo's wound is the first of many he receives in the course of his journey, and it is symbolically important. It is much more than a mere injury to the flesh, and it is made by no ordinary knife blade. Rather, Frodo's wound strikes his inner self. Indeed, the physical wound barely affects Frodo's outer self at all; Tolkien does not focus on the blood, scar tissue, or any external harm it causes. Rather, he focuses on the internal activity of the knife blade, which breaks off inside Frodo and moves toward his heart. The blade of the Nazgûl is alive inside Frodo, like a kind of cancer. We learn that if the knife had reached Frodo's heart, it would have been the end of him—but not, interestingly, the death of him. Frodo would have become an undead wraith like the Ringwraiths. He may have continued functioning under the knife's influence, but he would no longer be the Frodo we have known thus far. Once again, we see that personality and selfhood are key in *The Lord of the Rings,* and in some cases even more important than life and death.

The insidious power of the Ring to infect healthy relationships with greed and selfishness comes to affect one of the happiest bonds in the novel—the friendship between Bilbo and Frodo. It is sad enough to see the Ring's effect on the already-corrupted Gollum, but it is grievous to see its effects on those we feel we know well, such as Bilbo. The bond between Bilbo and Frodo represents more than an enjoyable union between like-minded Hobbits; as Bilbo and Frodo are related, it symbolizes the continuity of Hobbit culture itself. The aging Bilbo passes on his role to the younger Frodo in just the same way that myths and traditions are always passed down from generation to generation, especially in oral cultures. Therefore there is something sacred about Bilbo and Frodo's relationship that makes it all the more painful to see the Ring come between them. When Frodo watches the strange transformation of Bilbo's face from that of friendly advisor to that of rapacious, power-hungry manipulator, our shock is as great as Frodo's. The horror of this corrupted friendship never quite fades, even after Bilbo comes to his senses and apologizes, and even after Frodo accepts the apology. A deep suspicion remains, one of the hateful legacies of the Ring's power.

BOOK II, CHAPTER 2

SUMMARY — THE COUNCIL OF ELROND

In the morning, Gandalf summons Frodo and Bilbo to the Council. Messengers from many lands and races are there seeking Elrond's advice. Glóin says that the Dwarves are worried: the Dwarf-king Balin, who journeyed to the Mines of Moria under the Misty Mountains to reestablish the ancient Dwarf-kingdom that once flourished there, has not sent word for quite a long time. Furthermore, a messenger from Mordor has come offering the Dwarves an alliance, as well as new Rings of Power, in exchange for news about a certain Hobbit.

The wise Elrond tells of the origins of the Rings of Power, forged by the Elven-smiths in the Second Age, and of the One Ring, which Sauron made to rule the others. Elrond speaks of the great battle in which Isildur cut the Ring from the Dark Lord's hand, and of the loss of the Ring in the Anduin River when Isildur perished. Afterward, the realms of the Men of Westernesse went into decline: the northern realms were mostly abandoned, and though the southern realm of Gondor endured, it weakened as well. The Men of Gondor allowed Sauron's forces back into Mordor and had to cede territory to the Dark Lord.

At this point, Boromir, a powerful-looking warrior from Minas Tirith, the great city of Gondor, speaks. He tells of a rising power in Mordor that has recently dealt crushing losses to Gondor. Boromir tells of a dream he had that spoke of the Sword that was Broken, something called Isildur's Bane, and a Halfling. The meaning of Boromir's dream is suddenly made clear as Strider stands and reveals himself to be Aragorn, the heir and direct descendant of Isildur, keeper of Elendil's broken sword. The Halfling—another word for Hobbit—is Frodo, who stands and displays Isildur's Bane—the Ring.

Frodo and Bilbo relate their parts in the story of the Ring thus far. Then Gandalf tells how he managed to prove the identity of the Ring. He discovered that Sauron was gaining power again in Mirkwood, and that Saruman the White, the head of Gandalf's order of Wizards, advised against challenging Sauron. When the Wizards finally did decide to challenge Sauron, it was too late, as the Dark Lord had built up his forces in Mordor and fled there. Gandalf searched for Gollum but was unable to find the creature, so he went to the city of Minas Tirith, where Isildur had allegedly left a description of the Ring. From this description, Gandalf learned about the writing on the Ring. Then Aragorn tells the Council that he did in fact find Gollum after Gandalf left; the wizard adds that it is surely from Gollum that Sauron heard of Bilbo and the Shire. Legolas, an Elf from Mirkwood, interrupts with the alarming news that Gollum recently escaped from the Elves' dungeon with the help of an army of Orcs.

Gandalf tells how he journeyed to Orthanc, the tower of Saruman, where he was dismayed to learn that Saruman, the greatest of the Wizards, intended to join forces with Mordor or to wield the Ring himself. When Gandalf refused to join the side of Mordor, Saruman locked him in the tower of Orthanc until Gwaihir, the Great Eagle, came and rescued Gandalf, taking him to the horsemen of Rohan. There, Gandalf tamed Shadowfax, the swiftest of all horses, and rode him back to the Shire. Gandalf missed the hobbits and Aragorn at Bree, and then went on to Weathertop, where he battled the Nazgûl. The wizard then made his way to Rivendell, hoping to draw some of the Nine away from Strider and the hobbits.

The only remaining question—the most important one—is what to do with the Ring. The Elf-lord Erestor suggests they give the Ring to Tom Bombadil, over whom it seemingly has no power. Glorfindel counters that such a course of action would simply postpone the inevitable, as Tom alone could not defeat Sauron. Boromir brashly recommends that they use the power of the Ring to defeat Sauron. Gandalf and Elrond immediately dismiss this suggestion. As the Ring contains the power of Sauron, it is irrevocably evil, and anything done with it will ultimately turn to evil.

Glóin suggests that the Elves use the Three Rings of the Elves to fight Sauron, but Elrond silences this idea. Glóin asks what would happen if the Ruling Ring were destroyed. Elrond sadly replies that he thinks the Three Elven Rings would fail; their power and all that they have created would fade. However, the Elves are willing to endure that possibility in order to destroy Sauron.

Erestor suggests that it is despair and folly to go into Mordor to look for the fire that forged the Ring. However, Gandalf responds that despair is only for those who have no hope; as for folly, that may be their only chance. Sauron is wise, but he only thinks in terms of desire for power. That someone would pass up power by trying to destroy the Ring would never occur to him. Elrond agrees, adding that the road will be so hard that neither strength nor wisdom will be of much help; the weak are as likely to succeed as the strong. It is often true that the weak make all the difference in the world "while the eyes of the great are elsewhere."

At this, Bilbo pipes up, declaring that it is obvious that Elrond is saying that old Bilbo himself should take the Ring to Mordor. Gandalf disagrees. After a heavy silence, Frodo feels strangely compelled to speak up. He says he will take the Ring himself, "though I do not know the way." Elrond agrees, saying that it is a heavy burden, but it seems that Frodo is meant for it. Sam, who has been hiding in a corner, jumps up and demands to go along. Elrond smilingly assents.

***

ANALYSIS

Like the second chapter of Book I, the second chapter of Book II offers a lengthy historical context for the events to follow. Indeed, there is much overlap between the story Gandalf tells to Frodo in Bag End and the history described at the Council of Elrond; the only difference is that more has been learned over the course of Book I. Indeed, at the Council, much of the history that has only been hinted at or sketchily described earlier is laid out in full, and many of the pieces are fit together. As Tolkien's narrator likes to remind us, the story he tells is merely one episode in a long saga. However, the narrator does not explain all, but continues to hint at stories and myths that remain unexplained—Gandalf and the Necromancer, the story of Arwen's mother, and so on. To fully explain would provide a sense of closure, finality, or complete knowledge, which is apparently not Tolkien's intention. By leaving so many myths, stories, and characters only partly explained, or not explained at all, Tolkien gives Middle-earth an aura of mystery and vastness, leaving us with the sense that *The Lord of the Rings* is merely a small glimpse of the realm's history, geography, and inhabitants.

Elrond and Gandalf, however, are determined that the story of the Ring end with them. They reject any potential solutions that would simply pass the Ring along to others, whether Tom Bombadil, those who live across the sea in the Downs, or future generations. Gandalf and Elrond assert that the responsibility to deal with the Ring is theirs and theirs alone. As Gandalf says to Frodo earlier in the novel, "All we have to decide is what to do with the time that is given us." History assigns tasks, and Tolkien's heroes must rise to meet them.

Such a conception of heroism sets up one of the central oppositions of *The Lord of the Rings*: the conflict between selflessness and selfishness. Heroism demands selflessness, a willingness to give oneself to a larger cause. For the Elves, the sacrifice required is especially acute, since, in fighting for the Ring's destruction, they may bring about the end of their own power and all that they have built with it. Sauron, by contrast, as Gandalf explains, understands only the desire for power. This characteristic is the weakness that those who fight Sauron might exploit in order to defeat him. Anyone who dares to try to destroy the Ring, thereby denying himself its power, would be acting in a way that Sauron would neither understand nor expect. Of course, to destroy the Ring, or even merely to resist its powerful appeal, is easier said than done, as Isildur, Gollum, Bilbo, and now Frodo have discovered.

Tolkien's idea that resisting evil means, in part, resisting desires reflects his Christian sensibility. Christianity demands the subjugation of one's own desires—whether sensual, material, or even merely a greed for knowledge—before the word of God. Indeed, excessive thirst for knowledge can be the most dangerous desire. In the biblical book of Genesis, this danger appears in the form of the forbidden fruit of the Tree of the Knowledge of Good and Evil, which offers the irresistible promise of forbidden knowledge that leads to Adam and Eve's expulsion from Eden. In Middle-earth, there are similar examples of forbidden knowledge: the Elven-smiths, ensnared by Sauron with promises of great learning, and the corrupted wizard Saruman. Indeed, even the Dwarves whom Glóin describes to Frodo, who dig too deep in Moria in search of the precious metal *mithril* and awaken "the nameless fear," serve as a symbol of the dangers of reckless and greedy curiosity.

Tolkien's warning against the greed for knowledge appears to be based on the distinction between mere knowledge and wisdom. We are offered a clue as to exactly what differentiates the two in Gandalf's rebuke to Saruman when he discovers that the latter's deep study of Ring-lore has corrupted him: "he that breaks a thing to find out what it is has left the path of wisdom." Wisdom implies an added moral dimension that mere knowledge lacks: wisdom involves thinking of the *consequences* of actions. Gandalf and Elrond, among others, embody wisdom, while Saruman, the Elven-smiths, and the Dwarves of Moria have sought only knowledge.

Another notably Christian element in the text is Elrond's pre-diction of the great part that "the weak," including Hobbits, are to play in the coming battle. Indeed, it is Frodo's physical weakness that makes him the ideal Ring-bearer, as he is not powerful enough to wield the Ring in a truly dangerous or destructive fashion. However, Frodo's temperament suits him to the great task before him. As Elrond and Gandalf both point out, physical strength and wisdom will not carry the day in the quest. Resisting the temptation of the Ring is a matter of conviction and inner strength. Elrond's description of the ideal Ring-bearer—who is not necessarily physically unimpressive, but is morally steady,

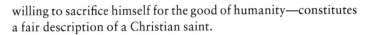

willing to sacrifice himself for the good of humanity—constitutes a fair description of a Christian saint.

BOOK II, CHAPTER 3

SUMMARY — THE RING GOES SOUTH

Elrond sends out his scouts to determine the movements of the Enemy. Meanwhile, the hobbits bide their time. Bilbo asks Frodo to help him finish a book recounting the elder hobbit's adventures, and start the next book, which will describe Frodo's. Elrond chooses the company that will set out with the Ring-bearer. All told, there will be nine in the Fellowship: Frodo, Sam, Gandalf, Legolas, Gimli, Aragorn, Boromir, Merry, and Pippin. Elrond is hesitant to send the last two, as he is unsure of what they could contribute. However, he consents after Gandalf points out that not even an Elf-lord's power would be able to guarantee success, and that Merry's and Pippin's feelings of loyalty to Frodo count for much.

The Company prepares to depart after Elrond's scouts return two months later. As a parting gift, Bilbo gives Frodo a beautifully crafted coat of mail and the short sword, Sting, that Bilbo used on his own adventures. Aragorn has his broken sword reforged, and he renames the sword Andúril. Finally, the group takes along the old pony the hobbits bought from Bill Ferny, whom Sam has named Bill and who now looks healthy and strong. After quick goodbyes, the Fellowship sets off.

The Company heads south out of Rivendell, along the foothills of the Misty Mountains. One day, they see a suspicious flock of birds flying overhead, which Aragorn fears are servants of Mordor sent to spy on them. The group tries to decide how to cross the Misty Mountains, which impede their path. They settle on the pass of Caradhras, which enables passage beside one of the range's tallest peaks. Caradhras is Aragorn's choice, although Gandalf fears the pass may be watched. The wizard mentions a darker and more secret path—one that Aragorn is loath to try.

As the group climbs higher, the road becomes a treacherous path along a cliff face. Snow begins to fall. Only Legolas remains undeterred, for as an Elf he can walk lightly over the snow, leaving hardly a footprint. The farther the group goes, the heavier the snow falls. Before long, boulders start to tumble down the mountain all around them as well. Eventually, they are forced to turn back. The snow has built up many feet deep behind them, so the men must burrow a way out for the hobbits. The snow stops soon after they retreat. As Gimli notes, evidently some force in Caradhras—the mountain has a reputation for evil—does not want them to pass.

ANALYSIS

The Fellowship of the Ring is chosen to represent all the Free Peoples of Middle-earth: Hobbits, Elves, Dwarves, and Men. Such an assembly of races in cooperation—now one of the most common, staple elements of the fantasy genre—emerged in large part because of Tolkien's works. Although Tolkien never considered himself a fantasy writer—in fact, he spoke of the genre with disdain—an enormous amount of fantasy literature and gaming is derived from his writing. Tolkien thought of his work, with its concern for the origins of mankind and the fullness of its scope, as far more than fantasy; he envisioned it as something between fiction and mythology. On a narrative level, this cooperation of races allows Tolkien to act out in miniature some of the historical conflicts of Middle-earth, such as the traditional animosity between Elves and Dwarves, which we see in the early interactions of Legolas and Gimli. The diversity of the Fellowship also allows Tolkien to personify some of the traits he earlier describes only on a more general, archetypal level: the lightness and quickness of the Legolas the elf, the stolid determination of Gimli the dwarf, and so on. Some readers may find this stereotyping a bit limiting, but Tolkien does flesh out his characters beyond the stock traits of their particular races.

This chapter reminds us that nature is not merely a neutral backdrop to the adventures recounted in *The Lord of the Rings,* but is an active participant in them. Nature is endowed with moral qualities in the novel—sometimes good, sometimes evil. We see in the second volume, *The Two Towers,* a powerful example of nature's goodness: the Ents, a tribe of treelike beings who rouse themselves from dormancy to aid the Fellowship. Within *The Fellowship of the Ring,* Sam's pony, Gwaihir the Windlord, and Shadowfax are smaller examples of how the world of nature can offer aid. But this chapter also offers potent examples of how evil nature can be. The sinister birds flying overhead are not just a part of the landscape, but a suspicious reminder that Sauron is spying on the Fellowship, suggesting that nature itself may be a secret agent. The heavy snowfall encountered here, which at first seems like mere bad luck as it impedes the group's progress through the pass of Caradhras, is finally judged by Gimli to be an evil influence. The clouds above the pass are, in effect, snowing on purpose, in order to keep the Fellowship from passing through Caradhras. Everything in Tolkien's world is part of the central saga of good opposing evil.

BOOK II, CHAPTER 4

SUMMARY — A JOURNEY IN THE DARK

Gandalf feels that the group's only remaining option is a path beneath the mountains, through the Mines of Moria. Many in the group tremble at the mention of Moria, which is widely reputed to be an evil place. Only Gimli is eager, as Moria was once one of the greatest places in the realm of the Dwarves, and he is eager to enter Moria to look for any sign of the Dwarf-king Balin. Aragorn makes a mysterious comment, saying that Gandalf in particular should beware of Moria. The rest of the Company is forced to agree with Gandalf's decision to enter Moria, however, when they hear the howling of wolves nearby and realize they must move on quickly. Indeed, that very night they barely stave off an assault by the wolves. Everyone in the group fights valiantly: Legolas with his bow, Gimli with his axe, Aragorn and Boromir with their swords, Gandalf with a spell that sets the circle of trees around them on fire.

In the morning, the Company proceeds to the western Door of Moria, which is near a dark lake by the side of the mountain. At this point, they decide, much to Sam's chagrin, that they must let Bill the pony go. The Door is sealed with ancient magic, and it takes Gandalf some time and a great deal of thought to figure out the password—which, as it turns out, is actually written in a deceptively simple riddle on the Door itself. Just as the Company is about to pass through the Door, it is attacked by a tentacled creature from the lake that tries to drag Frodo into the water. The Company rushes through the entrance. The creature slams the Door behind them and piles on boulders and uprooted trees. The group is now committed to the journey through Moria.

Once inside the Mines, the Fellowship is glad to have Gandalf's guidance, as the caves are vast and intricate. Since the wizard has been through Moria before, he leads the way, lighting the passages ahead with his glowing staff. They walk for miles, through twisting passages and over great, gaping pits. Frodo thinks he hears a strange pattering sound behind them, like quiet footsteps.

After several hours of walking, the Company comes to a fork in the path that stumps Gandalf. They decide to stop for the night while the wizard mulls the problem over. They spend the night in a room off to one side of the path. Pippin raises Gandalf's ire by carelessly tossing a pebble down a seemingly bottomless well in the room; the noise of the pebble falling appears to awaken something far below. Later that night, Gandalf relieves Pippin of his watch, as the wizard cannot sleep for all of his worrying over which path to take. Gandalf decides that he needs a smoke to soothe his nerves, so he lights a pipe.

The next morning, Gandalf chooses a path. When the group finds itself in an enormous, splendid underground hall with great pillars and shining walls, the wizard says he has chosen correctly. The group stops, and Gimli and Gandalf tell of the history of Moria. The Dwarves mined the caves for *mithril,* a metal of almost magical beauty and strength. Gandalf mentions that the dwarf Thorin once gave Bilbo a shirt of mail made of *mithril*—a gift worth more than all the Shire put together. Frodo realizes that this shirt is the gift Bilbo gave him earlier in Rivendell. That night, Frodo thinks he sees two luminous eyes off in the distance, but he cannot be sure.

The next morning dawns, and some light shines into the hall from windows built into the side of the mountain. Gandalf believes he knows the correct path, but he decides he wants to take a look around first. The group comes upon a large, square chamber, dimly lit by the sun through huge shafts in the mountain above. In the middle of the room is a block of stone, inscribed with runes—it is the tombstone of Balin, the Dwarf-king. Gimli casts his hood over his face in mourning.

ANALYSIS

Aside from Frodo, the character whom we get to know the best during this chapter is Gandalf. The Mines of Moria test the wizard from the start and, as we see in the upcoming chapters, continue to test him until the end. In his deep thought and even frustration, he tries mightily to keep the Fellowship on the right track through Moria. Both at the gate and then at the confusing fork in the path, we see Gandalf stymied by problems that must be solved not with powerful spells but simply with riddles and a good memory. One of the most memorable and human moments in the novel is when Gandalf, wondering why he is so jumpy, realizes he simply needs a smoke. It is this mix of timeless wisdom and short-temperedness, great power and wry humor, that makes Gandalf one of the most enduring characters in *The Lord of the Rings.*

The first stage of the Ring's journey from Rivendell to Mordor provides several new examples of nature at its cruelest. Like Old Man Willow, Caradhras is powerful and malevolent for no apparent reason. When the Fellowship is not dodging falling boulders and slogging through heavy snow, it must hide from spying birds and fend off fearsome wolves. Tolkien's nature is not the sort of Darwinian world in which every animal is out for itself, but is rather a magical place in which every bird, tree, and mountain is aligned either with the side of good or with the side of evil. Again, as we see in the episode in the Old Forest earlier in the novel, Tolkien draws a clear distinction between domesticated nature, which results in pleasant settings such as the Shire, and wild, untamed nature, which can be either good or evil, but always unpredictable and therefore dangerous.

Tolkien also uses this section to better acquaint us with the Dwarves, about whom we have heard little in the novel before this point. The history of the Dwarves is long and dramatic, and as a race they are not only the traditional rivals of the Elves, but their opposites in many ways. The Elves are tall, slender, and fair; the Dwarves short, stout, and dark. The Elves make their home in the light, among the trees; the Dwarves live largely in the dark, mining deep within the earth. Perhaps most important, the Elves live in harmony with the natural world, whereas the Dwarves mine the earth for its riches. It is this mining that has perhaps led to the Dwarves' doom, at least that of the Dwarves of Moria. Their skill at building and forging is great, but we learn that they also have been greedy, and their greed has had high costs for them. Not only have the Dwarves been driven from Moria in the first place, but furthermore, the Dwarf-king Balin, who insisted on returning to reclaim the Dwarves' glorious realm of old, has met with an untimely end. This history of the Dwarves, especially their great desire for *mithril*, which leads them to dig too deep and wake something evil in the earth, is a manifestation of one of Tolkien's central concerns in the novel: desires that are not in themselves evil can nonetheless lead to evil ends.

BOOK II, CHAPTERS 5–6

SUMMARY — CHAPTER 5: THE BRIDGE OF KHAZAD-DÛM

Inside the chamber containing Balin's tomb, Gandalf finds a half-burned book among bones and broken shields. The tome is the record of Balin's people in Moria; it tells of their last days, when they were besieged both by hordes of Orcs and by a mysterious force much more ominous than Orcs. The final page of the record, hastily scrawled, is terrifying in its vagueness: "We cannot get out . . . drums in the deep . . . They are coming."

The Company, scared and saddened, is about to leave the chamber when they suddenly hear the booming of a drum deep below them, along with the noise of many running feet. They bar the west door of the chamber just as a troop of Orcs arrives, along with a great cave-troll. The cave-troll forces its way through the door, but Frodo stabs its foot with Sting and the monster withdraws. Then the Orcs break through the door, but many are slain by the Company and the rest retreat. Gandalf sees a chance to escape, so he leads the Company out through the unguarded east door—but not before an Orc-chieftain stabs Frodo in the side. The rest of the Company is amazed to see Frodo still alive.

Gandalf holds the door shut with a closing spell while the others flee, but he feels a powerful counter-spell from the other side. The ensuing battle of spells collapses the doorway, and then the entire room. The wearied wizard rejoins the Company and leads them down toward the lower halls. Finally, they come to the Second Hall, just opposite the gate that leads out of Moria. The Company runs across the Bridge of Khazad-dûm, a slender arch of rock over a seemingly bottomless chasm. As they turn to look back, though, Legolas cries out in horror and Gimli covers his eyes.

Out of a band of Orcs leaps a great shadowy form, wreathed in flame and yet surrounded by shadow and darkness. It is a Balrog. Gandalf commands the others to flee while he holds the bridge. The Balrog swings a flaming sword and leaps forward, but the wizard stands firm. With a mighty spell, Gandalf breaks the bridge in two. The Balrog tumbles down, but in falling, casts its whip around Gandalf's ankles and pulls him down into the depths of the cavern. As Gandalf falls, he shouts to the Company, "Fly, you fools!" Aragorn hurriedly leads the Company out of the Great Gates of Moria. They stumble a mile or so away from the mountain and then all collapse in grief.

SUMMARY — CHAPTER 6: LOTHLÓRIEN

With Gandalf lost, Aragorn assumes command of the Company. Hopeless though they all feel, the Ranger leads them away from the Misty Mountains and toward the Elvish forest of Lothlórien (often simply called Lórien). Stopping briefly to tend to Frodo's injury, Aragorn is amazed to find Bilbo's coat of *mithril,* which saved Frodo from his spear wound in Moria. Moving on, the Company comes to a deep well of crystal-clear water. Legolas and Aragorn are relieved to arrive at Lórien, but Boromir is wary; among Men, the name of the forest is surrounded by strange rumors.

Legolas tells the others of the history of Lothlórien: sorrow came in the Dark Days, when the Dwarves awakened the evil in Moria that then spread out into the hills and threatened Lórien. Gimli bristles at this mention. The Company enters the woods as night falls but is suddenly stopped by a group of Elves, led by one named Haldir, who have been watching from the trees. Luckily, the elves recognize Legolas as kindred and have also heard something of Frodo's quest, so they bring the strangers up to their tree-platforms. After night falls, a company of Orcs passes under them, chasing after the Fellowship, but the creatures are waylaid by the Elves. Frodo and the others then see another strange creature—a small, crouching shape with pale eyes—but it slips away into the night.

In the morning, the Company walks further into Lórien, reaching the river Silverlode. At one point, the Elves tell Gimli that he must be blindfolded so that he does not know where he is walking, especially because the Dwarves and Elves have not gotten along since the Dark Days. Gimli strongly objects, and the dispute nearly comes to blows. Thinking quickly, Aragorn demands that all the Company, even Legolas, be blindfolded. Gimli assents, so all the members of the Fellowship are led blindfolded into the Naith, or heart, of Lórien. Once they arrive, Haldir receives word that the Lady Galadriel, queen of the forest, has decreed that the Fellowship's blindfolds may be removed.

When the blindfolds are taken off, the strangers behold a forest that seems to belong to another age. Its trees and flowers surpass the beauty of any other growing things, and the light and colors are ethereal golds and greens. They are at Cerin Amroth, a hill with a double ring of trees that is, in Aragorn's words, "the heart of Elvendom on earth." Haldir takes Frodo and Sam up to a platform on top of the trees, from which they gaze at the enchanted land surrounding them, noticing also the forbidding lands beyond. When the hobbits descend, they find Aragorn in a powerful and blissful daydream.

ANALYSIS — CHAPTERS 5–6

"The Bridge of Khazad-dûm" contains the longest stretch of continuous action in *The Fellowship of the Ring,* and Tolkien's skill at sustaining the dramatic action in the chapter is remarkable. He sets the scene with the ominous entries in the Dwarf journal that mention "drums in the deep." Then, moments later, the Company itself hears those same drums, and Legolas and Gimli, perhaps unwittingly, echo the scrawled last words of the journal: "They are coming" and "We cannot get out." The drums themselves owe some of their frightfulness to the fact that Tolkien evokes their sound with the word "doom" (or sometimes "doom-boom") rather than the more typical "boom." The throbbing pulse of the Orc drums punctuates the action and hints at something that has been awakened from its dormancy deep beneath Moria. Tolkien's visual descriptions further the sense of drama. In the previous chapter, the Fellowship moves from the quiet, spooky tunnels into the dark, silent hall, occasionally hearing strange, distant noises. As the tension builds throughout Chapter 5, so do the noise and the visuals, until finally at the bridge itself there converge roaring Orcs, flying arrows, leaping flames, Trolls, a fearsome demon, a sword and whip of fire, and the bridge itself, thin and arching over a gaping chasm of nothingness. After Gandalf and the Balrog fall, the flames die and the noise fades accordingly. Like a director, Tolkien adds significance to the action of his characters by augmenting the scene with the equivalent of stage directions of all kinds.

With Gandalf's plunge into the chasm, which is arguably the climax of *The Fellowship of the Ring,* we see the fulfillment of one of the many prophecies that are told throughout *The Lord of the Rings.* In the chapter before Gandalf's battle with the Balrog, Aragorn makes a strange warning when he reluctantly consents to Gandalf's plan to enter Moria: "I will follow your lead now—if this last warning does not move you. It is not of the Ring, nor of us others that I am thinking now, but of you, Gandalf. And I say to you: if you pass the doors of Moria, beware!" It is unclear whether Aragorn recalls some prophecy he has heard in the past, or whether he has had a prophetic insight of his own. In any case, he is proven prescient when Gandalf falls into the chasm.

Aragorn's prediction is one of many prophecies throughout Tolkien's novel, many of which are contained in songs or verses that link present and future occurrences to the past—often the distant, ancient past. These prophecies not only create a sense of anticipation that moves the plot forward, but also tie *The Lord of the Rings* to the mythological tradition that precedes it. Greek myth is one of the most familiar arenas of prophecy, as seemingly every mortal and god in Greek myth is subject to the predictions of the fabled oracles. Numerous characters in the Greek myths live out prophecies made long before their births, usually unwittingly. Tolkien, in his inclusion of similar prophecies in the mythological world of Middle-earth, emphasizes and explores the importance and nature of fate. Many of the events prophesied in *The Lord of the Rings* happen for seemingly no reason, or at least not for a reason that is immediately clear. Though Tolkien does not explicitly refer to any gods or higher powers that may govern the workings of Middle-earth, these prophecies, in a sense, imply an overarching consciousness or direction that controls the events that transpire in the universe of the novel.

After the tumult and tragedy of the journey through Moria, Tolkien leads us into the near-heavenly quiet and peace of the Elvish forest of Lothlórien. This pattern of hairbreadth escapes followed by intermissions of peace is a recurring structure throughout the novel: we see it first in the flight to the Ford of Bruinen followed by a respite in Rivendell, and now in the escape from Moria to Lórien. In both cases, the peace comes in the realm of the Elves. The Elves live in a world set apart and protected—a world out of the past, as Frodo notes during the stay in Lórien. Tolkien's pattern of action followed by respite serves, in part, to propel the narrative along without inundating it with a series of frenzied battles or chases that go on without interruption. This pacing also mirrors the embattled, tumultuous state of Middle-earth. As Elrond says, Middle-earth is increasingly a place in which small pockets of goodness and safety are surrounded by a sea of darkness. To move from one to another of the islands is to move from safety to danger and back again.

Tolkien's Middle-earth is, of course, entirely the author's own creation, but his intimate knowledge of the natural world allows him to ground it and lend it an everyday immediacy. We especially see this blending of the real and the invented in the forest of Lórien. Along with the mystical *athelas* and *mellyrn* trees, Lórien contains the more familiar fir-trees, harts-tongue, and whortle-berry; along with Orcs and Trolls, there are wolves and ponies. This blending of the authentic and the fantastic not only makes the landscape more believable and not so completely whimsical, but also allows Tolkien to sustain the conceit that Middle-earth—with its magic and great deeds and battles between good and evil—is the earlier universe that has somehow become the more banal and mundane world we know today. Some elements of this older world remain, but many have disappeared. Tolkien leaves the reasons for this transformation intentionally unexplained, allowing our own imaginations to take over.

BOOK II, CHAPTER 7

SUMMARY — THE MIRROR OF GALADRIEL

That night, the Company is taken to Caras Galadhon, the main city of Lórien. There, they are brought before Lord Celeborn and Lady Galadriel, the rulers of Lórien. The great hall of the Lord and Lady is built on a platform in the largest tree in the forest. The Lord and Lady are tall, beautiful, and timeless, seeming neither old nor young. Aragorn tells them of the loss of Gandalf in Moria. It is a grave blow, as Galadriel knew Gandalf well. Celeborn initially blames the Dwarves for waking the Balrog, and he regrets having let Gimli into Lórien. Galadriel, however, quickly tells Celeborn that it is not Gimli's fault. She goes on to say that she knows the purpose of their quest and the burden that Frodo bears. As the Company stands before her, she looks upon each of its members for a time, searching his heart. Afterward, they all feel as though Galadriel has read their minds and offered them the thing they wanted most—but could get only if they turned aside from the quest and returned home. But some among the Fellowship, especially Boromir, are reluctant to say what it was that Galadriel offered them.

The Company rests in Lórien, where the days pass almost without notice. The entire forest of Lórien seems outside of time. Legolas and Gimli spend much time together, and they become fast friends. They all grieve for Gandalf, and Frodo writes a song in the wizard's memory. As the day approaches when the Fellowship must leave, Galadriel takes Frodo and Sam to a basin in the middle of an enclosed garden. She calls the basin her mirror. Looking into it, one can see visions of far-off places and times, but interpreting these visions is dangerous. Galadriel fills the basin with water from the nearby stream. When Sam looks in the mirror, he sees parts of Hobbiton being torn up and what looks to be a factory spewing dark smoke. For a moment, he wishes to run back home, but then he masters himself. Frodo sees many things—a bent, old figure clad in white; ships on the sea; a white fortress—before a final vision of a great, dark eye rimmed in fire. Frodo realizes the eye is searching for him.

Afterward, Galadriel comforts Frodo, telling him she can perceive the mind of Sauron and can resist his efforts to perceive hers. As she speaks, Frodo notices a ring on her finger. Galadriel tells him it is one of the three Elvish Rings of Power; Sauron does not yet know that she is its keeper. She tells Frodo that, should he fail, Sauron will overpower her. Nonetheless, even if Frodo succeeds, the power of the Elves will fade. Either way leads to sadness, but Galadriel greatly prefers the latter. Frodo, overwhelmed by her wisdom, beauty, and power, offers her the Ring to keep. Galadriel refuses, knowing that the Ring would corrupt her as well, leading her simply to replace Sauron herself.

ANALYSIS

Lothlórien is, in Aragorn's words, "the heart of Elvendom on earth," and Tolkien spares no superlative in describing it. All in the forest is light, pure, fair, clear, timeless, soothing—generally perfect. The Elves have magical gifts aplenty: they bestow upon the Fellowship long-lasting food and enchanted, chameleonic cloaks with seemingly endless versatility. However, as much as Tolkien evokes a sense of perfection in Lórien, he also kindles an elegiac sense of loss. As Frodo notes, "[i]n Rivendell there was memory of ancient things; in Lórien the ancient things still lived on in the waking world." Therefore, the loss and the fading that the Elves repeatedly describe will be felt most acutely here in the heart of their realm. Here is the Eden of Middle-earth, the paradise that will inevitably be lost whether or not Frodo succeeds.

Even the near-celestial Elves are not above getting bogged down in a mutually distrustful relationship with their former neighbors, the Dwarves. In a sense, the opposition between these two races offers two different conceptions of art and craft. The Dwarves dig deep into the earth and work in long-lasting stone and metal. The Elves of Lórien live above the ground in trees, and their art tends to be more organic. Of course, there are Elven-smiths like those who made the Rings of Power; on the whole, however, the Elves are associated with moving water and blooming plants—quicker, more ephemeral aspects of nature that fade, change, or disappear. This transience embodies the paradox of the Elves: they are immortal, but their creations are fragile and dependent on their magic. Without out the power of Galadriel's ring, Lothlórien will inevitably fade.

However, the forest will continue to exist in the memories of those who have seen it. For the Elves, memory is a central and powerful force. As Gimli tells Legolas, he has heard that memory is especially vivid for Elves, more like waking life than a dream state. Of course, one would need a good memory to store an eternity's worth of recollections, and in this sense, the Elves' ability to remember and their instinct for elegy and nostalgia link them closely with Tolkien himself. All the free races of Tolkien's universe—Men, Hobbits, Dwarves, and Elves—value songs and stories, but the Elves seem to place the highest regard in such words and records.

The mirror of Galadriel is a powerful image of prophecy—and the limitations of prophecy—that foreshadows the appearance of Sauron's *palantír* in *The Two Towers,* the next volume of *The Lord of the Rings.* Galadriel's water-filled basin can provide images of things to come: by the end of Tolkien's saga, we will recall the ship glimpsed in the water and realize it has foretold the ship that bears the Elves away to the West. Sam's glimpse of a disfigured Hobbiton foreshadows the trouble that the Shire ultimately faces when the Fellowship returns there after their adventures are over. But while Galadriel's mirror is undoubtedly powerful and accurate, it is also of limited usefulness. Galadriel herself warns that it is dangerous to try to interpret what one sees in the mirror—yet without an interpretation of what is seen, evaluation and action are not possible. Like the Ring that allows Frodo to see the Riders but not to fight them, the mirror allows seers to glimpse the future but does not empower them to do anything about it. We see again that magic implements may be wondrous, but that ultimately active courage and determination may count for more.

Book II, Chapter 8

Summary — Farewell to Lórien

> *For so it seemed to them: Lórien was slipping*
> *backward, like a bright ship masted with enchanted*
> *trees . . . while they sat helpless upon the margin of the*
> *grey and leafless world.*
>
> (See QUOTATIONS, p. 85)

The time comes for the Company to set off. Celeborn gives each member the option of staying in Lórien, but they all choose to go onward. Their next destination, however, is undecided. Boromir wants to go to the city of Minas Tirith, but it is on the other side of the river from Mordor, where the Ring must ultimately go. Luckily, the Company does not have to decide for a few days, as the Elves have provided them with boats to use to float down the Great River, Anduin, which leads out of Lórien. Only when they reach a point where they cannot go farther on the Great River will they have to choose whether to go east or west. During their debates, Frodo says nothing and Aragorn says little, and the Company as a whole remains undecided. Boromir, however, shows a strange reluctance to destroy the Ring at all.

The Elves present the Fellowship with many gifts, including *lembas*—wafers of long-lasting meal that have a pleasant taste and provide a day's worth of energy—along with ropes and magic cloaks that provide warmth in the cold and cool in the heat, are light and strong, and change color to conceal the wearer. The Company then has one last meal with the Lord and Lady on the banks of the river.

Galadriel then presents the Fellowship with additional gifts. To Aragorn she gives a sheath for his sword, Andúril, and a green gem in a silver brooch. Boromir, Merry, and Pippin each receive belts of silver or gold, while Legolas receives a longer, stouter bow. Sam, the gardener, gets a box of dirt from Galadriel's orchard that, sprinkled anywhere, will cause the earth to burst into bloom. Galadriel asks Gimli to name his request. To the great shock of the Elves, the dwarf reluctantly asks only for a strand of Galadriel's hair as a memento and a token of good faith between their races. The Lady gladly agrees. Lastly, Galadriel gives Frodo a phial of water in which is caught the light of Eärendil's star. The time has come for the Fellowship to leave, and Galadriel sings to them as they float down the river and out of sight of Lórien. With heavy hearts, they turn and look to the journey ahead.

ANALYSIS

In this chapter, we begin to see the first signs that Boromir is wavering from the goal of destroying the Ring. The corruptive power of the evil object is no longer merely a *potential* threat to the Fellowship, but may be an actual threat if Boromir becomes a traitor to the cause. We see in him hints of moral indecision and, though not an inherent evil, a capacity for corruption. Of all the Company, Boromir appears the least contented with Gandalf's and Elrond's explanations as to why the Ring must never be used, even as a weapon in the fight against Sauron. Boromir makes it clear that his goal is to reach Minas Tirith, not to head for Mordor where the Ring must be destroyed. He even declares that he will journey to the city alone if need be—a strong urge toward individualism that is one of the telltale signs of the Ring's wicked influence. It is, of course, far too early to accuse Boromir of outright treachery, or even of plotting it. But our suspicions linger, and the Fellowship appears a more fragile alliance than it ever has before.

The gifts Galadriel offers to the group are useful and urgently needed: the *lembas* cakes provide nourishment, and the cloaks warmth. But many of the gifts also symbolize what is missing from the bleak landscape of the war-threatened Middle-earth. Galadriel gives Frodo her phial of light, reminding us of the "dark times" (as a character in the next volume of the novel describes them) that currently prevail in Middle-earth. Her gift of magic soil to Sam reminds us of how little regeneration and growth there has been in this time of warfare and destruction. Finally, Galadriel's gift of a strand of her hair to Gimli—who may have a small crush on the Lady—is not merely a gesture of reconciliation between the Elves and Dwarves, but also a reminder of how few females there are in Tolkien's work (a fact upon which many readers have commented). In Tolkien's universe, women and girls are associated with times of peace, prosperity, and happy home life—none of which can survive the wide-ranging disturbances of Sauron. As such, Galadriel's gifts are more than just a fairy-tale addition to the adventure. Rather, they remind us of all the fruits of civilized and peaceful life for which the Fellowship is fighting.

BOOK II, CHAPTER 9

SUMMARY — THE GREAT RIVER

For several days, the Company passes swiftly down the Anduin without incident. The landscape, especially on the eastern bank facing Mordor, gets more and more barren and foreboding. One night, Sam thinks he sees two pale eyes shining out of a log floating nearby, which seems to be heading straight for Gimli's boat. Sam mentions this observation to Frodo, who puts it together with the pattering noises in Moria and the strange creature in Lórien, and suspects that Gollum himself has been following them. The next night, Frodo keeps watch, and, as expected, he sees a dark shape swim up close to the boats. The hobbit draws his sword and the shape disappears.

Aragorn confirms Frodo's suspicions and says that he, too, has seen Gollum, and has even tried, unsuccessfully, to catch him.

The next day, the Company paddles more swiftly, fearful that their tracker will inform the Enemy of their whereabouts. Indeed, when they find themselves suddenly in the rapids of Sarn Gebir, they are forced to turn around and make for the shore with Orc arrows whistling over their heads. Just as the Company reaches the shore, a dark shape in the sky comes speeding up from the south, filling the Company with terror. Frodo suddenly feels the pain of the old wound in his shoulder. Legolas grabs his new bow, lets fly an arrow, and sends the flying form crashing down on the other side of the river. They hear no more from the Orcs that night. Frodo refuses to say to the others what he thinks the flying shape might have been.

The next morning, though Boromir tries mightily to convince the Company to make for Minas Tirith, they decide to push on further along the river. To get past a set of rapids, they use an old portage road to carry the boats and gear to where the river runs smooth again. The current takes them swiftly onward to the Gates of Argonath, a narrow passage between two immense cliffs, guarded by two gigantic statues—likenesses of Aragorn's ancestors Isildur and Anárion. The Gates mark the ancient northern border of the realm of Gondor, one of the realms of Men. Passing through Argonath, the Company comes to the three great hills before the Falls of Rauros—Amon Lhaw on the east, Tol Brandir in the midst of the river, and Amon Hen on the west. They draw up the boats at the foot of Amon Hen, as they can go no further on the river. They must now, at last, choose to go either west to Minas Tirith or east to Mordor.

SUMMARY & ANALYSIS

ANALYSIS

As the first stage of the Ring's journey winds down, it is worth pausing to note how exactly Tolkien has brought the Company this far. There is, of course, plenty of action, many songs, and a great deal of recounted history, but much of the novel simply consists of descriptions of the Company walking through countryside. Tolkien's eye for scenery, and his talent for making that scenery reflect mood, make the natural environment almost another character in itself, whether it is the sleepy Shire, the enchanted Lothlórien, or the bleak Brown Lands. In the case of Old Man Willow or the pass of Caradhras, the natural world actually does become a character. Each land through which the Company passes has its own topography and its own flora and fauna. Indeed, though some might find

Tolkien's characters a bit two-dimensional and his dialogue at times implausible with its mythic-biblical tone, the richness and fullness of the world surrounding the action make up for it.

In addition, such lush description allows Tolkien to demonstrate just how thoroughly he has thought out his realm of Middle-earth. If inclined, we can follow the trail of the Fellowship, from its seeds in the Shire to its dissolution at the foot of Amon Hen, on maps enclosed in the novel. Each river the party fords is there, as is each mountain range they cross. The maps add an aura of the arcane, giving us the feeling that we are poring over an ancient manuscript. They add to the sense that the novel is a record of a past age and place. At the same time, the maps serve a practical function, allowing us to follow the quest geographically and mark its progress toward Mordor, the final destination. Tolkien realizes the importance of providing this sort of bird's-eye view for us: all along the way, first the hobbits and then the Fellowship stop at high places to mark their progress, whether in the Old Forest, at Weathertop, or on the tree-platform in Lothlórien. These vistas give us a sense of where the Fellowship is going, how far it has come, and an overall impression of direction and order in what might otherwise seem an incessant slog through unending terrain.

Gollum's stalking of the group is one of the most notable examples of the constant anxiety the Fellowship experiences on the journey. Indeed, the various skirmishes with Barrow-wights and tentacled monsters certainly provide the Fellowship with a series of challenges and violent encounters. However, it could be argued that unceasing dread, rather than isolated bursts of incident, is more characteristic of the travelers' everyday experience—and more of a drain on their energies. An unknown and unseen enemy is far more terrifying than one clearly viewed and recognized. Gollum, like the dark shapes of the Ringwraiths, is frightening more in his obscurity and elusiveness than in the actual harm he causes. He haunts and stalks rather than ambushes or attacks, so his threat is never-ending. Gollum's pale, staring eyes and the ever-present patter of his footsteps in the distance symbolize the constant paranoia with which the Fellowship is forced to live in the name of safety.

BOOK II, CHAPTER 10

SUMMARY — THE BREAKING OF THE FELLOWSHIP

That night, Aragorn is uneasy and wakes during Frodo's watch. He asks Frodo to take out his sword, Sting. The sword glows faintly, indicating that Orcs are near—though they do not know how near.

The next morning, Aragorn declares that Frodo must decide where the Ring is to go; the rest of the Company may continue where they will. Frodo asks for an hour alone to decide, and he walks up through the woods on Amon Hen. Secretly, Boromir follows, and, once in the isolation of the woods, he approaches Frodo. Boromir tries to convince the hobbit to turn toward the safety of Minas Tirith, and not to throw the Ring away when it could be used as a weapon against Sauron. When Frodo disagrees, Boromir grows angry and is suddenly taken with an uncontrollable desire for the Ring. He leaps toward Frodo, who is forced to put the Ring on his finger and disappear. The madness then leaves Boromir. Realizing what he has done, he falls to the ground and weeps.

Frodo runs breathless to the top of Amon Hen. From this high point, and with the vision the Ring gives him, he can see many things—but mostly war, gathering on all fronts. He looks toward Mordor and beholds Barad-dûr, the Dark Tower of Sauron, and he feels Sauron's Great Eye searching for the Ring-bearer. The Eye has almost found Frodo when a voice suddenly comes into his head, telling him to take the Ring off his finger. Frodo struggles between the two forces, the Voice and the Eye, before he suddenly realizes that the choice is ultimately his to make. He removes the Ring, and the Great Eye does not find him. Frodo now knows that he must go on to Mordor alone. The Ring has already corrupted one of the Company—Boromir—and Frodo loves those whom he can trust too much to lead them to what seems a certain death. Going back into the cover of the forest, the hobbit slips the Ring on his finger again.

Meanwhile, the others down at the shore begin to worry, debating among themselves where the Ring should go and wondering why Frodo is taking so long to decide. Boromir returns, sad and grim, and tells them that he scared Frodo off, though Boromir does not reveal that he tried to take the Ring from the hobbit. The Company, filled with concern, scatters and calls out for Frodo. In vain, Aragorn insists that they divide up into pairs and search. He runs off after Sam and sends Boromir to look after Merry and Pippin.

Aragorn quickly catches up to Sam and tells him he thinks there is danger near. The Ranger decides to go up to the top of Amon Hen to look around. Sam hurries after Aragorn for a bit, but soon loses sight of him. Sam stops, realizing that Frodo is probably making for the boats, intending to go to Mordor alone. He quickly dashes down to the shore and sees a boat slipping into the river, seemingly on its own. He tries to run after it, nearly drowning himself. Frodo is forced to save Sam and to come back to shore and take off the Ring. Sam refuses to be left behind; Frodo, with some relief, accepts his friend's company. Sam grabs his pack, and they push off from shore, toward Mordor.

ANALYSIS

We get an interesting insight into Frodo's self-discovery when he sits at the top of Amon Hen wearing the Ring. With the special sight the Ring gives him, he sees much around him, but he also opens himself up to Sauron's searching Eye, with its "fierce eager will" that urges him to keep the Ring on his finger. Then Frodo hears a voice telling him to take off the Ring. For a long moment, he is caught between those two forces: "perfectly balanced between their piercing points, he writhed, tormented." Then, suddenly, he becomes aware of himself: "Frodo, neither the Voice nor the Eye: free to choose, and with one remaining instant in which to do so." We might read this conflict in a straightforward Freudian manner. Sigmund Freud was a doctor and philosopher who, around the turn of the twentieth century, created the field of psychoanalysis, which developed and popularized the notion of the unconscious mind. In a Freudian reading, the Eye of Sauron, with its fierce will and desire for the Ring, becomes what Freud called the id, the part of the psyche that is all instinctual, animal desire. The Voice, with its stern command to take off the Ring and defy Sauron, is effectively the superego, the part of the psyche that is rational and obedient to societal demands for what is right and just. Frodo himself—"neither Voice nor the Eye"—is the ego, the part of the psyche that must negotiate between the id and superego.

Though Tolkien—who resisted highly theoretical interpretations of his work—would likely find any reading linking him to Freud somewhat inappropriate, the point remains that the scene at Amon Hen serves as a dramatic representation of the role of free will and the part it plays in the battle between reason and desire. Frodo, in saying that he is affected by duty and desire, but not totally identified with either, describes the condition of every human being, pointing out the basic conflict that Freud discerned at the core of human nature. What makes Frodo unique is that he is willing to meditate on the matter. His introspective moment at Amon Hen is a time of self-exploration, which in turn is a sign of wisdom. It is impossible to imagine an evil warlord like Sauron meditating on his conflict between duty and desire. Frodo's wisdom also distinguishes him from characters like Boromir, for example, who are inordinately subject to stormy fits of passion and desire. Though we are given indications throughout *The Lord of the Rings* that Frodo is fated to be the Ring-bearer, Tolkien uses episodes such as the one at Amon Hen to remind us that self-knowledge, and the wisdom that springs from it, make Frodo worthy of his destined role.

Frodo and Boromir are the two focal points of the conclusion of *The Fellowship of the Ring*, and the contrast between them shows us the diverging developments they have undergone in the story thus far. At the beginning, Frodo and Boromir are committed to the same cause, and they appear to be of more or less similar character. Frodo, however, has kept his original honesty, as we see from his sincere conversation with himself at Amon Hen, while Boromir has become deceptive, not admitting to the rest of the Fellowship that he has tried to take the Ring from Frodo. Frodo has also kept his original selfless devotion to the Fellowship, which has led him to break away from the rest of the group in order to spare them the dangers and hardships he knows they would face if they stayed with him. Sam shows a similar sense of devotion in insisting on following his master, come what may. Boromir, by contrast, has become selfish, betraying his companions for the goal of possessing the Ring. The contrast in moral attitudes between Frodo and Boromir could hardly be greater. *The Fellowship of the Ring* ends with the struggle between Frodo and Boromir not only for reasons of plot, but also for symbolic meaning. Two examples of opposite moral paths bracket the closing of the first volume of *The Lord of the Rings*, hinting at the enormous moral opposition to come.

SUMMARY & ANALYSIS

Important Quotations Explained

1.   *"I wish it need not have happened in my time," said Frodo.
     "So do I," said Gandalf, "and so do all who live to see
     such times. But that is not for them to decide. All we have to
     decide is what to do with the time that is given us."*

This exchange occurs in Book I, Chapter 2, as Gandalf explains the history of the Ring to Frodo. The "it" to which Frodo refers is the finding of the Ring by Gollum, as well as the return of Sauron. Gandalf's response to Frodo's lament is at once heroic and fatalistic. The wizard's words are heroic because they insist that one must rise to the challenge offered by one's time. At the same time, however, there is also the suggestion that one is born at a particular time and in a particular place for a certain preordained purpose. The decision is, of course, not one's own to make; however, Gandalf does imply that it is a decision that is made somewhere—that Gandalf and Frodo's "time" has been "given" to them. This sense of purpose, of fate assigning roles to certain people, surfaces in many other such passages in The Lord of the Rings, in which ancient prophecies assign characters to certain tasks. Indeed, as Aragorn says, the War of the Ring is fated to be Gandalf's greatest battle. These pervasive references to preordainment and prophecy link Tolkien's novel to earlier epics and mythologies, most notably those of ancient Greece. Like many of the characters in The Lord of the Rings, the Greek gods and mortals are at the mercy of fate, often in the form of prophecies made long before the characters were even alive. Despite this emphasis on fate, however, free will does play a significant part in Tolkien's novel. Frodo is perhaps the ideal Ring-bearer, as his strength of character enables him to accept his fated role, yet also to retain a sense of free will in the face of the powerful, corrupting influence of the Ring.

2. *"Many that live deserve death. And some that die deserve life. Can you give it to them? Then do not be too eager to deal out death in judgement. For even the very wise cannot see all ends."*

Later in the same conversation in Book I, Chapter 2, Gandalf again explores—though this time more dimly—the hand of fate in the world of Middle-earth. The wizard's words are again a gentle rebuke to Frodo, who bemoans the fact that Gandalf did not kill Gollum when he had the chance, even though the wretched creature "deserves" death. Though Gandalf does not know how exactly, he does have a sense that Gollum has some further role to play in the story of the Ring. Indeed, as we see later in The Two Towers and The Return of the King, the wizard is correct. On a plot level, predictions such as Gandalf's serve to maintain suspense and create a sense of foreboding or anticipation, foreshadowing coming events but not telling us whether they are near or distant. On a more figurative level, however, Tolkien uses these prophecies and predictions to remind us of the presence of fate, which has assigned roles to all of the characters—roles that even the wisest and most powerful among them do not yet know or understand.

3. *"[Bilbo] used to say there was only one Road; that it was like a great river: its springs were at every doorstep, and every path was its tributary."*

The Lord of the Rings is a quest narrative, as the characters spend much of their time on the road, traveling toward the various destinations to which the quest takes them. Indeed, this tradition of the road narrative is a staple of Western literature. Texts ranging from the Danish epic Beowulf to Cervantes's Don Quixote to Kerouac's On the Road feature protagonists who take to the road in search of something. Here, as Frodo quotes Bilbo just as the hobbits set out in Book I, Chapter 3, Tolkien creates an image of the road as a river, carrying its travelers along in its current. This current works at the narrative level to advance the plot, keeping the Fellowship moving into fresh encounters and oftentimes into the unknown. Furthermore, the road serves as one of the most potent and charged metaphors in all of The Lord of the Rings. In part, the road represents the passing of time and the ages that time sweeps into the past, just as the road sweeps travelers off into the distant horizon. The road also

QUOTATIONS

represents the interconnectedness of all things, the fact that even the smallest footpath in the Shire leads, through many merges and branches, to the most distant and sinister places in Middle-earth. Though the Shire itself may be a place of comfort and familiarity, the road serves as a subtle yet constant reminder that the unknown outside world is present, and merely a journey away.

4.   *All that is gold does not glitter,*
      Not all those who wander are lost . . .

These lines are the beginning of a poem about Aragorn, quoted by Gandalf in his letter to Frodo in Book I, Chapter 10, and offered as a means for the hobbit to determine whether Strider is indeed Aragorn. The poem demonstrates not only Tolkien's facility with language, but also the central place of poetry, lore, and prophecy in the world of Middle-earth. The verse functions as a sort of seal of authenticity for Aragorn, one that defines him not only through his past and lineage, but also through his future—the destiny that awaits him. Stylistically, the poem shows Tolkien at his mythic-poetic best. In opening the poem with an inversion of a widely known aphorism ("all that glitters is not gold")—a move that also sets the metric rhythm for the poem—Tolkien grounds the poem in the known before using it to lay out part of his own created mythology. In this case, the mythology is the story of the return of the king to Minas Tirith and the reforging of the sword of Elendil. Tolkien uses this technique of grounding the mythic in the known many times throughout the novel. Perhaps the most notable arena for this technique is in Tolkien's descriptions of the natural world of Middle-earth, which mix familiar elements, such as birds, horses, and willow and fir trees, with the unfamiliar or scary, such as Orcs, athelas and mellyrn trees, and the Balrog. This blending of elements enhances the believability of Tolkien's Middle-earth, making it easier to swallow than a world in which literally everything is unfamiliar—and perhaps even characterizing Middle-earth as a sort of ancient predecessor to our own world.

5. *For so it seemed to them: Lórien was slipping backward, like a bright ship masted with enchanted trees, sailing on to forgotten shores, while they sat helpless upon the margin of the grey and leafless world.*

This passage describes the Fellowship's departure from the mystical forest of Lothlórien in Book II, Chapter 8. Here, they look back from their boats as the Great River, Anduin, carries them away from the Elven realm. Lórien is, as Aragorn names it, "the heart of Elvendom on earth"—the most enchanted place in all of Middle-earth. Leaving the beautiful realm is painful for all of the members of the Fellowship, even Gimli, whose people, the Dwarves, have a long-standing animosity with the Elves of Lórien. The departure of the Company also has a broader significance, as it represents the more general fading away of the Elves and their realm. Tolkien uses the flowing Anduin to good effect in this description of transience and impermanence. To the departing travelers, it seems as if Lórien itself is sailing away like a ship, rather than the Company sailing away from it. This manner of description alludes to the fact that the Elves, if they survive the War of the Ring, plan to take to ships and cross the sea away from Middle-earth forever. The river's current also symbolizes the passage of time—a convention of countless songs and poems—that sweeps the world before it, but leaves the Elves behind. Indeed, throughout the novel, the Elves occupy an unusual position as immortal beings whose creations are often nonetheless fragile and impermanent. The members of the Fellowship, in their boats, are acutely aware of the fact that the world without the Elves will be "grey and leafless," a drab and less magical place.

QUOTATIONS

KEY FACTS

FULL TITLE

The Fellowship of the Ring, being the first part of The Lord of the Rings

AUTHOR

J.R.R. Tolkien

TYPE OF WORK

Novel

GENRE

Epic; heroic quest; folktale; fantasy; myth

LANGUAGE

English, with occasional words and phrases from various languages of Middle-earth that Tolkien invented

TIME AND PLACE WRITTEN

1937–1949; Oxford, England

DATE OF FIRST PUBLICATION

1954

PUBLISHER

Allen and Unwin

NARRATOR

The whole of The Lord of the Rings is told by an anonymous, third-person narrator. The Prologue and later notes are somewhat academic in nature, and are presumably added by the same narrator.

POINT OF VIEW

The Fellowship of the Ring is narrated in the third person, following Frodo throughout most of the narrative, but occasionally focusing on the points of view of other characters. The narration is omniscient, which means the narrator not only relates the characters' thoughts and feelings, but also comments on them.

Tone

The narrator's tone varies somewhat over the course of The Fellowship of the Ring, though it maintains an aura of myth and nostalgia throughout. During the opening episodes in the Shire, the tone is light and casual, but it quickly becomes more serious as the Company moves into the perils of the world beyond—especially in the Mines of Moria, the darkest section of the novel. The episodes in the Elven lands, most notably the forest of Lothlórien, feature a more elegiac tone, seemingly mourning the inevitable passing of the Elves and their beautiful creations from Middle-earth.

Tense

Past

Setting (time)

The end of the Third Age of Middle-earth

Setting (place)

Various locales in the imaginary world of Middle-earth, including the Shire, Bree, the Old Forest, Rivendell, Moria, Lothlórien, and the Anduin River

Protagonist

Primarily the hobbit Frodo Baggins, though the Fellowship with whom he travels might be considered a single protagonist

Major Conflict

Frodo struggles with the opposing forces of the Ring's corrupting influence and pull and the responsibility and burden fate has placed upon him as the Ring-bearer. Frodo's uncertainty, reluctance, and perceived weakness work against his inner heroism and strength of character. As he continues on the quest, he feels the burden of his responsibility grow stronger, but also feels increasingly resigned to the role fate has given him.

rising action

Bilbo's handover of his ring to Frodo; Gandalf's identification of the ring as the One Ring; the Council of Elrond and the formation of the Fellowship; Gandalf's sacrifice of himself in Moria; the Fellowship's debate about whether to take the Ring to Minas Tirith or to Mordor

KEY FACTS

CLIMAX

Boromir tries to seize the Ring from Frodo, causing Frodo to realize that the Ring has the power to corrupt his companions and compelling him to shoulder responsibility for destroying it on his own.

FALLING ACTION

Frodo and Sam's departure toward Mordor; Boromir's shame and regret about betraying Frodo

THEMES

The corrupting influence of power; the inevitability of decline; the power of myth

MOTIFS

Songs and singing; the road; prophecy

SYMBOLS

The Rings of Power; the sword of Elendil; the mirror of Galadriel

FORESHADOWING

Gandalf's prediction that Gollum still has a part to play in the fate of the Ring; Elrond's prediction that the quest will only be completed successfully by someone weak and largely disregarded; Aragorn's warning that Gandalf, in particular, should not enter Moria; the visions Frodo sees in Galadriel's mirror

KEY FACTS

STUDY QUESTIONS & ESSAY TOPICS

STUDY QUESTIONS

1. *In what ways is* THE LORD OF THE RINGS *a typical quest narrative? In what ways is it not?*

The Lord of the Rings draws heavily from the literary tradition of the quest narrative, but it also inverts and reimagines significant aspects of the archetypal quest. Perhaps the most prominent element of the traditional quest in Tolkien's novel is the journey, the road the Fellowship takes through many lands as it makes its way to Mordor, the ultimate destination in the quest. Many of the great literary quest narratives that precede *The Lord of the Rings*—from *Beowulf* to the *Odyssey* to *Don Quixote*—are built around exactly this concept of the hero who embarks on an epic journey in search of a goal. The journey typically is a trying one, with many tests for the hero as he or she passes through unknown lands and previously unimaginable dangers. *The Lord of the Rings* follows this conceit from the start, as Frodo and his companions encounter dangers from the moment they leave the familiar confines of the Shire.

The hero at the center of Tolkien's quest, however, is quite atypical—a far cry from Odysseus or Beowulf. Whereas archetypal epic heroes draw upon incredible strength and bravery in overcoming the hardships of their quests, Frodo is an ordinary fellow. There is no particular glory or great power associated with him; indeed, from the beginning, he is characterized as "weak." He is shouldered with an epic task, but he is reluctant to accept it, wondering why the responsibility has fallen upon him. Furthermore, Frodo relies on strength of character rather than strength of arms to endure the hardships he faces. He does not feel the thrill of adventure and does not yearn for glory and recognition. Rather, he views the quest as merely a burden, and a seemingly impossible one at that. He maintains a bearing of great humility throughout the novel, and we sense that it is this very humility, along with his strength of character, that may enable him to succeed in the end.

2.   *The novel is full of songs, most of which are transcribed in full. Discuss the significance of these songs and the way in which they are presented.*

The frequent appearance of songs in *The Lord of the Rings*—and the length of these included verses—is one of the most distinctive and noteworthy aspects of the novel. The presence of these songs works toward a number of different ends. Perhaps most important, the songs add the weight of mythological history and tradition to the events that Tolkien describes. The songs link the present action of the novel—Frodo's quest—to noble, epic events of a distant past. We sense that the events that are unfolding before our eyes are destined to become part of this mythic history themselves—that, ages after the events of the novel take place, the quest of the Fellowship will be similarly immortalized in song. These included songs add such epic weight to the events of the novel because they link the novel to the oral tradition of myth and storytelling in human history. In the time before written literature was ubiquitous throughout much of the world, myths and tales were, by necessity, memorized and passed along orally. Tolkien's use of song links *The Lord of the Rings* to this ancient oral tradition. Furthermore, the songs Tolkien includes also highlight the importance of language in the world of the novel. Tolkien, a trained philologist, built much of the world of Middle-earth around the various linguistic systems he created to give it character and color. The songs the characters sing foreground these various languages, adding to the depth and realism of the universe Tolkien has imagined.

3.   *Discuss Tolkien's depictions of the natural world in the novel. How do the various societies of Middle-earth interact with the nature that surrounds them? Is nature a benevolent or malevolent force?*

As the Fellowship travels throughout a number of different realms during the journey toward Mordor, Tolkien includes a wealth of descriptive passages about the changes in the surrounding landscape and its natural features. Despite the remarkable diversity of these landscapes, one common element is maintained throughout: the distinction between wild, untamed nature and domesticated natural landscapes in various forms. The Shire, the first setting to which we are introduced in the novel, is seemingly a model of harmonious interaction between society and nature. The landscape is domesticated, but gently and beautifully so; the Hobbits appear to have a clear and profound respect for nature. As we see later, Tom Bombadil and the Elves share this respect for nature: the grounds of Tom's house, along with the Elven realms of Rivendell and Lothlórien, are beautiful and peaceful respites from the rigors of the quest. However, Tolkien implies that not all such domestication and harnessing of nature is beneficial. The Dwarves, for instance, appear to overstep their bounds in mining for the precious metal *mithril* in the Mines of Moria. They ultimately pay a price for this irresponsible use of nature, as they awaken the terrifying Balrog that sleeps deep in the earth. All of these examples of domestication, whether responsible or irresponsible, sharply contrast with realms in which nature is untamed and feral. Allowed to run wild, nature is unpredictable and sometimes very dangerous, as we see in the encounters with Old Man Willow and the pass of Caradhras. Nature never appears to be a wholly neutral force: Middle-earth is a mystical world in which each natural element is aligned with either good or evil. This moral alignment, however, is haphazard and unpredictable: the reasons why one tree is good while another is evil are thoroughly unclear.

SUGGESTED ESSAY TOPICS

1. *How would Tolkien define good? How would he define evil? Use examples from the text to support your answer.*

2. *Explain the distinction Tolkien makes between knowledge and wisdom.*

3. *Tolkien was a devout Catholic. What elements of his novel might be traced to a Catholic worldview?*

4. *Discuss the significance of the fact that Frodo, the Ring-bearer, and his closest companions are Hobbits rather than Elves, Men, or some other, more powerful race.*

5. *What does Sauron's Ruling Ring signify?*

QUESTIONS & ESSAYS

Review & Resources

Quiz

1. How are Bilbo and Frodo Baggins related?

    A. Bilbo is Frodo's father
    B. Bilbo is Frodo's grandfather
    C. Bilbo is Frodo's cousin
    D. Bilbo is Frodo's uncle

2. Which birthday does Bilbo celebrate at the beginning of *The Fellowship of the Ring*?

    A. His 100th
    B. His 101st
    C. His 110th
    D. His 111th

3. What effect does Bilbo's ring have on its wearer?

    A. It makes him invisible
    B. It enables him to see in the dark
    C. It gives him great strength
    D. It has seemingly no effect

4. How did Bilbo come into possession of his ring?

    A. He inherited it
    B. He won it in a battle
    C. He found it in a cave
    D. He found it at the bottom of a river

5. To which of the following is the landscape of the Shire most similar?

    A. The Scottish highlands
    B. The French Riviera
    C. The Swiss Alps
    D. The English countryside

6. Which of the following hobbits does *not* set out on the quest with Frodo?

    A.   Merry
    B.   Fatty
    C.   Sam
    D.   Pippin

7. How many Black Riders are there?

    A.   Seven
    B.   Nine
    C.   Eleven
    D.   Thirteen

8. What type of tree ensnares Merry in the Old Forest?

    A.   A larch
    B.   An oak
    C.   A willow
    D.   An elm

9. What are Tom Bombadil's origins?

    A.   He is from the unknown West across the Great Sea
    B.   He is the brother of Old Man Willow
    C.   He is a being from deep inside the earth
    D.   His origins are unknown

10. What is the name of the inn at Bree?

    A.   The Red Lion
    B.   The Golden Goblet
    C.   The Prancing Pony
    D.   The Hungry Traveler

11. Which important character do the hobbits meet at the inn?

    A.   Bilbo
    B.   Elrond
    C.   Aragorn
    D.   Gandalf

REVIEW & RESOURCES

12. What is the name of the fiery mountain where the One Ring was forged?

    A. Caradhras
    B. Orthanc
    C. Orodruin
    D. Dúnedain

13. Of what races are Legolas and Gimli, respectively?

    A. Man and Dwarf
    B. Elf and Dwarf
    C. Elf and Man
    D. Dwarf and Elf

14. What is Legolas's weapon of choice?

    A. A bow and arrows
    B. An axe
    C. A sword
    D. A spear

15. Moria was once an ancient realm of which race?

    A. Trolls
    B. Orcs
    C. Elves
    D. Dwarves

16. Which terrible creature does Gandalf battle during the journey through Moria?

    A. The Barrow-wight
    B. The Balrog
    C. The Uruk-hai
    D. The Nazgûl

17. What are Gandalf's final words before he falls into the chasm?

    A. "Fly, you fools!"
    B. "All that is gold does not glitter!"
    C. "Behold Isildur's Bane!"
    D. "Fare Well!"

REVIEW & RESOURCES

18. Over which realm does Galadriel rule?

    A. Gondor
    B. Lothlórien
    C. Rivendell
    D. Rohan

19. Which of the following does Frodo *not* see in Galadriel's mirror?

    A. An old figure dressed in white
    B. A glowing sword
    C. A dark eye rimmed in fire
    D. A white fortress

20. Why does Galadriel reufse the Ring when Frodo offers it?

    A. It does not fit on her finger
    B. She dislikes its appearance
    C. The metal from which it is made is fatal to Elves
    D. She knows it would corrupt her

21. To which city does Boromir suggest the Fellowship go?

    A. Minas Anor
    B. Minas Ithil
    C. Minas Morgul
    D. Minas Tirith

22. What are *lembas*?

    A. A type of Elvish food
    B. A type of flower that grows in Lothlórien
    C. Elvish coins
    D. Elvish arrows with magical properties

23. Which creature does Aragorn assert has been following the Fellowship throughout the journey?

    A. Gollum
    B. Gwaihir
    C. A Balrog
    D. A cave-troll

REVIEW & RESOURCES

24. Which of the following best characterizes Boromir's attitude toward the Ring?

    A. He cannot see the importance of it
    B. He thinks its power is merely a myth
    C. He begins to be corrupted by it
    D. He cannot stand the sight of it

25. With which companion does Frodo set out at the end of *The Fellowship of the Ring*?

    A. Aragorn
    B. Merry
    C. Pippin
    D. Sam

ANSWER KEY:
1: C; 2: D; 3: A; 4: C; 5: D; 6: B; 7: B; 8: C; 9: D; 10: C; 11: D; 12: C; 13: B; 14: A; 15: D; 16: B; 17: A; 18: B; 19: B; 20: C; 21: D; 22: A; 23: A; 24: C; 25: D

THE TWO
TOWERS

PLOT OVERVIEW

THE TWO TOWERS opens with the disintegration of the Fellowship, as Merry and Pippin are taken captive by Orcs after the death of Boromir in battle. The Orcs, having heard a prophecy that a Hobbit will bear a Ring that gives universal power to its owner, wrongly think that Merry and Pippin are the Ring-bearers.

Several other members of the Fellowship, including Gimli, Legolas, and Aragorn, resolve to pursue Merry and Pippin. They follow the hobbits' tracks through fields and forests, always on the lookout for Orcs. The group encounters the Riders of Rohan, led by Éomer.

Meanwhile, Merry and Pippin are being conveyed back to Orc headquarters when Orcs from another tribe, the Uruk-hai, kidnap them in pursuit of the Ring they believe the hobbits to be carrying. Pippin and Merry escape the Orcs and travel through the forest near the Entwash River, where an Ent (a giant treelike creature) named Fangorn befriends them. Fangorn offers the hobbits nourishment and conveys them to an Ent assembly. There, the Ents resolve to go to war against the Orcs of Isengard (creatures controlled by the corrupted wizard Saruman), who have been cruel to them.

Meanwhile, Saruman haunts Aragorn and his group as they travel the forest. Gandalf then appears to them, reborn after his earlier death in *The Fellowship of the Ring* as Gandalf the White, also known as the White Rider. Gandalf guides Aragorn's group to Edoras, the Golden Hall of King Théoden. There, Gandalf exposes Théoden's counselor, Wormtongue, as a spy for the evil Saruman. Gandalf also facilitates a reunion between Théoden and Éomer.

The group then proceeds to confront Saruman at Isengard, where they are surprised to find Merry and Pippin at the gates of Saruman's headquarters. The hobbits tell Gandalf that the Ents wish to meet with him, to offer their aid in the struggle against Saruman. The group finds Wormtongue in Saruman's tower, Orthanc. Wormtongue tries to kill Gandalf by throwing an object down on him from a window. That object is a *palantír,* a magic seeing-stone that transmits images. Pippin looks into the *palantír,* which allows the Dark Lord Sauron to discover where Pippin is and pursue him.

The second half of *The Two Towers* rejoins Frodo and Sam just after they separate from the rest of the Fellowship and begin making their way to Mordor to destroy the Ring. As they travel, they meet the creature Gollum, whom they tame and force to be their guide to Mordor. Sam and Frodo are wary of Gollum—they know he owned the Ring before and wishes to regain it—but they desperately need someone to direct them to their destination.

Frodo, Sam, and Gollum journey through a smelly marshland in which they can see the faces of slain warriors haunting the waters. They travel by night, as Gollum cannot stand the sun, so they are cold and hungry most of the time. They finally reach the Black Gate of the realm of Mordor and see Sauron's Dark Tower rising overhead. The Gate is well guarded, and the hobbits wonder how they will be able to get inside. Gollum directs them to a different, hidden path into Mordor, where the guards will likely be sparser. On the way, the hobbits are frightened by dark shapes flying overhead—the Nazgûl, the Black Riders of Sauron who are searching for the Ring.

Along the way, Frodo meets a band of Men led by Faramir, the younger brother of Boromir. The men are suspicious of the hobbits at first, believing they are responsible for Boromir's death. Frodo avoids telling Faramir that his brother betrayed the Fellowship by attempting to seize the Ring for himself, but Sam blurts it out. Faramir is shocked, but grateful to learn the truth, so he offers support to the hobbits' journey. Faramir's men nearly kill Gollum, who is caught as an intruder, but Frodo intercedes to save the creature.

Gollum leads Frodo and Sam up the mountain called Cirith Ungol and into tunnels inhabited by Shelob, a giant, deadly female spider. Shelob paralyzes Frodo with her sting, but Sam wounds the spider. Frodo and Sam are separated, however, as Orc guards find Frodo and proceed to take him off to their headquarters, where they plan to search him for the Ring. Sam believes Frodo to be dead, so he accepts the responsibility of carrying the Ring by himself.

Surrounded by Orcs, the terrified Sam dons the Ring and finds that it enables him to understand the Orc language. Sam follows the guards who carry off the paralyzed Frodo. Upon hearing them mention that Shelob only devours living creatures, Sam is shocked to realize that his friend is alive. He chastises himself for taking the Ring for himself, unaware that he has actually saved the Ring and kept it from Sauron by taking it from Frodo. Sam realizes that Frodo is alive at the very moment when the guards enter Mordor, slamming the gates in Sam's face. As *The Two Towers* ends, Sam is anguished by the thought that he and Frodo are separated.

CHARACTER LIST

THE FELLOWSHIP

Frodo Baggins The Ring-bearer and main protagonist of *The Lord of the Rings*. Frodo, a lowly Hobbit, has accepted the tremendously dangerous task of returning the Ring to the fires of Mordor in which it was created—the only place where it can be destroyed. In the later stages of the novel, the Ring becomes a difficult burden for Frodo, who relies increasingly on his friend, Sam, for support.

Samwise (Sam) Gamgee The Hobbit who serves Frodo, traveling with his master on his quest to return the Ring to Mordor. Sam is more practical and sensible than Frodo, but is also more emotional and less able to control himself—as when he blurts out to Faramir that Faramir's brother, Boromir, was a traitor.

Gandalf the White A Wizard of supreme good and a staunch enemy of the corrupted Saruman and the evil Sauron. Gandalf the Grey, seemingly killed in *The Fellowship of the Ring* when he falls into a chasm, returns from beyond the grave as Gandalf the White, or the White Rider. The enormously powerful wizard aids the Hobbits in their quest to destroy the Ring.

Legolas The only Elf in the Fellowship, possessed of superhuman eyesight that serves him well in warning his traveling party of approaching Orcs.

Gimli A fierce Dwarf hero, expert in wielding his axe against Orcs, fond of caves and rocks, and unhappy in forests. Gimli follows Aragorn and Legolas in pursuit of the hobbits.

Aragorn   A human warrior, the heir of Isildur. Aragorn is in league with Gimli and Legolas to aid the Hobbits in their mission to destroy the Ring. Aragorn is the last to see Boromir alive.

Boromir   The Lord of Gondor and the elder brother of Faramir. Boromir enters the Fellowship to help convey the Ring to Mordor, but he becomes corrupted by the Ring's power and ultimately attempts to seize the Ring for himself. Boromir repents, however, just before his death in battle against the Orcs.

Peregrin (Pippin) Took   A Hobbit who, along with his friend Merry, is cut off from the rest of the Fellowship during a battle with Orcs. Pippin and Merry spend much of *The Two Towers* trying to rejoin Gandalf's group.

Meriadoc (Merry) Brandybuck   Pippin's companion, also separated from the Fellowship at the beginning of *The Two Towers*. Merry and Pippin make their way to join their companions, pursued by Orcs who mistakenly believe them to be in possession of the Ring.

ENEMIES AND MALEVOLENT BEINGS

Sauron   The Dark Lord of Mordor, the primary antagonist in *The Lord of the Rings*. Sauron, who created the One Ring, is driven only by his desire to retrieve the Ring. He never appears during the novel; we see only his Great Eye and his Dark Tower in Mordor. Sauron's rule has made the land of Mordor barren and inhospitable.

The Nazgûl   Nine messengers of Sauron who soar above Middle-earth on fearsome winged steeds, constantly searching for the Ring. The Nazgûl—also known as the Ringwraiths, the Black Riders, or the Nine—rely on intimidation and terror, striking fear into the hearts of those who see them flying above.

Saruman the White The most powerful Wizard in Gandalf's order. Saruman, once a force of good and a cohort of Gandalf, becomes corrupted by power and takes over the realm of Isengard. There, Saruman plots to seize the Ring and breeds a new race of evil Orcs that do not fear sunlight.

Gríma Wormtongue The wicked and deceitful advisor of King Théoden. Wormtongue, who is secretly in the employ of Saruman, is exposed by Gandalf, and flees to Saruman's headquarters.

Gollum (Sméagol) A strange, froglike creature. Gollum once carried the Ring himself, but lost it, and now attempts to get it back. Though at times pathetic and even somewhat sympathetic, Gollum is deceitful and treacherous to the core, feigning humility to his masters Sam and Frodo after they tame him, only to then lead the hobbits to danger in Shelob's lair.

Shelob An unimaginably ancient, enormous, and evil female spider that lives in the tunnels near Mordor, ever hungry for prey. Shelob, who is even older than Sauron, serves as a kind of guard for one of the entrances to Mordor. Gollum deceitfully leads Frodo and Sam into Shelob's lair, where the spider paralyzes Frodo and nearly kills both hobbits before Sam drives her away.

Orcs Squat, swarthy, wretched creatures that serve the purposes of Sauron. Orcs, unable to withstand daylight, attack at night, by force of numbers.

The Uruk-hai A fearsome breed of Orcs specially created by Saruman to be able to withstand daylight.

Uglúk An Orc warrior and captor of Merry and Pippin in the early chapters of *The Two Towers*. Uglúk is killed in battle at the hands of Éomer.

Gorbag and Shagrat Two Orc warriors who carry Frodo's paralyzed body away into Mordor.

MEN

Éomer   One of the Riders of Rohan, the horsemen to whom the Lord of Gondor has given land in exchange for guarding his territories. Éomer encounters Aragorn's traveling party early in *The Two Towers*, giving Aragorn information implying that Merry and Pippin are still alive.

Théoden   The King of Rohan and keeper of the Golden Hall. Théoden is a good man, but his wily and two-faced counselor, Wormtongue, has misled him, urging him to support the evil Saruman. Gandalf reveals the truth of Wormtongue's deception to Théoden, who then supports the members of the Fellowship.

Éowyn   The Lady of Rohan. Éowyn in Theoden's niece and Éomer's sister.

Faramir   The Lord of Gondor after the demise of his elder brother, Boromir. Faramir initially distrusts Frodo, whom he suspects of having killed Boromir. When Faramir learns the truth, he aids the hobbits in their mission.

Mablung and Damrod   Two of Faramir's warriors. Damrod threatens to kill Gollum upon finding the creature bathing in a pool in Gondor.

Háma   The doorman at the gates of the Golden Hall, who is initially very suspicious of Gandalf and company.

OTHER ALLIES AND BENEVOLENT BEINGS

Fangorn   One of the Ents, a race of giant, mobile, treelike creatures. The fourteen-foot-tall Fangorn is one of the oldest creatures in Middle-earth. An authority figure to the other Ents, he shows great hospitality to Pippin and Merry, who are given food by him in his Ent-house.

Bregalad   A younger Ent who befriends Merry and Pippin during
the Ent assembly.

Shadowfax The swiftest of all horses, whom Gandalf has
borrowed from Théoden and who later becomes an
outright gift from the king to the wizard.

ANALYSIS OF MAJOR CHARACTERS

FRODO BAGGINS

Like the other Hobbits in the novel, Frodo is not so much a born hero as one who has had heroism thrust upon him. Compared to the other heroes—the stout-hearted Gimli, the far-seeing Legolas, or the noble Théoden, for instance—Frodo appears almost absurdly underqualified for the pivotal role he plays in *The Lord of the Rings*. We never see him act with overt valor or fearless courage. Frodo's bravery, on the rare occasions when we witness it, seems almost involuntary: his seemingly bold action of reaching for the Ring when he fears the Enemy has seen him in Mordor, for instance, is not really courageous, as his hand is described as reaching for the Ring on its own. The last image we see of Frodo in *The Two Towers*—paralyzed and comatose—is pitiable, a far cry from heroic. Furthermore, Frodo possesses a readiness to trust others, which, though perhaps a noble instinct, gets him into trouble in his dealings with Gollum. Frodo goes out of his way to prove to Gollum that the hobbits are trustworthy masters, only to be betrayed later when Gollum leads Frodo and Sam into the lair of Shelob. Frodo is a bit too unassuming and unintimidating to be powerful, but he is all the more endearing to us for that reason.

Despite his lack of heroic stature—or perhaps because of it—Frodo is well liked by those who know him intimately. His closest friend is his servant Sam, whom Frodo refuses to treat as a servant, always addressing him as an equal. When Sam gazes on Frodo sleeping, Sam's feelings of fondness push him to tell himself how much he cares for Frodo—a private moment of genuine sentiment. Sam is quite simply devoted to his master. Even the wretched and untrustworthy Gollum displays what appears to be genuine affection for Frodo. Gollum caresses Frodo as he sleeps, not because Gollum is sneaking around his master (as Sam suspects), but simply because he likes Frodo. Frodo is a sympathetic character whose ordinary failings are our own, and whose goodness and steadiness make him undeniably likable.

SAM GAMGEE

In the early parts of *The Lord of the Rings,* Sam comes across as a rather flat character, a sidekick to the more interesting and dynamic Frodo, whom he serves. But from a psychological point of view, Sam is among the most interesting and complex characters in the novel. Like his probable namesake, Pickwick's servant Sam in Charles Dickens's *The Pickwick Papers,* Frodo's Sam is earthy and common-sensical, fond of his beer and his bread, clever though sometimes forgetful—as when he forgets he has a magic Elf rope in his bag. Over the course of *The Two Towers,* Sam changes more than any other character. Initially, he is subservient and not quite capable of independent judgment. His constant references to Frodo as "Mister Frodo"—a formal title that other characters do not use even when addressing kings or Wizards—makes us wonder whether Sam suffers from a sense of inferiority. Frodo never orders Sam around as a master would command a servant, yet Sam continually speaks of himself as serving Frodo.

Eventually, Sam is a servant no more. By the end of *The Two Towers,* when his master lies speechless and paralyzed, Sam is forced to affirm his own strength and assume the role of Ring-bearer himself. In being forced to make his own decisions, he becomes his own master, thereby becoming a symbol of the potential for leadership and heroism that may lie dormant in the most unsuspecting people, perhaps even ourselves.

GANDALF THE WHITE

Gandalf is the supreme force of good in the novel, a worthy opponent of the evil Saruman and Sauron. Gandalf's goodness and power are such as to make him seem a near-religious figure at times; indeed, there is Christian symbolism attached to the wizard, even though the mythology of *The Lord of the Rings* is primarily pagan. Wearing a white cloak and riding a white steed, Gandalf is associated with the Christian color of spiritual purity. In a distinctly Christlike resurrection, the wizard has died and returned from the grave, having fallen to his death in the preceding volume of the novel. Gandalf has passed through the greatest trial of existence—that of death—and has survived with his powers enormously enhanced. Furthermore, the wizard's timely arrival with military backup during the siege of Hornburg makes him seem almost a miracle worker.

However Christlike Gandalf may seem, though, he is no transcendent figure floating over the action. He maintains firm personal connections with all the characters, regardless of race or rank; he addresses even the lowliest members of the Fellowship by their full names and with great respect. Tolkien reminds us that even the immensely powerful Gandalf occasionally needs human help, as when the wizard asks Théoden to give him the horse Shadowfax. This human connection brings Gandalf down to earth, enabling us to identify with him more than we might have expected.

Pippin Took

Pippin, together with his companion Merry, represents the entire Hobbit race in the first half of *The Two Towers,* as Frodo and Sam do not appear in this portion of the story at all. Pippin is typically Hobbitlike in his kindness, humility, and ordinary mixture of flaws and fears. He is more clever and quick-thinking than he is bold or courageous—as when he engineers his escape from the Orcs not by attacking them, but by profiting from a knife that falls near his hand bindings. Still, even if Pippin is not a typical adventure hero, he shows a firmness of purpose and a quick-wittedness that make him a valuable member of the Fellowship.

The honorable Pippin is a highly likable character. He is thoughtful and generous, as when he loans his beloved tobacco pipe to Gimli, who yearns for a good smoke. Pippin likes to relax, as we see when Gandalf comes upon him and Merry smoking and chatting at Saruman's headquarters. Pippin values companionship highly; one of his few moments of relief during his Orc captivity is when he happens to be thrown on the ground near Merry, with whom he is able to enjoy a brief conversation before being silenced. Pippin and his friend Merry are a refreshing presence in *The Two Towers,* largely because they are *not* superhuman or larger than life, as so many of the others are. Instead, these two hobbits are simple creatures with simple pleasures and failings. Their ordinary natures help us to identify with their mission, as we can picture ourselves in their places.

Gollum

While a wide variety of creepy nonhuman creatures populate the world of *The Lord of the Rings*—ranging from the dark Nazgûl to the revolting Shelob—Gollum stands out from the rest as psychologically intriguing. Capable of speech, he is quite forthcoming in sharing his inner thoughts with anyone who cares to hear them, even talking out loud when no one is there to hear. As such, Gollum is something more than a mere monster. By the same token, he is not quite a villain either, as he lacks the grand stature of Sauron or Saruman, or even of Wormtongue. We cannot imagine any of these other wicked figures splashing around in the water in search of fish or whining about how bread burns his throat. Moreover, though Gollum acts like a servant, it is hard for us to believe that he kowtows to Frodo only in order to win the hobbit's trust. Rather, this wretched subservience seems to be Gollum's natural state—at least, his natural state after years of the deleterious effects of possessing the Ring. On the whole, Gollum's morality is almost completely impossible to guess for most of the novel. While other characters are clearly evil or clearly good, Gollum acts as if he is on the side of good, but he may perhaps be treacherous. Until the end of *The Two Towers,* we are never quite sure.

Gollum's fondness for Frodo is one of the mysteries of the creature's personality. Of course, Gollum willingly leads Frodo to a probable death at the end, and he is no true friend to the hobbit. But still there is a striking and surprising display of real affection for the one whom Gollum calls master, even beneath the false flattery he issues to Frodo in order to gain trust. When Sam catches Gollum fondly caressing the sleeping Frodo, there is no other explanation for what the creature is doing than showing that he loves his master. Sam may suspiciously describe Gollum's activity as "sneaking" around Frodo, but we feel that, strangely enough, Frodo's betrayer loves and respects him in his own odd way. We may be inclined to think that at these moments, Gollum's original nature—his lost identity as Sméagol—shows through, perhaps in response to seeing his earlier self in Frodo.

Themes, Motifs & Symbols

Themes

Themes are the fundamental and often universal ideas explored in a literary work.

The Decay of Civilization

The world that the members of the Fellowship glimpse on their wanderings through Rohan, Isengard, Entwash, and Mordor is not a happy one. Everywhere the Fellowship goes, it finds evidence of how the civilized world has fallen from a peaceful and noble earlier state into a present degradation threatened by warlords and general bleakness. Isengard and Gondor are both described as formerly beautiful realms, once full of orchards and blossoming gardens, that have deteriorated into desolate and barren places that smell terrible and are littered with poison pits. It is not merely the landscape, however, that has disintegrated. Moral and noble ideals have fallen away as well. Earlier norms of hospitality toward strangers have been abandoned because of the new dangers of the modern age, as Éomer notes when he refers to the "dark times" as an explanation for why he cannot treat the hobbits with customary courtesy. Stopping the onslaught of Sauron is, therefore, much more than merely thwarting an enemy: it is also saving an entire civilization from a slow slide into chaos.

The Value of Fellowship

Fellowship is mentioned often in *The Lord of the Rings,* not merely because the group of freedom fighters struggling to destroy the Ring calls itself the Fellowship of the Ring. The Fellowship, in a sense, is the collective protagonist of Tolkien's novel, a group representing all the free races and realms of Middle-earth in the struggle against the evil of Mordor. Fellowship is an important ideal for these characters, standing for a sense of camaraderie that depends on mutual support, cooperation, and solidarity in which no single member is considered more essential than any other. Even Gandalf, though the unofficial leader of the Fellowship, does not order around or act superior to the others. He is clearly far more powerful than any of the others, but still he needs them, and therefore treats them all with respect—referring even to low-rankers like Merry and Pippin by their full honorific names. There is also a mutual kindness that unites the members of the Fellowship, as we see when Pippin gives Gimli his precious pipe simply out of a desire to make the dwarf happy. It is this sensitivity toward others that the villains of the novel—all of them egomaniacs—noticeably lack.

Duty

When Aragorn and his group finally reach Isengard and penetrate Saruman's stronghold of Orthanc, they are surprised to find Merry and Pippin casually lying by the gates, smoking and chatting. From this memorable scene, we get an impression of the hobbits as easy-going and fun-loving creatures who do not thrive on the hardship and struggle that the mission of Ring-bearing entails. They would clearly prefer to be sitting on a hillside, quietly passing the time.

But this does not make the hobbits appear inferior to the task assigned them, nor does it diminish our respect for them in the novel. On the contrary, it heightens our respect, as it reminds us how deeply they have resisted their natural tendencies in taking on the weighty mission entrusted to them. Sometimes Frodo needs to pause in the journey—as on the endless steps of Cirith Ungol—but only because he is exhausted, never because he simply wishes to dawdle. His urgent desire to reach his goal becomes stronger as he nears the destination. When Gollum tells Frodo there is no way into Mordor, Frodo insists bluntly that he must enter the kingdom, and his intensity is impressive. However easygoing the hobbits may be naturally, the quest to return the Ring brings out a self-disciplined and unwavering determination in them, and we never once see them question the necessity of fulfilling their duty.

Motifs

Motifs are recurring structures, contrasts, or literary devices that can help to develop and inform the text's major themes.

Songs and Singing

Many songs are sung in *The Two Towers*, and Tolkien nearly always provides us with the complete lyrics, set off in italics from the rest of the text. Songs are clearly very important in Tolkien's novel. It is not

MOTIFS

enough for us simply to be told that a character sings about something; the author must tell us exactly what words are being sung. As a scholar of early cultures, Tolkien was aware that, before the advent of published books and the spread of literacy, culture and religion were largely kept alive through the singing of songs—not merely for entertainment, but to preserve the very memory of a culture. We find songs fulfilling such a function in *The Two Towers,* as when Fangorn sings about his childhood at the dawn of the world, preserving memories far older than any other living creature. Songs also have an emotional impact that stirs characters to action, as when Aragorn sings about Gondor in Book III, Chapter 2, concluding with the appeal to the others, "Let us go!" For Tolkien, songs represent everything noble and good about ancient cultural traditions.

THE NATURAL WORLD

In a sense, it is unavoidable that a fantasy novel set in ancient times, involving much wandering over meadows and mountains, focuses significant attention on the natural environment. Indeed, *The Two Towers* is full of forests, fields, pools, mountains, gorges, and caves—a loving attention to natural scenery that made Tolkien a favorite writer of the back-to-nature activists of the 1960s. Yet nature in *The Lord of the Rings* is more meaningful than merely a scenic backdrop to the plot. The state of nature closely mirrors the state of the world, reflecting the time of crisis leading to the War of the Ring.

In this regard, Tolkien borrows ideas from Romantic poetry, most notably the idea that the external world often reflects the minds of men. Where conditions are bad and conflict imminent, nature itself suffers visible scars. In Saruman's corrupt realm of Isengard, for instance, the landscape itself has become corrupted: the realm is barren and desolate where it once blossomed with greenery. Similarly, the land of Mordor has become sterile with the presence of Sauron's evil. Nature is a moral barometer measuring good and evil throughout Middle-earth, and is therefore a moral force itself, as we feel when we witness the trees of Entwash marching off to fight the evil Saruman. Even the very trees in the forest are part of the vast moral struggle taking place in Middle-earth.

SUSPICION

One of the bleaker aspects of *The Lord of the Rings* is the omnipresent aura of suspicion. Such suspicion surfaces frequently enough to give many characters (and us as readers) a gnawing sense of distrust toward others, even those we think we know well. *The Two Towers* opens with the death of Boromir, an ally-turned-traitor whose example reminds the members of the Fellowship that even vows of solidarity cannot guarantee lasting commitment to their cause; even a trusted colleague is open to suspicion. This ominous atmosphere of suspicion haunts *The Two Towers*. It is reaffirmed when strangers like Éomer and Théoden bluntly inform the travelers that, in dark times like these, no one is above suspicion, and all guests must be considered potential enemies. The final betrayal by Gollum carries this lesson home with tragic force.

However, it is clear that the current pall of suspicion cast over Middle-earth is due to the malevolent activities of Sauron. Therefore, there is hope that if the Dark Lord is defeated, trust will return to the world. This possibility makes it crucial that the members of the Fellowship continue to trust one another, despite the treachery of Boromir. When we see Gandalf return with Éomer to reinforce the Fellowship's forces at the storming of the Hornburg, we are pleased not just because the side of good triumphs, but also because we confirm that Gandalf is trustworthy—a far cry from the corrupted Saruman. We are left with the hope that a final victory of the Fellowship will reaffirm that trust is still a reliable presence in the world and will make suspicion no longer necessary.

SYMBOLS

Symbols are objects, characters, figures, or colors used to represent abstract ideas or concepts.

THE TWO TOWERS

The title *The Two Towers* refers to Barad-dûr and Orthanc, Sauron's stronghold in Mordor and Saruman's citadel in Isengard, respectively. These two towers can be seen as a physical embodiment of the two visions of evil that Tolkien explores throughout *The Lord of the Rings*. In the novel, we see a number of examples of evil as an external, elemental force that exists independent of and outside the human mind; however, we also see instances of corruption and perversion, in which evil is an internal force that humans create.

Sauron exemplifies the former notion, the vision of evil as an essential force that simply exists as part of the universe. The Dark Lord's evil physically spreads out over the land of Mordor and, later, over the rest of Middle-earth as well. Tolkien never implies that Sauron was once a good being who merely became perverted to the side of evil—the Dark Lord is evil by his very nature. The wizard Saruman, on the other hand, represents the latter vision of evil. He was once a figure of good, the leader of Gandalf's order. Saruman was not born evil; rather, he has become corrupt out of arrogance and ambition.

The two towers in which these villains reside mirror the respective natures of their owners' evils. Barad-dûr has always been evil; Sauron built it himself and has used it for no other purpose than as a refuge from which to use his Great Eye to watch and pervert Middle-earth. Orthanc, on the other hand, existed long before Saruman. We learn that Orthanc was constructed by the ancient lords of Gondor; as the narrator states, with a note of elegy, "long had it been beautiful." It was only when Saruman "slowly shaped it to his shifting purposes" that Orthanc became a place of corruption, mirroring its new master. Ironically, though Saruman believes he has improved the tower by using it as the citadel of his ambition, the narrator tells us that Orthanc "was naught, only a little copy, a child's model or a slave's flattery . . . of Barad-dûr." Tolkien implies that human evil, though at times powerful, arises merely from illusion and self-deception, and is much more easily defeated than inherent or elemental evil. Indeed, as we see, Saruman's defeat is an easy one, requiring only a rebuke by Gandalf and a misstep by Wormtongue. The defeat of Sauron, on the other hand, can only be accomplished by destroying the Ring—a monumental task.

THE PALANTÍR

The *palantíri* are seven ancient seeing-stones, crystal globes that show visions and communicate information to Sauron. Gandalf, upon discovering that Saruman owns a *palantír,* understands for the first time how communication occurs between the various evil parties in Middle-earth. In this sense, the *palantír* symbolizes a network of wickedness that mirrors the Fellowship, which is in effect a network of good. The *palantír* is a tangible symbol of the conspiracy of malevolence that Gandalf and the Fellowship are fighting. On a deeper level, the *palantír* also symbolizes the distinction Tolkien draws between knowledge and wisdom—the *palantír* offers knowledge and a glimpse of the future to those who look into it, but this knowledge comes at the price of direct communication with Sauron, the embodiment of evil in Middle-earth.

When Gandalf utterly breaks Saruman's power, Wormtongue, the corrupt wizard's servant, flies into a fit of madness and rage, throwing the *palantír* out of the window of Orthanc. Wormtongue does not know how valuable the magic globe is to Saruman, who moans at the loss. In this regard, the *palantír* symbolizes the dangers of rashness and rage, the loss of one's self-control to base emotions. Similarly, when Pippin takes the *palantír* from under Gandalf's cloak in order to peer into it, the hobbit too succumbs to the pull of curiosity, thereby committing a misdeed and earning a stern reprimand from Gandalf. In this sense, the *palantír* is not only a physical symbol of evil in *The Lord of the Rings,* but also a symbol of the moral failings and the potential for corruption in all of the characters.

PIPPIN'S PIPE
Soon after his reunion with Aragorn, Legolas, and Pippin following the Orc battle, Gimli expresses a yearning for a good smoke. Pippin remembers that he has a spare pipe that he has been carrying with him throughout his travels. It is clearly of great personal value to the hobbit: he calls it a treasure, "as precious as Rings to me." Yet Pippin offers this pipe to Gimli, who says that he is deep in the hobbit's debt for such a gift. This little pipe is much more than just a trinket given by one friend to another; it is, rather, a symbol of the mutual caring that binds the Fellowship together. Gimli's desire for a pipe is no matter of life and death, which makes Pippin's eagerness to please the dwarf all the more endearing. Pippin simply wants his friends to be as happy and comfortable as possible, especially in light of the burden of the quest. In this regard, Pippin's pipe symbolizes the very best aspect of the Fellowship, the bond that gives its members strength and may help them prevail in the end.

THE DEAD MARSHES
As Frodo and Sam make their way to Mordor, Gollum leads them through an unpleasant region known as the Dead Marshes. As they pass through the swampland, Sam is deeply disturbed to see flickering lights in the corner of his eye, images of faces that come and go fleetingly. Frodo says that he sees the lights and faces as well. Gollum informs the hobbits that the lights are the "candles of corpses"; he tells them not to look, so as not to be seduced into following the lights. The corpses to which Gollum refers are the bodies of slain warriors—Orc, Man, and Elf—who died in a battle on the site long before.

In this sense, the Dead Marshes are a physical reminder of the way in which the present is bound to the past in the world of *The Lord of the Rings*. The past constantly haunts the present in the novel, whether in the form of powerful traditions, ancient songs, prophecies, or memories of those who died long ago. Moreover, the union of former enemies in death—Orcs and Men fight each other in life, but join each other in death—suggests the deep unity of creation that often goes forgotten or ignored in the world of the living. The differences and divisions that lead to war are flimsy and meaningless compared to the everlasting togetherness of death.

SUMMARY & ANALYSIS

BOOK III, CHAPTER 1

SUMMARY — THE DEPARTURE OF BOROMIR

The narrative picks up just after Frodo and Sam have left the rest of the Fellowship and have headed toward Mordor to destroy the Ring. Aragorn races in pursuit of Frodo, but he finds it difficult to follow the hobbit's tracks. Suddenly, Aragorn hears the voices of Orcs going into battle, followed by the battle horn of Boromir, the other human warrior in the Fellowship. Aragorn fears that Boromir is in danger. Indeed, the Orcs wound Boromir fatally, and when Aragorn reaches him, Boromir is nearly dead. Boromir confesses to having tried, unsuccessfully, to take the Ring from Frodo earlier. Boromir dies, and Aragorn weeps over his friend's body.

Legolas the Elf and Gimli the Dwarf join Aragorn. Legolas regrets that he has been chasing the wrong group of Orcs, leaving Boromir without defense. Aragorn announces that Boromir is dead, having been killed defending the hobbits. Gimli, Legolas, and Aragorn carry Boromir's body on a bier to the river and launch a funeral boat. Legolas and Aragorn sing bits of prophetic songs that concern the death of Boromir and his role in the larger scheme of destiny.

Legolas asks where the hobbits are now, but Aragorn says he does not know. He explains that he sent Boromir to follow Merry and Pippin, but neglected to ask whether Frodo was with them. Aragorn now realizes his error. He speculates that Frodo separated from his colleagues because he did not wish to expose them to the dangers of the quest. Aragorn says that the Dwarves, Elves, and Men must stick together in their mission to find Frodo.

ANALYSIS

The opening chapters of *The Two Towers* mark the first time in *The Lord of the Rings* in which the hobbits are absent from the narrative. The other characters—Aragorn, Boromir, Gimli, and Legolas—constantly talk about the hobbits, however, and try to find them. This absence of the hobbits continues throughout much of *The Two Towers,* as the hobbits are at the center of everything that occurs, yet are kept offstage, leaving us in doubt about what is happening to them. Through Aragorn's eyes, we study the tracks on the forest floor, hoping in vain for a glimpse of the hobbits. Tolkien, in structuring the narrative in this manner, keeps us in suspense about what is happening to Frodo, Sam, Pippin, and Merry; our interest is inevitably aroused by creatures whom everyone is pursuing, but who are kept offstage. Ironically, it is the hobbits' very absence that contributes to their status as the focus of the narrative, the center of the plot as bearers of the Ring.

Moreover, Hobbits in general are intriguing simply because of the fact that, as a race living in a sheltered corner of Middle-earth, they are relatively unfamiliar to many of the other inhabitants of Tolkien's world. Although we as readers have been introduced to Hobbit lore and culture in *The Hobbit* and the Prologue to *The Fellowship of the Ring*, many of the characters in *The Two Towers*—such as Éomer (whom we meet later)—are unclear about what exactly a hobbit is. Gimli must explain to Éomer that Hobbits are neither children nor Dwarves, but Halflings—a hybrid reference that makes us realize that even we, for all the background knowledge Tolkien has provided, do not really understand the true origin and nature of the Hobbit race.

As we have seen thus far in the novel, the Hobbits, unlike many of the other races and creatures of Middle-earth, do not appear to possess any special gifts or powers. Others have such special abilities, which Tolkien often showcases in dramatic moments of the plot. Legolas has the incredibly acute eyesight for which the Elves are famous. Gimli demonstrates the considerable Dwarf skill in wielding an axe. Aragorn displays the honor, courage, and masterful horsemanship that mark the best of the race of Men. Gandalf and his order of Wizards are immensely powerful; the Ents, the tree-like creatures whom we meet later, have both great strength and seemingly limitless endurance and patience. The Hobbits—though they attract the close interest of all these other races, placed as they are at the center of the plot—display no comparable strengths or talents, making them rather unique among the canon of epic heroes.

Tolkien's characterization of the villains in these opening chapters reveals much about the moral universe he has created. The evil of the Orcs is evinced not just by their cruelty, but also, we see, in their inability to fight in close union with each other. In the next chapter, Aragorn notes that some of the slain Orcs he passes on the battlefield appear to have been killed by fellow Orcs from a more northerly tribe. Unlike Gandalf's alliance of Elves, Dwarves, Hobbits, and Men, who overcome long-standing animosities (most notably, that between Elves and Dwarves) to fight under vows of unity and solidarity, the Orcs kill each other in addition to their common enemy. This idea of evil as a tendency toward treachery is perhaps most notable in the character of Boromir. This noble and tragic figure dominates the opening of the novel; though he has fallen prey to the lure of the Ring, desiring it for himself, he appears noble and is mourned because he realizes the scope of his error, humbly repenting to Aragorn. The fact that Boromir is killed in battle so quickly after his attempt to commandeer the Ring suggests that his death may be a fated punishment of sorts for his lapse into selfishness and reckless ambition.

BOOK III, CHAPTER 2

SUMMARY — THE RIDERS OF ROHAN

Looking on the ground, Gimli, Legolas, and Aragorn at first see only their own tracks and those of Orcs; they are unable to tell whether the hobbits have passed by. Aragorn is at a loss, without a clue as to where the hobbits have gone. Suddenly, however, he notices some Hobbit prints near the river, but he is not sure when they were left.

At the foot of a steep slope, the group finds five Orc corpses huddled together. Aragorn notices that the slain creatures are from a different Orc tribe, and guesses that the Orcs have been quarreling among themselves. Gimli hopes that the captive hobbits have not suffered as a result of the Orc quarrel. Legolas, with his incredible eyesight, sees an eagle flying twelve leagues away, and guesses that the Orcs are there. If true, this suggests that the Orcs are moving with the greatest possible speed, proceeding not just at night but also by daylight, against their nature.

Aragorn, Legolas, and Gimli notice that the earth becomes greener as they enter the fields of Rohan. Aragorn spots Hobbit footprints on the ground and guesses them to be Pippin's. He also finds a brooch from an Elf cloak on the ground. As it is unlikely that the brooch was dropped by chance, Aragorn reasons that Pippin left it as a sign for his rescuers to find. They all rejoice in this proof that one of the hobbits, at least, seems to be alive.

Through the cold uplands of Rohan, the group follows the swiftly moving Orcs, whose speed is remarkable. Suddenly Legolas sees horsemen moving in the distance, though he glimpses no Hobbits among them. The riders are not Orcs, but Men. Though Gimli is cautious, Aragorn asserts that the horsemen—presumably the Riders of Rohan—are mighty but just; they would not assault strangers without listening to them first.

The horsemen approach, and the leader introduces himself as Éomer, Third Marshal of Riddermark. Aragorn announces that he is hunting Orcs, and Éomer admits that he mistook Aragorn's group for Orcs themselves. Aragorn explains that he is in the service of no man, but is merely searching for his Hobbit friends, whom the Orcs have taken captive. Éomer relates that a great battle has just taken place between his riders and the Orcs. The Orcs were destroyed, with no sign of any Hobbit bodies among the slain.

It is not clear, however, whether Éomer even knows what a Hobbit is. Gimli explains that Hobbits are neither children nor Dwarves, but Halflings. Éomer, having thought that Halflings were merely characters from old tales, is surprised to learn that they actually exist. Éomer explains that the powerful wizard Saruman has been corrupted and is now a dangerous enemy preparing for war in nearby Isengard. Aragorn relates to Éomer that Gandalf the Grey, who has greatly aided the Fellowship, has been killed.

Éomer states that it is not customary for strangers to be allowed to wander freely in Rohan, but he permits passage to the group, and even gives them all horses to ride. They ride all day, but still find no trace of Pippin or Merry. In the forest of Fangorn, they build a fire with wood the Riders gathered earlier. Legolas tells of the treelike Ents rumored to live in Fangorn. Gimli has a vision of an old man in a large cloak and a wide-brimmed hat, whom he takes to be Saruman. When the group wakes, they find that their horses are gone.

ANALYSIS

As Aragorn, Legolas, and Gimli search for the hobbits, we see how the bonds between members of different races—such as Dwarves, Elves, and Men—can be as strong or stronger than the bonds between members of the same race. This fact is apparent when Aragorn meets another human. We might expect him to feel relief or joy at finally meeting one of his own kind, but we find that his attitude toward Éomer is not one of joyful identification. In fact, it is quite the contrary, as Aragorn is even a bit cold toward Éomer, telling him bluntly that he serves no man, but is only hunting for his Hobbit friends. The message is clear: Aragorn has deeper connections of loyalty and solidarity with Hobbits than with a member of his own race. In terms of historical context, Tolkien wrote large parts of *The Lord of the Rings* during World War II, a conflict in which racism and group identification reached dangerous extremes. His portrayal of heroes who look beyond their own kind, finding friends and allies among different races or peoples, is enlightened.

The meeting between Aragorn's group and Éomer also suggests the confused and chaotic climate in Middle-earth that provides the backdrop for *The Lord of the Rings*. No one is sure who anyone else is, or whether a stranger is a friend or foe. Even appearances cannot be trusted, as Éomer admits that he mistook Aragorn's group—composed of a Dwarf, an Elf, and a Man—for an Orc contingent. Hobbits, too, are confused with Men and with Dwarves. There are few reliable indicators of whom one can trust and whom one must oppose. Even group identification is not enough, as the northern Orcs have apparently had a fatal quarrel with other Orcs, demonstrating that even one's own kind may be an enemy. This climate of wariness and suspicion is evidence of the widespread reach of the evil of Sauron, the Dark Lord attempting to retrieve the Ring.

Gimli's vision of Saruman indicates the power and danger of the corrupted wizard. While Gandalf and other attendees of the Council of Elrond discuss Saruman in *The Fellowship of the Ring*, Saruman himself does not appear as a character in the first volume of the novel. Gimli's bizarre dream, then, is our first direct contact with Saruman—and even this contact is bizarre and hallucinatory. This first encounter is a mysterious one, highlighting the elusiveness of the corrupt wizard. We are unsure, as is Gimli, whether the dwarf has really seen Saruman or whether the wizard has used some magic power to appear in Gimli's mind. The dwarf's vision, along with the warnings of Éomer and the mysterious disappearance of the horses, sets Saruman up as a fascinating, ominous figure whose first real, tangible appearance we begin to anticipate greatly. Furthermore, the supernatural aura of Saruman's visit reminds us, by contrast, of how basically realistic the rest of the story is. Though *The Lord of the Rings* obviously operates in the realm of the fantastical, real traits such as bravery and loyalty are more important—and far more frequently witnessed—than the fireworks of a magic wand.

Furthermore, the fact that Saruman's appearance and dress—as an old man in a cloak, with a staff and a wide-brimmed hat—is strikingly similar to Gandalf's highlights the ambiguous nature of good and evil and the often ill-defined line between them. Indeed, when Gandalf reappears later in *The Two Towers*, the Company is initially frightened of him, believing him to be Saruman. Tolkien stresses the similarity between the good Gandalf and the corrupt Saruman to show that good and evil are very close—indeed sometimes nearly indistinguishable. Saruman is evil not by innate nature, but by choice. He has betrayed the principle of good in the universe, choosing instead a path of selfishness and power-hungry ambition. As Gandalf notes later in *The Two Towers,* Saruman could have remained a force of good, likely more powerful than even Gandalf himself, were it not for his decision to embrace wickedness. This exploration of the nature of evil—more precisely, the question of whether evil is an internal matter of choice or an external influence and innate force—is one of Tolkien's primary objects of focus throughout the whole of *The Lord of the Rings.*

Book III, Chapter 3

SUMMARY & ANALYSIS

Summary — The Uruk-Hai

While Aragorn's group hunts for the hobbits, Pippin and Merry lie captive in the Orc camp, bound hand and foot. Pippin has a dark dream in which he calls out to Frodo but sees only Orcs around him. Pippin recalls the great battle in which Boromir appeared, at first causing great fear among the Orcs, but then unable to summon any other warriors with his horn. Pippin's last memory of the battle is of seeing Boromir trying to pull an arrow out of his own body. Pippin regrets that Gandalf ever asked him to come along, as he feels like little more than a burden.

Pippin hears the Orcs talking among themselves. One orc asks why the hobbits cannot simply be killed. Another answers that orders have been given not to kill, search, or plunder the hobbits; they must be captured alive. Pippin is aware that the two orcs are speaking the Common Tongue, as the different Orc tribes cannot understand one another. Nevertheless, he notes that the various Orcs sometimes lapse back into their native tongue when speaking with their own; in these instances, he cannot follow their speech, which sounds angry and snarling to him.

There is apparently some hostility among the various Orc tribes. Uglúk, an orc from the Uruk-hai clan, is proud to call himself the servant of Saruman the Wise, the White Hand. The other orc insults Saruman, and a fight breaks out in which one orc dies, falling on top of Pippin. Pippin is able to rub his hand bindings against the blade of the fallen orc's knife, thus freeing his hands. Not noticing that Pippin's hands are free, Uglúk orders the hobbits to move quickly in march with the rest of the Orc horde. Suddenly, the hobbits are snatched up by the Isengard Orcs, who double their speed and pull out ahead of the others. The Isengard Orcs attempt to leave behind the other Orcs, who pursue them unsuccessfully.

Finally losing the other Orcs, the Isengard Orcs, stop to give Pippin and Merry Orc-liquor, which allows them to march a long distance. The Orcs halt and throw Pippin to the ground. They begin to search the bodies of the two hobbits, believing Pippin and Merry to be the possessors of the Ring. The hobbits demand to be untied before they will offer anything to Grishnákh, the Isengard orc who is searching them.

Suddenly, a rider appears and kills the hobbits' Orc captor. Pippin and Merry lie frightened on the ground, covered by their Elf cloaks, which make them invisible. They eat some *lembas* cakes to regain their energy, and they decide to leave an Elf-brooch behind in the hopes that a rescuer might find it (as Aragorn indeed finds it later). The hobbits flee into the woods, not seeing that the rider kills Uglúk.

ANALYSIS

Our first glimpse of the hobbits in this volume of the novel is dark and troubling: Pippin and Merry are bound and captive, tormented and mistreated by their captors. In light of their small size, they are treated like pieces of baggage—carried around, picked up, and flung down without any courtesy. Pippin overhears several orcs wondering why they should take so much trouble for the sake of the hobbits, instead of simply killing them. Once again, the hobbits are a far cry from the traditional picture of heroism; they are important to the Orcs, but only as suspected bearers of the Ring, not as characters or identities in their own right. Even Pippin's self-liberation from the Orcs' bonds is not an act of courage, but a bit of very good luck: the dying orc falls in such a way that his knife rubs up against Pippin's hand bindings.

Despite the hobbits' ignoble introduction, however, their positive characteristics emerge clearly. Pippin begins the chapter dreaming that he is calling out for Frodo, reminding us of the strong bond among the four hobbits—the bond that Gandalf predicts will count for much when he argues for Pippin and Merry's inclusion in the Fellowship in the previous volume of the novel. Though Pippin and Merry never complain about the physical hardships they undergo, they do suffer when they are out of contact with each other. The narrator describes the hobbits' great sense of relief when they are near enough to each other to talk quietly for a while, taking pleasure in the simple camaraderie of being together even when bound and in captivity.

The importance of camaraderie is emphasized through contrast, in the the almost total absence of it among the Orcs. The Orcs simply do not get along well together, squabbling constantly and at times even fatally. Their frequent lapses into their native Orc dialects, incomprehensible to the Orcs of different tribes, is one sign of how little the creatures care about communication and unity with each other. The Isengard tribe's betrayal of the other Orcs is the most obvious example of this disunity, but we see considerable quarreling and dislike even within the Isengard tribe itself. We see the Isengarders snarling at each other in their camp, cursing each other with a bitterness that we would expect from enemies, not cohorts. When Pippin is being searched, he senses that his searcher might be attempting to double-deal his companions and seize the Ring for himself. While the two hobbits would do anything for one another, the Orcs seem barely able to hold together long enough to accomplish their kidnapping mission.

BOOK III, CHAPTER 4

SUMMARY — TREEBEARD

> *Could it be that the trees of Fangorn were awake, and*
> *the forest was rising, marching over the hills to war?*
> *(See* QUOTATIONS, *p.* 161*)*

Speeding through the forest, Merry and Pippin stop to drink water from the Entwash River. Munching on some of their few remaining *lembas* cakes, they worry about their lack of food and supplies. To their surprise, Merry and Pippin are suddenly addressed by what appears to be a fourteen-foot-tall walking tree. The creature is an Ent, an ancient treelike creature, named Fangorn or Treebeard. He is kind to the hobbits, and he explains his history to them. Treebeard identifies himself as one of the oldest creatures in Middle-earth. He is the shepherd of the other trees in the forest, many of which are Ents like him. Fangorn offers to carry Merry and Pippin to his home and to give them food and drink. On the way, Fangorn provides information about the Ents and their history. Many trees in the forest are simply Ents that have fallen asleep, who must be roused to action by some stirring motivation. The Ents have lost their wives, as the Ent-wives wandered off one day long ago. As a consequence, there are no young Ents in the forest.

As Pippin and Merry are being carried to the Ent-house, they ask Fangorn why they have heard stories warning them about the Ent forest. Fangorn agrees that it is an odd land, and expresses surprise that the hobbits ever made it into the forest in the first place. During the hobbits' meal at the Ent-house, Fangorn gives them some Ent food, a nourishing liquid that they drink greedily. Pippin and Merry learn about the Ents' growing fury at the Orcs and at Saruman, who has been mutating the Orcs into a new breed of monsters unafraid of sunlight (most Orcs fear the sun, and therefore come out only at night). Fangorn says that Saruman is evil and that Saruman's Isengard forces must be stopped through an alliance between Rohan, the Ents, and Aragorn's group.

After a night's sleep, Fangorn takes the hobbits to an Entmoot, or gathering of the Ents, in which the tree beings discuss a possible alliance with Rohan. The hobbits discover a variety of tree creatures of different shapes and sizes assembled. While the Ents debate in a low murmur, Merry and Pippin wonder how the Ents could possibly move on Isengard, which is a ring of rocky hills with a pillar of rock in the middle—not a place that trees could reach easily.

Merry and Pippin are invited to the home of an Ent named Bregalad or Quickbeam, who explains that the Orcs have been cruel to the Ents, cutting down trees for no reason. The hobbits suddenly hear the mighty roar of the Ent assembly, which has been stirred to action. Pippin at first cannot believe his eyes when he thinks he sees trees in motion, but it is true—the forest itself begins to move. The tree creatures all march toward Isengard to wage battle with Saruman and his Orc forces. Bregalad marches next to Fangorn, who reflects that the Ents may be marching to their doom. Fangorn points the way on to Isengard.

ANALYSIS

The introduction of the Ents effectively broadens the scope of the battle brewing between the Fellowship's forces and the Enemy, as the natural world itself becomes involved. What is taking shape is more than just warfare among the various races and peoples of Middle-earth. As Saruman's Orc armies have begun an assault on nature itself, destroying the forest for no reason, nature itself fights back.

The dramatic scene of the Ents marching into battle is a powerful moment, as well as a subtle nod to Shakespeare's *Macbeth,* in which one of the prophecies relating to Macbeth's demise is that a forest will physically move toward a castle. The episode of the Ents, in reminding us that evil in *The Lord of the Rings* is a universal force, touching even the lives of trees, forests, and entire landscapes, is an important component of the rich portrayal of the natural world that Tolkien has created in the novel. Tolkien wrote *The Lord of the Rings* in the 1940s, before the blossoming of the modern environmental conservation movement, but he foreshadows this era of ecological concerns in his critical portrayal of the evil Orcs' thoughtless destruction of trees for no practical purpose. The tree creatures have been patient for centuries, but now that they feel a significant threat to their environment, the power of their anger is formidable.

The Ents offer an example of a benevolent element in the natural world. Continuing the pattern we have seen in *The Fellowship of the Ring,* nature is rarely just an indifferent backdrop: it is either a force of evil (as in the previous volume's episodes with Old Man Willow and the pass of Caradhras) or good (as we see here with the Ents)— almost never neutral. Fangorn is willing to help Merry and Pippin from the first moment he meets them, offering to convey them through the forest and treating them nobly and hospitably thereafter. Both Fangorn and Bregalad offer Ent food and shelter to Merry and Pippin out of sheer benevolence, expecting nothing in return. As always in *The Lord of the Rings,* good brings creatures together and evil drives them apart. The display of hospitality, such as we see here with the Ents, is an important idea in Tolkien's work, and is one of the ways in which the world of Middle-earth imitates the ancient Greece depicted in epics such as Homer's *Odyssey.* In Homer's world, the true measure of a person's nobility is the generosity with which he receives guests. While the Orcs are objectionable hosts to Merry and Pippin, the Ents show an ancient and epic regard for giving strangers food and shelter.

The full dimensions of the imminent standoff between Gandalf and Saruman become clearer in this chapter, as the Ents provide crucial insight into the scope of the war that is brewing. Fangorn issues the first unequivocal call to arms in the novel, declaring Saruman to be evil and announcing the necessity of a large-scale alliance among all of Saruman's enemies. The fact that this initial call to arms is issued by a tree creature, rather than one of the Fellowship's leaders like Aragorn or Gandalf, is a measure of the urgency of the conflict at hand. The Ents are very deliberate, patient creatures who have been dormant for centuries, and they are not at all political beings. They seem capable of shrugging off nearly any provocation. However, the offenses to which Saruman's Orcs have subjected the Ents cannot be ignored. The enthusiasm of the Ents when roused to action shows us that this battle is not just a skirmish among minor, transitory figures, but an epochal clash of the primal forces of Middle-earth.

BOOK III, CHAPTERS 5–6

SUMMARY — CHAPTER 5: THE WHITE RIDER

> *"The Dark Lord has Nine. But we have One, mightier than they: the White Rider. He has passed through the fire and the abyss, and they shall fear him."*
> (See QUOTATIONS, p. 162)

Meanwhile, Aragorn, Gimli, and Legolas suffer from freezing weather on the trail of Merry and Pippin. They fear that the hobbits may have perished in the fierce battle between the Riders of Rohan and the Orcs. Gimli and Aragorn find the knife and the cut ropes that bound the hands of Pippin, giving them hope that the two hobbits are still alive somewhere in the forest. They find Hobbit tracks and follow them up to the river where the hobbits bathed.

Debating what to do next, Aragorn, Gimli, and Legolas are suddenly surprised by an old man in a cloak and wide-brimmed hat in the forest. Taking him for the evil Saruman, they are about to shoot him when Aragorn advises them to address him first, to be sure who he is. The stranger speaks to them familiarly, as though he knows them all. Gimli implores the old man to tell them where their friends are. Rather than answer, the old man jumps on a tall rock and throws off his gray clothes, revealing white garments beneath. Aragorn, Gimli, and Legolas are stunned to recognize their former companion Gandalf the Grey, reborn as Gandalf the White. Gandalf mysteriously says that he has "passed through fire and deep water" since his plunge into the chasm with the Balrog in the Mines of Moria (as recounted in *The Fellowship of the Ring*).

Gandalf explains Saruman's evil intention to seize the Ring for his own use. Sauron, the great Enemy, had asked for Saruman's help, but Saruman betrayed Sauron by dividing the Isengarders against Rohan, thereby aiding Gandalf's forces. Gandalf notes that Sauron's mistake is in concentrating his forces abroad in search of the Ring-bearing Frodo, rather than guarding the entrance to Mordor so that Frodo's entry might be blocked. It has apparently not occurred to Sauron that Frodo might be trying to return the Ring to Mordor to destroy it. Gandalf also predicts that the Ents, now fully roused to action, will be powerful in a way no one can foresee. Aragorn is confident that Gandalf will be a superb leader of their forces, and he hails Gandalf as the White Rider. Gandalf mounts his horse, Shadowfax, and they all make their way toward Isengard.

SUMMARY — CHAPTER 6:
THE KING OF THE GOLDEN HALL

The Company, led once again by Gandalf, marches toward Isengard, camping at night. The next morning, Legolas glimpses a golden building far in the distance, which Gandalf identifies as Edoras, the court of Théoden, King of Rohan. Gandalf cautions them to ride carefully, as war is afoot and the Riders of Rohan are always on the watch.

As Gandalf and the group arrive at the court of Edoras, guards ask them to identify themselves, addressing them in the local language of Rohan rather than in the Common Tongue. The guards declare that no one is welcome in Edoras in times of war, explaining that someone named Wormtongue has issued these orders. Hearing the name Wormtongue, Gandalf becomes angry and demands to speak to Théoden himself. Gandalf and his companions are allowed entry, although they are forced to leave their weapons with the doorman, Háma, despite Aragorn's protests. When Gandalf refuses to leave his staff at the door, Háma is suspicious, but allows the wizard to keep the staff with him.

Entering the royal hall, Gandalf's group meets the aged King Théoden, his wily counselor Gríma Wormtongue, and Theoden's niece, Éowyn. Wormtongue immediately issues a verbal attack on Gandalf, accusing the wizard of always seeking favors and never offering aid. Gandalf erupts in a rage, using his staff to bring down a powerful thunder that sends Wormtongue to the floor. Gandalf denounces Wormtongue, explaining to Théoden that his counselor had given advice that allowed the Isengarders to become stronger. Gandalf calls upon Théoden to recover his rightful strength as king and to fight off Saruman. Gandalf asks Théoden whether the king is holding Éomer prisoner. Théoden admits that it is so, and that he did so on the advice of the deceitful Wormtongue. Gandalf asks Théoden to release Éomer and to array forces against Isengard.

Théoden confronts Wormtongue, accusing him of treachery. Wormtongue tries to defend himself, but Théoden remains firm, and gives his advisor the ultimatum of either fighting alongside him against Isengard or leaving the country immediately. Wormtongue flees. Gandalf asks for Shadowfax as a gift (the horse was merely borrowed from Théoden before). Théoden offers weapons and coats of mail to everyone in Gandalf's group, though the wizard himself rides unprotected. From the hall, Éowyn watches the group ride off.

Analysis — Chapters 5–6

In the description of King Théoden and the court of Edoras, Tolkien draws upon the mythical tales of King Arthur and his court of Camelot. Edoras is more than a royal residence. It is described as a "Golden Hall," giving it a fantastical feel. Théoden's Riders evoke Arthur's Knights of the Round Table. In nodding to ancient British myth in this manner, Tolkien signals his intention for *The Lord of the Rings* to be not a mere fantasy novel, but a tale with the feel of ancient myth. Like the old stories about King Arthur, Tolkien's novel aims not just to tell a thrilling story, but to reveal something deeply symbolic about human nature and fate.

The preternatural power and wisdom of Gandalf are in the foreground in these chapters, and we begin to see the reasons why his character is the most revered in Tolkien's novel. The wizard is highly insightful about the psychology of both good and evil characters, as we see in his subtle understanding of the wicked Sauron's psychology. Gandalf knows that Sauron would never imagine that the present possessor of the Ring might want to destroy it rather than use it for his own benefit. The wizard contends that Sauron, in failing to consider this possibility, has made the error of searching for the Ring abroad rather than guarding the border of Mordor so that the Ring may not reach Mount Doom. Here, Gandalf shows his ability to think like the Enemy and to use this knowledge strategically. The wizard's acute understanding of human personality and motivation is also evidenced in his delicate dealings with Théoden. Gandalf has the difficult task of convincing the king, whom he barely knows, that the king's long-trusted advisor, Wormtongue, is in fact a traitor. Gandalf pulls off this sensitive task with poise and diplomacy. He foresees that Wormtongue, if provoked, will lose his cool and reveal his dark side, enabling the wizard to achieve the desired end without criticizing Théoden's judgment.

Gandalf's wisdom appears somehow related to his experience of death, as he has come back to life after his death in Moria. Like many figures in myth who gain superhuman understanding by passing through the underworld, Gandalf's demise at the end of the preceding volume of the novel is not a mark of failure, but is paradoxically a mark of power, as the wizard reappears stronger than ever. Like the ancient Roman hero Aeneas in Virgil's *Aeneid,* who gains wisdom from a trip through the realm of the dead, Gandalf too possesses an enhanced power now that he is reborn. Furthermore, as in the Christian tradition of rebirth, Gandalf returns as a purified being, no longer Gandalf the Grey but Gandalf the White. He has been cleansed, as if earlier weaknesses have been completely eradicated.

The idea of trust is central to the episode at Edoras. The major crisis of the chapter is Théoden's inability to realize that his long-trusted counselor is a spy and traitor who has undermined the welfare of the kingdom he purports to serve. Wormtongue's smooth-talking attempt to discredit Gandalf and to reaffirm his own trust-worthiness to the suspicious Théoden demonstrates the power of language to deceive and misguide. Trust is also an issue for Gandalf's party, as the members are all strangers in Edoras who must prove that they can be trusted. The guards' reluctance to allow Gandalf passage emphasizes that Sauron's evil has cast a pall of suspicion and mistrust on all of Middle-earth. Every stranger is automatically suspect. The value of trust is underscored by Gandalf's borrowing of the horse Shadowfax from Théoden. Tolkien could have easily structured the novel so that the horse was Gandalf's own property, but he instead chose to make the horse a loan from Théoden. In making this narrative choice, the author emphasizes that even the powerful wizard must rely on others, which both humanizes Gandalf and underscores the importance of trust in the Fellowship's quest.

BOOK III, CHAPTERS 7–8

SUMMARY — CHAPTER 7: HELM'S DEEP

Gandalf's group rides south of the River Isen. Legolas sees shapes moving in the distance, but he is unable to distinguish them clearly. The next day, Gandalf becomes alarmed, and with a word to his trusty horse, Shadowfax, speeds off, ordering the group to proceed to Helm's Deep and to stay far from the plains of Isen.

Obeying Gandalf without knowing his reasoning, the group goes to the Deep, a narrow gorge in the mountains on the far side of the Westfold Vale. Théoden reveals that Saruman knows the region very well, and he foresees that there will be a great battle between the Orcs and the armies of Rohan. Théoden and his Riders arrive at the Deeping Wall, a great fortification near Helm's Deep. They do not have enough provisions for a long encampment, having prepared for a quick battle rather than a long siege.

Suddenly, the battle begins with a great thunder, as the area around the Deeping Wall is flooded with Orcs. Many arrows are launched on both sides, and Legolas and Gimli fight valiantly. After many hours, the forces of Rohan grow tired. Aragorn is worried to see that the Orcs have crept beneath the Wall and have lit a flaming trail of Orc-liquor below the Riders. Aragorn goes into the Hornburg, the nearby citadel, to find that Éomer has not arrived. Aragorn learns that the Orcs have used their flaming liquid to blast through the Wall and seize it. Aragorn feels demoralized even though he is told that the Hornburg has never once been taken. The Orcs jeer at the Riders in the citadel, telling them to come out and meet their fate at the hands of the Uruk-hai. Suddenly, the roar of trumpets is heard, and King Théoden appears in martial splendor. The Orcs, gripped with fear, begin to retreat, dispersing throughout the land surrounding Helm's Deep. The Hornburg yet again remains safe. Suddenly, a horseman clad in white appears in the distance. The Riders of Rohan hail Gandalf, the White Rider, on the back of Shadowfax.

SUMMARY — CHAPTER 8: THE ROAD TO ISENGARD
Éomer, Théoden, Gandalf, Gimli, Legolas, and Aragorn all gather on the plain near Helm's Deep after the victory over the Orcs. Éomer expresses wonder that Gandalf came at just the right time. Though the men are weary from battle, Gandalf urges the King to assemble a party to ride with him to Isengard to meet Saruman. Théoden chooses Éomer and twenty Riders to accompany them. Gandalf rides in the company of Aragorn, Legolas, and Gimli. They sleep in preparation for the journey the next day. The slain Orcs are gathered on the fields.

The party sets out for Isengard the next day, passing through a forest of strange trees along the way. Gimli praises the beauty of caves to Legolas, who prefers the woods. Legolas is surprised to see eyes among the trees, and Gandalf explains that the forest is full of Ents, who are not enemies. The Riders of Rohan grieve over their slain fellow warriors, whose bodies litter the fields around them. Eventually, they reach the Misty Mountains. They sense that the area known as Nan Curunír, or the Wizard's Vale, is burning. They see a strange black liquid pass over the ground near them. Gandalf orders his men to ignore it and wait until it passes.

Riding on for several days, the group finally arrives at Saruman's stronghold at Isengard. They see the great stone tower called Orthanc, where Saruman lies in wait, surrounded by a deep gorge on all sides. Once Isengard was abloom with gardens and orchards, but ever since it has been under Saruman's control, it has been barren and desolate. At the gates of Isengard, Gandalf's group is surprised to find Merry and Pippin lounging and smoking. It is the first time Théoden has ever seen Hobbits. After a brief chat, Merry and Pippin deliver the message that Fangorn is waiting to meet with Gandalf on the northern wall of Isengard. Gandalf sets out to meet the Ent, accompanied by Théoden.

ANALYSIS — CHAPTERS 7–8

The appearance of Théoden at just the right moment to save the Hornburg from the Orc forces is the most dramatic battle scene in the novel thus far. Tolkien's masterful depiction of the battle displays all the classic characteristics of narrative suspense. The scene unfolds with Aragorn's sinking feeling that the Orc forces are too numerous to withstand. But then, with a clap of thunder and a roar of trumpets, Théoden appears, Gandalf guiding the king to the scene. The thunder and trumpets are less realistic details than mythic additions to the tale that enhance its legendary feel. Real battles may not take place in this somewhat melodramatic fashion, as the grim war scenes in great literature from Homer's *Iliad* to Tolstoy's *War and Peace* remind us. But in *The Lord of the Rings*, Tolkien aims for the more abstract level of myth, in which events do not necessarily happen as they do in real life.

Tolkien symbolically expresses the universality of the struggle for the Ring in some of the physical details of his description of the defense of Hornburg. All of the four traditional mythical elements of creation—earth, air, fire, and water—are present in the battle scene. The air is full of Orc arrows, the earth is covered with slain bodies, and the Orcs attempt to undermine the wall of the Hornburg by pouring a flaming liquid underneath it. Danger threatens Aragorn's men from above and below in what is not merely a fierce battle, but a mythical portrayal of the threat of total devastation, symbolic of the collapse of life itself. Only an overwhelming savior like Gandalf can counter such an overwhelming destructive force.

The natural beauty of the environment arises here as an important symbol of the state of the universe of Middle-earth. As Gandalf's traveling party passes through a forest of remarkable trees on its way to Wizard's Vale, Gimli and Legolas comment on the trees and then have a seemingly trivial conversation about whether caves or woods are more beautiful. The two disagree, as the dwarf naturally prefers underground rock formations to the leaves and greenery beloved to the elf. However, the conversation reveals more about what Gimli and Legolas share than about how they differ, as it is clear that both of them value the natural environment very highly. As it is hard to imagine a villain like the forest-destroying Saruman appreciating either caves or woods, an implied parallel is made between moral good and a love for nature. This connection is confirmed later, when the group rides through Isengard and finds that the once-blossoming realm, full of gardens and orchards, is now bleak and barren ever since it has fallen under the sway of Saruman. When evil takes over a place, natural beauty fades, as evil scars the earth itself.

The surprising appearance of Merry and Pippin at Saruman's stronghold of Orthanc shows us the humor of which Tolkien is capable. Though *The Lord of the Rings* is famous for its grand epic tone and serious treatment of the nature of good and evil, it also includes its share of humorous, human moments. The humor in the scene at Orthanc arises from the juxtaposition of the solemn and dramatic setting—the immense stone tower standing amid a gorge of rock—and the leisurely, nonchalant attitude of the hobbits who sit there. Merry and Pippin appear oblivious to the brewing battle—lounging, smoking, chatting, and generally enjoying themselves as if in their natural element. They are more eager to talk about different varieties of tobacco than about the events that shake the world around them. Once again, the portrayal of the hobbits challenges traditional notions of what epic heroes should be like. Tolkien, as we have heard through the words of Gandalf, Elrond, and others, suggests that history may be in the hands of the little people, those who go unnoticed among the grander dealings of the world.

SUMMARY & ANALYSIS

BOOK III, CHAPTERS 9–11

SUMMARY — CHAPTER 9: FLOTSAM AND JETSAM

Gandalf and Théoden leave Isengard to meet Fangorn. Aragorn and his cohorts, staying behind, are given human food obtained by the Ents, a welcome change from the Orc food that disgusts them. The two hobbits offer Gimli some tobacco from barrels they have discovered at Isengard. The dwarf regrets not having a pipe with which to smoke the tobacco, but Pippin gives Gimli a pipe of his own, which Gimli may keep. Gimli is grateful.

Pippin tells the tale of his adventures since he was separated from his friends. Aragorn returns the hobbits' knives and the Elf-brooch that he found on the way. Merry tells of the Ent assembly and the trees' decision to go to battle against Saruman, describing the Ents' speed and great strength in destroying the stone walls of the wizard's fortress. The hobbits also relate Gandalf's meeting with Treebeard to seek help. The Ents responded by breaking the dams nearby and flooding the earth under Isengard with water. The Orcs in the lower areas were wiped out.

SUMMARY — CHAPTER 10: THE VOICE OF SARUMAN

> *"You have become a fool, Saruman, and yet pitiable.*
> *You might still have turned away from folly and evil…*
> *But you choose to stay and gnaw the ends of your own*
> *plots."*
>
> *(See* QUOTATIONS, *p. 163)*

Gandalf and his group set off for the gates of Orthanc to try to make contact with Saruman. Watching the windows of the tower, Gandalf calls out Saruman's name, but gets no response. Finally, a window opens and they hear the voice of Gríma Wormtongue, Saruman's a spy in Théoden's court. Wormtongue asks what the visitors want. Gandalf impatiently demands to speak to Saruman himself. Finally Saruman speaks. He addresses the travelers in a sad and self-pitying voice, using his powers in an attempt to persuade and placate them.

Saruman first speaks to the Riders of Rohan, claiming that he only wants peace for all. Théoden and his men are initially dazzled by Saruman, but Gimli interrupts the wizard to accuse him of deceit. Saruman tries to maintain his cool, but he explodes in rage when Gandalf rebukes him. Gandalf responds by breaking Saruman's staff. Saruman falls down. The enraged Wormtongue, hidden from view, seeks revenge by throwing a glowing crystal sphere out of the tower window. The globe misses Gandalf and rolls along the ground. Pippin picks it up.

The group prepares to leave Orthanc. As they do, they hear a piercing cry from Saruman's quarters. Gandalf knows that Saruman has realized the loss of the precious globe that Wormtongue threw out the window. As they leave the gates, Gandalf introduces Fangorn to Legolas and Gimli. Gandalf asks the Ent to fill the gorge around Orthanc with water, ensuring that Saruman can never escape. Fangorn promises that the Ents will do so.

SUMMARY — CHAPTER 11: THE PALANTÍR

As Gandalf and Théoden retreat from Isengard, the wizard carries Merry with him on Shadowfax, while Aragorn carries Pippin. Merry and Gandalf chat. They ride late into the night and then stop to camp. Pippin asks Merry whether Gandalf seems different now that he has come back from the dead, and Merry replies that the wizard seems both happier and more serious.

Merry is sleepy and tired of Pippin's questioning, and he soon falls asleep. But Pippin, unable to sleep, is tormented by curiosity about the crystal globe Wormtongue threw out of the tower. Pippin sneaks over to the sleeping Gandalf and snatches the globe. Gazing into it, Pippin is appalled by the sight of a dark flying creature approaching him, and then an image of an evil figure addressing him. He drops the globe and cries out in fear.

Gandalf awakens, angered at Pippin, as the globe is a *palantír*, one of the seven ancient seeing-stones that Sauron has turned to evil uses as devices to communicate with his minions from his tower in Mordor. Pippin's glimpse into the *palantír* not only enabled the hobbit to see visions, but allowed Sauron to see Pippin and into the hobbit's thoughts. Aragorn notes that the *palantír* explains how Saruman was able to communicate with Sauron, and Gandalf notes that the *palantír* likely played a large part in the corruption of the formerly good Saruman. Gandalf also says that the sight of Pippin in the globe will confuse the Dark Lord, and that the group can make good use of the delay caused by this confusion. The wizard explains that the winged creature Pippin saw in the globe is one of the Nazgûl, the Ringwraiths who pursued the hobbits earlier in the novel. Gandalf proposes to take Pippin away on Shadowfax and to ride as far as the court of Edoras.

ANALYSIS — CHAPTERS 9–11

The scene in Chapter 9 in which various trivial items (the "flotsam and jetsam" of the chapter's title) are exchanged forms a rather static interlude between episodes of action, but it reveals a great deal about the personalities of the heroes. When Pippin gives Gimli his tobacco pipe, we glimpse the everyday world of small pleasures and minor details that is just as important as the drama of catastrophic conflict and heroic action in *The Lord of the Rings*. Pippin's pipe is a far cry from the Ring, having no bearing on the outcome of history, ignored by kings and wizards, and uninvolved in any prophecies or destinies. Yet the pipe is nevertheless a significant object, a symbol of the values of caring and friendship that make the Fellowship possible in the first place. Pippin gives Gimli a pipe, a tool of brief respite from the burden of the quest, as a gesture of good will, simply because Pippin cares for Gimli and wants him to be comfortable. Though perhaps a humble, overlooked gesture, the gift of the pipe embodies the selflessness that is central to the whole novel.

The portrayal of Wormtongue speaking from the window of Orthanc broadens Tolkien's exploration of evil. Wormtongue is not an impressive, powerful villain like Saruman, but a much lesser figure who embodies corruption and evil on a small scale. Tolkien, as he often does in his fiction, associates a facility with sweet words and eloquent phrasing with corruption and deceit in his presentation of Wormtongue. When Gandalf reveals Wormtongue's role as spy against Théoden, Wormtongue's response is to use a fine speech to sway Théoden against Gandalf. This deliberate language is precisely what Gandalf uses against Wormtongue when he calls the spy a "jester." A jester deals with language rather than actions, using words playfully for entertainment—an accusation that strikes a raw nerve in Wormtongue. Equally important, Tolkien portrays Wormtongue as completely unable to control his emotions. Wormtongue's rash toss of the *palantír*—a great loss to Saruman, as the sphere is a valuable tool—suggests the danger of emotional outpouring. The emotional instability of Wormtongue emphasizes, by contrast, the moderation and self-control that Tolkien values as heroic.

Pippin's succumbing to his urge to gaze into the *palantír* shows us the "human" side of this endearing character, as well as another example of the corrupting power of Sauron's evil. While Pippin does not steal the *palantír* from the sleeping Gandalf, it is clear that the hobbit knows he is doing something he should not be doing. Yet Tolkien structures the scene to enable us to sympathize easily with

Pippin, making clear the allure of the *palantír*. Tolkien narrates the scene from Pippin's point of view to enhance our understanding of the hobbit's motivations. On one level, Pippin is simply bored, unable to sleep, and fascinated by a mysterious object. His moral failing here is nothing more than the common human flaw of curiosity, augmented by the pull of the *palantír*. Gandalf later notes that Sauron appropriated the seeing-stones, which were originally tools used for good by the ancient kings of Gondor, for evil purposes—yet another example of the Dark Lord's corruption.

Pippin's glimpse of the frightening Nazgûl in the seeing-stone etches the reality of Mordor more clearly in our minds. Prior to this moment, the only character to have actually seen Mordor is Frodo, who glimpses it from the top of Amon Hen at the end of *The Fellowship of the Ring*. For the other characters, and for us as readers, Mordor has primarily been only a vague idea of evil far in the distance, a general destination to reach eventually. As the novel progresses, Mordor's presence is felt more strongly. Gandalf's words remind us that, though at times the evil of Sauron may slip from the characters' minds, Sauron is constantly watching and searching for the characters, focused obsessively on the Ring.

BOOK IV, CHAPTER 1

SUMMARY — THE TAMING OF SMÉAGOL

> *"Yess, wretched we are, precious.... Misery misery!*
> *Hobbits won't kill us, nice hobbits."*
> (See QUOTATIONS, p. 164)

The narrative returns to Frodo and Sam on the third day after they departed from their companions at the end of *The Fellowship of the Ring*. The hobbits wander the barren slopes of the mountains called Emyn Muir, striving to make their way to Mordor, but frequently getting lost and having to retrace their steps. Standing on the edge of a tall cliff, they can see the way down into Mordor, but have no way to descend the cliff. Sam complains to Frodo about their desperate situation. He has been lugging cooking gear for days, but there is nothing to cook. The hobbits survive only on old *lembas* cakes, and Sam yearns for a pint of beer and a chunk of bread. He expresses his hope that they have lost Gollum, the creature who has been pursuing them for some time. Frodo agrees, but says that he is more troubled by the unending hills of the landscape, which torture his feet. He observes that there is no turning back, as Orc warriors now patrol the banks of the river they have crossed.

Sam and Frodo continue to follow the cliff northward for several more days, finally arriving at a spot where it appears they might be able to climb down. Sam insists on going first, against Frodo's objections. Sam lowers himself down the cliff, when suddenly a great dark shape appears overhead with a horrible wind and a crack of thunder. Sam loses his hold on the rock and falls, but is saved by a narrow ledge below. Frodo tries to hide his face in fear, but he loses his foothold and falls down onto a ledge below. It begins to rain. Sam suddenly remembers that he has a strong, thin Elf rope in his bag. He measures it out, and finds that it is long enough to allow the two hobbits to lower themselves to the ground below.

After descending safely, Sam and Frodo prepare to go onward to Mordor. Sam regrets abandoning the rope, which is still attached to a rock overhead and cannot be untied. Suddenly, as if by magic, the rope is released and falls into his hands. Frodo suspects that the knot was not tied well, but both wonder whether it was perhaps enchantment that freed the rope.

As the hobbits huddle in the cold, Frodo spots a crawling insect-like creature on a distant cliff, clinging to the wall by its hands. Sam realizes the creature is Gollum. As the creature draws nearer, he leaps on Sam. They wrestle. Frodo draws his knife Sting from its sheath and thrusts it against Gollum's neck, demanding obedience from the creature. Gollum is suddenly subservient and vows total servitude, but Frodo does not trust him entirely. Gollum suddenly bounds away, attempting escape. The hobbits get him back and harness him with the Elf rope, which causes Gollum great pain. Gollum again vows obedience, and this time he seems sincere. The creature leads his Hobbit masters onward to Mordor.

ANALYSIS

A sense of frustration and hopelessness colors our first glimpse of Frodo and Sam in *The Two Towers,* much like our first glimpse of Merry and Pippin in Book III. As we have seen frequently, the hobbits are not epic heroes who have great powers at their disposal to solve their dilemmas. Rather, they are shrewd and adaptable, using modest means and a bit of luck to yield impressive results. Indeed, in virtually all of the hobbits' dilemmas in *The Two Towers,* the hobbits depend on something stronger than themselves to extricate them from their problems. Pippin profits from the fortunate fall of an Orc knife near his hand bindings in Book III, much as Frodo and Sam profit from the magic rope woven by Elves to lower themselves down the cliff in Book IV.

This chapter returns us to the fascinating character of Gollum, whom we have not seen up close since Bilbo's encounter with the creature in *The Hobbit*. Gollum proves to be one of the most complex and indefinable characters in Tolkien's novel. He is literally a slave to the Ring, as his mind focuses on his "Precious" at the exclusion of all else. Gollum's moral nature is split quite drastically, an inward reflection of the division between Sméagol, his identity before he encountered the Ring, and Gollum, the creature he has since become. Gollum's long-standing habit of talking aloud to himself, debating with himself in a near-neurotic manner, indicates his inner conflict and his lack of a strong sense of identity. When Gollum is subservient after Frodo tames him, he is genuinely convincing in his proclamation that he wishes to guide his new masters. Indeed, as we see many times in the upcoming chapters, Gollum stays with Frodo on many occasions when he could easily escape. Nonetheless, Gollum also proves himself treacherous on numerous occasions. Even at the very end of the novel, we are still somewhat divided between a view of Gollum as an innocent but selfish child and a view of him as a depraved and evil monster.

Frodo's taming of Gollum highlights a potential for sternness and authority in the hobbit that we have not yet seen, as he uses the knife in a fearless and even somewhat violent manner. As we continue to see in the following chapters, Frodo displays a surprising and forceful mix of suspicion and compassion in his interactions with Gollum, fully aware of the creature's motivation to retrieve the Ring, but sensing that he would not do anything to harm the hobbits overtly. This aura of suspicion and mistrust parallels, on a small scale, the overall atmosphere of apprehension that Sauron's evil has cast over the whole of Middle-earth. In the character of Gollum, Tolkien injects a significant element of uncertainty into the plot, as even Gollum himself appears unsure of what he will do or what his goal is. This sense of utter unpredictability and potential danger pushes the narrative forward, keeping us in suspense throughout the entire remainder of *The Two Towers* as Gollum travels with the hobbits. Tolkien's technique effectively places us in Frodo's and Sam's shoes: much like the hobbits, though we are aware that the wretched Gollum has selfish intentions, we have no idea when or how he might act upon them.

BOOK IV, CHAPTER 2

SUMMARY — THE PASSAGE OF THE MARSHES

Gollum guides Frodo and Sam through the marshland that surrounds Mordor. The creature was once on the run from Orcs in the area, so he knows it well. Gollum is fearful of the sun, which he calls the "Yellow Face," so he prefers to travel by night. The hobbits continue to feed on *lembas* cakes, and they offer some to Gollum, but he finds Elf products painful to eat. He chokes and spits out the cake, constantly yearning for fish and complaining that he will soon starve. As the hobbits get ready to camp for the night, Sam worries that Gollum may trick them while they are sleeping, so he waits until Gollum falls asleep first. Sam whispers the word "fish" in Gollum's ear, and when he gets no reaction, he is satisfied that the creature poses no danger, at least not on this night. Frodo and Sam both fall asleep, despite Sam's insistence on keeping one eye open, fixed on Gollum.

The next morning, the hobbits awaken to find Gollum gone. They again discuss their concerns about their food supply. Sam repeats that while he is not fond of *lembas* cakes, they are at least nourishing and keep him on his feet. But even the *lembas* are running out; Sam calculates that they have only enough left for three more weeks. Suddenly, Gollum reappears and says he is hungry. He leaves again, but soon returns with his face dirty with mud. The hobbits believe that they can trust him.

Gollum leads Frodo and Sam through the foul-smelling Dead Marshes, which are haunted by the slain warriors of a great past battle. Ghostly, floating lights surround them on the path. Gollum tells the hobbits to ignore the lights, which could lead them into the realm of the dead. They proceed onward for several days, nearly fainting from the stench of the marshes. One night, the dark shape of a Nazgûl flying overhead strikes fear into all three of the travelers. Gollum warns that the Nazgûl see everything, and report back to their master, the Dark Lord. Frodo is deeply disturbed by the idea that a great power is constantly watching him.

On the fifth morning, they wake to see that they are very close to Mordor. The land is desolate and unwelcoming, full of poison pits. Even the stinking marshland dries up, leaving an expanse of completely barren ground. That night, Frodo hears the dozing Gollum in conversation with himself, torn between his need to get his "Precious" and his conflicting vow to obey the hobbits. Gollum recognizes that Frodo is the master of the Ring, and that he must serve the master of his "Precious." Frodo realizes that Gollum knows the Nazgûl are searching for the Ring just as he is. Gollum says something about never letting the servants of the Dark Lord get the Ring.

The next morning, Frodo, Sam, and Gollum have nearly arrived at the gates of Mordor. The hobbits thank Gollum for fulfilling his promise of guiding them to the gates. A Nazgûl flies overhead for the third time, which Gollum claims is a very bad omen. Gollum refuses to proceed, and Frodo must threaten him with a knife to make him go forward.

ANALYSIS

In this chapter, Gollum's character becomes more mysterious and complicated just as the question of his trustworthiness becomes more crucial. When Frodo initially tames Gollum in the previous chapter, the creature is clearly the hobbit's inferior, and the issue of his reliability does not matter much. But as the group gets closer to Mordor, Gollum assumes more control in relation to the hobbits. No longer merely a passive slave under Frodo's knife, he is now their guide, whom they must trust—a slave with the power of a master. Gollum's refusal to travel by the light of the sun reminds us that he is a creature of darkness, a corrupted opposite of Frodo. Tolkien continues to create suspense by playing with our suspicions along with the hobbits' as Gollum briefly disappears and then reappears. Even after Gollum returns, claiming total loyalty to the master of his "Precious," our apprehension about his motivations lingers.

The image of Gollum guiding Frodo and Sam through a barren landscape on their way to fulfill their mission echoes similar images from the ancient Greek and Roman epics. Tolkien, who was well studied in the classics, was very familiar with epic tales like the *Odyssey* and the *Aeneid,* in which the protagonists must suffer through a distressing journey to the underworld, often guided by somewhat shady or unsavory characters. On these ancient journeys, the heroes often must confront the dead, along with the possibility that they themselves may die as well. In *The Two Towers,* Gollum leads the hobbits through the Dead Marshes, a realm of the dead, with waters that contain ghostly images of the faces of slain warriors. Much like the realms of the dead in the classical epics, the landscape of the Dead Marshes is deeply unpleasant, devoid of life and growth. Yet passage through this barren landscape is a necessary step for the ultimate completion of the quest. As Gollum emphatically points out, there is simply no other way to reach Mordor, just as in the classical epics there was no way for the heroes to complete their quests without a sojourn in the underworld.

Mordor continues to become an ever stronger and darker reality in the novel. As the hobbits approach the dark land, it becomes a clearly felt presence. The landscape bordering Mordor is noticeably nasty, full of poison pits and barren stone outcrops, with an overwhelming stench saturating the air. The frightening Nazgûl flying overhead are a constant reminder of the proximity and threat of Sauron. Even the normally solid Gollum is deeply spooked when the Nazgûl flies overhead for the third time, taking it as a very bad omen. This growing atmosphere of evil, along with the uncertainty surrounding Gollum's trustworthiness, increases yet further the suspense that propels Book IV forward.

BOOK IV, CHAPTER 3

SUMMARY — THE BLACK GATE IS CLOSED

Frodo, Sam, and Gollum finally arrive at the gates of Mordor. They behold the Teeth of Mordor, the tall towers built earlier by the Men of Gondor after the fall of Sauron, but then later reoccupied by the Dark Lord upon his return to power.

At the sight of the closely guarded gate, Sam wonders how they will enter. Gollum replies that they must not enter, prompting Sam to ask why they bothered traveling to Mordor in the first place if they cannot go inside. Gollum replies that he fulfilled his part of the agreement, guiding the hobbits to the gate. Sam is angry, again asking why they bothered going to Mordor at all. Frodo affirms that he must enter Mordor at all costs. At the hobbits' insistence, Gollum admits that there is another way into the kingdom, a secret way that he discovered earlier. Sam distrusts Gollum, but the hobbits have little choice but to follow the creature's lead. Frodo reminds Gollum that he has sworn by his "Precious" to guide them safely and not betray them.

Gollum directs Sam and Frodo toward a road that bends south around Mordor, telling them that the road extends for a hundred leagues, but warning that they should not go that way. Frodo asks if there is a third way. Gollum admits that there is a third path running around to the back of the kingdom, past a fortress built long ago by tall Men with shining eyes. Frodo realizes that Gollum refers to the former fortress of Isildur, the warrior who defeated Sauron and won the Ring from him. Part of the fortress is a tall tower called the Tower of the Moon. Sam asks whether the tower is occupied, and Gollum replies that it is guarded by Orcs and by even worse creatures called Silent Watchers. Sam remarks that this third path sounds just as risky as the first one, but Gollum says the Dark Lord is focusing his attention elsewhere. Gollum admits that the rear path past the Tower of the Moon is dangerous, but that it is worth trying. The hobbits are suspicious, but they accept Gollum's advice.

Four Nazgûl appear in the sky overhead, and the hobbits know that Sauron is observing them. Frodo and Sam grab their knives, but they know that escape is impossible. Gollum senses that other Men are heading toward Mordor too—Men with long dark hair, gold rings, and red flags. He describes them as very fierce, saying that he has never seen anything like them. There are always Men entering Mordor now. Sam asks whether the men have "oliphaunts" with them, as he has heard the creatures described in old poetry. Gollum has never seen an oliphaunt. He urges the hobbits to sleep through the daylight hours, and proceed again at night.

ANALYSIS

The Teeth of Mordor and the fortress of Isildur are further reminders of the idea that evil can overtake and corrupt goodness. According to the moral system Tolkien puts forth, good and evil are not necessarily inherent qualities. The good can become rotten, as we have seen with Saruman and Boromir. This possibility of transformation from good to evil is also true of the buildings of Mordor. The Teeth of Mordor and the fortress of Isildur are reminders of the fragility of goodness, as the gentle and peace-loving Men of Gondor originally built them. Frodo is startled to realize that the ghastly fortress of Isildur, which Gollum reports to be full of murderous Orcs and the even more horrible "Silent Watchers," was originally the property of the Lord of Gondor. Ironically, the building of the one who fought against evil is now possessed by that very evil. Good is not guaranteed in Tolkien's universe, but must forever be actively guarded and defended.

The impossibility of entering the final destination directly, and the necessity of following a roundabout route to get inside, is a common element of ancient epics from which Tolkien has borrowed. For instance, in the *Divine Comedy*, Dante is, like Frodo, a traveler who is motivated by good but who is forced to go into the mouth of hell in order to reach heaven later. Dante cannot simply take the shortest path toward his goal of reaching heaven, but must travel through realms of evil he would otherwise never visit. Similarly, Frodo and Sam must travel to the heart of evil in Mordor in order to ensure the ultimate triumph of good. The hobbits, as usual, attain their goals not by direct confrontation; they plan to take the back road to a hidden entrance to Mordor rather than fight the guards at Mordor's gates. Though the safety of this alternate route is doubtful at best, Frodo and Sam have little choice but to follow Gollum's advice.

The danger contained within the gates of Mordor continues to become ever more real, both to us and to Frodo and Sam. In this chapter, we glimpse for the first time the humans associated with the evil kingdom. Prior to this moment, Mordor was at first merely an idea of evil, and then a place largely associated with the fantastical, especially the dark shapes of the flying Nazgûl. Now Mordor is connected to the more real, yet equally terrifying, world of human evil. The Men of Mordor, with long dark hair, gold rings, and red flags, present yet another reminder that evil is not necessarily inherent, but can corrupt even the seemingly familiar realm of the human world to an almost unrecognizable degree.

BOOK IV, CHAPTER 4

SUMMARY — OF HERBS AND STEWED RABBIT

Sam, Frodo, and Gollum proceed through the desolate landscape of Mordor. Gradually, they notice that the land is becoming greener, more fragrant, and less barren, and they welcome the change. As always, they travel by night and rest by day. They do not travel on the open road, but near it. They worry about their dwindling food supply. After several days, they arrive in a country full of woods and streams once known as Ithilien. Gollum coughs and sputters in the verdant setting, but the hobbits rejoice in the reappearance of greenery and water. They stop at a stream to drink and bathe. Again, they are troubled by hunger. Sam sends Gollum off to hunt some food for them all, reminding him that Hobbit food is different from the food the creature is accustomed to eating. Sam watches the sleeping Frodo, observing the fine lines visible on Frodo's aging face. Sam acknowledges that he feels deep love for Frodo.

Gollum returns with rabbits, which he does not want to cook, preferring to devour them raw. Sam proceeds to make a nice dinner for himself and Frodo, calling upon Gollum again to gather wild herbs for his rabbit stew. Frodo awakens and sees the cooking fire burning. Sam informs Frodo of the nice dinner being prepared, but Frodo warns Sam about the dangers of fire in the open field.

Suddenly Frodo and Sam hear voices nearby, and they see four tall Men wielding spears. The warriors wonder whether the hobbits are Elves or perhaps Orcs. One of the Men identifies himself as Faramir, Captain of Gondor. The hobbits identify themselves as halflings. Faramir says that the hobbits cannot be travelers, as uninvited travelers are not allowed in his land. Frodo explains the hobbits' separation from Aragorn and Boromir. At the mention of the name of Boromir, Faramir is startled and becomes stern.

Two men named Mablung and Damrod guard Frodo and Sam, telling the hobbits of their enemies, the Southrons, who threaten to attack. Sam wonders where Gollum is. Suddenly, they hear noises of battle and the name of Gondor called out. Damrod announces that the Southrons are attacking and that Faramir's men are setting out to meet them. The hobbits climb into a position where they can see what is going on, and they witness their first battle among Men.

Suddenly, Damrod calls out for help from a large elephant-like creature called the Mûmak, which arrives from the forest and crushes the enemy. Sam is pleased that he has seen his first oliphaunt, as the creature is called. Damrod tells the hobbits to sleep, as the Gondor captain will soon return and they will have to flee the enemy. Sam replies that the troops of Gondor will not disturb him when they leave. Damrod answers that it is not likely that the captain will allow Sam to stay, but will instead force him to travel with the troops.

ANALYSIS

The relationship between Frodo and Sam, already at the center of the novel, is deepened by Sam's expression of affection for Frodo. Sam seems almost surprised by his feelings of solicitude toward Frodo when he notes the wrinkles appearing on his master's aging face. As Sam's thoughts are only a private musing, we know that they are sincere. Sam's concern for Frodo, along with his noting of Frodo's increasingly haggard and weak appearance, foreshadows the ever-greater role and responsibility Sam must bear in the remainder of the quest. Sam gains no profit or benefit from his attachment to Frodo, and, in fact, his dedication brings him only great hardship. Again, Tolkien, in his depiction of the relationship between the two hobbits, emphasizes the importance of loyalty and selflessness as essential traits for his brand of epic hero.

The narrator's careful attention to the food preparation of Sam, Frodo, and Gollum brings us down to earth somewhat, again reminding us of the ever-present mundane concerns within the grander scope of the quest. The author even gives Chapter 4 a title referring to the stewed rabbit and wild herbs that Frodo and Sam prepare for dinner. In part, this chapter name is a Homeric touch. In the *Iliad* and the *Odyssey,* Homer devotes long passages to seemingly trivial concerns such as the size and smell of the roast ox the warriors eat. Such material details ground the epic quest in reality and remind us that, however spiritual or lofty the heroes' final goals may be, the heroes themselves are still very human, creatures with bodies that must be fed. Further, the food episode once again shows us the hobbits' uneasy reliance on Gollum. Their food supplies dwindling, Frodo and Sam are nonetheless unable to catch rabbits themselves, so they must rely on their guide to do so. In such passages, Tolkien yet again reminds us of the hobbits' odd status as epic heroes, with their relative frailty and inexperience in an environment and role typically filled by great warriors and Wizards.

The appearance of the oliphaunt, or giant elephant creature, is yet another small detail in the story of the journey to Mordor that reminds us of the completeness with which Tolkien has imagined the world of *The Lord of the Rings.* Sam and Frodo have inquired about the existence of oliphaunts when talking to Gollum, who claims never to have heard of or seen such creatures. But then, in the battle between Faramir's men and the attacking Southrons soon afterward, this very creature is glimpsed and vividly described. The imagined turns out to be real, and Sam is thrilled. This little detail reminds us that in Tolkien's universe, the potential for amazement is always present. Unlike other works of fantasy, in which the characters are never surprised by anything within their fantastical world, in *The Lord of the Rings,* the characters of Tolkien's Middle-earth are often awestruck by what they see. Sam is amazed by oliphaunts, Faramir's men are amazed by Gollum, and many humans throughout the novel are startled by the hobbits, whose like they have never glimpsed before. In such episodes, Tolkien constantly reminds us that the surprises of the imagination are always available to us, an essential and often enjoyable part of the experience of life.

BOOK IV, CHAPTER 5

SUMMARY — THE WINDOW ON THE WEST

"[I]t was Gondor that brought about its own decay . . .
thinking that the Enemy was asleep, who was only
banished not destroyed."

(See QUOTATIONS, *p. 165)*

Sam falls asleep and awakens to find Faramir interrogating Frodo. Faramir wants to know why the hobbits originally set out from Rivendell, and under what circumstances they parted with Boromir. Faramir knows of a prophecy that states that a Halfling will arrive bearing something of great value, and he asks Frodo what this object is. Frodo answers only that he is on an errand to deliver the object elsewhere. Frodo makes a great effort not to speak ill of Boromir, even though Boromir tried to seize the Ring for himself. Faramir, knowing that Boromir is dead and attempting to trick Frodo, announces that Boromir will clear up everything when he arrives. Frodo, however, is unaware of Boromir's death. Faramir hints that he suspects Frodo of betraying Boromir.

Faramir reveals to Frodo that Boromir is his brother. He asks Frodo whether he recalls any particular object Boromir possessed, and Frodo remembers Boromir's horn. Faramir recounts how once he was staring at the sea, and either in a dream or in real life he saw Boromir floating by on a boat, his horn broken. Faramir says he knew that Boromir was sailing to the land of the dead, and that he had been killed. Frodo says that it must have been a mere vision, as Boromir had undertaken to go home across the fields of Rohan, far from water. Faramir addresses the dead Boromir in deep grief, asking for answers to his questions about what happened to Boromir before death. Faramir knows that there has been some wrongdoing, but he no longer suspects Frodo.

Faramir announces to the hobbits that he must take them back to Minas Tirith, the great city of Gondor. On the way, Faramir commends Frodo's truthfulness, though fully aware that Frodo has withheld the fact that the hobbits did not like Boromir. Faramir tries again to extract information about the valuable object—which he knows only as Isildur's Bane—that he knows Frodo is carrying. Faramir suspects that Isildur's Bane killed Boromir, perhaps because it caused contention among the men. Frodo answers that there was no fighting in the ranks, and Faramir understands that the cause of the problem was Boromir alone.

When the woodlands begin to grow thinner, Faramir orders his men to blindfold Frodo and Sam so that they will not know the location of the hideout where they are headed. When the blindfolds are removed, the hobbits see the splendid Window of the Sunset, as Faramir calls the waterfall-covered window of the cave in which they are hiding.

Faramir offers Frodo and Sam food and drink. While they eat, Faramir recounts the former glory of the kingdom of Gondor and its later slide into weakness as the kingdom offered land to the Rohirrim in exchange for military defense. As they talk, Sam accidentally blurts out the fact that Boromir had sought to get the Ring. Faramir is shocked that his brother was guilty, but he appreciates Sam's honesty, and affirms that he has no interest in getting the Ring for himself. Frodo tells Faramir of his own mission to throw the Ring into the Crack of Doom to destroy it. Faramir is astonished.

ANALYSIS

Frodo's tense encounter with Faramir, who initially suspects the hobbit of being responsible for the death of Boromir, is an important plot development in several ways. First, the episode brings unity to the two disparate halves of *The Two Towers* by bringing us back to the first chapter, in which Boromir's death is recounted. Now, near the end of this volume of the novel, we hear about the death of Boromir once again, but from a different perspective that gives us information we were not offered before. In circling back in the novel in this manner, Tolkien again reminds us that everything in *The Lord of the Rings* comes back to where it started—the Ring. Moreover, the new point of view on Boromir's demise reminds us of the emotional consequences of the bloodshed in the novel, an aspect that sometimes is overlooked. We hear of the death of Boromir in the first chapter of *The Two Towers*, but do not grieve over it much, having little familiarity with Boromir, even after reading *The Fellowship of the Ring*. We judge Boromir's death mainly in terms of what it means for the hobbits' mission. But here, when we watch Faramir sorrowfully address his dead brother, begging for answers to his questions about Boromir's death, we are reminded that the death carries with it a great emotional burden for Faramir. In a novel in which death is so widespread, Tolkien does well to remind us that these deaths, however numerous and sometimes anonymous, have an emotional importance above their status as mere plot points.

The episode with Faramir also shows us a new side of Frodo. The hobbit has suffered all manner of hardships in the novel, but he has never had to face an interrogation of the sort that Faramir forces upon him. Frodo could easily escape Faramir's suspicions simply by stating the truth: that Boromir was a traitor who sought possession of the Ring himself, betraying the Fellowship. But Frodo refuses to admit the truth out of regard for Faramir's honorable memory of his late brother. Of course, Boromir was not completely evil, and for a while he was the solid ally of the hobbits; in this regard, Frodo may be attempting to pay tribute to his former colleague. But the fact remains that, in his conversation with Faramir, Frodo sacrifices his own comfort and honor to preserve the good memory of someone who betrayed him. The nobility of Frodo's act is impressive indeed. When we watch how well he holds up under pressure from the accusatory Faramir, we develop a deeper respect for the hobbit's empathy and strength of character.

Faramir's reaction to the news of his brother's ignoble behavior is itself highly noble. Faramir does not curse Frodo and Sam as the bearers of bad tidings, nor does he label them liars, unable to believe or process the fact that his beloved elder brother could be capable of treachery. On the contrary, Faramir accepts the hobbits' story with grace and calm. His acceptance of the distressing truth about his brother may suggest that Faramir is, on some level, well aware of the possibility of good turning to evil in the world. Faramir continues to exhibit this awareness in his touching recount of the fall of Gondor from a land of peace and prosperity to a realm of wickedness and corruption. The inhabitants of Gondor, Faramir explains, grew spoiled by their easy lives, and forgot about the necessity of constantly striving for good and defending themselves against evil. Faramir does not mention his brother in his tale, but indeed we might say the same things about Boromir—a good man who, in the face of temptation, became open to corruption and evil.

BOOK IV, CHAPTER 6

SUMMARY — THE FORBIDDEN POOL

Frodo is awakened late in the night, as Faramir seeks advice on a matter. Frodo asks whether it is morning already, and Faramir tells him the dawn is just breaking, but that they must leave right away.

Faramir takes the hobbit to a cliff by the river, and Sam joins them. For a while, Frodo wonders why he was roused from sleep to come watch the river. Sam, too, is curious. He remarks on the beauty of the landscape, but suggests it is not enough to justify getting up so early in the morning. Faramir says that the landscape is not the reason they have come. He tells Frodo to look down and identify a small, dark creature moving in the water. Frodo gazes down and recognizes Gollum, who has followed them, unseen by Faramir's men until now. Faramir asks what kind of a creature it is. His men inquire as to whether they should try to kill it or not. Frodo begs them not to do so.

Faramir asks whether Gollum knows about the treasure Frodo is carrying. Frodo replies that Gollum does know about it, and indeed carried it himself for some time. Now, Frodo explains, Gollum just wants fish to eat. Faramir's guard reminds his lord that the punishment for anyone trespassing in their kingdom is death. Frodo offers to speak to Gollum instead. Frodo goes down to the water and addresses the creature, who pouts about having been abandoned and refuses to come. Finally, Frodo persuades Gollum to leave the water, leading him toward the area where Faramir's men are waiting for him. The men apprehend Gollum, who feels betrayed by Frodo and spits on him as he is led away.

Faramir demands to interrogate Gollum, who initially refuses to cooperate. Frodo tries to persuade the creature to trust him. Faramir asks whether Gollum has ever been in this area before. Gollum claims he has not. Faramir does not believe Gollum, but he ultimately accepts the truthfulness of the creature's statement. Frodo sticks with his assertion that Gollum should not be harmed, begging Faramir's men not to hurt Gollum. Faramir agrees, on the condition that Gollum be considered Frodo's servant.

However, Faramir privately warns Frodo to be wary of Gollum, whom he still does not trust. Faramir says that there is evil growing in Gollum, and that he is curious about how this "creeping thing" came into the possession of the Ring earlier. Faramir says that one day, when he and Frodo are old and chair-bound, Frodo can tell him the story. Faramir also warns against Frodo's passing over the mountains, saying that there is great danger there. Frodo replies that this is the only way he can go, as he must avoid the gates of Mordor that they passed earlier. Faramir says it is a hopeless task.

ANALYSIS

In this chapter, Tolkien explores the idea of treachery from a surprising new angle, as Frodo is forced to betray—or at least to trick—Gollum into leaving the water and walking right up to where Faramir's men are waiting for him. Ironically, though Frodo does indeed save Gollum's life—Faramir's guards are ready to kill the creature for trespassing in their realm—in doing so he is forced to betray Gollum. The fact that Gollum, for all his whining and seeming deceitfulness, still manages to elicit our pity when Frodo betrays him highlights the creature's complex character. Tolkien's portrayal of Gollum as a somewhat childish creature who resorts to simple flattery of the hobbits makes him somewhat pitiable and pathetic, helplessly enslaved to the lure of the Ring. Furthermore, our identification with Frodo is somewhat complicated by the fact that this episode is the first time we have ever seen Frodo do anything willfully deceitful to another individual. When Gollum spits in Frodo's face after his capture, it is hard not to feel a bit sorry for the creature. On the whole, this episode contributes to Tolkien's exploration of the ambiguity of good and evil and marks the psychological and moral complexity of which Tolkien is capable.

The hobbits are wrong in their initial thought that Faramir is forcing them awake in the wee hours of the morning merely to look at beautiful scenery, but the episode does nonetheless remind us that the beauty of the landscape is a significant feature in *The Lord of the Rings*. Here, in Faramir's realm, the landscape is overwhelmingly beautiful, a sharp contrast to the barrenness and outward evil of Mordor. The waterfall known as the Window on the West, which functions as a cover for Faramir's hideaway, creates a natural panorama that even the tired and hungry hobbits are delighted to admire. Indeed, perhaps the most significant aspect of Tolkien's portrayal of the natural world in this section is that the characters within the novel themselves—not merely the narrator—are struck by the beauty of the world around them, rather than taking it for granted. Frodo and Sam are awed by the beauty of the early dawn on the cliffs even though they are still half-asleep. Here, as we see with the Ents, Tolkien infuses the novel with a powerful ecological awareness prescient for its time.

Tolkien often uses techniques of literary flashback and flash-forward that keep us in tune with the overall course of the novel, rather than sweeping us away in the drama of the moment. When Faramir, for instance, tells Frodo that he would like to find out how Gollum came to possess and then lose the Ring, we are reminded of that sequence of events as it transpired in *The Hobbit* and was recounted in *The Fellowship of the Ring*. Furthermore, Faramir says that perhaps one day, when he and Frodo are old, Frodo can tell him Gollum's story. This idea expands the novel's horizon to the distant future, opening our imagination to what these characters will be like many years off. Tolkien gives us, then, more than just the hobbits' quest to Mordor, but also a vast saga that stretches on far beyond the bounds of the novel.

BOOK IV, CHAPTERS 7–8

SUMMARY — CHAPTER 7: JOURNEY TO THE CROSS-ROADS

Faramir bids farewell to Frodo and Sam as the hobbits continue their journey into Mordor. He warns them to beware of the territory nearby, and never to drink from any of the waters flowing out of Imlad Morgul, the Valley of Living Death. Faramir presents Frodo and Sam with packed food for their journey, as well as staves to support them in their fatigue. Gollum is brought out of captivity, and all three are blindfolded as they are taken out of Faramir's hideaway.

As the journey continues, Gollum reports that the area is dangerous and full of watching eyes. Frodo asks whether a dark shape in the distance is the valley of Morgul. Gollum answers that it is indeed the valley, and says that they must move quickly to a place called the Cross-roads.

One night, Frodo and Sam awaken to find Gollum gone. Sam expresses relief that they are finally free of him, but Frodo reminds him of the help Gollum has given them in the past. Sam is suspicious, believing Gollum to be capable of tricks. Meanwhile, the atmosphere is changing; the daylight is somewhat dark and the air feels heavy and warm. One afternoon, Gollum wakes Frodo and Sam with an urgent entreaty to get moving as soon as possible. He directs them eastward, up a slope to the Southward Road, which leads to the place he calls the Cross-roads. Gollum asserts that this is the only way to go. As they proceed toward the Southward Road, they spot a headless statue of one of the ancient kings of Gondor, now desecrated with graffiti. Sam finds the head lying nearby, a crown of golden flowers growing on it. Frodo comments that the forces of the evil Sauron cannot hold sway forever in the realm.

Summary — Chapter 8: The Stairs of Cirith Ungol

Gollum draws Sam and Frodo away from their rapt contemplation of the statue, telling them that time is short. He guides them along the Southward Road until they reach the valley of Minas Morgul. All three are momentarily transfixed by the sight of the Tower of the Moon rising in the distance, but Gollum finally urges them onward again. The way is hard, and the land is full of a horrid stench that makes it hard for the hobbits to breathe. Frodo begs for a moment's rest, but Gollum and Sam insist on continuing. As they start moving again, Minas Morgul erupts in a deafening thunder, and troops appear. Frodo sees a great mass of cavalrymen all dressed in sable, guided by a horseman whom Frodo identifies as the Lord of the Nazgûl.

Suddenly, the horseman stops, and Frodo fears that he has spotted them. Frodo stands still, but almost against his will his hand moves toward the Ring hanging on his neck, which would give him the strength needed to confront the Lord of the Nazgûl. Frodo also touches the phial of Galadriel, which he had forgotten. Luckily, the Ringwraith ends his watchful pause and continues on his way.

Frodo remains extremely distressed, however. He fears that he has taken too long to reach Mordor and that it is too late to fulfill his mission of destroying the Ring. Gollum, however, urges the hobbits steadily onward, up an interminable set of stairs. Frodo becomes dizzy and feels that he cannot go on, but Gollum forces them to continue. Frodo looks down and sees that they are above Minas Morgul.

After what seems like miles uphill on the stairs of Cirith Ungol, as the twisting mountain is called, Gollum leads Frodo and Sam into a dark crevice to rest. They discuss the question of whether there is water at these heights and whether it is drinkable. The two hobbits fall into a discussion of the old songs and prophecies, wondering whether they themselves will become characters in future songs, sung by their own children perhaps.

Frodo and Sam also talk about how trustworthy Gollum is. Frodo asserts that no matter how selfish Gollum may be, he is no friend of the Orcs, and therefore may be considered a reliable guide. One night, Sam awakens to find Gollum caressing the sleeping Frodo. Sam accuses Gollum of sneaking around in the dark. Gollum is offended, saying he was not sneaking. Frodo wakes and settles the argument, telling Gollum he is free to go off by himself if he wishes. Gollum affirms that he must guide the hobbits to the end.

ANALYSIS — CHAPTERS 7–8

The headless, graffiti-covered statue the hobbits discover on the way to Mordor is an example of the poetic moments that are sprinkled throughout *The Lord of the Rings*. The statue has no importance whatsoever to the plot, and Frodo and Sam learn nothing they need to know from it. They simply see the statue and continue on their journey. Yet the statue nevertheless has an aura of deep meaning, not only for the hobbits, who pay it such rapt attention that Gollum must drag them away, but for us as well. The broken statue of an ancient king of Gondor may be Tolkien's reference to the poem "Ozymandias" by Percy Bysshe Shelley, one of the most prominent figures in the Romantic movement in English poetry in the early nineteenth century. Tolkien, a professor of Anglo-Saxon literature at Oxford, was certainly familiar with the poem, which tells of a wanderer in the desert who comes upon the beheaded statue of a once-great Egyptian king now forgotten. Shelley's poem is a meditation on how worldly power vanishes with time, and how the mighty are fallen. In this regard, the headless statue is a fitting symbol of the kingdom of Gondor, where wicked usurpers have replaced the once-powerful noble lords.

The Cross-roads to which Gollum leads the hobbits may be another sly literary reference on Tolkien's part. As the word cross-roads suggests, Gollum is leading the hobbits to a place where one thing will meet another, where an encounter will take place. Indeed, Frodo does have an encounter of sorts, with the Lord of the Nazgûl—the embodiment of all against which Frodo and the Fellowship have been fighting against. In literature, the concept of the crossroads has another meaning as well, relating not to other people, but to oneself. It is on a crossroads that Oedipus, perhaps the most famous Greek tragic hero, kills a stranger who turns out to be his father. Later, as king of Thebes, Oedipus strives to identify the killer, and is horrified to learn that it is none other than himself—a revelation that leads him to misery and exile. Oedipus's experience at the crossroads teaches him the power of fate, the fact that no one can escape responsibility for his or her actions. Frodo has a similar revelation at the Cross-roads in the novel, when, in his fear of the Lord of the Nazgûl, he finds himself reaching for the Ring. Frodo has not felt the Ring's pull or been tempted to put it on for quite some time in the journey. For the first time in a long while, he confronts his own power, which could prove dangerous as he gets ever closer to Mordor.

The importance of songs and singing resurfaces again in Chapter 8 in an interesting new way, as Sam and Frodo explicitly speculate that their own quest might someday be the subject of songs. Songs have been sung in the novel frequently, never as mere entertainment but as a record of historical or prophetic knowledge. Tolkien knew from his study of ancient cultures that before the invention of writing, cultures maintained their traditions and myths through the oral performance of their sacred stories. Such deeply important cultural communication was passed on through songs and poems rather than through manuscripts. Gandalf reminds us of this role of oral storytelling when he gives Legolas and Aragorn important messages about their fates by reciting bits of poetry to them in Chapter 5. Here, Sam and Frodo discuss the cultural importance of songs, but they do so with the awareness that they themselves might be characters in songs sung by their own offspring. This speculation on the hobbits' part is a key moment that makes us realize that *The Lord of the Rings* is itself a chronicle, just like the songs of Middle-earth, and that the characters realize that they might themselves end up in a narrative very much like the one we are reading.

We see an intriguing aspect of Gollum when Sam awakens to find the creature caressing Frodo with the appearance of love and affection. It is no surprise that Sam views Gollum's action with suspicion, and accuses Gollum of "sneaking" around his master. What is surprising instead is that Gollum really does appear innocent. We have been so used to viewing the creature with uncertainty, doubting his loyalty to the hobbits he is serving, that it is a shock to encounter the possibility that he may genuinely care for Frodo. Of course, we find out later that Gollum plans to kill the hobbits, but in the world of the Ring, it is no surprise that murder and affection can go hand in hand. For the moment, at least, Gollum seems truly fond of the master whom he leads to death.

BOOK IV, CHAPTERS 9–10

SUMMARY — CHAPTER 9: SHELOB'S LAIR

Gollum leads Sam and Frodo to a dark stone wall and to a cave within it, which they enter. The smell is overwhelmingly bad. Gollum reports that the cave is the entrance to a tunnel, but he does not say its name, Shelob's Lair. Despite the possibility that the cave is filled with Orcs, Sam and Frodo know that they must enter.

The tunnel is totally dark, and the hobbits proceed by feeling the walls. Strangely, Gollum disappears, leaving the hobbits to find their way themselves. Suddenly, Frodo is aware of an intense feeling of hostility and danger emanating from the darkness. They hear a bubbling hiss, but can see nothing. Sam shouts to Frodo to raise the phial of Galadriel, a small container blessed by Galadriel that Frodo wears around his neck. The phial shines a strong light that illuminates hundreds of tiny eyes, all of them staring at the hobbits. The eyes belong to Shelob, a giant spider-monster ever hungry for creatures to devour, used by the evil Sauron to guard his passages.

Frodo is terrified, but he walks boldly toward the eyes, which retreat as he advances. The hobbits head for the end of the tunnel, but are held up by cobwebs stretched across the passageway. The cobwebs are too strong to be cut by a knife, and the hobbits fear they are trapped until Frodo remembers Sting, his Elf-made knife. They cut their way through, and the hobbits are within view of the exit from the tunnel. Frodo shouts that they should run and pulls ahead. Sam lifts the phial to see, notices that there are orcs ahead, though, and hides the phial. Suddenly Shelob attacks, moving swiftly between Sam and Frodo. Sam shouts a warning to his master, but he is silenced by the clammy hand of Gollum, who has betrayed the hobbits by leading them to Shelob. Sam removes himself from Gollum's grasp and threatens to stab him, but Gollum moves quickly away.

SUMMARY — CHAPTER 10: THE CHOICES OF MASTER SAMWISE

In the midst of the struggle with the spider-monster Shelob, Sam discovers Frodo lying face up, paralyzed by the spider's poison. The sight of his master in such an awful state fills Sam with courage and rage, and he charges Shelob. He manages to stab her in one eye, which goes dark. Heaving her belly up over Sam, Shelob prepares to crush the hobbit, but instead impales herself on his sword. Shelob shudders in pain and withdraws. Sam rushes to Frodo, and then charges Shelob again. The defeated spider flees. Sam calls out to Frodo, whom he at first believes to be asleep.

When Sam suddenly realizes that Frodo may be dead, he is stricken by the thought that he himself must now carry out the mission of destroying the Ring. He is upset by the idea of taking the Ring from Frodo's body and carrying it himself, remembering that it was originally entrusted only to Frodo. But Sam decides that, as Frodo's companion, he may legitimately inherit the mission. Sam takes the Ring. He attempts to flee, but hears Orc voices surrounding him. Without reflecting on his actions, Sam puts on the Ring, and feels as though the world has changed. As a result of wearing the

Ring, Sam can understand the Orc language perfectly. The Orcs take up Frodo's paralyzed body and carry it away.

Sam follows behind, listening to the guards' conversation. One Orc, named Shagrat, is telling the other, Gorbag, that Shelob has been wounded. Gorbag is impressed that any creature was able to hurt Shelob and cut through the cords of her cobwebs. He imagines that the creature must be very powerful indeed. Shagrat announces that the orders given from above are to retrieve Frodo safe and sound, with a careful examination of all his possessions. Gorbag wonders whether Frodo is even alive at all, but Shagrat affirms that Shelob only eats living flesh, so that Frodo must still be living, although stunned. Sam is amazed to hear that Frodo is alive. The Orc guards carrying Frodo slam the doors behind them. Sam still has the Ring, but is separated from his friend.

ANALYSIS — CHAPTERS 9–10

Frodo and Sam's encounter with the revolting monster Shelob is the culminating danger of their journey. The spider represents a danger different from their previous trials in several ways. For one thing, the hobbits' encounter with Shelob marks the first time that any character in the novel has tricked them into danger. Before this point, the dangers they face have always been obvious and undisguised: the Nazgûl flying overhead to spy on them, the Uruk-hai kidnapping them, and the guards of Gondor mistaking them for fugitive murderers. Those tests of endurance have been difficult, but overt. With Gollum's treachery comes a new case of a trial, one that stems from deception and wrongful trust. Gollum does not attack the hobbits or threaten them, as their previous enemies have done, but tricks them by winning their confidence over an extended period. As an enemy, the pathetic Gollum now appears more dangerous than all the others, as he has played upon the natural goodness of the hobbits and exploited it to his own advantage. In a sense, Frodo recalls the tradition of the tragic heroes of ancient Greek drama, as he suffers because of his tragic flaw of excessive trust.

As Frodo's nemesis, Shelob is different from previous villains in the novel in a variety of other ways. Unlike Saruman or Wormtongue, the giant spider-monster is incapable of speech, and even perhaps of rational thought. She is a creature of instinct, following only her hungry stomach. She does not care for world domination like Sauron; in fact, we learn that she is much older than Sauron, and dwelt in her cave long before the Dark Lord ever came to rule over Mordor. Shelob is a surprising figure of evil as she is an animal, and it is somewhat hard for us to imagine animals being so thoroughly and inherently evil. Moreover, the great danger Shelob represents is the first and only appearance of an evil female force in *The Lord of the Rings*. The narrator hammers home the point that Shelob is female, repeatedly calling the spider "She." Furthermore, the narrator explicitly tells us how Shelob devours her babies, making her a perverse mother figure. Readers of Tolkien often remark on how few women appear in his works, so it is noteworthy that Frodo's closest and most fearsome brush with death comes at the hand of a female.

As the title of Chapter 10 indicates, the novel ends with a surprising focus not on Frodo, who has been the protagonist and Ring-bearer for all of the novel thus far, but rather on Sam. It is Sam who cuts through Shelob's web with his knife Sting, and it is Sam who assumes possession of the Ring—and takes on all the responsibility that goes along with it. The servant steps into the limelight and accepts the burden, no longer a follower but a hero. Indeed, the decisions Sam makes in this chapter arguably demonstrate more quick thinking and courage than anything we have seen from Frodo. For all his sense of inferiority and servility, Sam may be made of stronger stuff than the hobbit he considers his master. The larger moral lesson of this revelation is clear: anyone may have the inner potential for heroism, no matter how insignificant his or her social rank may seem. In a moment of hardship and challenge, even the lowliest person may emerge as the figurative Ring-bearer and the savior of the world.

The last pages of *The Two Towers* leave us in great suspense, making us rush to start reading the third volume in Tolkien's novel. In part, the suspense is simply plot-related, as we want to find out whether Sam is capable of handling the Ring-bearer role and whether he has what it takes to fulfill the hobbits' mission. The personal and emotional aspect of the novel's conclusion, however, is equally suspenseful. Sam and Frodo have been such a close team throughout Book IV that it is hard to imagine what might happen now that they are separated. When the Orc guards slam the gates in Sam's face, denying him access to Frodo, we wonder whether Sam's extraordinary devotion to Frodo will be an impediment in the grand role he has assumed for himself. Now that Sam has the Ring, he could go his own way. Yet his attachment to Frodo may keep him from doing so. The choice between commitment to one's friends and the need to follow one's own destiny will no doubt be a difficult one for Sam.

Important Quotations Explained

1.   *Pippin looked behind. The number of the Ents had grown—*
     or what was happening? Where the dim bare slopes that
     they had crossed should lie, he thought he saw groves of
     trees. But they were moving! Could it be that the trees of
     Fangorn were awake, and the forest was rising, marching
     over the hills to war?

The march of the army of treelike Ents at the end of Book III, Chapter 4, indicates the universality of the War of the Ring in the context
of the entire realm of Middle-earth. The struggle for the Ring is not
a mere squabble between greedy parties who yearn for a magic
object to enhance their personal power. Nor is the Ring an ancient
heirloom fought over in some otherworldly realm that has little to
do with the more immediate world of Men. Rather, the struggle for
the Ring involves the whole cosmos, the entire scale of creation from
top to bottom. Even the trees, which normally sleep through the various disturbances and conflicts of Men, as Fangorn tells us, cannot
remain uninvolved in this battle. Their march to war here symbolizes not just another party joining the action, but rather the involvement of all creation in the struggle against evil.

Pippin's amazement at the spectacle of the moving trees is also
our amazement, as the hobbit reflects our reaction to the extraordinary events of Middle-earth. Unlike other fantasy novels in which
the characters are accustomed to the events that occur in their
world—however bizarre they may seem to us as readers—Pippin is
just as flabbergasted as we are. Tolkien emphasizes the psychology
of the scene by allowing us to read Pippin's thoughts as they appear
in his mind. "Or what was happening?" and "Could it be that . . . ?"
are not the authoritative statements of the narrator, but private
questions that Pippin is asking himself. This inward, psychological
focus helps us keep a more personal perspective on the surreal and
epic events unfolding in the novel.

2.   *"[Y]ou are our captain and our banner. The Dark Lord has Nine. But we have One, mightier than they: the White Rider. He has passed through the fire and the abyss, and they shall fear him. We will go where he leads."*

Aragorn pays this homage to Gandalf in Book III, Chapter 5, revealing much about what leadership and warfare mean in this novel. The struggle between good and evil is clearly no conventional military encounter, as Aragorn makes no mention of the number of troops on the field, their weaponry, or their deployment in battle lines. The fact that the Enemy has eight more military commanders than his own army does not trouble Aragorn in the slightest. The traditional concerns of warriors appear to be of no interest to him. The war between the West and Sauron is a higher sort of struggle, requiring spiritual rather than material forces. It is a highly symbolic war, which explains why Aragorn calls the West's effective leader, Gandalf, not just a captain but a "banner" as well. It is unusual for a single person to be described as a banner, as banners advertise the abstract emblems or causes for which an army or other group is fighting. But, in fact, Gandalf is his own emblem, as he is fighting for good and is himself a powerful symbol of good.

The quotation also reveals much about what inspires trust in Gandalf's followers. There is no mention of the wizard's military skill or brilliance at tactical maneuvers. What seems to inspire Aragorn the most is that Gandalf "has passed through the fire and the abyss." In this regard, personal suffering defines a great leader. Gandalf's fire-tempered resolve and will are what will terrify his enemies, says Aragorn—not the wizard's talents at warfare. This characterization is a psychological benchmark by which to judge a good commander, but it is precisely the point of the entire novel, which values spiritual ideals of goodness and fellowship over outward accomplishments. Tolkien's tale emphasizes that one's inner life and personality determine one's success far more than external achievements—or, rather, they make those achievements possible. The highly developed inner spirit that Gandalf displays is enough to command the servitude of even a great leader such as Aragorn.

3. *"I did not give you leave to go," said Gandalf sternly. "I have not finished. You have become a fool, Saruman, and yet pitiable. You might still have turned away from folly and evil, and have been of service. But you choose to stay and gnaw the ends of your own plots."*

Gandalf's fierce rebuke of Saruman in Book III, Chapter 10, shows us the relationship between the good wizard and his former superior, now his enemy. Gandalf speaks "sternly" to Saruman, as a parent might speak to a disobedient child, telling the corrupt wizard that he does not have permission to leave until the lecture is over. Adults of similar rank do not speak to each other in this condescending manner, even when they are angry. Rather, Gandalf's is the tone taken by one who clearly feels superior to the person he is addressing. Indeed, Gandalf does feel superior to Saruman, and he is not ashamed to say as much. Gandalf's superiority is not based on power or prestige; after all, Saruman was the leader of Gandalf's order, and Gandalf addresses even those below him with extreme respect. Instead, Gandalf's sense of superiority stems from the incorrect moral choices Saruman has made, which have cost him considerable respect. Gandalf's association of "folly" with evil reflects this lack of esteem, as if only fools play at being wicked.

Tolkien implies here that evil is something chosen, rather than a cosmic force that sweeps innocent people up and corrupts them. Gandalf stresses that, until recently, it was still possible for Saruman to repent his ways: "You might still have turned away from folly and evil. . . ." Saruman might have, but he did not: he made a choice, and it was the wrong one. After that, Gandalf again emphasizes, "[Y]ou choose to stay." Such a conception of morality as free choice is important in Tolkien's universe. As grand and dramatic as the tale of *The Lord of the Rings* is, its definition of good and evil is very traditional. Every being, from the humblest Dwarf to the mightiest Wizard, chooses a course of action in life and then accepts the consequences.

4. *"Yess, wretched we are, precious," [Gollum] whined.*
    "Misery misery! Hobbits won't kill us, nice hobbits."
       "No, we won't," said Frodo. "But we won't let you go,
    either. You're full of wickedness and mischief. . . ."

This dialogue between Frodo and Gollum, when the hobbits first
encounter the creature and tame him in Book IV, Chapter 1, gives us
a clear picture of Frodo's characteristic frankness. The hobbits do
not owe Gollum any explanations about why they are forced to
keep him captive. Other creatures, such as Orcs, kidnap the hobbits
without giving them the slightest indication of why they are being
captured or where they will be taken, as with Merry and Pippin's
capture in Book III. Frodo, however, is an honorable character, and
he insists on being straightforward with Gollum about his impres-
sions of the creature's wickedness and mischief. Frodo is neither
silent nor evasive, but upfront and honest. Moreover, he never creates
the impression of being intoxicated with his own power. His casual
way of saying "But we won't let you go, either" displays none of the
grandiose posturing that Saruman, for instance, would show if he had
the opportunity to inform someone of his captivity. For Frodo, power is
just a fact, not a justification for complacency or bullying.

This passage also showcases Gollum's sneaky and deceptive personality, which distinguishes him from the other evil characters in
the novel, who, for the most part, are just what they appear to be.
Gollum's self-abasing remarks, such as "wretched we are," along
with his incessant whining, are not imaginable in other evil characters, such as Saruman. Gollum whines and puts himself down in
order to play on the hobbits' sympathy—a tactic that works better
on the trusting Frodo than on the skeptical Sam. Frodo's goodwill is
his weak point, as we find out later, when Gollum ultimately betrays
the hobbits. Indeed, this tiny conversation between Frodo and Gollum is an ironic foreshadowing of the creature's final treachery in
Shelob's lair. Here, Frodo tells Gollum that he is "full of wickedness," and we realize later how tragically true this assertion is.

5. *"[T]he old wisdom and beauty brought out of the West*
    remained long in the realm of the sons of Elendil the Fair,
    and they linger there still. Yet even so it was Gondor that
    brought about its own decay, falling by degrees into dotage,
    and thinking that the Enemy was asleep, who was only
    banished not destroyed."

Faramir recounts the history of the fall of Gondor to Frodo and Sam in Book IV, Chapter 5. Faramir's words remind us of the constant sense throughout the novel that the world of Middle-earth is changing. Nearly all the characters the hobbits encounter on their wanderings remark that they cannot afford to be as hospitable to strangers as they used to be—they are living in "dark times," as Éomer puts it. The world is a more confusing place than it was before, and visitors are not always who they seem. The old ways and traditions do not apply as they used to, for a new world order is emerging. This change is not always for the better, as the history of Gondor illustrates. The ancient Lords of Gondor were once proud and free, but the entire realm now lives in fear of Sauron. Gondor was once a blossoming land of orchards and gardens, but is now barren and deteriorating. The reality of decay is symbolized in the headless and graffiti-covered statue of an early king of Gondor that Frodo and Sam come upon in their travels.

The causes for these changes in the world of Middle-earth are not concerns of economics or politics, which we never hear about in the course of the novel. We do not see or hear of merchants' disputes or groups clamoring for recognition by states or governments. Indeed, economics and politics are almost entirely absent from Tolkien's worldview. The main motivating force behind world history in The Lord of the Rings is morality and the strength that supports it. The "wisdom and beauty" of which Faramir speaks here are really shorthand terms for moral good and strength of character. The fall of Gondor was caused by rulers who took the morality of their kingdom for granted, forgetting that it needed to be defended against evil, as the Fellowship is now trying to do. The clash between good and evil keeps history moving, and keeps the world in constant flux as the balance between the two opposing forces changes over time.

KEY FACTS

FULL TITLE
  The Two Towers, being the second part of The Lord of the Rings

AUTHOR
  J.R.R. Tolkien

TYPE OF WORK
  Novel

GENRE
  Epic; heroic quest; folktale; fantasy; myth

LANGUAGE
  English, with occasional words and phrases from various
  languages of Middle-earth that Tolkien invented

TIME AND PLACE WRITTEN
  1937–1949; Oxford, England

DATE OF FIRST PUBLICATION
  1954

PUBLISHER
  Allen and Unwin

NARRATOR
  The whole of The Lord of the Rings is told by an anonymous,
  third-person narrator.

POINT OF VIEW
  The Two Towers is narrated in the third person, primarily
  following the exploits of Merry and Pippin in Book III and the
  exploits of Frodo and particularly Sam in Book IV. The narration
  is omniscient, which means the narrator not only relates the
  characters' thoughts and feelings, but also comments on them.

TONE
  The narrator is unobtrusive, not allowing himself any authorial
  commentaries on the fate of the characters or any exclamations
  about the story as it unfolds. The tone is somewhat reminiscent
  of the tone used in the Odyssey and other ancient poetic epics: it
  focuses on actions in a simple, direct manner, and generally

avoids psychological explorations in the narrative. There are minor exceptions to this rule, especially in the narration of the thoughts and feelings of the hobbits at moments of crisis, but these are infrequent.

TENSE
Past

SETTING (TIME)
The end of the Third Age of Middle-earth

SETTING (PLACE)
Various locales in the imaginary world of Middle-earth, including Rohan, the Forest of Fangorn, Edoras, Helm's Deep, Isengard, and Mordor

PROTAGONIST
Primarily Merry and Pippin in Book III and Frodo and Sam in Book IV, though the Fellowship as a whole might be considered a single protagonist

MAJOR CONFLICT
Frodo struggles with the ever-heavier burden of the Ring as he and Sam convey it to Mordor. Meanwhile, Gandalf attempts to obstruct Saruman's quest to gain power in support of Mordor.

RISING ACTION
Boromir's death; Aragorn's attempt to reunite his group with the hobbits after the battle separates them; Aragorn's meeting with Gandalf, and later Pippin and Merry; the group's collective pursuit of Frodo and Sam; Frodo and Sam's wanderings, and their acceptance of Gollum as a guide; Frodo and Sam's passage into Mordor

CLIMAX
Gollum's betrayal of Frodo and Sam; the hobbits' struggle with the spider-monster Shelob

FALLING ACTION
Frodo's paralysis from Shelob's bite; Sam's assumption of the role of Ring-bearer; Sam's anguished uncertainty about how to proceed with the quest

THEMES
The decay of civilization; the value of fellowship; duty

KEY FACTS

MOTIFS
Songs and singing; the natural world; suspicion

SYMBOLS
The two towers; the palantír; Pippin's pipe; the Dead Marshes

FORESHADOWING
Frodo's assertion that Gollum is full of wickedness; Sam's repeated doubts about Gollum's trustworthiness

KEY FACTS

STUDY QUESTIONS & ESSAY TOPICS

STUDY QUESTIONS

1. *Tolkien chooses to keep Frodo entirely absent from Book III, directing our attention instead to the wanderings of Merry, Pippin, and Aragorn's group. Why does the main protagonist of the novel not appear in Book III at all?*

One reason Tolkien chooses to focus on characters other than Frodo in Book III may simply be to create suspense and reader involvement in the story. A missing major character in a novel always arouses our curiosity, keeping us turning the pages to find out what has happened to him or her. Furthermore, our lack of awareness of the whereabouts of Frodo, and of the Ring as well, makes us sympathize more closely with the other characters, who are in search of Frodo. We are just as clueless as to his location as the others are, and the similarity of our situations causes us to feel as though we are part of the group pursuing the missing hobbit.

Another possible reason for Frodo's absence is more symbolic, related to the idea of fellowship that gives the first volume of the novel—*The Fellowship of the Ring*—its title. A constant focus on Frodo throughout *The Two Towers* might give the mistaken impression that Frodo matters more than the other characters—that he is the main figure, while Sam, Pippin, Merry, Aragorn, and the others are minor background characters. But Frodo is not any more heroic than the others are. He is just one part of the whole, as are all the members of the Fellowship. They work together, unlike their enemies, such as Saruman and Sauron, who follow only their own private ambitions. Focusing on the other characters throughout Book III helps remind us that the Fellowship as a whole is more important than any individual member.

2. *Though there are several figures of powerful evil in the novel, such as Sauron and Saruman, the greatest and most immediate danger to Frodo is arguably Gollum, one of the weakest characters in the novel. Why do you think Tolkien has Frodo fall prey to such a small, pathetic creature rather than a much more powerful evil force?*

It is indeed noteworthy that Frodo's downfall comes in the guise not of the dark Lord of the Nazgûl or the sinister Saruman, but in the somewhat ridiculous Gollum. Gollum is not at all a majestic figure: Tolkien emphasizes the creature's absurd side by showing us how he constantly whines and pouts, and how he squirms and squeals when he feels uncomfortable. As Gollum seems more interested in getting fish in his belly than in ruling the universe, we hardly expect him to be the one to cause Frodo's undoing. In part, Tolkien may choose Gollum as the culprit just for the sake of our surprise. It is more thrilling to have the danger come from an unexpected source than it would be to have Frodo attacked by an Orc-chieftain or a Nazgûl.

Tolkien may also select Gollum to be Frodo's undoing for more psychological reasons. As we have frequently observed, Frodo is a kind and generous soul, and Gollum preys upon Frodo's kindness by flattering the hobbit, making himself appear weak and vulnerable, and pretending to be a loyal servant. Unlike the wary Sam, Frodo is all too ready to see the positive side of Gollum and to try to ignore the wickedness in the creature, of which he is nevertheless aware. Frodo is not stupid, and he clearly knows Gollum to be capable of horrid deeds, but his innate kindness leads him to trust a traitor. In a sense, then, Frodo causes his own downfall, making him something of a tragic hero whose fatal flaw is that he is too trusting. This sort of downfall is more complex and interesting than if Frodo were simply captured by a horde of Orcs.

3. *Saruman is arguably the primary adversary in* THE TWO
   TOWERS, *yet we learn that he and Gandalf used to be
   allies. Why does Tolkien choose to make Gandalf's
   opponent a former colleague?*

It is interesting that Saruman is not a mysterious stranger from a
wicked land, but is someone whom Gandalf knows well. A faraway
invader with evil intentions is easier to accept, as we never expect
the familiar to be as evil or mysteroius as the unfamiliar. But Tolkien
chooses to maximize the shared background of the two wizards in
order to show how little separates them, and how similar they could
still be. They are not that different, as we see from the fact that Gimli
mistakes Gandalf for Saruman when the wizard appears in the forest. Both wizards are old men who wear broad-brimmed hats and
cloaks. This physical similarity is significant, reminding us that
Saruman could be like Gandalf if he chose to be. Gandalf's former
affiliation with Saruman emphasizes the fact that magic is magic,
and that great Wizards may have similarly profound skills even
when they differ in the ways they choose to apply these powers.
Good magic and evil magic both derive from the same origin. Gandalf and Saruman do not differ in blood, brains, or background—
the only difference is in the moral choices they make.

SUGGESTED ESSAY TOPICS

1. *Which of the main characters in* THE TWO TOWERS *changes the most throughout the course of the story? Does Frodo change by the end in any way?*

2. *Though Gollum is clearly hateful and scheming, Tolkien emphasizes a childish, even innocent side to Gollum as well. At times, the creature appears almost sympathetic. Why do you think Tolkien shows this soft side of Gollum?*

3. *Critics often note how few of the major characters in* THE LORD OF THE RINGS *are female. Why do you think Tolkien's Middle-earth is so male dominated? Does the absence of women change the world in which the characters live?*

4. *Discuss the role of prophecy in the novel. Why are prophecies so important, but frequently also so vague?*

5. *Cooperation and fellowship figure prominently in the novel, as characters of many races cooperate in the war against Sauron. Conversely, characters who act on their own— Boromir, Saruman, and Sauron, for instance—often do so corruptly. Does this pattern imply that Tolkien is against individualism in general? Or is he only against a certain kind of individualism?*

REVIEW & RESOURCES

QUIZ

1. Who kills Boromir?

    A. A horde of Orcs
    B. Shelob
    C. Gandalf
    D. Pippin

2. Whom is Aragorn pursuing at the opening of *The Two Towers*?

    A. Faramir
    B. Merry and Pippin
    C. Gandalf
    D. Saruman

3. What is Legolas's special ability?

    A. Extraordinary hearing
    B. Extraordinary eyesight
    C. An ability to predict the future
    D. Incredible running speed

4. What are the Uruk-hai?

    A. Magic weapons
    B. A special breed of horses used in battle
    C. A special breed of Orcs
    D. The inhabitants of the Entwash

5. What type of creature is Fangorn?

    A. An Orc
    B. An Ent
    C. A Nazgûl
    D. A Hobbit

6.   What is an Entmoot?

    A.   An Entish article of clothing
    B.   A meeting of Ents
    C.   An Entish household
    D.   A traditional Entish meal

7.   What is the final decision of the Ent assembly?

    A.   To denounce Gandalf
    B.   To march against Saruman
    C.   To expel Pippin and Merry
    D.   To befriend the Uruk-hai

8.   What is the relation between Gandalf and the White Rider?

    A.   They are cousins
    B.   They are brothers
    C.   They are enemies
    D.   They are the same person

9.   Who is most closely associated with the Golden Hall?

    A.   Gandalf
    B.   Saruman
    C.   Théoden
    D.   Sauron

10.   Who controls the realm of Isengard?

    A.   Sauron
    B.   Gandalf
    C.   Théoden
    D.   Saruman

11.   Who is Éowyn?

    A.   Théoden's niece
    B.   Pippin's sister
    C.   Gandalf's daughter
    D.   Aragorn's fiancée

12. For what does Gandalf denounce Wormtongue?

    A. Destroying the Ring
    B. Betraying Théoden
    C. Misleading Pippin
    D. Killing Boromir

13. What is a *palantír*?

    A. An amulet worn around the neck
    B. An artifact of Rohan
    C. A healing potion
    D. A crystal sphere

14. How is Saruman's *palantír* separated from its owner?

    A. Orcs steal it in battle
    B. It falls off of a cliff by accident
    C. Gandalf raids the Enemy's camp and steals it
    D. Wormtongue throws it out of a window in a rage

15. Which two characters are the primary focus of the second half of *The Two Towers*?

    A. Frodo and Sam
    B. Gandalf and Saruman
    C. Merry and Pippin
    D. Théoden and Éowyn

16. For what food does Gollum frequently yearn?

    A. Bread
    B. Fish
    C. *Lembas*
    D. Chickens

17. How are Boromir and Faramir related?

    A. They are brothers
    B. They are cousins
    C. They are father and son
    D. They are not related, but are very close friends

REVIEW & RESOURCES

18. Why does Faramir blindfold Frodo and Sam?

    A.   He is about to execute them
    B.   He does not want them to see each other
    C.   He is taking them to a secret hideout
    D.   He does not want them to see his face

19. What is Gollum doing when Faramir's men spot him?

    A.   Fishing
    B.   Sleeping
    C.   Killing rabbits
    D.   Cooking

20. To what do the stairs of Cirith Ungol lead?

    A.   Shelob's lair
    B.   The top of Orthanc
    C.   The Mines of Moria
    D.   The Golden Hall

21. What does Gollum call the Ring?

    A.   His "Beloved"
    B.   His "Darling"
    C.   His "Beauty"
    D.   His "Precious"

22. What is Shelob?

    A.   A giant worm
    B.   A giant snake
    C.   A giant spider
    D.   A giant scorpion

23. What does the phial of Galadrial provide?

    A.   Light
    B.   Healing
    C.   Prophecy
    D.   An endless supply of water

24. How do Sam and Frodo overcome the obstacle of Shelob's cobwebs?

   A. Sam dissolves the webs with Orc-liquor
   B. Frodo cuts through the webs with Sting
   C. Sam finds a hidden passage below the webs
   D. Frodo unties the webs

25. In what state does Sam find Frodo after Shelob's attack?

   A. Alive, but paralyzed
   B. Unharmed, but terrified
   C. Alive, but bleeding profusely
   D. Dead

ANSWER KEY:

1: A; 2: B; 3: B; 4: C; 5: B; 6: B; 7: B; 8: D; 9: C; 10: D; 11:
A; 12: B; 13: D; 14: D; 15: A; 16: B; 17: A; 18: C; 19: A; 20:
A; 21: D; 22: C; 23: A; 24: B; 25: A

THE RETURN OF
THE KING

PLOT OVERVIEW

THE RETURN OF THE KING, the third and final volume in *The Lord of the Rings,* opens as Gandalf and Pippin ride east to the city of Minas Tirith in Gondor, just after parting with King Théoden and the Riders of Rohan at the end of *The Two Towers.* In Minas Tirith, Gandalf and Pippin meet Denethor, the city's Steward, or ruler, who clearly dislikes Gandalf. Pippin offers Denethor his sword in service to Gondor, out of gratitude for the fact that Denethor's son Boromir gave his life for the hobbits earlier in the quest.

A blanket of gloom—which Gandalf calls the Darkness—begins to issue from Mordor and soon obscures the entire sky over Minas Tirith. Meanwhile, Aragorn realizes that the Riders may not reach the city in time to defend it from the imminent conflict with Mordor. Aragorn parts company with Théoden and decides to take the legendary Paths of the Dead to Gondor. As he travels through the Paths, accompanied by Legolas and Gimli, a huge army of the Sleepless Dead heeds Aragorn's commands and follows him southward.

In Gondor, Denethor sends his other son, Faramir, to hold off the approaching armies of Mordor at Osgiliath. Faramir holds his position as long as he can, but he ultimately gives up the field, despite Gandalf's help. Retreating to the city, a poisoned arrow of the Nazgûl—the Black Riders—strikes Faramir down, though it does not kill him. Later, as the fierce battle wages outside Minas Tirith, Denethor goes mad and locks himself in a crypt with the ailing Faramir. Denethor plans to destroy the remnants of the line of Gondor's Stewards.

The army of Mordor nearly breaks through Minas Tirith's defenses, but the Riders of Rohan arrive just in time to fight the army off. The Lord of the Nazgûl, the Black Captain, kills King Théoden. In heroic defense, Lady Éowyn and Merry slay the Black Captain, though Éowyn is grievously wounded. The forces of Mordor regroup, but Aragorn arrives via the Anduin River on the black ships of the Enemy, which he has conquered with the help of the Dead.

Pippin finds Gandalf, and together they stop Denethor from killing his son. The old Steward throws himself on a burning pyre and kills himself. Having rescued Gondor, Aragorn enters Minas Tirith and heals those whom the Black Captain wounded during the battle. In so doing, Aragorn fulfills an ancient prophecy concerning the coming of the next king of Gondor.

The leaders of the armies of the West decide to put together an assault on Mordor in order to distract Sauron from the quest of Frodo, the Ring-bearer. Aragorn's forces march to the Black Gate of Mordor and confront Sauron's Lieutenant. The Lieutenant claims that the hobbit spies—Frodo and Sam—have been captured in Mordor. Gandalf rebukes the Lieutenant, who flees inside the Gate and unleashes the great armies of Mordor.

In the meantime, Sam manages to rescue Frodo from the tower of Cirith Ungol. With the aid of the Ring and his sword, Sam scares off the Orcs he encounters. The hobbits don Orc clothing and begin the arduous trek through Mordor. The Ring grows heavier around Frodo's neck with each step.

After several long and weary days of travel, the two hobbits reach Orodruin, or Mount Doom. Sam carries Frodo to the top. Just as they reach the Cracks of Doom, Frodo refuses to give up the Ring, overcome by its power. Gollum appears and struggles with Frodo. Gollum bites the Ring off Frodo's finger, but then he stumbles and falls into the Cracks of Doom. Sauron's power breaks, and Aragorn's forces at the Black Gate defeat the panicked servants of Mordor. Gandalf flies to Orodruin on the back of Gwaihir, the giant eagle, and rescues Frodo and Sam.

The Darkness dissipates from Gondor. Aragorn is crowned King of Gondor, and he marries Arwen, Elrond's daughter from Rivendell. Minas Tirith and the surrounding areas begin to recover and rebuild.

The hobbits return to the Shire, where they find their homes ravaged. A group of Men have entered and set up an oppressive police state. The four companions organize a rebellion and rout the intruders, discovering that the secret leader of the destruction is Saruman, the deposed wizard, who seeks revenge on the hobbits. Frodo spares Saruman's life, but the wizard's browbeaten servant, Wormtongue, betrays and kills his cruel master.

The hobbits rebuild the Shire and return to their ordinary lives. Sam marries a hobbit named Rosie Cotton, and together they have a daughter. Frodo, wounded by the burden of the Ring-quest, decides to leave the Shire. He sails away over the Great Sea with Gandalf, Bilbo, and the other Ring-bearers to the peaceful paradise in the unknown West.

CHARACTER LIST

THE FELLOWSHIP

Frodo Baggins The brave but unassuming hobbit who bears the Ring back to Mordor. Frodo has a quiet determination and a strength of character that establish his distinctive heroism. Increasingly affected and burdened by the Ring's power, Frodo assumes a more passive role in *The Return of the King* than in the first two volumes of *The Lord of the Rings*. Nonetheless, Frodo's ultimate struggle to overcome the temptation and burden of the Ring reminds us that an individual with less courage and moral fiber would be unable to complete the quest.

Samwise (Sam) Gamgee Frodo's loving friend and dutiful support throughout the quest, especially in its final stages. Over the course of the journey, Sam grows from an insecure sidekick to the determined and shrewd guardian of his master. Sam emerges as the true hero of *The Return of the King*, performing the physical and sacrificial deeds expected of a great hero while maintaining his humble and lighthearted nature.

Gandalf the White The great wizard, also known as Mithrandir, who leads the forces of the West. Gandalf, resurrected from his seeming death in *The Fellowship of the Ring*, functions as a soldier and a mystic, but more often as an advisor to the political rulers of the world of Men. While Gandalf possesses supernatural abilities, his powers of speech remain his greatest tool for admonishing his counterparts and rebuking his foes.

Legolas The lone Elf member of the Fellowship. Legolas, like his friend Gimli, plays a smaller role in *The Return of the King* than he does in *The Fellowship of the Ring* or *The Two Towers*. Nevertheless, he bravely represents the Elf race in Gondor's march against Mordor.

Gimli   The lone Dwarf member of the Fellowship. The headstrong Gimli dutifully traverses the Paths of the Dead with Aragorn, but he is crippled with fear throughout the journey. The trip through the Paths is narrated from Gimli's perspective.

Aragorn   The heir of Isildur and the throne of Gondor, the king to which the title *The Return of the King* refers. Aragorn, also known as Elessar or Elfstone, claims his right to the throne near the end of the novel, and takes the elf Arwen Evenstar as his queen.

Peregrin (Pippin) Took A young Hobbit member of the Fellowship. Pippin, stranded from the other hobbits in Book V, abandons his troublesome ways and acts as the intermediary between Gandalf and Denethor. Pippin is the primary focus of the narrative in the scenes in Minas Tirith in Book V.

Meriadoc (Merry) Brandybuck The fourth hobbit in the Fellowship. Merry, also stranded from his counterparts, desperately seeks the approval of King Théoden, to whom he offers his service. Merry, who sacrifices his safety for Théoden in slaying the Black Captain, is the primary focus of the chapters concerning the Riders of Rohan.

ENEMIES AND MALEVOLENT BEINGS

Sauron   The Dark Lord of Mordor and creator of the One Ring. While we never encounter Sauron himself in the novel, the far-reaching effects of the Darkness of Mordor suggest Sauron's overwhelming presence throughout Middle-earth. Sauron's Great Eye, which scans the land from his home in the Dark Tower of Barad-dûr, acts as a manifestation of his will. The destruction of the Ring ultimately empties Sauron of his power.

The Lord of the Nazgûl The leader and most powerful of the nine Ringwraiths, or Black Riders, who serve Sauron in search of the Ring. Though the Black Captain embodies undefeatable evil, he is ironically struck down by a small hobbit, Merry.

Gollum (Sméagol) A black and bestial creature who owned the Ring prior to Bilbo. Gollum incessantly pursues Frodo throughout *The Lord of the Rings* in hopes of regaining the Ring. Throughout the novel, Gollum acts as a strange double to Frodo. The shriveled creature represents what Frodo might become under the Ring's influence. As Gandalf predicts, Gollum's evil ultimately serves a good purpose. Gollum completes the Ring-quest, biting the Ring off Frodo's finger and falling into the Cracks of Doom.

The Lieutenant of the Dark Tower A deputy to Sauron who confronts Gandalf and Aragorn at the gates of Mordor. Although the Lieutenant is a living creature, his face is a skull, and fire burns in his eye sockets and nostrils. The Lieutenant taunts and mocks the assembled army of Gondor, but Gandalf rebukes him and sends him fleeing back into Mordor.

Saruman the White The deposed wizard and the enactor of the Shire's brief police state. Out of pride, Saruman refuses forgiveness at the hands of Gandalf or Galadriel. Saruman's power is so diminished that the hobbits easily overthrow his regime, after which the wizard's dejected slave, Wormtongue, kills him.

Gríma Wormtongue Saruman's servant and agent, who earlier posed as an advisor to Théoden in *The Two Towers*. t the conclusion of *The Return of the King,* Wormtongue turns on Saruman and kills him.

Shagrat and Snaga Two Orcs whom Sam and Frodo encounter in the tower of Cirith Ungol.

CHARACTER LIST

MEN

Denethor   The Steward of Gondor and the father of Boromir and Faramir. Denethor undergoes a painful descent into madness that Tolkien uses to explore the complexity of human evil. Proud and wise, Denethor fails not because he is inherently evil, but because he allows the evil lies of the *palantír* to convince him that he is incapable of saving Minas Tirith from Mordor's power.

Faramir   The son of Denethor, brother of the deceased Boromir, and future husband of Éowyn. Faramir appears confident and assured when Frodo and Sam encounter him at Ithilien, outside Mordor. Denethor's attempts to burn Faramir alive are the extreme manifestations of the Steward's suppression of his dutiful son. In contrast to his father, Faramir displays the depth of his nobility by immediately recognizing Aragorn's long-awaited claim to the throne of Gondor.

Théoden   The King of the Mark and the leader of the Riders of Rohan, or Rohirrim. Théoden functions as a foil, or counterpoint, to Denethor. Whereas Denethor neglects the fate of Minas Tirith by committing suicide, Théoden bravely sacrifices his own life on the battlefield for the sake of the West.

Éowyn   The Lady of Rohan and future wife of Faramir. Éowyn, driven by a desire for combat and for Aragorn's affection, disguises herself in men's clothing and endangers herself to challenge the Lord of the Nazgûl. With the passing of the Shadow of Mordor, Éowyn is freed from her desire for war, and she turns her affections to Faramir.

Éomer   The son and declared heir of Théoden and the brother of Éowyn. Éomer, who initially urges his father not to go east to battle Mordor, joins the battle himself and bravely leads the Rohirrim after his father's death.

Beregond   A member of the Tower Guard at Minas Tirith and Pippin's friend. Beregond breaks the law of the Guard of the Citadel by leaving his post, but he successfully delays Denethor from killing his son Faramir.

Bergil   Beregond's son. Bergil becomes close with Pippin after the hobbit joins the Guard of Minas Tirith.

Imrahil   The Prince of Dol Amroth, the proudest of the captains of the Outlands who arrive to aid Minas Tirith. Imrahil is appointed interim leader of Gondor after Denethor's suicide.

Barliman Butterbur   The innkeeper at the Prancing Pony in Bree. Butterbur welcomes Gandalf and Frodo back to the inn on their return journey to the Shire.

ELVES

Elrond Halfelven   The wise Master of Rivendell. Elrond travels with the other Elves and Frodo to the West beyond the Great Sea at the end of the novel.

Arwen Evenstar   The beautiful daughter of Elrond. After the defeat of Sauron, Arwen marries Aragorn to become Queen of Gondor.

Elladan and Elrohir   The sons of Elrond. Elladan and Elrohir are members of the Dúnedain of the North, who make their way to Minas Tirith in response to a message requesting that they come to Aragorn's aid.

Celeborn and Galadriel   The Lord and Lady of Lothlórien. Celeborn and Galadriel arrive at Minas Tirith after Sauron's defeat, and then later sail to the West.

HOBBITS

Bilbo Baggins Frodo's cousin and mentor, the previous keeper of the Ring. Bilbo spends much of the latter part of *The Lord of the Rings* in Rivendell, writing his memoirs— ostensibly the source material Tolkien uses in writing the novel.

The Shirrifs Hobbit policemen who attempt to arrest Frodo, Sam, Pippin, and Merry as they reenter the Shire. The Shirrifs warn the Company that the "Chief" who has taken over the Shire has a large army.

Lotho Frodo's greedy and corrupt relative, whom Frodo suspects is the "Chief" to whom the Shirrifs refer.

Farmer Tom Cotton One of the oldest and most respected hobbits in the Shire. Farmer Cotton explains how a police state formed in the Shire after Frodo and the Company left.

Rosie Cotton Farmer Cotton's daughter. Rosie marries Sam Gamgee at the end of the novel, and together they have a daughter, whom they name Elanor.

OTHER ALLIES AND BENEVOLENT BEINGS

Gwaihir, the Windlord The leader of the Great Eagles, who bears Gandalf to Mount Doom, where the wizard rescues the exhausted Frodo and Sam after they complete the quest.

Shadowfax Gandalf's mythically swift horse. Shadowfax bears Gandalf to Minas Tirith, where the wizard saves Faramir and his men from the Nazgûl.

Treebeard The Ent who keeps the corrupt Saruman imprisoned at Isengard. Treebeard, however, ultimately frees Saruman because he does not wish to keep the miserable, defeated wizard caged.

ANALYSIS OF MAJOR CHARACTERS

FRODO BAGGINS

Frodo's role as the main protagonist of *The Lord of the Rings* changes significantly in the novel's final volume. Frodo no longer leads the quest, but is increasingly led by others and by circumstance. We wonder in what sense Frodo remains the true Ring-bearer if he himself must be borne by others in order to carry on his quest. For a brief time at the opening of Book VI, Frodo does not even possess the Ring. Lying naked in the tower of Cirith Ungol, Frodo appears a lifeless shell with little control of the Ring's movement toward Mount Doom. After the quest is completed, Frodo looms in the background of the events in Middle-earth and slips into irrelevance in his home, the Shire. Frodo explains to Sam in the last chapter that he is "wounded" in a way that will never heal. Certainly, Frodo is far from morbid or pitiful. His once-youthful nobility now appears a weathered reticence. Rather, Frodo is wounded because all the experiences after Mount Doom seem like a trite footnote. More important, Frodo feels wounded because he has completed a grand quest in which the goal—to get rid of something—was distinctly negative. In this, Frodo remains the true hero, for he has succeeded in a task that no one really wanted. The quest is both futile and yet the most important deed of all. Frodo's loss of vigor and identity after such a strange accomplishment propels his desire to sail away to the paradise of the West.

SAM GAMGEE

Sam's remarkable heroism in Book VI consists of courageous action that is tempered by love and spontaneity. Aragorn and the Riders of Rohan fight without restraint, as though they have always done so and know little else. As a Hobbit, Sam tends merely to stumble into adventurous deeds, and his plodding pursuit to save Frodo echoes with the running self-commentary Sam performs in his head. We do not just watch Sam run through the gates of Cirith Ungol brandishing the phial of Galadriel; we hear Sam prepare himself and see him shrug his shoulders and fumble absentmindedly for the magic phial. We know that Sam is not really an imposing Elf-warrior, as the Ring's power causes the Orcs to see him. Instead, we see the Orcs from Sam's perspective, sharing his dismay when they turn to run from him in fear. Sam offers a model of the hero whose heroism lies not in impulse, but in the choices he constantly and consciously makes to perform heroic deeds. Sam's heroism is comical, for he is consistently surprised by his success.

Sam's playfulness as a surprised hero is tempered by his genuine devotion to Frodo. All heroes must have first principles—the inspiration of their actions. Sam possesses such a strong tacit love for Frodo that he becomes united with the object of his service. As Sam climbs Mount Doom, carrying Frodo, the comrades appear to be only one hobbit climbing, not two. The ascent of Mount Doom is emblematic of Sam's friendship with Frodo. Sam's sacrifice produces true friendship, for he loses all thoughts of himself in his devoted care for his companion and master.

GANDALF THE WHITE

Gandalf is a formidable and intimidating Wizard who uses his powers sparingly and cares primarily for the individuals around him. He takes Pippin with him to Minas Tirith, as though both he and the hobbit might soften each other's behavior. Gandalf spends each night answering Pippin's unending questions and allaying the hobbit's fears. The wizard is patient and stern with Pippin, but he always has time to listen to the hobbit, and he values Pippin's perspective on the Steward of Gondor. Gandalf's attention remains divided between the political and the private, between the cosmic future of Middle-earth and the immediate personal needs of those around him. Tolkien uses Gandalf to establish the importance of redemption in the novel, showing that present, personal dilemmas always supercede responsibility to the larger, mystical crises of the world. For instance, Gandalf turns from rebuking the Black Captain of Mordor at the city gates to deal with the crazed Denethor, who has locked himself in the Citadel to attempt suicide.

Like Frodo, Gandalf—whom we later learn is a bearer of one of the three lesser Rings—distinguishes himself from the evil Sauron in that he does not perceive his life or destiny to be fixed. Sauron has limited himself to evil, and evil has become for him a necessary logic. Gandalf rarely plays the role of the enchanting wizard, and he uses his power sparingly. Rather, Gandalf uses his wisdom to imagine new possibilities in his counsel to others, offering others redemption by imagining their potential for good. Gandalf believes that it is possible for even the Lieutenant of Mordor or the dejected Saruman to turn from their evil ways and follow a new, unexpected path.

ARAGORN

The title of the third volume, *The Return of the King,* refers to Aragorn, or Strider, and his return to claim the throne of Gondor. When the hobbits first encounter Strider in *The Fellowship of the Ring,* he is a cloaked and mysterious Ranger of the North, a mercenary who patrols the borders of Middle-earth against bandits and evildoers. As the novel progresses, we learn that Strider is Aragorn, the heir of Isildur, the last and greatest king of Men who led the forces of Middle-earth against the armies of Mordor. To the hobbits, Strider appears rugged yet strangely stately, an ideal combination for the ruler of the great realm of Gondor. As time passes, however, Strider becomes quiet and aloof. He increasingly refers to himself as Aragorn, and his attention is fixed mainly on the throne he will claim if the quest to destroy the Ring succeeds.

In Books V and VI, Aragorn ceases to be a character who reveals himself through conversations, personality quirks, or limited knowledge of events. Aragorn becomes the opposite of the hobbits, who represent the common individual's perspective and for whom the quest is a journey of self-understanding and discovery. Aragorn's character reveals itself in the roles he plays, and particularly in the symbolic actions he performs. Aragorn emerges as a Christ figure—one whose experiences resemble those of Christ and who performs a sacrifice that redeems others. Interestingly, Tolkien's Christ figure does not sacrifice himself for anyone in the novel. Aragorn heals people, like Christ in the biblical Gospels, but he suffers no wounds on their behalf. Tolkien opens the sacrificial role to all characters, particularly the most humble ones, the hobbits. Aragorn represents the eschatology of Christ—the belief that Christ will return to establish a kingdom on earth for his faithful.

THEMES, MOTIFS & SYMBOLS

THEMES

Themes are the fundamental and often universal ideas explored in a literary work.

THE AMBIGUITY OF EVIL

Tolkien offers a conflicted picture of evil in *The Lord of the Rings*. As the literary scholar T.A. Shippey argues, the images of evil Tolkien portrays in the novel depict two traditional explanations for the existence of evil. The first, Manichaeism, was a view deemed heretical by the early Christian church. In Manichaeism, good and evil are two opposing forces or powers at war in the world. The second view, embraced by early Christian theologians, is that evil does not exist as a positive force. Evil is, instead, a human creation—that which is produced by humankind's lack of goodness.

The Shadow, the chief metaphor for the evil of Mordor, exemplifies this ambivalent depiction of evil. On one hand, shadow is nothing but the absence of light; it has no substance, and its qualities are ambiguous even to those who perceive it. At the same time, shadows are real objects, with clearly visible shapes and edges. With the Shadow that blankets Mordor and extends outward later in *The Lord of the Rings,* Sauron's evil spreads as various groups of Men and Orcs obey his will. In this sense, Sauron's evil is not a force or a thing, but a form of human behavior. Even so, Sauron's Darkness affects the physical world itself. The land of Mordor lies destitute and barren because of Sauron's residence there, and the flying Nazgûl represent the physical embodiment of a mystical evil force.

While Tolkien does not clarify this ambiguous picture of evil, he suggests that the evil of human behavior precedes the physical force or power of evil in the world. Sauron creates the Ring out of malice and pride; the Ring does not cause Sauron's evil. Similarly, the evil Saruman never actually loses his mystical powers when ousted from Isengard. Saruman's hatred and bitterness cause his psychological deterioration, and his physical loss of power follows suit.

THE IMPORTANCE OF REDEMPTION

Redemption—the ability to renew another's life—is a capacity that few of the Fellowship's members possess. As the rightful King of Gondor, only Aragorn can redeem another by his power, as his words possess the ability to direct, by royal edict, the fate of his subjects. Nevertheless, throughout *The Lord of the Rings*, the protagonists are faced with opportunities to extend mercy to others, often at the risk of losing sight of the goal of their larger mission. Tolkien suggests that mercy must always be extended to others, regardless of the risks such an offering poses.

Gandalf and Frodo, more than any other characters, repeatedly offer mercy and the possibility of redemption to others. At Minas Tirith, Gandalf turns from pursuing the Lord of the Nazgûl to save Faramir from the burning pyre and to offer aid and a second chance to the desperate Lord Denethor. Gandalf continually offers redemption to the corrupt wizard Saruman up through their last meeting. Time and again, Frodo offers mercy to Gollum, pardoning Gollum's offenses and entrusting his journey to the creature and his devices. Often, the offer of redemption jeopardizes the success of the quest itself.

By having Gandalf and Frodo extend second chances to others again and again, Tolkien emphasizes the importance of free will. Gandalf's intervention in *The Two Towers* transforms Théoden, who suddenly realizes that evil is not his only available choice. Denethor's evil, in contrast, stems from his belief that Sauron's evil lies are an inescapable necessity. Furthermore, Tolkien suggests that the act of offering redemption demonstrates a trust in the justice of providence or fate. Gollum ultimately betrays Frodo's confidence, trying to destroy Frodo to gain the Ring. Frodo's patience with Gollum, however, prompts the creature to follow Frodo all the way to the Cracks of Doom. In the end, good does come of Gollum, as, in a cruel twist of irony, his mischief destroys the Ring in the Cracks of Doom.

THE PRIORITY OF FRIENDSHIP

The common concept of friendship might appear too simple or trite to have such great importance in an epic novel, but Tolkien's picture of true friendship is at times grave and demanding. Tolkien suggests that even the all-important quest itself should be suspended for the sake of devotion to one's friends. Sam's deeds in Mordor display the ultimate courage, for he must constantly decide between fidelity to his friend Frodo or the forward movement of the Ring. In the dead silence of Mordor, Sam risks discovery by singing aloud in order to

THEMES

find his way to Frodo's hidden cell. For Sam, true friendship means absolute devotion to another person. This absolute devotion involves a denial of the self and the willingness to sacrifice one's own life for one's friend.

At the same time, Tolkien's exploration of friendship remains refreshing in its lightheartedness. The companions of the Fellowship make few vows of deep or serious friendship to each other. Rather, friendship in the novel frequently means being content with the company of another person. As Frodo leisurely tells Sam while Mordor collapses around them, "I am glad you are here with me . . . at the end of all things." Gandalf closes the novel by quietly bidding Sam, Merry, and Pippin to return home, "for it will be better to ride back three together than one alone."

MOTIFS

Motifs are recurring structures, contrasts, or literary devices that can help to develop and inform the text's major themes.

GEOGRAPHY

As the British poet W. H. Auden observes, quest narratives like Tolkien's use the image of the physical journey as a symbolic description of human experience. Tolkien's intricate design and mapping of Middle-earth suggest the significance of the realm's geography. In general, Tolkien draws upon the traditional associations of the distinction between East and West. In the Bible, Adam and Eve are exiled from Eden to the East for their sins. In Tolkien's epic, Mordor dominates the East—a vast, dark region of mystery. Good lies to the West and grows greater as one passes through the Shire, and finally on to the Grey Havens and the paradise beyond the Great Sea.

Tolkien's geography, however, has not only a broad significance, but also an importance specific to each area through which the protagonists pass. Like the city of Minas Tirith, which decays because of the spiritual depravity of its ruler, each land the hobbits traverse is analogous to the travelers' experiences. The Old Forest highlights the hobbits' fresh bewilderment; the fords of the Anduin River parallel the tough choices Frodo must make regarding the future of the Fellowship. In Book VI, Mordor's wretched plains mirror the evil of Sauron and the physical and mental destitution of the Ring-bearer. Mount Doom itself symbolizes the spiritual ascent that Frodo and Sam must make to destroy the Ring.

RACE AND PHYSICAL APPEARANCE

In part, Tolkien uses the different races of Middle-earth—Hobbits, Elves, Dwarves, Men, Orcs, and Ents—to display the diversity of the realm and variety in characterization. As C.S. Lewis notes, Tolkien's characters wear their individual distinctiveness in their stature and their outward appearance. Legolas is soft-spoken and ethereal, like his "fair race" of Elves; Gimli is brutish and proud in his behavior, which mirrors his stocky size and the stalwart character of the Dwarves in general. The Ents, like the trees they resemble, are slow yet strong and wise with years. Men remain complex, as they have great physical strength proportionate to their size, yet are confused and ill-defined, as though their history lies mostly ahead of them.

Hobbits are popularly interpreted as Tolkien's depiction of the common man, modern yet preindustrial. Certainly, Tolkien wishes us to identify more with the Hobbit protagonists than with the Men of his tales. The Men are mythic, like the giants or heroes of old who will later produce humankind as we know it. The four hobbits, on the other hand, venture forth from the sheltered Shire and experience the fantastical quality of Middle-earth. Their size reveals much about their qualities—their humility, love for common things, and jovial, amicable social habits. Their small size also emphasizes our sense that the creatures we encounter in Middle-earth are larger than life.

THE CHRIST FIGURE

Frodo and Gandalf each fill the sacrificial role of a Christlike character at various points in *The Lord of the Rings*, but Aragorn's fulfillment of the prophecies surrounding the return of the King to Gondor casts the Ranger as the most explicit Christ figure of the novel. Aragorn's journey through the Paths of the Dead parallels Christ's purported descent into hell after his death on the cross. Aragorn's healing of the wounded in Minas Tirith—with only the touch of his hand and his kiss—equally recalls Christ's work with the sick as recorded throughout the Gospels. Aragorn's Christlike nature does not indicate that the third volume of *The Lord of the Rings* is intended to be a systematic analogy for the Christian narrative. Rather, the biblical overtones in Aragorn's rise to the throne are more properly a motif, providing a structure for discerning the images of sacrifice, redemption, and rejuvenation in the Zion-like city of Minas Tirith. These principles and archetypes carry Christian meaning in Tolkien's text.

Symbols

Symbols are objects, characters, figures, or colors used to represent abstract ideas or concepts.

THE RING

As a physical object with a mysterious claim over its owner, the Ring acts as a concrete symbol of the ambiguity of evil that Tolkien explores in the novel. The Ring has a tangible presence and it maintains easily observable powers. The Ring causes its wearer to physically disappear, but it also weakens the owner's personal sense of identity with each use. In Mordor, the Ring appears to be an undeniable symbol of the physical force of evil. It grows progressively heavier with Frodo's each step toward Orodruin, and it causes the violent eruption and dissolution of Mordor's power with its deposit in the Cracks of Doom. At the same time, the Ring's weight is perceivable only to the wearer, for Sam carries Frodo and his Ring with surprising ease. The Ring, in its ambiguity, symbolizes both the power and the horror attributed to it, in the pride of its owner and the physical destruction that the owner's pride delivers upon himself and others.

MINAS TIRITH

The great city and fortress of Gondor situated on the border with Mordor, Minas Tirith symbolizes the precarious condition of the West in the conflict against Mordor. As a city, Minas Tirith evokes a sense of human history and the hope of future progress. Its survival determines the survival of humankind. The white walls of Minas Tirith, organized into the beauty and order of seven concentric circles, symbolize the ability for moral choice among the denizens of the West. The white exterior can be marred or preserved. Recalling the Arthurian myth of the Fisher King, in which the physical condition of the ailing king is mirrored in the barrenness of the land, Sauron's corrupting influence over Denethor has caused the walls of Minas Tirith to deteriorate. The White Tree, the city's symbol, remains broken. Aragorn's rise to the throne leaves physical marks of his spiritual and political renewal of Gondor on the city of Minas Tirith. The city walls are restored, and a new sapling of the White Tree is replanted in the Court of the Fountain.

THE GREAT EYE OF SAURON

Like the Ring, the Great Eye of Sauron indicates both the physical force of evil and the elusive quality of evil. Perched atop Sauron's Dark Tower, behind Mount Doom, the Eye scans the borders of Mordor, but its gaze is not exhaustive. Frodo and Sam slip under its searching glance to reach the Cracks of Doom. The Eye is distracted by the forces of Aragorn to the north. Nevertheless, as Frodo and Sam approach the Cracks, the Eye becomes strangely aware of the hobbits' presence, and the dark land underneath trembles. Through the Eye, Sauron appears capable of directing his will toward the physical world in a stream of power. As with with other forms of evil in the novel, the extent of the Eye's real power remains elusive. It provides a physical image for Sauron, but, at the same time, Sauron remains only a shapeless idea behind the Eye. The only thing we know definitely is that the Great Eye is constantly open and searching. The final moments of Mordor indicate that, just as Denethor believes everything Sauron shows him through the *palantír,* so Sauron believes everything the Great Eye sees occurring outside the Dark Tower.

SYMBOLS

Summary & Analysis

Book V, Chapter 1

Summary — Minas Tirith

Having parted from Aragorn and the Riders of Rohan at the end of Book III, Gandalf and Pippin ride swiftly east from Isengard to Gondor, the southeastern land inhabited by Men and bordering the dark region of Mordor. Gandalf and Pippin head toward Minas Tirith, the major city of Gondor. They travel by night to elude the searching Nazgûl—the Ringwraiths, now mounted on horrific winged steeds that fly overhead—whose eerie cries echo throughout the land.

Gandalf and Pippin gain entrance to Minas Tirith. The white stone city is built on seven tiered levels along one side of an immense hill, each tier surrounded by one of seven concentric semicircular stone walls. Upon the crown of the hill is the great Citadel, and within the Citadel is the High Court, at the feet of the White Tower. The sight of the iridescent city amazes Pippin. The Hobbit notices, however, that Minas Tirith is slowly falling into decay.

The two reach the gate of the Citadel, which opens to a court in which a pleasant green fountain trickles water off the broken branches of a dead tree. The Tower Guards, who still wear the ancient symbol of Elendil, an image of the White Tree, allow Gandalf and Pippin entrance without question. Approaching the court, Gandalf warns Pippin to watch his words and to avoid mentioning the subject of Aragorn, who maintains a claim to the kingship of Gondor.

In the Hall of Kings, the high throne remains empty. Denethor, the Steward (Lord) of Gondor, sits upon a black stone chair at the foot of the steps to the throne. While his body appears proud and healthy, he is an old man and stares blankly at his lap. Denethor holds the broken horn of his dead son, Boromir, who died at the hands of the Orcs in *The Two Towers*.

From the outset, there is a palpable yet unspoken tension between Gandalf and Denethor. Denethor takes great interest in Pippin, however, wishing to hear of Boromir's last stand in defense of the hobbits. Pippin realizes he owes Gondor and its Steward a debt; driven by a strange impulse, the hobbit offers his sword to

Gondor in service and payment. Denethor, flattered and amused, accepts Pippin into his Guard.

Denethor asks Pippin questions about the Company, deliberately ignoring Gandalf. Pippin senses Gandalf growing angry beside him. The two old men stare at each other with intensity. Pippin ponders Gandalf and is perplexed about the wizard's role and purpose. Finally, Denethor bitterly accuses Gandalf of being a power-hungry manipulator. Denethor says he will rule alone until the day the King returns to Gondor. Gandalf responds that his only goal is to care for the good in Middle-earth during the current period of evil.

After the interview, Gandalf explains to Pippin that Denethor possesses the ability to read men's minds. Gandalf praises Pippin for kindly offering service to Denethor in spite of the Steward's rudeness, but he warns the hobbit to be wary around Denethor. Gandalf expresses his longing for Faramir, Denethor's other son and Boromir's brother, to return to Gondor.

Pippin meets a soldier, Beregond, who is instructed to give the hobbit the passwords of the city. Looking over the city walls, Pippin perceives—either because of a cloud wall or a distant mountain—a deep shadow resting in the East, beyond the Anduin River toward Mordor. Beregond expresses little hope that Gondor will survive the ensuing conflict. The two hear the far-off cries of a flying Nazgûl, riding a terrible steed with enormous wings that darken the sun.

Pippin descends to the outermost ring of Minas Tirith, where Beregond's young son, Bergil, shows the hobbit to the gate. The captains of the Outlands arrive with reinforcements, the proudest of whom is Imrahil, Prince of Dol Amroth. The reinforcements prove smaller than expected, as the Outlands are under attack from the south by a large army of Men of Umbar, allies of Mordor.

That night, a black cloud settles over Minas Tirith and enshrouds it in a terrible gloom. Gandalf ominously explains to Pippin that for some time there will be no dawn, for the Darkness has begun.

ANALYSIS

The opening chapter of Book V begins where Book III left off in *The Two Towers,* immediately accelerating and making more urgent what previously appeared to be a far-off conflict with Sauron. As Gandalf and Pippin race eastward to the border of Mordor, the quest shifts from a meandering journey of self-discovery through the various realms of Middle-earth to a head-on confrontation with the Enemy just outside the gates of Mordor.

The idea of darkness and obscurity is important in this chapter, as Gandalf and Pippin ride to Gondor in darkness. Darkness appears as an important element throughout much of the rest of the volume. On one hand, the darkness is metaphorical, suggesting the protagonists' growing sense of uncertainty and dread. Pippin only perceives a gloom of darkness in the East, unsure whether it is a cloud wall or a mountain shadow—a confusion that suggests a broader fear and uncertainty regarding the imminent conflict with Sauron. On the other hand, the darkness indicates the increasing proximity of an actual, physical evil force. The wings of the Nazgûl's steed darken the sun, creating terrifying and ominous shadows on the earth below. Gandalf claims that evil has the next move in a grand, metaphysical game of chess. We see that evil acts as a physical substance, spreading out over Gondor, and enveloping Minas Tirith in darkness at the end of Chapter 1. In this regard, the natural world itself is affected by the conflict between Gondor and Mordor, as the apocalyptic Darkness spreads over the landscape. Gandalf's ominous words at the close of the chapter—"The Darkness has begun. There will be no dawn"—create a sense of dread that propels the narrative.

The city of Minas Tirith stands on the brink of Gondor and Mordor as a symbol of good and hope, particularly for the race of Men. The cities of Elves and Hobbits we have seen in *The Lord of the Rings* are hidden within forest glens or countryside, offering peaceful reprieve for their visitors. Minas Tirith, in contrast, boldly rises above ground, carved into seven circles out of the side of a mountain—a picture of the boldness, resilience, and lofty ambition of the race of Men. In many ancient religions, the number seven was considered the number of perfection, and the city's rise from the ground suggests that it is straining upward toward heaven. Moreover, the city is white, in stark contrast to the darkness of Mordor, reminding us of the Christian association of the color white with purity of spirit and recalling the fact that Gandalf is reborn as the White Rider. In every sense, Minas Tirith represents good and idealism, gathering together humans in political unity with a sense of history and future progress.

However, there are many signs that the city, while aspiring toward greatness, is not reaching its aim. Pippin notices that the tree over the courtyard fountain is dead, its branches broken, and that the city suffers from decay and vacancy. The image of the beautiful city falling into decay also reminds us of Celeborn and Galadriel's realm of Lórien in the first volume of the novel. That realm is similarly good, pure, and noble, yet it is losing its strength, unable to summon an inner vitality to match its outward elegance. In this portrayal of Minas Tirith, Tolkien draws upon the idea, frequently explored in ancient mythologies, of a kingdom suffering decay because of the deteriorated condition of its king. The popular story of the Fisher King, depicted variously in the Arthurian romances, tells of a wounded king so closely united to the land that the kingdom remains barren and unfruitful until the king's health is renewed. In similar fashion, Minas Tirith's empty houses and sad trees mirror its downtrodden Steward, Denethor, and its empty throne, devoid of a king.

Much like the city under his command, Denethor possesses a bearing and an appearance that belie the presence of inner decay, paranoia, and trepidation. This ambiguity and conflict within Denethor's character contrast with the simpler tensions we see in the chapter—between light and dark, good and evil, West and East, Gondor and Mordor, and so on. Denethor is neither wholly admirable nor wholly detestable: he remains dignified enough to prompt Pippin to offer his service to the Steward's court, yet he also appears curt and distracted, as though something suspect lurks beneath his appearance and behavior. Furthermore, the fact that Denethor so obviously dislikes Gandalf—a figure whom we have grown to know closely and trust unequivocally so far in *The Lord of the Rings*—warns us that all is not well with the Steward.

The encounter between Denethor and Gandalf parallels the wizard's earlier confrontation with Théoden in *The Two Towers*. Upon Gandalf's intervention, Théoden radically transforms from an evil, decrepit king to an emboldened, magisterial ruler. Denethor, however, does not take to Gandalf's influence so readily. Whereas we have seen that Théoden's evil stemmed largely from the power of Saruman and the false counsel of Wormtongue, Denethor's dark side comes from within. The two troubled kings embody the dual picture of evil that is a pervasive element of Tolkien's novel—the image of evil as that which comes from within the human heart versus the image of evil as that which is an external power or force.

BOOK V, CHAPTER 2

SUMMARY — THE PASSING OF THE GREY COMPANY

As Gandalf and Pippin ride toward Minas Tirith, Aragorn, Théoden, and the Riders of Rohan return from Isengard. Aragorn cryptically explains to Gimli, Legolas, and Merry that he must proceed to Minas Tirith by a darker, as yet undetermined route. On the way to Rohan, the group encounters thirty Dúnedain of the North—Rangers and friends of Aragorn, including Elrond's two sons, Elladan and Elrohir. The Dúnedain are gruff but proud, clad almost entirely in gray. They have received a mysterious message requesting that they come to Aragorn's aid. Théoden welcomes the Dúnedain to his company, and Elrohir conveys a message to Aragorn from Rivendell: "If thou art in haste, remember the Paths of the Dead." After a time, the group reaches Helm's Deep, the refuge of the Riders of Rohan. Théoden asks Merry to ride with him for the rest of the journey. Merry is delighted, as he feels out of place among the Riders and wishes to be useful. He offers Théoden his sword in service of Rohan, and the king gladly accepts.

As Théoden prepares the group to resume the journey, the group suddenly realizes that Aragorn is missing. He reappears exhausted and sorrowful. Aragorn knows that the Riders will not arrive at Minas Tirith in time. He has decided to take the Dúnedain with him to Minas Tirith via a terrifying road—the Paths of the Dead. It is said that no living man may travel the Paths, but Aragorn says that the proper heir of Elendil may safely pass. Meanwhile, Théoden and the Riders take a slower, safer path east through the mountains to Edoras.

Aragorn informs Legolas and Gimli that he has consulted the *palantír,* the Stone of Orthanc that Saruman used to communicate with Sauron. Aragorn has confronted Sauron through the *palantír* and claims he has successfully subdued the stone's power to his own will. In doing so, however, Aragorn has alerted Sauron to his existence as Isildur's heir to the throne of Gondor. Gimli guesses Sauron will now release his forces sooner because he knows Isildur's long-awaited heir exists. Aragorn, however, hopes such a hasty move may weaken the Enemy's attack.

Aragorn explains the history of the Paths of the Dead, citing a legendary song. In the early days of Gondor, Isildur set a great black stone upon the hill of Erech. Upon this stone, the King of the Mountains swore allegiance to Isildur. When Sauron returned and waged war on Gondor, Isildur called upon his allies for aid. The Men of the Mountains broke their oath, as they had begun to worship Sauron. Isildur condemned the Men never to rest until their oath was fulfilled. According to the verse, the Sleepless Dead, or Oathbreakers, must fulfill their oath to Isildur's heir when he returns to call them from the Stone of Erech. Rallying the Rangers, Aragorn rides through the plains of Rohan and reaches Dunharrow by morning. Théoden has not yet arrived, but his niece, Éowyn, begs Aragorn to avoid the Paths of the Dead. Aragorn refuses.

Outside Dunharrow lies the entrance to the Paths of the Dead, which run beneath the mountain. Spurred only by the strength of Aragorn's will, the Company enters the dark path. Gimli is nearly paralyzed with fear, as he can hear the whispering voices of an unseen host following the Company in the dark. At a clearing, Aragorn turns and speaks to the Dead, summoning them to follow him to the Stone of Erech.

After creeping in the darkness for what seems like ages, the Company emerges from the Paths and rides quickly through the mountain fields with the Men, horses, and banners of the Dead following behind. The inhabitants of the surrounding countryside flee in fear, calling Aragorn the "King of the Dead." Arriving at the large, black Stone of Erech, the legion of the Dead—the Oathbreakers—announce their allegiance to Aragorn. Aragorn unfurls a black flag and pronounces himself the heir of Isildur's kingdom. The Company rides on to the Great River, Anduin.

ANALYSIS

The events of the first three chapters of *The Return of the King* follow each other in parallel, tracing the separate paths of Gandalf, Aragorn, and Théoden, with their respective parties, in the moments leading up to the day the Darkness settles. These synchronized chapters convey the experience of parallax—the observation of the same cosmic or heavenly event from different locations. Merry and Pippin watch the Darkness arrive from opposite ends of Middle-earth. Their different vantage points further emphasize the vast effect of Sauron's evil on the natural world. While each chapter is narrated in the third person, the narration is typically limited to the perspective of each group's most diminutive member: Pippin at Minas Tirith, Gimli in the Paths of the Dead, and Merry with the Riders of Rohan. Tolkien's narrative voice implies that the most important aspect of the quest and the war against Mordor is not the outcome of these cataclysmic events, but each character's personal, subjective experience of the events—even that of the smallest or most frightened character.

This chapter also highlights the importance of song and myth, a motif that surfaces frequently throughout the novel. We may tend to think of songs and stories as entertainment to help pass the time, separate from the urgent and practical matters of everyday life. But in the early cultures Tolkien studied and upon which he modeled Middle-earth—cultures dominated by the spoken rather than the written word, before the advent of widespread literacy—songs and stories were vital and indispensable tools. They conveyed information that was not recorded anywhere else, keeping that legacy alive for future generations. We see the importance of song here when Aragorn cites an ancient song to teach his companions about the Paths of the Dead and the menacing Oathbreakers. When Aragorn emerges from the Paths, one could can say that he literally owes his success to his memory of the songs and the information conveyed in them.

Tolkien often insisted that *The Lord of the Rings* was not an allegory—a symbolic or contemporary rendering of established tales and archetypes. Nevertheless, the mystical trip through the Paths of the Dead depicts Aragorn as a Christ figure, and the events of Chapter 2 as a whole reflect the Passion of Jesus Christ as portrayed in the Gospels. Traditionally, the early Christian church affirmed that Christ, after his death on the cross, descended into hell to redeem those believers who had already died and to preach to the lost souls held captive there. After doing so, Christ rose again on earth, eventually to ascend into heaven. Similarly, Aragorn descends into the underground Paths of the Dead, where he speaks to the animated spirits of the Dead. He leads the Dead out into the waking world, where they affirm their devotion to Aragorn, renouncing their broken promise to Isildur at the altar-like Stone of Erech. Like the Bible's foreshadowing of Christ in the Old Testament, Elrohir's secret message and the legendary song about the Paths of the Dead act as prophetic underpinnings for Aragorn's deed; Aragorn himself has a keen sense of the ominous task that he "must" do. Moreover, Aragorn repeatedly affirms that his feats are accomplished not by heroic skill, but by divine right and by the strength of his will.

The presence of these biblical parallels does not mean that Tolkien misrepresented his intentions for *The Lord of the Rings*. The comparisons to Christ are far from a systematic allegory, and more than one character fits the role of a Christ figure in the trilogy. Gandalf also recalls Christ's sacrifice and resurrection when he dies in Book II and returns in Book III as Gandalf the White, purified and godlike. Frodo and Sam perform additional sacrificial duties in their quest to save and redeem Middle-earth. Rather than create Christian parallels, Tolkien wanted to create in *The Lord of the Rings* an ancient mythology for contemporary England. The history of Middle-earth in the novel and in the tales of *The Silmarillion* depicts a pre-Christian world before the flowering of humankind's dominance. As mythology, *The Lord of the Rings* promotes a specific moral and religious understanding, implying that the Christian principles of sacrifice, redemption, and forgiveness are central to the way the world is and has always worked—even before the appearance of Christianity as a religion.

BOOK V, CHAPTER 3

SUMMARY — THE MUSTER OF ROHAN
Meanwhile, Théoden and the Riders reach the outer hills of Rohan after a hard three days' journey. Éomer, Théoden's son, urges his father not to go further east, but Théoden insists on going to war. Gathering the remaining Riders of Rohan, Théoden decides to ride to the Hold at Dunharrow, where the people of Rohan have taken shelter in anticipation of war. He finds Éowyn, the Lady of Rohan, waiting there among her people, and he orders the host to rest for the night.

At dinner, Merry waits at Théoden's side, fulfilling his duties as the king's new squire. Théoden further explains to Merry the legend of the Paths of the Dead, speculating about whether or not Aragorn will survive. A messenger from Gondor enters the tent. Merry is startled by the man's armor, as it reminds him of Boromir. The stranger brings a red arrow—a summons, sent only in times of great peril—from the Steward of Gondor. Théoden states that six thousand Riders will set out for Minas Tirith in the morning, but that they will not reach Minas Tirith for a week.

There is no sunrise the next morning; a great Darkness has descended, and all the land is buried under a terrible gloom emanating from Mordor. As the host prepares to leave, Théoden asks Merry to stay behind when they pass the city of Edoras. The ride to Gondor will be hard and swift, and none among the Riders can afford the burden of carrying the hobbit along. Merry is sorely disappointed, but the king has made up his mind. Éowyn, however, escorts Merry to a small booth and outfits him as best she can in the armor of the King's Guard. She bids Merry farewell and returns to her tent.

In Edoras, Merry loses all hope of going to Gondor until a young and slender Rider offers to carry Merry with him secretly to battle. The Rider introduces himself as Dernhelm. Merry gratefully accepts, and soon Théoden's host departs for Minas Tirith.

ANALYSIS

The terrible gloom emanating from Mordor reminds us that the war brewing in Middle-earth is more than a political wrangling. It is not just a dispute over stolen property (the Ring) or a battle over territorial claims (the realm of Gondor). Rather, the war is portrayed as a cosmic battle with universal implications. The darkening of the sky is strikingly reminiscent of the transformation of the heavens described in the Book of Revelation in the Bible, associated with the Day of Judgment. We have already seen the Dead returning to life in the parade of the Oathbreakers in the Paths of the Dead, mirroring the resurrection of the deceased—one of the events linked to the Day of Judgment in Christian doctrine. On Judgment Day, a fierce battle and a darkened sky foreshadow a cataclysmic change not just in the political setup of nations on earth, but also in the nature of existence. Tolkien makes clear references to the Book of Revelation to heighten the cosmic importance of the War of the Ring and to underscore its moral and philosophical import.

Merry's touching insistence on marching to Minas Tirith with the warriors provides a moment of lighthearted sentimentality to balance the gloom of the war preparations. Théoden's fighters are grave and determined, rugged in their fixation on the battle looming before them; Merry, in comparison, seems as childlike as his name—like a toddler who wants to accompany the adults. The soldiers' rejection of Merry's wish to participate emphasizes the gravity of the war. It also shows us that the mission of the Ring is more than a series of steps to be taken by the Company, but a rite of passage for the hobbits. Up to this point, they have led a rather sheltered existence in the Shire, but now they are called on to perform an act of maximum universal significance. In doing so, they have the potential to attain a heroic status they have never held before. If Merry seems like a child trying to grow up, so are all the hobbits on their journey.

BOOK V, CHAPTER 4

From the beginning of the chapter to Gandalf's words about Gollum

SUMMARY — THE SIEGE OF GONDOR

Back in Minas Tirith, Pippin receives his new uniform and gear as a member of the Tower Guard. He spends a long day serving Lord Denethor, Gandalf, and the Captains of the West. Pippin chats with Beregond at the outer wall of the Citadel amid heavy darkness and a stagnant air. Suddenly, they hear the terrifying shriek of a Black Rider. Beyond the outermost gate, they can see five dark Nazgûl swooping over a small, rapidly approaching group of Men on horseback. The leader of the horsemen sounds his horn; Beregond recognizes the trumpet call of Faramir, Denethor's son.

The men, thrown from their terrified horses, run for the city gate on foot. Just as a Nazgûl descends on Faramir, Pippin sees what appears to be a brilliant white star in the north—it is Gandalf on his horse, Shadowfax. Gandalf raises his hand and sends a shaft of light shooting upward into one of the Nazgûl. The Nazgûl cries and circles away, the other Ringwraiths following. Gandalf returns to the city with Faramir slumped in the saddle.

Faramir is escorted into Denethor's chambers, where he is shocked to see Pippin (Faramir has already had a strange encounter with two other hobbits—Frodo and Sam—in *The Two Towers*). Gandalf erupts when he learns from Faramir that Frodo and Sam are heading to Mordor by way of Cirith Ungol. Faramir notes that he bid farewell to the hobbits only two days ago; they could not have reached Cirith Ungol yet. The men surmise that Sauron's new movement on Gondor is not related to Frodo's approach to Mordor.

Denethor upbraids Faramir for showing cowardice in defending the outposts. The Steward bitterly remarks that Boromir, his other son, would have brought him a "mighty gift"—meaning the Ring. Gandalf points out that Boromir would have kept the "gift" for himself. The two men argue, and Pippin again senses the strain between them. Denethor opposes sending the Ring with a Hobbit into the hands of Sauron, believing that he himself should have been given the Ring for safekeeping. The gathering disperses. Pippin asks Gandalf why, as Faramir has indicated, Frodo and Sam are traveling with Gollum. Gandalf fears Gollum's treachery, but notes that perhaps some good may yet come of Gollum's actions.

ANALYSIS

Now that Pippin is a member of the Tower Guard, we realize how much his status has changed throughout the novel. When we first meet him, he is content to smoke and lounge about; as recently as *The Two Towers,* he has seemed more interested in leisure than in warfare, as when Aragorn's group comes upon Merry and Pippin smoking their pipes at Isengard. The Pippin of this volume of the novel, however, is a warrior, or at least an aspiring one. His passage from the simple pleasures of food and conversation to the grave obligations of fighting mirrors the rite of passage that all the hobbits of the Fellowship are undergoing on the quest. Nonetheless, at this point Pippin is still not much of a fighter. His close association with the slender young warrior Beregond reminds us that Pippin is no seasoned soldier. Moreover, we see that his role in this chapter is basically observational rather than active. He sees the white star heralding Gandalf's arrival on the back of Shadowfax, carrying Faramir with him—but Pippin only witnesses this heroism; he does not play any part in it. Nevertheless, his presence on the scene is a kind of achievement for him.

Denethor's misappraisal of his two sons, Boromir and Faramir—his wrongful condemnation of Faramir and praise of the treacherous Boromir—recalls an earlier scene from *The Two Towers.* Previously, Faramir captured Frodo and Sam on suspicion that the hobbits had something to do with the death of Boromir, who perished under mysterious circumstances. Faramir hinted that the hobbits had betrayed Boromir, ironically unaware that it was actually Boromir who was the betrayer. While Frodo remained silent on that earlier occasion, unwilling to destroy Faramir's faith in his deceased brother, Sam eventually spoke up to tell the truth, which Faramir ultimately accepted gratefully. Here, the situation is similar, as Denethor is unable even to imagine that Boromir would have kept the Ring for himself rather than presenting it as a gift to his father and lord. On this occasion, it is Gandalf who reprises Sam's earlier role of truth-teller, revealing Boromir's betrayal to a shocked family member. This parallel between the two scenes is one of many in *The Lord of the Rings,* serving as a unifying force that reminds us that *The Lord of the Rings* is one novel with three volumes, rather than three separate novels.

Book V, Chapter 4 (continued)

From Faramir's expedition to Osgiliath to the end of the chapter

Summary — The Siege of Gondor

> *"You cannot enter here. . . . Go back to the abyss prepared for you! Go back! Fall into the nothingness that awaits you and your Master. Go!"*
>
> *(See* QUOTATIONS, *p. 242)*

The next morning, Denethor sends Faramir to protect the outlying ruins of Osgiliath, where Mordor's armies are likely to strike first. Faramir dutifully accepts the perilous—possibly suicidal—assignment from his father. News arrives the following morning of a battle for the nearby Pelennor Fields.

The Lord of the Nazgûl, the Black Captain against whom none can stand, leads the armies from Mordor. Gandalf rides off toward Osgiliath to help fight the Black Captain. The wizard returns the next day, leading many wounded men. Faramir remains at Pelennor, trying to hold his men together to execute a safe retreat.

Not long after, the armies of Mordor approach Minas Tirith. Thousands of black-clad Men and Orcs stream onto the plains. A small, beleaguered ensemble rides before them—the last of Gondor's rearguard in retreat. Lord Denethor, clad in armor, sends a small army of horsemen out to protect the retreat. Gandalf rides among them, using his white fire to deter the front lines of the Enemy. The retreating men reach the city safely, but one of the Nazgûl's poisoned arrows strikes Faramir.

Sauron's armies besiege the city in a vale of fire, cutting off all roads. They use huge catapults to lob blazing missiles into the first ring of the city. As the forces of Minas Tirith try to put these fires out, they realize to their horror that the Enemy's missiles are the burning heads of those who have died defending Osgiliath.

Stricken with sudden bitterness and grief, Denethor locks himself in the Tower with Faramir, who is now delirious with fever from his arrow wound. Pippin looks on as Denethor weeps, cursing Gandalf and bewailing the end of his lineage as Steward of Gondor. As Denethor is holed up, Gandalf takes over the defense of Minas Tirith. The army of Mordor launches an attack on the outer wall of the city.

Denethor instructs the desperate messengers who arrive in his court that everyone in the city should give up and burn in the fires.

Denethor calls for his servants. He has Faramir carried out of the Citadel to the Hall of Kings, where Gondor's leaders are laid to rest. Denethor places Faramir on a marble table and calls for dry wood and a torch. Pippin warns the servants not to obey Denethor's orders, as it is clear that the Steward has gone mad. Pippin breaks the rule of the Tower Guard by leaving his post. He sends Beregond up to the Hall of Kings to try to intervene with Denethor, and then the hobbit goes in frantic search of Gandalf.

The armies of Mordor, led by the Lord of the Nazgûl, approach the gate of Minas Tirith with a great battering ram. The servants of the Enemy strike the great iron door three times. On the third strike, the door shatters. The Black Captain enters the first ring of the city, and all flee in terror before him. Pippin watches as Gandalf alone stands before the Black Captain. Gandalf orders the Lord of the Nazgûl to return to Mordor—to nothingness—but the Ringwraith laughs. He throws back his hood to reveal a crown on a headless body. His sword bursts into flame, ready to strike. Suddenly, a cock crows, and a great clamor of horns emanates from the north. The Riders of Rohan have arrived.

Analysis

As some commentators have observed, one of Tolkien's great strengths in *The Lord of the Rings* is his ability to write convincingly about war. Tolkien not only fought and sustained injury in World War I, but he also wrote his novel in the years surrounding World War II—a war in which Germany bombed the heart of England. Tolkien writes about the battle generally, without graphic detail and only briefly from the viewpoint of those actually fighting. As such, his descriptions of war maintain a refreshing sense of perspective. "The Siege of Gondor" is narrated in the usual third person, but it is limited to the perspective of the chapter's only hobbit, Pippin. We are not occupied with Pippin's thoughts and emotions; the only information available to us is that which Pippin overhears in Denethor's court, discusses with Gandalf, or observes as might a citizen of Minas Tirith. From this perspective, we watch from afar as retreating men stumble frantically for the city gates, their pursuers close behind. We learn in horror, alongside the occupants of Minas Tirith, that some of the Enemy's firebombs are not actually bombs, but human heads. This restricted knowledge of events increases our sense of suspense and fear. Tolkien's account seems realistic, for it depicts war against the backdrop of the human city.

Recalling the image of Nero fiddling as Rome burned, Denethor's actions in the midst of impending doom reveal much about his character. While a war for the freedom of Middle-earth rages outside Gondor's walls, Denethor turns his attention inward, locking himself in the Citadel and mourning his own demise. Denethor desires complete power or none at all; with the destruction of Minas Tirith seemingly at hand, he feels he must exert control over the only things he is still able to control—his and Faramir's lives. Denethor believes that he would have safely hidden the Ring had Boromir procured it for him. Gandalf, however, notes that Denethor, like Boromir, would have coveted and used the Ring for himself. In truth, Denethor appears to want to use the power of the Ring to return glory to Gondor. Denethor's desire for the Ring leads to his descent into madness, paranoia, and insecurity. As critic Rose Zimbardo notes, the Ring's wicked effect on individuals in *The Lord of the Rings* is a loss of personal identity. Just as those who wear the Ring become invisible, so those who focus their energies on obtaining the Ring lose their sense of self in the overwhelming desire to harness power to control others.

BOOK V, CHAPTER 5

SUMMARY — THE RIDE OF THE ROHIRRIM

Four days into their journey to Minas Tirith, Merry remains hidden among the Riders of Rohan. He worries that he is a burden to the Rohirrim (as the Riders are sometimes called), and he feels unwanted and small. While the group rests, the Riders encounter the Woses, the Wild Men of the Woods. Troubled by Orcs, the Woses offer their services to Théoden. They are a little-known yet ancient people, stumpy and brutish. The Woses' leader informs Théoden that all roads to Minas Tirith are blocked, save the secret ways the Woses know. The Wild Men promise to show the Riders through these paths, though they will not fight alongside Rohan.

The Riders emerge from the forest just north of Minas Tirith, and the Woses bid them farewell and vanish. To Théoden's dismay, the Riders discover two dead bodies, one of them the earlier messenger from Gondor, still clutching the red arrow. Apparently, Minas Tirith does not know the Riders are coming to its aid. Dernhelm, still carrying Merry, breaks rank and draws closer to Théoden as the Riders reach the out-walls of Gondor.

Théoden looks sadly upon the destruction of Minas Tirith. Suddenly, a great flash of light springs from the city with a booming sound. Reinvigorated, Théoden commands his Riders into battle with a great cry "more clear than any there had ever heard a mortal man achieve." The shouting Rohirrim rout the Orcs and armies of Mordor. The Darkness dissipates with a fresh wind from the sea.

At the arrival of the Rohirrim, the Black Captain senses the Darkness fading and the tide of battle turning. He vanishes from the city gate to enter the fray. Meanwhile, Théoden rides in fury ahead of the Rohirrim. The chieftain of the Southrons—allies of Mordor—leads his men against Théoden. Though outnumbered, Théoden and Éomer charge through the line of enemy scimitars handily, striking down the Southrons' chieftain.

ANALYSIS

The Woses, or Wild Men, are reminiscent of the Ents in *The Two Towers*. Both are tribes associated with nature who have had little contact with the civilized world, but who are induced to aid the Fellowship as a way of countering the Orcs. As with the Ents, the Woses are unable to remain neutral in the war—a measure of the all-encompassing gravity of the conflict. Running into the forest offers no escape, as even the forest-dwellers have been forced into the fray, compelled to offer their support to one side or the other. There is nothing heroic about the Woses, who are dumpy and brutish in appearance and show none of the grace or nobility of other races the Fellowship has encountered. The Woses make no gracious offer to aid the Fellowship further when their job is done; they vanish after the group has found its way. However, the commonness of the Woses enhances the value of the aid they provide: they are not typical heroes in the knightly style, but ordinary folk whose participation shows how large the scope of the War of the Ring has become.

The rejuvenation of Théoden in the midst of battle provides the boost in morale that the king's warriors have needed—the extra push that allows them to rout the Orcs. Théoden's resurgence illustrates the importance of character in a leadership position, and suggests the tremendous mystical potential of the mind when prompted by the right psychological motives. The king gazes gloomily at the destruction of Minas Tirith until the blast from the city jolts him, prompting him to utter a cry of more clarity than seems mortally possible. It is as if Théoden himself is becoming immortal, at least in the sense that the moment of his battle cry will endure in the memory of the Rohirrim. No doubt, he is stirred to this superhuman intensity by his sentimental attachment to Minas Tirith—a connection he feels deeply but never explicitly describes in words. Tolkien was fascinated by the hidden psychological impulses that prompt humans to superhuman deeds and bring the potential for heroism within the grasp of everyone capable of intense emotion.

BOOK V, CHAPTER 6

SUMMARY — THE BATTLE OF THE PELENNOR FIELDS

Suddenly, a massive black beast swoops down upon Théoden, hitting his horse with a poisoned dart. The steed rears up, and the king falls beneath his horse, crushed. The Lord of the Nazgûl looms above on the back of his flying steed. Terrified, Théoden's guards flee in panic—all but Dernhelm. Thrown from his horse but unharmed, Dernhelm challenges the Black Captain. Merry, crawling on all fours in a daze, hears Dernhelm speak, and he recognizes the warrior's voice. Dernhelm throws back his hood and reveals to the Nazgûl that he is in fact Éowyn, the Lady of Rohan, in disguise.

The winged steed strikes at Éowyn, but she deals it a fatal wound. The Black Captain leaps off his dead mount and shatters Éowyn's shield with a blow from his club, breaking her arm. He raises his spiked club again, but just before he strikes, Merry sneaks up behind him and stabs the Nazgûl through the leg. Bowed over, the creature lets out a terrible shriek. Éowyn, with her final strength, slashes at his face with her sword, the blade shattering upon impact. The Black Captain's armor falls shapeless at Éowyn's feet, and his crown rolls away. Éowyn collapses on top of the Nazgûl's remains.

The dying King Théoden appoints Éomer as his heir. Éomer, seeing his sister Éowyn's fallen body, leads the Rohirrim in a furious attack. The men of Minas Tirith, led by Imrahil, Prince of Dol Amroth, emerge from the city and drive the enemy from the gate. Théoden's body is taken to the city, along with Éowyn, but Imrahil alerts her rescuers that she is not dead.

The allies of Mordor reassemble as new soldiers of Sauron arrive from Osgiliath. The men of Rohan and Gondor dwindle. As the tide turns against Gondor again, a fleet of black ships appears on the Anduin River. The defenders of Gondor turn for the city at the sight of the enemy ships. Éomer, though he realizes he is defeated, continues to fight bravely, laughing in a mix of hope and despair.

Suddenly, the frontmost black ship unfurls a banner bearing the white tree of Gondor and the seven stars and crown of Elendil—the symbols of the ancient kingdom of Gondor. Aragorn has arrived in the black ships, along with the Rangers of the North, Legolas, Gimli, and reinforcements from the southern kingdoms. Wielding the legendary sword Andúril, reforged and burning like a star, Aragorn leads a fierce battle to save Gondor. The armies of Mordor are defeated, and Aragorn, Éomer, and Imrahil return to the city.

ANALYSIS

This chapter marks a turning point in *The Lord of the Rings*. The conflict established in *The Fellowship of the Ring* remains unresolved, but a great tension accumulated over the second and third volumes of the novel finds some resolution in these chapters. The forces of Men from the west have been slowly gathering and moving steadily to the east, just as the armies and allies of Sauron have equally organized and spread west, marked by the ever-expanding cloud of Darkness over the land. Gandalf's earlier metaphor of the chess game is apt, for the opposing forces have arrayed themselves and now make strategic moves in turn. In terms of chess, the armies of Gondor successfully capture Mordor's queen by killing the Lord of the Nazgûl, the Black Captain. The Darkness overhead dissipates as Mordor's forces retreat to huddle around their stationary king, Sauron.

Gondor's ultimate salvation, however, arrives in a manner that upsets the black-against-white, East-against-West conflict. Aragorn emerges from the South, aided by a sea breeze that the characters sense throughout the chapter. Moreover, he comes riding in Mordor's own dark ships, complicating the distinction between the forces of good and evil. Aragorn's unusual entrance via the Paths of the Dead suggests that his claim to the throne extends over both East and West, the living and the dead. Furthermore, Aragorn's sword, Andúril—reforged after centuries of remaining broken—symbolizes the reunification of the lands and peoples Sauron has divided.

As the most detailed account of hand-to-hand combat in Tolkien's third volume, this chapter offers numerous portrayals of heroic courage on the part of Théoden and his Riders. Personally, Tolkien was wary of the archetype of courage found in the heroes of the Norse sagas and myths he studied. Tolkien commented that heroic courage was a "potent but terrifying solution." The blind or impulsive courage of the unrestrained hero may be effective, but it is not necessarily admirable. Tolkien instead prefers to emphasize the heroism of those whose courageous deeds arise from their ideals and a sense of moral obligation. Éomer demonstrates great bravery in his maniacal drive to keep fighting even after Gondor seems lost. Yet the true heroes of the battle are those who sacrifice their lives in combat, not because it comes naturally, but because of their sense of responsibility and commitment.

Tolkien explores the ideas of valor and self-sacrifice by casting two unlikely candidates—Éowyn and Merry—in the role of hero. Both characters represent somewhat marginalized segments of the population of Middle-earth—Hobbits and women. The conspicuous scarcity of women in *The Lord of the Rings* highlights the irony of Éowyn's sacrifice for Théoden. The pampered and repressed Lady offers her life for Théoden and manages to slay the terrifying Lord of the Nazgûl, whom no man has been able to defeat. Éowyn, to secure the opportunity to act, has had to show cunning, care, and dedication to the cause of Rohan. Ironically, to become a hero she has had to resort to deceit, disguising herself to show that her deeds arise from the quality of her character rather than from the privilege of her position or her gender.

Merry also plays a role in slaying the Black Captain, though his heroism emerges from a sense of moral obligation and duty rather than stealth or cunning. When Merry and Dernhelm (Éowyn) are thrown from their horse before the Nazgûl, Merry finds himself crawling on the ground, crying and whimpering. In his heart, he berates himself for his lack of courage, thinking, "King's man! . . . You must stay by him." When Merry sees the Nazgûl strike Éowyn, he responds out of pity, wonder, and the "slow-kindled courage of his race." Merry's courage represents Tolkien's ideal of heroism— unobsequious, reflective, and unexpected. As T.A. Shippey notes, Tolkien's ideal—as represented in the novel's main protagonists, Sam and Frodo—is Hobbit heroism, not human heroism.

Book V, Chapters 7–8

Summary — Chapter 7: The Pyre of Denethor

> *"I would have things as they were in all the days of my
> life . . . and in the days of my longfathers before me. . . .
> But if doom denies this to me, then I will have naught:
> neither life diminished, nor love halved, nor honour
> abated."*
> (See QUOTATIONS, p. 244)

The narrative returns to the perspective of Pippin. When the Black
Captain disappears from the gate of Minas Tirith, Pippin runs to
Gandalf and tells him of Denethor's madness and the situation in the
tower. Gandalf wishes to pursue the Nazgûl but knows he must save
Faramir. As they race to the Citadel, Gandalf laments the Enemy's
ability to bring evil and discord to the inner circle of Minas Tirith.
Reaching the door to the House of Stewards, the two find
Denethor's servants bearing swords and torches, standing before
the lone figure of Beregond, who holds the door against them. Two
servants have already fallen to Beregond's sword. The men cower at
the sight of Gandalf, whose appearance is like a burst of white light.

Denethor throws open the door, drawing his sword, but Gandalf
lifts his hand and the sword flies from Denethor's grip. The wizard
decries Denethor's madness, but the Steward says that Faramir has
already burned. Rushing past, Gandalf finds Faramir still alive on
the funeral pyre. To Denethor's protests and tears, Gandalf lifts
Faramir and carries him away with a strength that surprises Pippin.
Denethor, the wizard says, does not have the authority to order
Faramir's death.

Denethor laughs. Standing proudly, he produces from his cloak a
palantír, similar to the Stone of Orthanc. He warns that the West is
doomed, as he has foreseen the black ships of the Enemy approaching. The Steward condemns Gandalf for bringing a young upstart
Ranger to replace him as ruler. Denethor wishes that things would
remain as they always have been in Minas Tirith. He springs for
Faramir, but Beregond stops him. Grabbing a torch from a servant,
Denethor lights the funeral pyre. He throws himself into the raging
fire, clutching the *palantír*.

Gandalf and Beregond carry Faramir to the Houses of Healing.
As they exit, the House of Stewards collapses in flames, and

Denethor's servants run out. Soon after, they hear a great cry from the battlefield—the sound of Éowyn and Merry's defeat of the Lord of the Nazgûl. A sense of hope returns as the sun breaks through the Darkness. Gandalf discusses Denethor's *palantír* with Pippin and Beregond. Gandalf says he had always suspected that the Steward possessed one of the seven seeing-stones. The wizard surmises that Denethor, in his growing distress, began to use the stone, and through it he fell prey to the lies of Sauron.

SUMMARY — CHAPTER 8: THE HOUSES OF HEALING

Crying and in pain, Merry accompanies the procession carrying Théoden and Éowyn into the city. As Merry ascends the city roads, he runs into Pippin, who is startled and glad, and notices that Merry is stumbling badly. Merry's arm has gone completely numb after he stabbed the Nazgûl. Pippin escorts Merry to the Houses of Healing.

After the battle, Aragorn furls his banner and orders his men to prepare tents outside the city. He refuses to claim his throne until the war with Mordor is decided, for good or ill. Aragorn plans to wait outside the gate until the Lord of Minas Tirith bids him to enter. Aragorn, learning of Denethor's fate, assigns Imrahil to act as the interim leader of Gondor. Aragorn, Éomer, and Imrahil secretly agree, though, that Gandalf is their true leader for the remainder of the war against Mordor.

At Gandalf's request, Aragorn enters the city in the guise of a Ranger. The wounded, including Merry, Faramir, and Éowyn, grow steadily sicker from the poison of the Enemy's weapons. One of the city's nurses recalls a legend of Gondor, which says, "The hands of the king are the hands of a healer, and so shall the rightful king be known." Only Aragorn can save those wounded by the Enemy.

Aragorn crushes the leaves of a common, seemingly useless herb that grows in Gondor and stirs the leaves in a bowl of warm water. The sweet scent of the herb awakens Faramir from his fever. Faramir immediately affirms Aragorn as his superior and king. Aragorn then tends to Éowyn and Merry, who both return to consciousness when Aragorn touches and kisses them. All through the night, Aragorn heals the wounded of the city. Rumors fly throughout the city that the King of Gondor now walks again, bringing healing in his hands. As foretold at Aragorn's birth, the people call him Elfstone, or Elessar, after the green gem that he wears around his neck, which Galadriel gave to him earlier.

ANALYSIS — CHAPTERS 7–8

The pall of Lord Denethor's suicide looms over these chapters, despite the arrival of Aragorn and the victory over the Black Captain. Tolkien places Denethor in sharp contrast to each of the West's other three prominent leaders—Théoden, Gandalf, and Aragorn. As Chapters 6 and 7 take place at the same time, though from different perspectives, Denethor and Théoden perish at the same moment. Gandalf and Beregond hear the cries of the Black Captain just as the House of Stewards crumbles in flames; Pippin watches Denethor place himself on the burning pyre just as Théoden prepares to speak his final words to Merry. The parallels between the two rulers show them to be true foils, or counterpoints. Théoden dies sprinting ahead of his men into battle, effectively drawing the attention of the Lord of the Nazgûl and allowing for Éowyn to strike down the Black Captain. Denethor, in contrast, removes himself from his people, withdrawing into isolation in the Citadel, high above the erupting conflict. Théoden displays the sort of forward movement necessary to lead and to improve the welfare of his kingdom, whereas Denethor's passiveness and self-involvement parallel the recent decay of Minas Tirith.

The scene just before Denethor's suicide is the third major confrontation between the Steward and Gandalf and it highlights the contrast between the two men. Pippin has been unable to understand the tension between Gandalf and Denethor since their first meeting. The hobbit even questions Gandalf's role, wondering what purpose or good Gandalf's wizardry serves in the broader scheme of Middle-earth. The wizard's role is clarified in his final standoff with Denethor. Gandalf's virtue as a wizard lies less in his mystical powers or even his sage-like wisdom than in his ability to perceive possibilities for change in each individual and extend charity in turn. Just as Gandalf offers Théoden forgiveness and redemption for the King's former misdeeds, so he offers counsel and a second chance to Denethor. Before Denethor commits suicide, Gandalf beckons to him, "Come! We are needed. There is much that you can yet do." Denethor, however, is a politician crippled by the weight of necessity; after years of pressure from Mordor on Minas Tirith, he feels that a hopeful solution for the West is impossible. While Denethor remains strong enough to resist Sauron's will, he does succumb to Sauron's lies through his use of the *palantír*. Whereas Gandalf is the paragon of wisdom, Denethor gains only knowledge—not wisdom—from the *palantír*. The sphere offers the Steward prescient images, such as that of the ships of the Enemy approaching, but it provides no explanation for these images. Denethor misinterprets the knowledge imparted to him by the *palantír*, thinking that the ships of the Enemy foretell the doom of Minas Tirith, when in reality the ships herald the arrival of Aragorn. In this regard, Denethor falls prey to his inability to distinguish between knowledge and wisdom—a distinction that characters such as Gandalf and Elrond make, and that Tolkien implies is crucial.

Aragorn also contrasts with Denethor, not as the Steward's opposite, but as a fulfillment of that which the Steward has failed to achieve. Aragorn enjoys a birthright to the throne, while Denethor struggles to retain the line of the Stewards—the interim leaders in Gondor. Aragorn has not only resisted Sauron's lies through the *palantír*, but he has also subordinated the power of the seeing-stone to his will. Finally, in Chapter 8, Aragorn emerges as the redeemer of Minas Tirith. Under Denethor, the city suffers decay analogous to the debilitated condition of its ruler. Aragorn, in contrast, brings renewed life to the city. Not only does he defeat the armies of Mordor, but he heals the wounded and the dying with his touch and presence. Once again, Aragorn fulfills the role of a Christ figure. He is perhaps the complete opposite of Denethor, who, rather than giving life to others, takes his own life and attempts to take the life of his son, Faramir. Aragorn's claim to the throne is finally manifest when Faramir wakes from his fever and immediately pronounces Aragorn king.

BOOK V, CHAPTER 9

SUMMARY — THE LAST DEBATE

Gimli and Legolas find Merry and Pippin in the Houses of Healing. The hobbits eagerly ask questions about the Paths of the Dead. Gimli refuses to speak of the experience, but Legolas describes it. According to Legolas, after setting out from the Paths of the Dead, Aragorn led the Company and the army of the Dead to the Great River, Anduin. Invading fleets of Sauron's allies prevented thousands of potential defenders from reaching Minas Tirith. At Aragorn's command, the legion of Dead swept over the Enemy's ships, causing the terrified sailors to throw themselves overboard. Aragorn released the Dead from their curse and then, gathering the local Men of Lamedon, set sail for Minas Tirith. At the end of the tale, Gimli and Legolas express their wonder that Mordor's allies were overthrown by darkness and fear.

While the four companions share their stories, Aragorn holds a meeting of the lords in his tent outside the city. Gandalf tells the assembled captains that Mordor has not yet unleashed the greater part of its army. Though Minas Tirith has fought back the first assault, the next will be much stronger. In addition, the Ring of Power is now somewhere within the borders of Mordor. Should Sauron seize the Ring, all hope would be lost. Gandalf suggests an assault on the Black Gate of Mordor, reasoning that it is impossible to defeat Mordor without destroying the Ring, and that the Eye of Sauron must be diverted from the Ring-bearer as long as possible. Gandalf predicts that Sauron will think that Aragorn has taken possession of the Ring and, rash with pride, has chosen to attack Mordor. Gandalf believes that while attacking Mordor may prove fatal, it is their duty to defend against evil while it remains in their power to do so. The Captains agree to this plan.

ANALYSIS

Legolas's tale is a departure from Tolkien's typical habit of depicting events firsthand, as they unfold. We hear the story of the Dead's assault on the forces of Mordor secondhand rather than directly through a narrator. This storytelling technique reminds us of the importance of oral tradition in the ancient cultures Tolkien studied and of the author's attempt to recreate this tradition in his portrait of Middle-earth. We sense that one day, many generations later, Legolas's tale will become a folktale or a myth, part of the cultural legacy of the Elves or Men. In an interesting twist, Gimli refuses to talk about what happened on the Paths of the Dead; while the Elf is willing to narrate in great detail, the Dwarf absolutely refuses all comment. Gimli states that he wishes to keep the memories of his journey on the Paths of the Dead in darkness forever and never bring them to the light of day. Hearing Legolas narrate the tale that Gimli refuses to utter reminds us of the fragility of the oral tradition—a story may be lost forever if it is not retold.

Tolkien also complicates the notion of good against evil in these chapters, exploring the fact that the Enemy, just like the forces of Gondor, experiences fear. Legolas, as he narrates the tale of the routing of Mordor's forces by the legions of the Dead, expresses his amazement that the troops of the Dark Lord were overcome by simple terror. The Dead overwhelmed the Enemy not with military maneuvers or well-aimed arrows, but by appearing on the ships. That even the soldiers of Mordor are scared reminds us that the battle between good and evil in *The Lord of the Rings*, however cosmic in scope, is still a battle between imperfect mortal creatures with their own limitations. Similarly, Gandalf highlights Sauron's limitations in the Dark Lord's assumption that Aragorn took control of the Ring, and that Aragorn will use it to attack Mordor vaingloriously. Sauron is able to imagine only the selfish and aggressive course of action, which is not the option the Fellowship chooses. Sauron's blindness to the possibility of selflessness and sacrifice—to the idea that someone might destroy the Ring willingly, giving up access to its power—is perhaps the only failing that the forces of good can exploit to overthrow him.

BOOK V, CHAPTER 10

SUMMARY — THE BLACK GATE OPENS

Two days later, the armies of the West set out for Mordor, numbering seven thousand. At Imrahil's urging, a small force remains in Minas Tirith to defend the city. Though the injured Merry cannot go to battle, Pippin marches as a soldier of Gondor. The army passes Osgiliath and makes camp; the horsemen move ahead, but they encounter no opposing forces. As the army draws closer to Mordor, Gandalf instructs the heralds to sound the trumpets and declare the coming of the King of Gondor. The army's stirring and brazen cheers meet little answer from Sauron aside from an eerie, watchful silence.

On the second day of its march, the army is nearly ambushed by a strong force of Orcs, but Aragorn and the Captains stop the ambush. Several Nazgûl begin to fly overhead, following the progress of the army. As Aragorn's army nears Mordor on the fourth day, the younger troops become paralyzed with fear. In pity, Aragorn permits them to turn back, but many decide to stay. On the sixth day, the host approaches Morannon, the Black Gate of Mordor, which is surrounded by reeking pools of mud and filth. Aragorn arranges his army upon two great hills.

Gandalf and Aragorn ride toward Morannon with a small envoy, including Gimli, Legolas, Pippin, Éomer, Imrahil, and Elrond's sons—representatives of each of the races of Middle-earth that are opposed to Sauron. The envoy calls for Sauron to emerge and submit to the justice of Gondor. After a long period of silence, the Lieutenant of the Dark Tower emerges with an embassy of black-clad soldiers. Although a living man, the Lieutenant has a face like a skull, and fire burns in his eye sockets and nostrils.

The Lieutenant laughingly mocks Aragorn and his army. When Gandalf admonishes him, the Lieutenant draws from his cloak Frodo's coat of *mithril,* Sam's sword, and a gray Elven cloak. The Lieutenant informs the anxious Captains that Sauron will spare the life of the captured Hobbit spy if they agree to certain terms. Gandalf, with a look of defeat, asks for the terms. The Lieutenant says that Gondor and its allies must never attack Mordor, that Gondor must become a tributary to Mordor, and that a suitable captain from Mordor must rule in Isengard over Rohan. Gandalf utterly rejects these terms.

The Lieutenant feels a sudden grip of terror at Gandalf's rebuke. He turns and retreats to the Black Gate. As he does, the host of Mordor—much larger than that of Gondor—pours out of the Gate. Drums roll, fires blaze, and the sun turns red. A great company of brutal hill-trolls charges into Pippin's company. One of the trolls pounces on Beregond, but Pippin stabs the troll with his sword. The troll topples forward and crushes the startled hobbit. Pippin begins to lose consciousness. He bids farewell to the world, and just as everything turns dark, Pippin hears a great clamor of voices shouting, "The Eagles are coming!"

ANALYSIS

As the famous Christian writer and friend of Tolkien C.S. Lewis observed, the chief differences between the good and evil characters in *The Lord of the Rings* involve imagination and logic. The evil forces, says Lewis, cannot imagine themselves doing anything else but evil; for them, evil is the only logical option—a necessary and impulsive inclination. The good, in contrast, can conceive of doing evil, but they *choose* to do good; for them, life is a series of free choices. As such, the good have the power to choose to take actions that are spontaneous or unexpected—a power that Sauron does not seem to have. Indeed, we see this ability to choose clearly in this chapter. Sauron expects a challenge from the Captains of the West, assuming that the new Ring-bearer—whom Sauron believes to be Aragorn—is moving in dangerous haste, driven by the vision of power that the Ring has surely fed to his ego. Greed backed by violence is the only line of reasoning Sauron can understand. He cannot imagine that the armies of the West might march toward Mordor as a smokescreen or with the motive of personal sacrifice.

This ability of the forces of good to foil Sauron's expectations sets the ground for the deep sense of irony that pervades the closing chapters of Book V. Legolas and Gimli, in the account of their journey, note the irony that Aragorn has defeated Mordor's forces on the Anduin River with the very spirits of the Dead who themselves once worshipped Sauron. In a strategic sense, the march to Mordor is ironic in two ways: first, an opposing force would approach enemy territory shouting and singing their claim over the land; second, Sauron thinks he is cunningly luring Aragorn's forces in, when it is actually Aragorn's forces who approach Mordor of their own accord, with the intention of playing into Sauron's hands.

The deepest irony of this section lies in the confrontation with the Lieutenant before the Black Gate. For one, we know that the Lieutenant's bold words are only a show. We recall that in the final moments of *The Two Towers,* Sam cast aside his sword in favor of Frodo's, and that the Orcs did not kill Frodo but only disrobed him of his *mithril* coat. Armed with his lies, the Lieutenant does not expect to be so coldly dismissed by a military force only one-tenth the size of his own. Gandalf uses a double entendre to toy with the Lieutenant's expectations: when the Lieutenant instructs the wizard to take or leave his demands, Gandalf shouts, "[T]hese we will take!" and takes the coat, cloak, and sword from the Lieutenant. Gandalf's spontaneous verbal irony yields an equally spontaneous reaction from the Lieutenant, whose look of sudden fear betrays his attempt to maintain his proud and evil demeanor.

Gandalf's words are not merely rhetorical, though, for they remain consistent with the wizard's overall approach to confronting evil throughout *The Lord of the Rings*. Both before the Balrog in the Mines of Moria and before the Lord of the Nazgûl at the gates of Minas Tirith, Gandalf abandons his formidable magic powers in favor of the power of words, confronting his enemies with speech and commanding them to turn from their violent intentions. Here, Gandalf similarly commands the Lieutenant, yelling, "Begone!" The wizard's authoritative words offer his adversaries the opportunity to choose between doing evil and relenting toward the side of good. In this regard, Gandalf implies that good and evil are not diametrically opposed forces or powers in the natural world, but rather two choices available to the mind and the will.

BOOK VI, CHAPTER 1

SUMMARY — THE TOWER OF CIRITH UNGOL

> *[H]e knew in the core of his heart that he was not large*
> *enough to bear such a burden. . . .*
>
> *(See* QUOTATIONS, *p. 245)*

As Book VI begins, the narrative returns to focus on Sam and Frodo, who are still in the Tower of Cirith Ungol in Mordor. Sam wakes to find himself in the dark, outside the Orc stronghold. He knows he needs to rescue Frodo, but a massive door blocks his path. He turns and makes his way through the tunnel behind him.

Without reason or purpose, Sam puts on the Ring. Immediately, he feels the great physical weight of the Ring's power. His hearing improves, but his sight becomes hazy. He hears the sound of savage fighting in the tower. He turns and runs back toward the door, hoping that the two Orc-captains have come to blows. Spurred by an intense love for Frodo, Sam takes off the Ring and approaches the main gate of Cirith Ungol. As he does, he sees Orodruin, or Mount Doom, in the distance to the east. He again feels the wild, heavy pull of the Ring and begins to fantasize about becoming "Samwise the Strong," a great hero. Remembering his love for Frodo, Sam shakes off such thoughts. He is convinced that he is too much of a plain hobbit and a humble gardener to control the Ring.

Pressing on with a shrug, Sam halts helplessly before the gate, as if held by a web. He is under the influence of the Two Watchers who forbid all entrance into Cirith Ungol. Sam unconsciously draws the phial of Galadriel from his breast and extends it forward. Its great light pierces the gloom, and Sam is able to pass quickly through the gate. The Watchers let out a shrill cry.

Inside, Sam notices the bodies of dead orcs as he reaches a narrow staircase. The dark figure of an orc moves down the stairs. The orc sees Sam and halts, perceiving Sam as a great, grey shadow brandishing an Elf blade that shines bitterly in the darkness. The terrified orc turns and runs up into the tower. Sam follows stealthily, jovially terming himself the "Elf-warrior." Upstairs, Sam can hear the orc, Snaga, speak to another, Shagrat; they are the only two orcs left in the tower. Shagrat orders Snaga to descend, but Snaga will not go back downstairs. Snaga runs into an unknown chamber of the tower, leaving the furious Shagrat alone. Sam reveals himself to

Shagrat and moves to attack, but the orc, overwhelmed by the power of the Ring, runs in panic around Sam and out the door.

Sam looks desperately around for Frodo, but cannot find him. He begins to sing to himself. His song draws a snarl from Snaga, who mistakes Sam's voice for Frodo's. Sam follows the sound of the snarl and finds the orc climbing a ladder through a hidden door in the ceiling. Sam climbs after Snaga and attacks him in the secret chamber. In a panic, the surprised orc charges Sam, trips over him, and falls through the hidden door to the hard floor below.

Frodo lies naked on a heap of rags in the middle of the room. He is surprised to see Sam and utterly elated to find that Sam has saved the Ring. Suddenly, Frodo demands that Sam hand over the Ring, calling Sam a thief. Grabbing the Ring, Frodo apologizes to Sam. Frodo and Sam outfit themselves in Orc gear and climb down the ladder. With the phial of Galadriel, the two hobbits move past the Watchers and out into Mordor. Suddenly, the terrifying cry of a Black Rider rends the sky above them.

ANALYSIS

The second half of *The Return of the King* opens with a different picture of evil from the one that closes the first half. In the final chapter of Book V, Gandalf offers a verbal challenge to Sauron's Lieutenant that suggests that evil is largely an internal force—the result of choice, corruption, and misdeed. When Sam awakens at Cirith Ungol, however, we immediately see a picture of evil as an external force, an outward manifestation of Sauron's inner evil that lies like a heavy blanket over Mordor. The sky is dark, the air thick and bitter, and the terrain a desert wasteland.

The physical presence of the Ring dominates the opening of Book VI. Once a symbol of the mixed blessings of power, the Ring is now a bane on Frodo's existence. His body and the Ring are one, and his body expires as the Ring grows heavier with each step toward Mount Doom. We are introduced to the Eye of Sauron, glaring as a potent symbol of Sauron's evil will as it extends across the land. From the Eye emanates a real physical stream of evil power and influence. Sauron's Eye imposes his inner evil qualities and corrupt condition onto the natural world of his realm.

Furthermore, the Ring begins to inflict trouble the only relationship that has remained pure and complete throughout the novel thus far—the devoted friendship between Frodo and Sam. We have never detected discord in the camaraderie of these two hobbits on their long journey through Middle-earth. But with Sam's sudden and unexpected possession of the Ring, the relationship falls victim to jealousy and wrongful accusations. When Frodo sees Sam with the Ring and demands it back immediately, calling his loving friend a thief, we witness the power of the Ring to distort reality and impart individuals with an illusory sense of power. Sam toys with mild delusions of grandeur when he wears the Ring, but these are more comic and endearing than evil, and they lead us to feel all the more strongly the unfairness of Frodo's accusations. The injury is even greater because it comes at a moment of reunion after extreme bravery on Sam's part. Although Frodo apologizes soon afterward and Sam accepts the apology, the memory of Frodo's unkind words lingers in our minds as further proof of the Ring's destructive power.

Sam's confrontation with the Ring's power reminds us why he emerges at the end of *The Lord of the Rings* as the unexpected hero of the novel. Sam wears the Ring and, to some degree, experiences the same delusions of grandeur and fame that all its wearers feel. He fantasizes about fame as "Samwise the Strong," thereby demonstrating his susceptibility to the insidious and powerful vanity that the Ring inspires. But Sam has the strength to remove the Ring when he thinks of Frodo. Love for others is precisely what the Ring destroys, setting all its wearers on courses of greedy individualism in which bonds of loyalty and love no longer matter. Sam's intense devotion to his friend is unmatched even by the good Frodo, who earlier took off the Ring through the strength of his own will, but not with the same heartwarming fondness for another. Frodo removed the Ring out of a sense of right—an honorable action, but not as selfless as that of Sam, who removes it out of love. The irony of Sam's thoughts—that, as an ordinary gardener hobbit, he is too common to wear the Ring—is that he is actually one of the Ring's safest keepers, relatively unaffected by the selfishness it provokes.

BOOK VI, CHAPTER 2

SUMMARY — THE LAND OF SHADOW

Sam and Frodo run away from Cirith Ungol as horns peal in the tower. They run onto a long bridge, but as they approach the other side, they hear a company of orcs quickly approaching. The orcs cannot see the two hobbits, but are heading straight for them. Frodo and Sam jump over the edge of the bridge, landing safely on the side of a cliff. With great difficulty, they clamber down to the valley below. Mount Doom lies to the east, but the hobbits travel north-ward, hoping to evade any Orc search parties.

Frodo and Sam have only some of Faramir's provisions, a few *lem-bas*, and no water. After a night of weary travel, they find a small stream and joyously refill their water bottles. The Ring grows heavier around Frodo's neck with every step. Mount Doom is still nearly forty miles to the east, across a great valley. Behind the mountain sits Barad-dûr, Sau-ron's home, from which the Dark Lord directs his will over Mordor. Scattered all over the valley, as far as the two hobbits can see, the armies of Mordor await the final battle. There is no hope of moving undetec-ted through so many enemies, but Frodo and Sam again have no choice but to go on. They continue moving northward, looking for a good place to leave the mountains and move east. They overhear two orcs quarrelling, speaking of a rumor about a great Elf in bright armor who is on the loose.

On the third day, Frodo and Sam turn into a narrow eastward road and travel over it for several miles in the darkness. After some time, they hear a great company of orcs approaching from behind. The hobbits are unable to move aside, and the company overtakes them, but in the darkness its leader assumes the hobbits are orcs and forces them into line with the others. For what seems like hours, they travel with the Orc company at an excruciating pace. Frodo is in agony from the Ring's increasing weight. After a time, they reach a busy crossroads. Armies from the south are moving in anticipation of Aragorn's army. In the confusion of the converging companies, Frodo and Sam jump aside and crawl behind a nearby boulder.

ANALYSIS
Sam emerges in these chapters as perhaps the most important hero of the entire novel. He represents the quintessential Hobbit hero, the vir-tues of which Merry displays briefly in Book V. Daring yet self-depre-cating, Sam succeeds because he approaches the heroic challenge with a certain lightheartedness, as though he is playing at being a hero. He jokes that he is an "Elf-hero" and shrugs his shoulders as he launches through the gate of Cirith Ungol. Sam remains centered and focused because, as he realizes, he cannot escape his "plain Hobbit-sense." That he is a gardener by trade has metaphorical significance, as Sam is used to dirtying his hands in the earth and does not think lofty thoughts of power or of reaching great heights. These correctives to Sam's pride help him focus on the proper goals of his quest—serving Frodo and guarding the Ring. At the same time, Sam's playfulness leads him to

trust his impulses, such as using the phial of Galadriel and unwittingly singing a song to lead him to Frodo.

Tolkien implies that love is an important aspect of heroism, as we see in the way Sam is inspired by his love for Frodo. It is not that Sam's attention to Frodo supersedes his commitment to the Ring-quest; rather, Sam implicitly understands that love and loyalty are essential to the success of the quest itself. Freedom, love, friendship, and the preservation of life are the goals of the Fellowship. Sam must save Frodo before he can carry out the destruction of the Ring, Gandalf must save Faramir from the burning pyre in order to prevent evil from gripping Minas Tirith, and Aragorn must set the captives free when he takes the ships by force from the allies of Mordor. Throughout *The Lord of the Rings,* Tolkien stresses the primacy of friendship and immediate social responsibility over more nebulous ideas of heroism or valor.

The closeness of Sam and Frodo to the Orc forces reminds us how the hobbits' nondescript appearance—and their modest ordinariness in general—is often an asset to them on their journey. A more noble and knightly presence, like that of Aragorn or Théoden, would have stood out from the Orc contingent, and would have been immediately destroyed. But Frodo and Sam, who are not much to look at, pass unnoticed even when they are swept along in the midst of the marching Orc army. Moreover, their proximity to the Orcs allows them to overhear the Orc discussion of the rumor that a great Elf in bright armor is on the loose. The hobbits are thus allowed to see what the knights like Aragorn cannot—the nervous and anxious side of the enemy they are preparing to meet. Elrond's words from the earliest parts of the novel, in Book II, ring true: the nature of the Ring-quest is such that the weak and the small are just as likely to succeed as the strong.

BOOK VI, CHAPTER 3

SUMMARY — MOUNT DOOM

> "[T]he Quest is achieved, and now all is over. I am glad you are here with me. Here at the end of all things, Sam."
>
> *(See* QUOTATIONS, *p. 246)*

The next morning, Sam gains new strength and a grim sense of responsibility. He wakes Frodo and pushes him on toward Orodruin. The land before them is cold and dead, dotted by countless craters and hollows. The hobbits crawl eastward from hiding place to hiding place. After a few miles, Frodo is nearly spent, his mind and body tormented by the terrible weight of the Ring. He refuses to give the Ring to Sam, for he knows he is held by its power. The two decide to take to the road once again. All eyes in Mordor are turned to the west, where the Captains march toward Morannon.

After three draining days of travel, Frodo's limbs give way and he falls, exhausted. Sam picks Frodo up and carries him on his back. Before nightfall, they reach the foot of the mountain. Sam carefully makes his way up the slope. It is nearly morning. For a moment, the shadows dissipate, and Sam can see the flicker of the piercing Eye from Sauron's Dark Tower. Its gaze passes by the hobbits and turns to the north, focusing on the Captains of the West. However, the glimpse of Sauron's power causes Frodo to panic. His hand grasps for the Ring around his neck, and he cries for Sam's help. Sam kneels beside Frodo and gently holds his master's palms together in his lap.

Afraid Sauron has spotted them, Sam takes Frodo upon his shoulders once more and continues up the mountain. With much difficulty, they finally reach the top. Sam looks down over a great cliff into the burning Cracks of Doom below. Suddenly, a cruel weight hits Sam from behind, and he falls forward. Behind him, he hears the voice of Gollum, cursing Frodo viciously for his treachery. Frodo and Gollum engage in a violent struggle, and Gollum proves stronger than the weakened Frodo. Suddenly, Frodo commands Gollum, "Begone, and trouble me no more!" and the creature falls to his knees. Frodo presses on to the Cracks of Doom. Sam, tempted to slay Gollum with his sword, refrains out of pity. Gollum slinks away.

Reaching the Cracks, Frodo turns to Sam and, with a voice clearer than Sam has ever heard, informs him that he will not complete the quest. The Ring, Frodo declares, is his. He puts the Ring on his finger and vanishes. Sam is once again flung aside, and then he sees a dark shape leap over him. Just as Sam looks up, the Great Eye of Sauron suddenly becomes aware of Frodo. The eight remaining Nazgûl hurtle toward the mountain at terrifying speed.

Sam sees Gollum struggling with an invisible enemy, biting at the air viciously. Frodo suddenly reappears, his hand bleeding from his severed finger. Gollum pulls Frodo's finger and the Ring from his mouth joyfully, but then steps backward, unaware that he is close to the edge of the cliff. Gollum then falls, along with the Ring, into the

Cracks of Doom. Mount Doom shakes violently as it accepts and consumes the Ring. Sam runs out into the daylight, carrying Frodo. The Nazgûl wither in the fiery ruin of the hill. Frodo stands by Sam's side, himself again. Sam feels overjoyed, and Frodo explains that, were it not for Gollum, he would not have been able to finish the quest. Frodo says he is glad to be with Sam "at the end of all things."

ANALYSIS

The completion of the quest marks the central climax of *The Lord of the Rings*. While the novel has included several separate, progressively larger climaxes—such as the overthrow of Saruman and the battle for Gondor at the Pelennor Fields—the deposit of the Ring into the Cracks of Doom resolves the major conflict presented at the outset of *The Fellowship of the Ring*. All of the markings we might expect from the climax of such a voluminous quest narrative are present: Mount Doom erupts, towers fall, and Sauron's dark shadow vanishes in the wind. In one sense, the effects of Frodo's success are endless. Middle-earth is freed from Mordor's evil influence, ensuring renewed hope and progress for its inhabitants. In another sense, however, Frodo himself gains little from depositing the Ring in the Cracks of Doom. The hobbit finds no treasure or maiden, and does not rescue any captives. He only emerges from Mount Doom with a greater self-understanding and the ability to say, as the world collapses around him, that he is content to be with his friend Sam.

Frodo and Sam continue to add to the picture of Hobbit heroism that Tolkien has developed throughout the novel. Notably, Frodo's heroism is purely passive. He must be carried up Mount Doom, almost against his own will, weeping and exhausted. At the end of his quest, he refuses to part with the Ring. Frodo announces to Sam, "I have come. . . . But I do not now choose what I came to do." This passage highlights once again the importance of choice in Tolkien's conception of good and evil. Choice has been the distinguishing factor of Frodo's heroism throughout the novel. Unlike Sauron, whose fate is bound to the Ring, Frodo possesses the power to choose whether to carry the Ring or not, and whether to wear it or destroy it. He remains a hero simply because he has *chosen* to carry the Ring for so long in a quest that aims only to destroy an object that offers him great power. That Frodo wills himself to move forward as far as the Cracks of Doom is evidence enough of his heroism. The success of the journey from the beginning has been doubtful; only a sense of providence and hope has suggested Frodo might accomplish the task. In an ironic twist of fate, the Ring's most possessive owner, Gollum, wrests the Ring from Frodo and inadvertently destroys it.

Sam's self-sacrificing heroism on the journey up Mount Doom complements Frodo's passivity in its loving gentleness. As Sam self-lessly carries Frodo up the mountain, he is struck that his master is lighter than he expected. When Frodo struggles with an uncontrol-lable urge to grasp the Ring, Sam gently removes his master's hand from his chest and holds his palms together. The image suggests two men praying, implying that Sam redeems Frodo in a spiritual sense. Sam's feet and controlling hands aid Frodo in the choice to move toward the Cracks of Doom, which Frodo indicates he still chooses to do only in his acquiescence.

The last leg of Frodo's journey also reveals much about the ambiguous nature of evil. At first blush, the Ring continues to sym-bolize actual physical evil. Frodo bears the immense physical weight of the Ring and its evil, eventually losing all bodily strength as he gets closer to Mount Doom. When Sam picks Frodo up—and thus picks up the Ring as well—he finds his friend to be light, and he is able to remove Frodo's groping hand from the Ring with a gentle tug. Tolkien suggests that only the Ring's wearer perceives its heavi-ness—its physical force remains a matter of perception, not of real weight. In this sense, we return to Tolkien's characterization of evil as a human creation; physical symbols of evil only display real power over those who are tempted by them.

Tolkien further examines the ambiguous nature of evil in the imagery of the land of Mordor. Sauron's Great Eye, fixed atop the Dark Tower, functions both as a symbol of the Dark Lord's will and as the source of his ability to enact his will on the physical world. The Great Eye itself does not cause any harm—it does not strike anyone down or emit any visible signal. The Eye only suggests where Sauron's attention is fixed. It focuses to the north while Sau-ron's mind remains occupied with the forces at the Black Gate, thus allowing Sam and Frodo to reach the goal of their quest.

BOOK VI, CHAPTER 4

SUMMARY — THE FIELD OF CORMALLEN

The narrative returns to Gandalf and those outside the Black Gate. To the north, the Captains of the West founder on the hills outside the Gate, surrounded by a dark, rolling sea of Orcs and Wild Men. Gandalf stands proudly, white and calm, with no shadow falling upon him. Suddenly, a great cry rises up: "The Eagles are coming!" Out of the north arrives a company of great eagles, led by Gwaihir the Windlord. The will of Sauron falters, and all the armies of Mordor quail in terror. A great roar shakes the hills. Gandalf cries in victory that the Ring-bearer has completed his quest, and that the reign of Sauron has ended. As Gandalf speaks, a huge shadow rises in the south, extending across the sky like a giant hand, and then vanishes in the wind with a great rush.

Aragorn leads the Captains in a great sweep over the plains. Gandalf then soars into Mordor on the back of Gwaihir. Meanwhile, Frodo and Sam, still in the heart of Mordor, have given up all hope of survival. As they talk quietly below the ruin of Mount Doom, Gwaihir spots them. Two eagles sweep down and lift the hobbits into the air.

When Sam wakes, he finds himself on a soft bed in Ithilien, the eastern lands of Gondor. He first comments on the extraordinary dream he has just had and then cries out in astonishment that his dream actually happened. Frodo sleeps next to Sam, and Gandalf watches over the two of them. The wizard says that a great Shadow has departed, asks the hobbits to dress in their worn and ragged attire, and escorts them out of the wood. They are to attend a reception hosted by the King of Gondor.

A great throng of people awaits the hobbits. At their emergence, the crowd bursts into thunderous applause, singing songs in praise of the hobbits. Frodo and Sam approach a great throne, where Aragorn welcomes them. He lifts them and sets them on the throne, and the joy of the people flows over them like a warm wind. In a regal ceremony, Frodo bequeaths his knife Sting to Sam, who initially resists but finally accepts the gift. That evening, Frodo and Sam attend a generous feast. They reunite with their old companions. Sam is greatly surprised by Pippin, who seems to have grown several inches. The next morning, King Aragorn prepares to enter the great city of Gondor as its rightful ruler.

ANALYSIS

This chapter, which marks the public acknowledgment of the end of Sauron's reign, features a number of prominent images of vanishing shadows. The great Darkness, extended outward like a giant hand over the land, suddenly vanishes. This sign of Sauron's fall is marked by the image of the hand, which is associated with Sauron's finger that wore the Ring and also suggests the reaching, grasping, greedy nature of the Dark Lord—the only aspect of him that we see, as he is never an actual character in the novel. But with the routing of Sauron, this hand dissipates like a shadow in the light, or like smoke in the air. The symbolism of this quick fading is clear. Sauron's power was never substantial or real, but was always just an airy illusion, a castle in the air that was fated to dissolve. When Gandalf stands outside the Black Gate, Tolkien explicitly tells us that no shadow falls upon the wizard—as a figure of supreme good, he is able to resist the pall of Sauron's evil.

The festivities at the court of Gondor mark an important step in the hobbits' development. Throughout the entire journey, they have not once been treated with anything remotely close to this level of respect and admiration. Earlier, their presence was met either with wary suspicion (as when the hobbits arrived at Éomer's court and Faramir's stronghold in *The Two Towers*) or with outright hostility (as at the inn at Bree in *The Fellowship of the Ring*). Though the hobbits have, since their first step out of the Shire, been pursuing a goal of value to all civilization, their significance has not been rightfully rewarded or even appreciated in any place they have visited. But here, at the reception in Gondor, the reunited hobbits are treated to rapturous praise and applause, with no shadow of suspicion or darkness falling over the ceremony. The Hobbit outsiders, whom others have often viewed as children not to be taken seriously, have now, in a sense, grown up. They finally receive due recognition, having shown the world their worth.

BOOK VI, CHAPTER 5

SUMMARY — THE STEWARD AND THE KING
The narrative jumps back to the time before the quest is finished, now focusing on the perspective of those in Minas Tirith. While Aragorn and the forces of Gondor are away, the city remains shrouded in fear. Faramir meets Lady Éowyn in the Houses of Healing. Éowyn longs for Aragorn and the chance to fight with the Riders against Mordor. Her sadness, mixed with pride and beauty, leads Faramir to fall in love with her. For days, they stare to the east, waiting for word of Gondor's success, until they eventually see the Darkness break. As sunlight breaks through the sky, the citizens of Minas Tirith break out in song. Messengers soon arrive telling of Aragorn's victory. The conflict resolved, Éowyn's longing for war fades, and she and Faramir agree to wed.

When Aragorn returns, Faramir rides out of the gate of Minas Tirith and offers him the keys of the city and an ancient crown. To everyone's amazement, Aragorn calls for the Ring-bearer and Gandalf. Frodo hands the crown to Gandalf, who places it upon Aragorn's brow.

The city of Minas Tirith begins to revive. Its walls are restored, and the city is filled with trees, fountains, and laughter. Ambassadors from many lands arrive in Gondor, and Aragorn shows mercy by rewarding both the faithful and the enemies of the West. Gandalf explains that the Third Age of Middle-earth has passed: the war against Sauron is over, and Aragorn's reign in the age of Men has begun. The group climbs up an ancient, snowy path, at the end of which, amidst a pile of debris, Aragorn finds a sapling of the great White Tree—the symbol of ancient Elendil, Gondor's kingdom. Aragorn takes the sapling back to the Citadel. The old, dead tree is removed and laid to rest, and the new one planted in its place.

The day before Midsummer, a group of Elves approaches Minas Tirith. Celeborn and Galadriel, Elrohir and Elladan, and all the Elf princes arrive in the city. Behind them, mightiest of all, is Elrond with his daughter, Arwen. On the day of Midsummer, Aragorn (now called King Elessar) and Arwen are wed. Queen Arwen, seeking to repay Frodo for his immeasurable service and suffering, offers him a gift. When the time comes, he may sail in her stead across the Great Sea to the unknown West, where the Elves dwell in eternal youth and joy.

Analysis

The revival of Minas Tirith marks the rise of the age of Men, as Gandalf announces when the city suddenly flourishes again. This notion of one age giving way to a new one is an ancient idea. The Greeks, for example, envisioned consecutive epochs symbolized by various metals—the Golden Age being the best and earliest. In Middle-earth, the transition of ages is foretold in *The Fellowship of the Ring*, when Galadriel sadly hints to Frodo that the power of the Elves will continue to diminish in the future, whether or not Frodo's mission is successful. The new age is also hinted at in *The Two Towers*, with the news that there are no young Ents, as the Ent-wives disappeared long ago. The era of the Ent race, like that of the Elves, appears to be passing away. Humans, represented by Aragorn, are to assume a place of primacy in the world during this new age, which presumably continues until our own present day. This transition to human rule allows us to picture our own world as a sequel to

Tolkien's Middle-earth, which is, in a sense, an ancient ancestor of the world as we know it. We may imagine that our lives have been made possible because of the heroism of Frodo and his cohorts. Aragorn's retrieval of the White Tree and its return to Minas Tirith furthers this idea of the beginning of the new age and the reclamation of history. The sapling tree is white in color, suggesting purity and a blank slate upon which the future of the new age of Men can be written. Though reappearing as a new sapling, the White Tree remains the ancient image of the city of Minas Tirith.

Aragorn's marriage to Arwen is a surprise in some ways, as there has been little focus on female characters in the novel thus far, and no romantic activity. Though the wedding is perhaps the last thing we might expect at this point, it fulfills several symbolic functions. On a literal level, it heartens us to see two such noble characters united. It is especially touching given that Arwen—who, as an Elf, has the opportunity to sail west across the Great Sea and live eternally—gives up her immortality out of a desire to remain with the mortal Aragorn. On a broader, mythical level, the wedding symbolizes the ideas of continuity and unity. As in Shakespeare's comedies, which nearly always conclude in a wedding, the marriage of Aragorn and Arwen suggests that life goes on and that past divisions are to be reconciled. The news of the wedding—a beginning in itself— represents the regeneration of a fresh, new world after the fall of Sauron. Though the marriage of Aragorn and Arwen is likely heartbreaking to Éowyn, who has longed after Aragorn, Éowyn ultimately finds comfort and love in Faramir. Éowyn's blossoming love for Faramir mirrors her own physical healing, the restoration of Minas Tirith, and the overall rejuvenation of Middle-earth after the overthrow of Sauron.

Book VI, Chapters 6–7

Summary — Chapter 6: Many Partings

After many days, when the festivities are over, the Company sets out for Rivendell. Aragorn tells Frodo that he knows the hobbit wishes for nothing more than to return home. Frodo answers that he wishes first to stop off at Rivendell to visit Bilbo one last time, as the older hobbit will likely die soon. On the way, they stop at Rohan and bid farewell to Éomer, honoring the memory of Théoden. After a brief stay in Rohan, they set off again.

Arriving in Isengard, they meet Treebeard, the Ent leader who orchestrated the march on Saruman in *The Two Towers*. The Ents had promised to guard Saruman's old stronghold of Orthanc, ensuring that the corrupt wizard would never escape. Treebeard tells them of the flight of many Orcs and the doom the Orcs met in the forest. He relates that he reported news regularly to Saruman, who would come to the window of Orthanc to listen. But then the wizard withered away. Treebeard, to Gandalf's dismay, has released Saruman, for he did not wish to keep such a miserable creature caged. Gandalf warns Treebeard that Saruman still has the power of his voice—a power he has used to his advantage in the past.

Proceeding onward, the group comes upon an old, ragged man leaning on a staff. They recognize him as Saruman. Another beggar in his company is Wormtongue, his former servant. The deposed Saruman is bitter but powerless. Galadriel and Gandalf offer Saruman mercy and reprieve. Their kindness irritates Saruman, who claims that with his demise, theirs will soon follow. After a few more days of slow and pleasant travel, Galadriel and Celeborn turn eastward and return home.

The remaining travelers reach Rivendell and the House of Elrond, and they find Bilbo. The old hobbit sits quietly in a small room, surrounded by bits of paper and pencils. The next day, all of Rivendell celebrates Bilbo's 129th birthday. After a fortnight, Frodo realizes that he must return to the Shire. Bilbo chooses to remain in Rivendell, for he is far too old for any more travel. Bilbo gives Frodo three books of collected lore entitled *Translations from the Elvish,* asking Frodo to finish editing them. Before Frodo leaves, Elrond takes the hobbit quietly aside, assuring him that in time he himself will visit the Shire, and he will bring Bilbo with him.

SUMMARY — CHAPTER 7: HOMEWARD BOUND

The hobbits are nearing home. Gandalf asks if Frodo feels much pain. Frodo answers that he has been wounded by a knife and by the other torments of his long and heavy burden. Gandalf is silent. The next day, Frodo feels happy, and they travel onward in relative ease. They arrive at Bree and speak to Butterbur, the innkeeper who aided them early in the quest. Butterbur, after welcoming them and making them comfortable by the warm fire, tells Gandalf and the hobbits that their strange warrior gear has scared many locals. Gandalf laughs at this. Gandalf assures Butterbur that now that Sauron has been vanquished, business at the inn will once again pick up, as people will feel more free to travel. Butterbur asks about the dangerous region known as Deadmen's Dike, which he imagines no one will be visiting. Gandalf asserts that the rightful king will return to that area, and it will become safe and prosperous again. He adds that the king is none other than Aragorn, once known in the inn as Strider. Butterbur is astonished at this news.

The next day, business in the inn is brisk, as many visitors, unable to restrain their curiosity, come to gawk at Gandalf's party. Many people ask Frodo whether he has written his memoirs yet. Finally, the Company sets off. Gandalf tells the hobbits that he will not accompany them to the Shire. His horse, Shadowfax, makes a leap, and Gandalf is gone. Frodo remarks that it feels as though he is falling asleep again, his adventures now over.

Analysis — Chapters 6–7

One complaint that readers of *The Lord of the Rings* sometimes make is that the denouement—the portion of the narrative following the climax—seems excessively long. Indeed, five full chapters follow Frodo and Sam's successful completion of the quest at the Cracks of Doom. This lengthy coda, however, highlights the important fact that *The Return of the King* cannot be considered an individual work, separate from the other two volumes of *The Lord of the Rings*; together, they form a single novel and narrative. Given the extraordinary length of the novel as a whole and the height of its climax, an exceptionally long coda is not out of line with the rest of Tolkien's work.

Furthermore, Tolkien does not use the remaining chapters only to tie up loose ends, but also to show the fulfillment of the images and themes he has introduced throughout *The Lord of the Rings* and *The Silmarillion* as a whole. The gradual return of the Company to the Shire frames the narrative, revisiting many characters and locales we have seen before. The Fellowship almost literally retraces its steps from *The Fellowship of the Ring* and *The Two Towers* in reverse order, giving us a chance to glimpse how these people and places have changed now that the burden of Sauron's evil has been lifted from Middle-earth. The town of Bree, for instance, is a far cry from the dark, suspicious, somewhat rough border town it once was. Whereas Frodo was earlier an object of great suspicion, especially after his accidental wearing of the Ring in the tavern in Book I, now he is the object only of great admiration and wonder, with throngs of people asking if he has written his memoirs yet.

Tolkien's inclusion of the idea of Bilbo's and Frodo's respective memoirs adds an interesting twist to the narrative structure of the novel. Tolkien implies, though he does not overtly say, that these memoirs form his source material for *The Hobbit* and *The Lord of the Rings*. As such, the author suggests that the mythology he has recorded is not his own modern creation, but a much older set of lore he has merely retold. This sense that the story of *The Lord of the Rings* existed before Tolkien's retelling connects the novel to the ancient mythological tradition, seemingly linking it to a narrative and a world that precede our own time.

BOOK VI, CHAPTERS 8–9

SUMMARY — CHAPTER 8: THE SCOURING OF THE SHIRE

The hobbits find the bridge at Brandywine closed with a large spiked gate. When they demand entrance, a frightened gatekeeper informs them that he is under orders from the Chief at Bag End to let no one enter between sundown and sunrise. Frodo guesses that the Chief must be Lotho, his greedy relative. Merry and Pippin climb over the gate. The four hobbits set out for Hobbiton and encounter a large group of Hobbit Shirrifs, who inform them they are under arrest. The four hobbits laugh and move on. One of the Shirrifs quietly warns Sam that the Chief has many Men in his service.

Leaving the Shirrifs behind, the four hobbits find a half-dozen Men who claim they do not answer to Lotho, the Hobbit Chief, but to another mysterious boss named Sharkey. The men threaten Frodo, but the other three hobbits draw swords. The men turn and flee. Sam rides on to find Tom Cotton, the oldest hobbit in the region. Farmer Cotton and his sons gather the entire village to fight. The band of Men returns, but surrenders after a brief fight.

After the battle, Farmer Cotton explains that shortly after the Hobbits first left, Lotho began to purchase farmland, causing a shortage of food in Hobbiton. Cotton says that a gang of Men from the south took over the town. The next morning, a band of nearly one hundred Men approaches Hobbiton. Pippin arrives with his relatives, and a fierce battle ensues. Seventy of the Men die in the Battle of Bywater, as the conflict is forever remembered.

The three remaining companions lead an envoy to Frodo's home, Bag End, to deal with the new Chief. To their surprise, the hobbits find Saruman standing at the gate to Bag End. Saruman—who, it turns out, is the mysterious boss Sharkey—pronounces a curse upon the Shire if any hobbit should harm him. Frodo assures his friends that Saruman has no power, but he forbids them to kill the wizard. As Saruman passes by Frodo, he draws a knife and stabs Frodo, but Frodo's armor shields him.

Frodo again demands that his companions show mercy on the old wizard. Frodo's clemency, however, enrages Saruman. Frodo asks about his relative Lotho, and Saruman informs Frodo that his servant, Wormtongue, killed Lotho in his sleep. Wormtongue, standing nearby, cries out that Saruman ordered him to do so. Saruman kicks Wormtongue, but Wormtongue stabs the old wizard. Wormtongue flees with a yell, but three Hobbit arrows kill him. From Saruman's corpse, a gray mist rises and blows away.

SUMMARY — CHAPTER 9: THE GREY HAVENS

> *"It must often be so, Sam, when things are in danger:*
> *some one has to give them up, lose them, so that others*
> *may keep them."*
>
> *(See* QUOTATIONS, *p. 247)*

The Shire's brief police state overthrown, the Hobbits rebuild the villages of the region. Sam opens the box Galadriel gave him and finds a small silver seed, which he plants. In the Party Field, a sacred tree springs up to replace the old one. Many children are born that year. Merry and Pippin become heroes in the Shire, but Frodo quietly retires. That spring, Sam marries Rosie Cotton, Farmer Cotton's daughter, and they live at Bag End with Frodo.

Frodo decides to travel to Rivendell to see Bilbo. Frodo entrusts to Sam a history of the War, written in part by Bilbo. Frodo, Sam, and others set out. As they enter the Woody End, they meet Elrond and Galadriel, who now wear two of the Three Elven Rings. Riding slowly behind the two elves is Bilbo himself. Sam and Frodo accompany the travelers to the Great Sea. When they reach the gates of the Grey Havens, they find Gandalf waiting for them. Beyond him is a great white ship, ready to sail to the West across the sea.

Pippin and Merry appear, wishing to be present at Frodo's departure. Frodo sadly bids farewell to his three friends and boards the ship. Gandalf entreats the three hobbits to enjoy each other's friendship as they quietly return to the Shire. Sam enters his warm home, where he finds Rosie waiting. She puts their young daughter, Elanor, in his lap, and Sam draws a deep breath and says, "Well, I'm back."

ANALYSIS

Although the final troubles of the Shire police state may seem out of place in the novel, they reinforce the ideas of corruption and temptation that Tolkien has frequently explored throughout the adventure. Ever since Pippin learned to control his curiosity after stealing the *palantír* from Gandalf, or since Frodo was torn between desire and duty when debating whether to put on the Ring or take it off, the ability to control one's urges and to understand oneself deeply has been of paramount importance. In the crisis in the Shire, Tolkien explores the problem of corruption on a social rather than an individual level. The hobbits have likely assumed—and we along with them—that while they journeyed to Mordor on their mission, the homeland they left behind remained quiet, peaceful, and safe. This assumption proves to be untrue: the familiar is just as open to corruption and danger as the faraway and the exotic. We see that even the wholesome Hobbit race is subject to the same failings as any other race in Middle-earth. In this episode, Tolkien stresses the fragility of good and the effort and self-control required to maintain it.

Sam's brief closing words neatly encapsulate the nature of the hobbits' return to the Shire in the final chapters of *The Lord of the Rings*. The hobbits are not home; they are "back." They have arrived at the place from which they started, but both the Shire and they themselves have changed drastically. When Gandalf leaves the hobbits to themselves—the first time the four of them have been alone together since they left the Old Forest early in *The Fellowship of the Ring*—they have only a vague feeling that they are now somewhat out of place back in the Shire. However, the Shire is indeed where they belong, and the new wisdom they have gained on the quest enables them to rebuild and restore order to their realm, just as they have restored order to Minas Tirith. The hobbits show that they have gained a set of skills from living with Men, Elves, and Dwarves. The hobbits speak with curt confidence to the Shirrifs and to Saruman's stooges and betray a knowledge of military strategy in the Battle of Bywater. Sam has become more forthright, and Merry and Pippin are actually taller. Later, Frodo, in his encounter with Saruman, displays the grace and forgiveness he has learned from Gandalf, from Sam, and in dealing with Gollum.

The Shire, much like the rest of Middle-earth, experiences fruitful growth and renewal after the troubles are eradicated. Things gradually return to normal after the police state is disrupted, and

Sam proceeds to live his life as if he had never left. Frodo's sacrifice stands in clearer relief than before, as we suddenly understand that his adventure has been less about improving life than about preserving it. Just as Frodo struggles upon the deposit of the Ring into the Cracks of Doom, the hobbits struggle to understand the experience of a journey for which the goal has been merely to allow Middle-earth to remain the beautiful realm it has been for so long. Frodo explains to Sam, "It must often be so, Sam, when things are in danger: someone has to give them up, lose them, so that others may keep them." Frodo, for his part, has given up his normalcy and commonness by his contact with the Ring's great power. In the end, he must join those whose lives are not common but mythic.

The company that boards the ship at the Grey Havens contains representatives of many of the races in Middle-earth. Those who board the ship, though different from each other, are now mythic heroes. According to Gandalf, the next age—the Fourth Age of Middle-earth—will be dominated by Men, led by Aragorn and Éomer. Tolkien uses the image of the sea as it is frequently employed in literature—to convey the notion of endless possibility, eternity, or obscurity. Just as the group on the ship sails away into the misty, indefinite horizon, so Tolkien attempts to imbue *The Lord of the Rings* with the qualities of long-lost, prehistoric lore.

Important Quotations Explained

1. *"You cannot enter here. . . . Go back to the abyss prepared for you! Go back! Fall into the nothingness that awaits you and your Master. Go!"*

Gandalf offers this dramatic challenge to the Lord of the Nazgûl at the close of Book V, Chapter 4. The old wizard confronts the Black Captain alone, recalling Gandalf's earlier confrontation with the Balrog in The Fellowship of the Ring. Initially, Gandalf's efforts fail in both instances: earlier, the Balrog pulls the wizard into the chasm of Khazad-dûm; here, the Black Captain sneers, turning away from Minas Tirith only because he hears the Riders' battle cry to the north. Nonetheless, the image of Gandalf standing firm before the Lord of the Nazgûl, unshaken and alone, lingers powerfully throughout The Return of the King.

While neither of these evil beasts directly cowers before Gandalf's commands, they both ultimately meet their demises. In this regard, the hand of providence or fate seems to direct events after Gandalf makes a sacrificial gesture. Gandalf scorns the opportunity to fight force with force, and he refrains from using his physical or mystical powers against the Nazgûl. Instead, the wizard uses human speech to invoke the powers of good over the powers of evil. Gandalf speaks with authority, as though performing a priestly duty, intervening with the unseen god or gods of Middle-earth on behalf of Minas Tirith. Interestingly, only Pippin, who observes the standoff, knows of the sins that Denethor, the Steward of Minas Tirith, is preparing to commit in the Citadel as Gandalf attempts to thwart the physical emblem of evil from entering the city.

In instructing the Lord of the Nazgûl to leave, Gandalf presents the Black Captain with a moral choice. The wizard offers brief redemption to the Black Captain, granting the creature the opportunity to make a moral choice in favor of good rather than completing the evil errand he has been sent to perform. However, the likelihood that the violent Ringwraith, given wholly over to evil, might change his mind because of a verbal rebuke is remote at best. Gandalf's words imply the assumption that the Lord of the Nazgûl has free will when it comes to choosing between good and evil. As servants of Sauron, however, the evil of the armies of Mordor resides in their corruption at the hands of the Dark Lord, their enslavement to his will, and their conviction they do not have such a choice to turn to the side of good.

2. "*I would have things as they were in all the days of my life . .
    . and in the days of my longfathers before me: to be the Lord
    of this City in peace, and leave my chair to a son after me,
    who would be his own master and no wizard's pupil. But if
    doom denies this to me, then I will have naught: neither life
    diminished, nor love halved, nor honour abated.*"

Denethor speaks this plea in the moments before he places himself on
the burning pyre in Book V, Chapter 7. In this quotation, Denethor's
tragic error appears obvious—he is overly fixated with power. On the
whole, however, Denethor's descent into madness is subtle, and his personal struggle with evil transcends the simpler distinctions—black
against white, East against West, evil against good—that abound in
The Return of the King. All told, Denethor wants honor and prosperity
for Minas Tirith and for Gondor. He wrongly assumes that he himself
must have complete power to accomplish such goals. Denethor could
rightly sit in the throne of Gondor, fulfilling his interim duties as Steward in place of the absent king. Instead, Denethor leaves the throne
empty, and his self-pity leads to the neglect of Minas Tirith that is evident in the city's decaying walls and vacant homes.

   As Gandalf later surmises, Denethor, under the growing pressure of
Mordor, has turned to the seeing-stone, or *palantír,* for power. The *palantír* itself does not symbolize evil; indeed, Aragorn claims he has
wrested control of the *palantír* and has used it to mislead and discour-
age Sauron. Rather, the *palantír* symbolizes knowledge—particularly
the ability to construe knowledge for the use of power or manipulation.
The distinction between knowledge and wisdom is important: Tolkien
implies that knowledge for knowledge's sake can lead to evil, whereas
knowledge tempered with wisdom—awareness of consequences—is
more responsible and virtuous. The *palantír* provides Denethor with
access to knowledge, but he does not have the wisdom with which to
temper this knowledge and recognize Sauron's lies. Through the stone,
Denethor does not become a servant of evil, but he succumbs to evil
lies. The effect of Sauron's evil on Denethor surfaces in the Steward's
stated belief that "doom denies" him a flourishing lineage. Denethor
accepts Sauron's misleading lie that the coming King of Gondor will
necessarily reduce Denethor's own political authority and restrict the
Steward's personal welfare. Indeed, as we see later in the novel, King
Aragorn grants Faramir, the new Steward, continued rule of Minas
Tirith. Denethor's tragic error lies in his belief that such unsolicited acts
of goodness can no longer happen in the world of Middle-earth.

3. *In that hour of trial it was the love of his master that helped*
    most to hold him firm; but also deep down in him lived still
    unconquered his plain hobbit-sense: he knew in the core of
    his heart that he was not large enough to bear such a burden,
    even if such visions were not a mere cheat to betray him.

This insight into Sam's thoughts about the Ring at Cirith Ungol in Book VI, Chapter 1, explains the key virtue of the hobbits as Ring-bearers and members of the Fellowship. Frodo's and Sam's small statures—both in terms of physical size and force of authority and personality—grant them a perspective that does not suit the Ring's overwhelming power. The small size of the Hobbit race also functions as a metaphor for their measured attitudes, their humility, and their unadorned goodness—attributes that appear to make them less vulnerable to the lure of the Ring. The Hobbits and the Shire are little known in Middle-earth; throughout *The Lord of the Rings*, the races of Men and Elves are surprised to learn that Hobbits actually exist. Frodo, by accepting the Ring, enters a history of war and conflict between Men and the forces of evil in which the Hobbits have had little part. As the symbol of that conflict, the Ring always seems like an awkward fit on a Hobbit hand.

Despite the seeming incompatibility of the Hobbit race as a whole with the lure of the Ring, we still get the sense that Frodo and Sam are exceptional Hobbits, with a strength of character that makes them less vulnerable to the Ring's power. After all, we know that Gollum, though once a Hobbit-like creature, was still corrupted by the Ring, and we have seen that the Ring is able to elicit erratic behavior and sudden fierceness in Bilbo. Frodo and Sam, on the other hand, are evidence that Hobbit virtues are only virtues insofar as one exhibits them. At Cirith Ungol, Sam proves that he has developed from a slightly dim-witted youth to a mature hobbit with a deep capacity for discernment and reflection. Deeply influenced by Frodo's experiences with the burden of the quest, Sam analyzes the Ring and immediately realizes and respects its subtle, destructive potential. Perhaps most important, Sam's desire to use the Ring himself springs only from his love for Frodo and his attempts to save his master. In this sense, Sam's affection for Frodo acts as a corrective to the Ring's power. Sam muses that, even if the tantalizing benefits of the Ring were an actual possibility rather than a false promise, they would not really be benefits if they involved losing his hobbit sense and his affection for Frodo. In this regard, Sam's resilient love for his friend precludes his fascination with the Ring's power.

QUOTATIONS

4.   *"But do you remember Gandalf's words: Even Gollum may*
     have something yet to do? But for him, Sam, I could not
     have destroyed the Ring. The Quest would have been in
     vain, even at the bitter end. So let us forgive him! For the
     Quest is achieved, and now all is over. I am glad you are here
     with me. Here at the end of all things, Sam."

Frodo shares this calm reflection with Sam at the end of Book VI, Chapter 3, as Mount Doom explodes and crumbles around them. Their somewhat leisurely conversation belies the fact that they have suffered from exhaustion and physical danger for so long, as well as the fact that Mordor is rupturing into a virtual apocalypse around them. The moment highlights one of Tolkien's strongest narrative devices—the juxtaposition of intimate personal moments against the backdrop of cosmic or earthly crises. This tension between the great and the small drives the entire plot of The Lord of the Rings— which revolves around the idea of two lowly hobbits not simply embarking on a quest but, as the critic Roger Sale puts it, descending into hell. Tolkien uses the device to emphasize the deep friendship between Frodo and Sam. Not only does the physical destruction of Mount Doom signal the climax of Tolkien's tale, but it also suggests that the moment represents the pinnacle of the two hobbits' friendship.

Frodo himself points out another irony: it is not he who finishes the quest they have traveled so far to achieve, but Gollum, the Ring's greatest hoarder, who has completed the task. Frodo cites Gandalf's prediction from the early chapters of The Fellowship of the Ring— that Gollum would invariably play a part in the fate of the Ring. Frodo has shown great patience and mercy toward Gollum throughout the second half of the quest. It remains unclear to what degree Gandalf's foreshadowing has remained in the back of Frodo's mind, inspiring his clemency for the miserable Gollum. Either way, a sense of divine providence and fate looms over the events that transpire at the Cracks of Doom, evoking a perfect blend of chance and retribution in Gollum's fall. In this regard, Frodo and Sam's calm discussion of Gollum's actions in light of the destruction around them hints that a greater, unknown power of good is protecting them.

5.   *"But I have been too deeply hurt, Sam. I tried to save the
        Shire, and it has been saved, but not for me. It must often be
        so, Sam, when things are in danger: someone has to give
        them up, lose them, so that others may keep them."*

Frodo speaks these words in his final farewell to Sam in Book VI,
Chapter 9—the final chapter of The Lord of the Rings. Frodo is
about to depart for the Grey Havens, where he will sail to the
uncharted West with the other Ring-bearers, in search of paradise.
As Frodo mentions, the quest has wounded him in an irreparable
way. He assumes that the safe deposit of the Ring in the Cracks of
Doom will save the Shire. The Shire does live on, but more so
because of the bravery of Merry, Pippin, and Sam in overthrowing
Saruman's destruction of the Hobbit lands. Though no one but Sam
has witnessed Frodo's deed, it has saved Middle-earth and has
allowed the Fourth Age to dawn and the kingdom of Men to take
root in Gondor. Such accomplishments, however, have little bearing
on Frodo or on the Shire. On the whole, his quest has been a negative one, a burden from the start. It has centered around giving
things up: not only the Ring, but also Frodo's innocence and mental
energy. Frodo has offered an absolute sacrifice, giving up a large
part of himself with minimal thanks from the hobbits for whom he
cares the most.

    In a sense, Frodo himself becomes a mythic character. As a hob-
bit, he is an everyman of sorts throughout the novel, experiencing
the events of his quest in wide-eyed, somewhat disbelieving fashion,
as if they are a fantasy story or a fairy tale. Frodo remains detached
from the Elves and the Dwarves, as they are beings whom Frodo has
encountered only in tales as a child. Now, Frodo's own greatest
deeds in life live on only in story and legend, symbolized by the
bound volume of tales he presents to Sam. It is fitting that Frodo
sails away into obscurity with the other Ring-bearers, whose fantastic lives in the coming age of Men will also attain a mythic, unreal
status.

QUOTATIONS

KEY FACTS

FULL TITLE

The Return of the King, being the third part of The Lord of the Rings

AUTHOR

J.R.R. Tolkien

TYPE OF WORK

Novel

GENRE

Epic; heroic quest; folktale; fantasy; myth

LANGUAGE

English, with occasional words and phrases from various languages of Middle-earth that Tolkien invented

TIME AND PLACE WRITTEN

1937–1949; Oxford, England

DATE OF FIRST PUBLICATION

1955

PUBLISHER

Allen and Unwin

NARRATOR

The whole of The Lord of the Rings is told by an anonymous, third-person narrator.

POINT OF VIEW

The Return of the King is narrated in the third person, following various members of the Fellowship, who by this point are separated. The early part of The Return of the King focuses on Pippin, Gandalf, and Aragorn, but then the focus switches to Frodo and Sam for much of the second half. The narration is omniscient, which means the narrator not only relates the characters' thoughts and feelings, but also comments on them.

TONE

The tone of The Lord of the Rings is in the epic tradition throughout, reinforcing a sense of myth through repeated references to characters' lineages and through spoken or sung prophecies that indicate the fates of various characters or the course of future events. The narrator makes few, if any, comments upon the unfolding story.

TENSE

Past

SETTING (TIME)

The end of the Third Age of Middle-earth and the beginning of the Fourth Age

SETTING (PLACE)

Various locales in the imaginary world of Middle-earth, including Minas Tirith, the Paths of the Dead, Osgiliath, Cirith Ungol, Mount Doom, the Shire, and the shore of the Great Sea

PROTAGONIST

Primarily Pippin in Book V, and returning to Frodo and Sam for most of Book VI, though the Fellowship as a whole might be considered a single protagonist

MAJOR CONFLICT

The Fellowship and the forces of Gondor battle the forces of Mordor, led by Sauron and the Lord of the Nazgûl. Frodo, meanwhile, struggles with the increasing torment of the Ring's burden, prompting Sam to take up a large part of the responsibility for the quest.

RISING ACTION

Gandalf and Pippin's arrival in Minas Tirith; Aragorn's journey through the Paths of the Dead; Denethor's madness and suicide; the battle of the Pelennor Fields; the death of Théoden; the slaying of the Lord of the Nazgûl; Frodo and Sam's weary journey to Mount Doom; Frodo's confrontation with Gollum

CLIMAX

Gollum's plunge with the Ring into the Cracks of Doom; the destruction of Sauron's power

FALLING ACTION

The crowning of Aragorn as King of Gondor; the dissolution of the Fellowship; the scouring of the Shire; Frodo's departure for the unknown West with the other Ring-bearers

THEMES

> The ambiguity of evil; the importance of redemption; the priority of friendship

MOTIFS

> Geography; race and physical appearance; the Christ figure

SYMBOLS

> The Ring; Minas Tirith; the Great Eye of Sauron

FORESHADOWING

> Aragorn's journey through the Paths of the Dead foreshadows his later Christlike ability to heal and restore the realm and residents of Gondor.

KEY FACTS

STUDY QUESTIONS & ESSAY TOPICS

STUDY QUESTIONS

1. *The cast of characters of* THE LORD OF THE RINGS *includes a number of pairs of characters who act as foils, or doubles, for each other. How is each character similar to, and different from, his or her foil? How do these foils relate to the broader themes Tolkien explores in his novel?*

As the two human political rulers in *The Return of the King,* King Théoden and Lord Denethor represent obvious character doubles. Tolkien emphasizes their doubled nature by alternating chapters devoted to Théoden and Denethor in Book V. When we meet them, both rulers are destitute, brought down by the influence of evil in their respective realms. Subsequently, each leader is the cause of further deterioration in his respective kingdom. Théoden, however, allows himself to be redeemed by Gandalf's counsel, whereas Denethor resists Gandalf's offer of redemption out of fear that the wizard wishes to infringe upon Denethor's political sovereignty in Minas Tirith. Both rulers leave their courts in order to die. Théoden rides to Gondor to die fighting for the cause of the West; Denethor commits suicide in the crypt of Gondor's ancient kings. Tolkien synchronizes their deaths, setting in relief the different outcomes of their demises. Théoden and his Riders ensure the survival of Gondor, and the king's body is carried in a somber procession from the battlefield. Denethor dies in self-pity, and his body is consumed in flames.

In a more profound way, Frodo and Gollum function as doubles as well, embodying the two opposite consequences of bearing the Ring. Both are small, but Gollum is smaller—a shriveled, black, and dirty version of a Hobbit. In one sense, they are opponents, united only by Frodo's mercy and forbearance. In another sense, Frodo and Gollum are one and the same. Gollum represents Frodo's id or inner self—the portion of Frodo that yearns for the Ring. Frodo, when he rebukes Gollum while ascending Mount Doom, appears to Sam as though dressed in white, as if he has mastered his darker, blacker self. When Frodo hesitates at the edge of the Cracks, he dons the Ring and disappears. In the ensuing struggle, Gollum is the only visible assailant, symbolizing the brief victory of Frodo's evil side. It is unclear who is responsible for Gollum's mistaken fall. What is apparent, though, is that the inner spiritual and external physical threats to Frodo's goodness are difficult to distinguish, rendering the portrayal of evil in *The Lord of the Rings* still more ambiguous.

2. *What are some of the physical symbols of evil in* THE LORD OF THE RINGS? *What do these symbols suggest about the nature or reality of evil? What is Tolkien's view of evil?*

In one sense, the physical symbols of evil in *The Lord of the Rings* depict evil as an overwhelming external physical force. At the opening of Book V, a thick blanket of gloom spreads out over the land of Gondor. The Darkness, or Shadow as it is often called, dulls the senses and makes the air stifling. The effects are similar to those of the Ring as Frodo nears Mordor and Mount Doom. Like a heavy magnet repelling its source, the Ring drags Frodo down, exhausting him until he can no longer walk. Furthermore, as Frodo and Sam approach the heart of Mordor, they increasingly feel the presence of the Great Eye of Sauron, fixed atop the Dark Tower where Sauron resides. The Eye conveys Sauron's will. The strength of Mordor's forces and the damage that is wrought upon the physical world all flow from the power source of the Eye.

In another sense, the physical symbols of evil seem to derive their evil quality from those who perceive them. A "physical symbol" cannot be entirely physical, as a symbol must possess a lingering quality that suggests there is more to the object than expected. The Darkness does not abate while Sauron rules; yet, as a shadow, the Darkness is immaterial, without power, and only a means of frightening onlookers such as Pippin. The Ring also manifests a certain ambivalence in its nature. Frodo feels the Ring is a giant weight, but Sam carries Frodo up Mount Doom with surprising ease, indicating that the Ring itself does not actually exert a real force. Evil is, in a way, a human creation, for while frightening or overwhelming events occur in the physical world, individuals must interpret these events and label them as evil. Tolkien, however, does not clarify this picture of evil. The physical world and the mental life of Middle-earth's inhabitants play reciprocal roles in defining evil.

3. *Is Aragorn a realistic character? Why or why not?*

In the third volume of *The Lord of the Rings*, Aragorn's character is inseparable from his actions and their significance. His words are few, and his calculated responses and decisions are rarely spontaneous. Aragorn's character is not realistic but idealistic—he embodies the moral principles, motifs, and plot conventions of Tolkien's text. The fact that Aragorn fulfills ancient legends about the long-awaited kingdom of Gondor does little to distinguish him as an individual, for Tolkien's legends are artificial, and we as readers have not been waiting long for the King of Gondor to return. Even the title of the third volume quashes Aragorn's realism. The title, *The Return of the King,* suggests that Aragorn's fate is fixed from the beginning of Book V.

Ironically, Tolkien's more fantastic characters are the ones who appear most convincingly real. Each character's race determines his or her personality and attitudes. Gimli is short and stout, and, as a Dwarf, a cave-dweller. Caves and stone, indeed, are major topics in Gimli's conversations. Gimli suffers embarrassment because he is the only member of Aragorn's group who is crippled with fear in the Paths of the Dead, despite the fact that dark trails and passages are Gimli's purported realm of comfort and expertise. Gimli's cowardice is rich and telling because it deviates so widely from his typical characteristics. His inconsistencies and exposed weaknesses deepen his character and make him more sympathetic. Aragorn, in his neutral appearance and impeccable prudence, lacks the ability to betray himself. Aragorn never exposes inner fears or a true self, for his true self is the role he plays as a Christ figure and eventually as King of Gondor.

SUGGESTED ESSAY TOPICS

1. Compare and contrast Frodo and Sam as heroes. What are their heroic virtues? In what ways are those virtues distinctively Hobbit-like?

2. What are some of the various powers Gandalf displays throughout the novel? Which of these is the most effective in the conflict against Mordor? What religious overtones, if any, surround the wizard's role and actions?

3. How does Tolkien use the geography of Middle-earth to contribute to the themes he explores in the Ring-quest?

4. Describe some of the various races of Middle-earth that Tolkien portrays in THE LORD OF THE RINGS. What are their distinguishing characteristics? How do their different physical appearances relate to their personalities, beliefs, customs, and so on?

5. Few female characters are mentioned in THE LORD OF THE RINGS. Describe some of the various appearances of female characters. How does Tolkien depict women? Is this depiction intended to be realistic? Idealistic? Ironic? Archaic?

6. In what sense might THE LORD OF THE RINGS be read as an allegory for Tolkien's Christian beliefs or the history of modern England? Are such readings of the novel apt or inadequate? What other methods does Tolkien use to convey his moral or religious intentions in the text?

QUESTIONS & ESSAYS

REVIEW & RESOURCES

QUIZ

1. Which of the following is not a distinguishing characteristic of Minas Tirith?

    A. Seven concentric city walls
    B. An empty throne
    C. Elaborate ruins
    D. A white tree

2. Why does Pippin offer his sword to Denethor in service of Gondor?

    A. Gandalf instructs him to do so
    B. He feels a debt to Gondor for Boromir's bravery
    C. He wishes to prove his valor as a warrior
    D. The Steward is dying and Pippin feels pity for him

3. How does Aragorn encounter Sauron?

    A. By traveling the Paths of the Dead
    B. In a series of prophetic dreams
    C. By consulting the Stone of Orthanc
    D. In the out-walls of Mordor

4. Who is the most frightened character in the journey through the Paths of the Dead?

    A. Gimli
    B. Legolas
    C. Merry
    D. Pippin

5. Why must the Sleepless Dead obey Aragorn's commands?

    A. They attribute to him a godly status
    B. They broke an oath to Aragorn's ancestor long ago
    C. Aragorn is dead also
    D. Aragorn casts a spell over them

6. How does Merry arrive at the Battle of the Pelennor Fields?

    A. He rides his pony alongside Théoden and his Riders
    B. He takes the Paths of the Dead
    C. He hides with a mysterious horseman, Dernhelm
    D. He rides with Gandalf on the back of Shadowfax

7. What does the Enemy catapult over the walls of Minas Tirith?

    A. A *palantír*
    B. Poisonous stones from Mordor
    C. The heads of Gondor's dead soldiers
    D. Faramir's armor

8. What strange guides lead the Riders of Rohan on a secret path to Gondor?

    A. The Woses
    B. The Dead
    C. The Ents
    D. The Uruk-hai

9. How does Gandalf defend the gates of Minas Tirith against the Lord of the Nazgûl?

    A. He strikes the Black Captain with his white fire
    B. He casts a spell on the Black Captain
    C. He causes lightning to strike the Black Captain
    D. He commands the Black Captain to return to Mordor

10. What does Denethor take with him to his fiery death?

    A. The sword Andúril
    B. The White Tree of Elendil
    C. The *palantír*
    D. His son Faramir

11. What is ironic about Aragorn's arrival in Gondor?

    A. Gondor has already won the battle against Mordor
    B. He has forgotten his sword, Andúril
    C. He is denied admittance to the city of Minas Tirith
    D. He arrives in the black ships of the Enemy

12. How does Aragorn heal the sick and dying in the Houses of
    Healing?

    A. He crowns himself King of Gondor
    B. He crushes the leaves of a common herb and touches
       the wounded
    C. He spits on his hands and touches the wounded
    D. His mere presence heals the wounded as he passes by

13. What is the goal of Gondor's advance attack on Mordor?

    A. To ambush Sauron before his forces are ready
    B. To distract Sauron from the Ring-bearer's activities
    C. To enact revenge for the death of Théoden
    D. To redeem the people of Middle-earth by their personal
    sacrifice

14. What does Sauron's Lieutenant use to threaten Gandalf and
    his envoy?

    A. The garments and sword of Frodo and Sam
    B. A pack of bloodthirsty Orcs
    C. His dark sword
    D. One of the other Rings of Power

15. How does Sam elude the Two Watchers at the gates of Ungol?

    A. He puts on the Ring and calmly passes through
    B. He sings a song to distract them
    C. He brandishes the burning phial of Galadriel
    D. He wears Orc clothing

16. How does Sam overpower Frodo's Orc captors?

    A. He brandishes the burning phial of Galadriel
    B. He scares them off
    C. He kills their two captains
    D. He casts a spell on the Orc guards

REVIEW & RESOURCES

17. How does Frodo respond when he learns that Sam has safeguarded the Ring?

    A. He snatches the Ring from Sam
    B. He believes Sam should continue to carry the Ring
    C. He worships his long-lost Precious
    D. He strikes Sam for his stupidity

18. What physical image of Sauron intimidates Frodo and Sam?

    A. Mount Doom
    B. The tower of Cirith Ungol
    C. The Great Eye
    D. The Darkness

19. How does the Ring end up in the Cracks of Doom?

    A. Frodo dives into the Cracks
    B. Frodo and Sam carry the Ring together and drop it in
    C. Gollum's wretched appearance awakens Frodo from the Ring's power and the hobbit lets go of the Ring
    D. Gollum bites the Ring from Frodo's finger and falls into the Cracks

20. Whom does Éowyn agree to marry?

    A. Legolas
    B. Éomer
    C. Aragorn
    D. Faramir

21. What does Arwen give to Frodo?

    A. A lock of her hair
    B. A mysterious book of tales
    C. An opportunity to sail to the West with the other Ring-bearers
    D. A crown, in recognition of his unrecognized bravery

REVIEW & RESOURCES

22. Who is the "Boss" of the Shire?

    A. Tom Bombadil
    B. Lobelia Sackville-Baggins
    C. Tom Cotton
    D. Saruman

23. How does Saruman die?

    A. Several Hobbits shoot him with arrows
    B. His servant, Wormtongue, kills him
    C. He dies fighting Gandalf
    D. He passes away of old age on the outskirts of the Shire

24. What improvement does Sam make to the Shire?

    A. He replants it with the trees of Lórien
    B. He builds several aboveground houses
    C. He tells great stories to the eager Hobbit children
    D. He invents a productive crop-sharing system

25. What do Frodo and Gandalf do at the end of the novel?

    A. They ride to Gondor to live with Aragorn
    B. They ride to Lórien to live with Galadriel and Celeborn
    C. They live alone in the woods near the Grey Havens
    D. They sail to the unknown West

REVIEW & RESOURCES

Suggestions for Further Reading

CARPENTER, HUMPHREY. *J.R.R. Tolkien: A Biography.* New York: Houghton Mifflin, 2000.

———. *The Inklings: C.S. Lewis, J.R.R. Tolkien, Charles Williams, and Their Friends.* London: Allen and Unwin, 1978.

HAMMOND, WAYNE G. *J.R.R. Tolkien: A Descriptive Bibliography.* Winchester, England: St. Paul's Bibliographies, 1993.

JOHNSON, JUDITH. *J.R.R. Tolkien: Six Decades of Criticism.* Westport, Connecticut: Greenwood Press, 1986.

KOCHER, PAUL HAROLD. *The Master of Middle-Earth: The Fiction of J.R.R. Tolkien.* Boston: Houghton Mifflin, 1972.

TOLKIEN, CHRISTOPHER. *The History of* THE LORD OF THE RINGS. New York: Mariner Books, 2000.

TOLKIEN, J.R.R. *The Silmarillion.* New York: Houghton Mifflin, 1977.

———. *The Book of Lost Tales.* New York: Del Rey, 1992.

———. *The Letters of J.R.R. Tolkien.* New York: Houghton Mifflin, 2000.

TYLER, J.E.A. *The Tolkien Companion.* New York: St. Martin's Press, 1976.

WEST, RICHARD C. *Tolkien Criticism: An Annotated Checklist.* Kent, Ohio: The Kent State University Press, 1991.

REVIEW & RESOURCES

SPARKNOTES
TEST PREPARATION
GUIDES

The SparkNotes team figured it was time to cut standardized tests down to size. We've studied the tests for you, so that SparkNotes test prep guides are:

Smarter:
Packed with critical-thinking skills and test-
taking strategies that will improve your score.

Better:
Fully up to date, covering all new features of the tests,
with study tips on every type of question.

Faster:
Our books cover exactly what you need to
know for the test. No more, no less.

SparkNotes™ Literature Guides